CHAUCER
AND THE LEGEND OF
GOOD WOMEN

CHAUCER
AND THE LEGEND OF
GOOD WOMEN

PHILIPPA MORGAN

CONSTABLE · LONDON

Constable & Robinson Ltd
3 The Lanchesters
162 Fulham Palace Road
London W6 9ER
www.constablerobinson.com

First published in the UK by Constable,
an imprint of Constable & Robinson Ltd 2005

A copy of the British Library Cataloguing in
Publication data is available from the British Library

ISBN 1-84529-093-3

Printed and bound in the EU

1

It was spring and the wind rushed down the river Arno, causing the water to shiver in the moonlight. Guido was shivering too and only partly from cold. He huddled further inside his cloak. The cloak was old and darned but it was better than nothing. He was standing on the northern side of the Ponte Rubaconte in the shadows of the newly built chapel to Our Lady, and looking down the length of the bridge. In front of him he could see little houses of stone at intervals on either side of the bridge. The moon, which was full tonight, shone cold on their walls and peaked roofs.

There was no one in sight yet he knew that he was probably being watched. The women who occupied these places were religious hermits, nuns who had chosen to move away from the loose living of convents and shut themselves up in solitude. It was a very strange kind of solitude, thought Guido. They received food and water through barred windows. They spent their time in prayer and devotion, their piety on public display.

Ten o'clock struck somewhere over his shoulder. It was the appointed hour. The wind dropped, as if it too kept time. Guido turned. From where he was standing he could see some of the city's bristling towers. They were grouped in clusters, as if trying to outdo each other in height. He knew that the towers had once reached even higher, before they were cut down by city ordinance like so many weeds. Those were the days when wealth and nobility had the complete run of the city, and ordinary people like himself lived under their thumb. It was to prevent an absolute return to such times that Guido was now standing close to Our Lady alle Grazie, shivering a little because of the cold and other things. It was almost impossible to imagine this spot during the baking days of summer, to recall the dazzling white stone of the bridge and the slow brown flow of the Arno. But it was easy for Guido to imagine the warmth of the bed he'd forsaken for this night, the warmth of Lisabetta by his side. He'd give quite a lot to be there, at this very moment.

The noise of an approaching wagon brought him back to himself. He felt his skin prickling. Was this it? He pulled further into the shadow of a wall. The wagon – no, it was more of a carriage – turned off the della Borsa and paused at the entrance to the bridge. From his position Guido saw the carriage-man turning his head from side to side. The fellow was wearing a cap pulled low over his brows. As he might have expected, the carriage was a smart new contrivance, designed for comfort and show. It was swaying slightly on its base and pulled by a pair of horses. The driver removed his cap and inspected it, with apparent pleasure. The moonlight glittered on his bald pate. Then he began to whistle a tune which Guido recognized. It was a song currently doing the rounds of the city, a ballad about a miller's daughter, a faintly bawdy ballad. The tune was the agreed signal.

Guido stepped away from the embrace of Our Lady alle Grazie. All at once he was reluctant to leave the cold wall for the more exposed, moonlit stretches of the bridge. But it was too late now. He was out in the open. The carriage-man, cap once more covering his shiny scalp, had spotted him. He smiled and Guido saw his teeth. He jerked his head towards the door of the carriage. Closer to, Guido observed that a black cloth was draped over the side of the door, covering the place where a coat of arms might have been displayed. Cloth hung over the window spaces too.

The door swung open. Guido, moving as if in a dream, climbed inside. The coach dipped under his weight.

2

"Close the door, it's cold tonight."

Guido's eyes were not yet accustomed to the dark. He sensed rather than saw a large man sitting on the opposite side. The man was breathing heavily as if the effort of opening the carriage door had tired him out. Guido pulled the door to after him and sat on a padded bench across from the other occupant. Wheels rumbling over the stone, the coach began to move forward along the bridge.

"Yes, it's cold all right," repeated the other man. "But you know what they say about this city . . . They say, even men's hearts are warmer than her stones."

"While her towers are taller than pride itself," said Guido.

"Just so," said the man, with a wheeze of approval that these preliminaries had been completed. "You are Guido Greco?"

"I am. And you . . . *messere?*"

"If you need to call me anything, you should call me Giuseppe," said the other. Guido waited for him to offer more but he said nothing.

The carriage swayed forward. By now they were off the Ponte Rubaconte, across the river and moving on one of the roads that led into the newer part of the city, the Oltrarno. Guido could tell by the change in the sound of the wheels from flagstone to cobble. He had never travelled so comfortably. To be honest, he had never travelled in anything except a farm cart, and this conveyance was as far removed from a cart as silk is from sackcloth. The seats were not only padded but quilted. He put out an experimental hand and it slid across the fine, worked surface of the material.

Yet for all the comfort and ease of his situation, Guido might have preferred to be perched on one of those farm carts at the mercy of wind and rain. Where he had shivered on the bridge, he now felt confined and sweaty.

The interior of the carriage was almost completely dark, with the merest glint of moon shining through when the curtains swayed in the draught from the unglazed windows. There was no sound either apart from the breathing of the man who'd announced himself as Giuseppe, and the grinding of the wheels on the cobbles.

After they'd been going for a short while longer, the carriage halted. By the time it had taken them to reach this point, he realized where they must be. This city was ringed by two walls, one inside the other. Like a belt whose owner has grown large and prosperous, the old wall had long outlived its usefulness. No longer a defence, it was pierced with gates whose number increased year by year. The true strength of the place lay in the outermost wall, six feet thick and the height of many men, and fortified with innumerable towers. The gates here were fewer in number – and they were manned day and night. Guido realized that they must be passing through this outermost wall. He waited to hear a muffled exchange from outside. If he'd been by himself and on foot, he'd have been stopped and questioned. In truth, he couldn't think of any business which would have permitted him to wander beyond the confines of the city after nightfall. But for a carriage such as this one, patently the property of a powerful family (even if the coat of arms was hidden by a folded cloth), no such obstacle applied. Outside, one person spoke, not the driver but a watchman, he thought, before the carriage rolled forward once more and quite soon started to travel uphill. The going became rougher.

There was the sound of a flask being uncorked and then gulping noises. The man sitting across from Guido swayed towards him.

"Here, have a swig of this, it is a cold night after all."

Guido grasped the leather flask. He paused a moment before raising it to his lips. Did he trust this man enough to share a drink with him? He swallowed a little. It was a fiery liquid which burned his gullet before settling down in the depths of his belly. He swallowed some more. That was better. Couldn't do any harm, after all, when his companion had already drunk from the flask. It was foolish to have doubts about a warming swig of liquor, since he had already entered the carriage and was permitting himself to be driven off to . . . God knows where exactly.

"Good, eh?"

"Yes, it's good," said Guido. "Where are we going?"

"You have an appointment."

"I know that," said Guido, the drink and the heat in his belly making him more assertive. "But who with?"

All he'd been told was that he was to meet someone important, someone who was on their side. Those had been Masetto's words. *On our side.* Guido had been willing enough to do Masetto's bidding. He'd been pleased, to be honest, to be entrusted with what Masetto Cennini had termed a delicate mission, particularly as he'd started to have some doubts about Masetto's commitment to the cause. The man was a fine speaker, much more skilled than Guido even when the drink was flowing through his veins and his tongue was singing with outrage. But Guido sometimes considered that Masetto was just a little too fluent and clever for his own good, that he perhaps put his own interests first.

One day Masetto had taken him aside and, seeming to penetrate to the bottom of Guido's soul with his direct gaze, had asked whether the younger man really trusted him. I do, I do, Guido had said. And the other's face had relaxed and Guido basked in the warmth of his smile. 'Because I trust you, my Guido. And to prove it, I want you to undertake a mission. A delicate one but not so difficult. All that is required is for you to judge for yourself whether a certain, ah, *gentiluomo* is prepared to offer us mere words or whether he will provide us with something more useful. Provide us with men or money or material. Of course, Guido, if you're not happy to undertake this task, I can offer it to one of the others. To Pasquino, for instance . . .' No, no, Guido had assured him, I can do this thing. Send me.

Very well, Masetto said, here's what you've got to do. You should wait by the chapel at the north end of the Ponte Rubaconte tomorrow night. After ten has struck, a carriage will appear. As a sign to you, the carriage-man will whistle the tune to *Figlia di Mugnaio*. You know it? Of course I know it, said Guido, all Florence is familiar with that miller's naughty daughter. Then you should board the carriage, said Masetto, which will take you to your appointment with this gentleman, after you've exchanged the necessary sentences with your escort. I could send one of the others, I could send Pasquino for example, but you are a wise head on young shoulders, Guido . . .

So, encouraged by Masetto's praise and eager to show that he did have faith in him, Guido had agreed to do this job. He'd been touched when, as a token of his esteem, Masetto had given him a clasp with an image of two joined hands. It was a fine ornament, more than Guido could ever have afforded. But then Masetto Cennini came of good family, which made his love of the common people all the more surprising – and inspiring. Guido was wearing the clasp at this very moment to fasten his old cloak. Mind you, he had kept the gift a secret from Lisabetta and only wore it when he was out of her company – if she'd seen it, she might have thought it was a gift from another woman! (But he would have been equally reluctant for her to know that it came from a man.)

Anyway, wearing Masetto's gift, he had waited at the end of the bridge, had heard the carriage-man whistle the tune, had boarded this very carriage. And now here he was, sitting in the darkness opposite a stranger who might have been more talkative. Why, it was very likely that 'Giuseppe' wasn't even his real name. Guido wasn't born yesterday. A wise head on young shoulders, that was what he had . . .

He took another mouthful from the flask and said, "You are with us? You are with the common people?"

6

"I am an educated man," said the the other, then quickly added, "but I am with you in spirit, naturally."

"Who am I meeting?" said Guido, not sure whether his earlier question had been answered.

"You lot call yourself the people of God, don't you? *Il popolo di Dio*."

"Yes. That is no secret."

"But other things may be secret, my friend," said the man called Giuseppe. "Let's just say that if you are one of the *popolo di Dio* then the person you are going to meet is *Dio*. As it were."

The man wheezed as though he was forcing the words out. Maybe it cost him an effort to speak, thought Guido, and that made him reluctant to engage in conversation, although he did make little chuckling sounds from time to time. Certainly as Guido's eyes grew more used to the darkness of the interior he had the impression of someone of considerable size, taking up most of the opposite bench.

The carriage continued its progress uphill but on a more gentle incline. Guido knew that in this area outside the city walls were the most lavish estates and villas, the most extensive orchards and avenues. If you were searching for a rich man – one who might jokingly be referred to as Dio, for example – it was here that you would begin.

Seeing that he wasn't likely to extract more information from Giuseppe he settled back and raised the flask again. It crossed his mind to return it but since the stranger hadn't asked for it, Guido kept tight hold of the thing. He had never been one to turn down a free drink. Even though she liked a draught or two herself, Lisabetta nagged him about his drinking, just as she nagged him about how his mouth ran away with him when he was in his cups. But Guido knew precisely how much he could absorb before becoming the worse for wear. To be honest, he reckoned he had a pretty hard head. And a wise one too, according to Masetto.

7

He stretched out his legs to brace himself against the tilt of the coach and wondered what were the chances of finishing off the liquor before they got to their destination, wherever *that* was. Maybe it was a long way away. Still, he told himself, better take it a little bit carefully, especially if he was going to meet Dio. Guido might know how hard his head was but other people sometimes got the wrong impression, they judged you to be not quite in your right senses when all the time you knew that everything was fine. And besides, having downed a flask full of liquor, he wouldn't want to be caught short . . .

There was something funny about the idea of being caught short in the presence of an individual referred to as God. Guido found himself snorting slightly, and quickly covered his mouth with his hand and turned it into a cough. And then to dampen down the cough he took another mouthful of the drink. By now the contents were having less effect, or rather they were having a different effect. Instead of warming his belly and giving him the confidence to speak out, the drink was beginning to make his limbs heavy. He felt sleepy. Time itself seemed to be passing more slowly. He'd give a lot – he'd give pretty much everything he possessed (which was little enough, God knew) – to be snuggled up next to Lisabetta, receiving her heat, lazily stroking her thigh. As for this 'delicate mission', well, it couldn't be so important, could it? Not at all important, to be honest. As far as Guido was concerned at this moment, the gentleman called Dio might go to hell.

And also at this moment the carriage drew to a halt, seeming to shudder as it did so.

Why were they stopping? Guido wondered. Surely they hadn't arrived already.

"Time to get out, my friend."

And the large man half raised himself from his seat and gestured – the movement of his arm just visible in the dimness – towards the door. As he did so, there was a thump and what sounded like a bottle rolled across the floor.

Guido exited the carriage clumsily, as if his limbs weighed him down. Someone else must have unlatched the door from outside. Who was it? Oh yes, the carriage-man with the large cap. As his passenger climbed down, the driver showed his teeth once more, civil fellow that he was, and bowed slightly.

Let's see where we are now, before we go off to a meeting with this important person, with this Dio.

Guido staggered forward on heavy legs, with his back to the carriage. The night air was cold on his face. They were on a piece of level ground across which ran a track, more of a path than a road. The track dropped out of view to one side. They were some distance from the city. He could see her towers and high buildings spread out before him, bathed in a dead white light. (Lisabetta was lying down there. Was she asleep?) He recognized this place although it seemed like somewhere in a dream. They were near the stone quarry on the edge of the city. It lay immediately below them like a giant's bite taken out of the hillside. He swung round, almost losing his balance. On Guido's other side was a line of trees, their black tops swaying in the night breeze. Above the trees hung the hard, bright moon. There was no sound apart from the shuffling of the horses and the sighing of the wind. As Guido shifted his head to look first down at the city and then at the woods behind him, he felt leaden and sluggish. Perhaps his head wasn't as hard as he'd thought. In fact, at this moment his head seemed to be filled with fog.

The carriage-man came to stand next to him and took hold of the leather flask which Guido was holding. Easing it from his grasp, the man placed it on the earth as if to prevent it coming to harm. Something about the gesture, its very gentleness, was disturbing. The fog in Guido's head blew away for a moment to reveal a disturbing prospect. What had he been drinking? He remembered the sound of a bottle rolling on to the floor of the carriage. A *bottle*? Had the large man inside kept

9

a bottle for himself and given him a flask? But why would he do that . . .?

And at once Guido knew that he had been enticed into a trap. He turned to move off to his right where the path dropped out of sight over the edge of the hill. But the carriage-man, unsmiling now, pushed him back by main force against the side of the carriage. Guido was a strong young man but whatever had been added to the liquor he'd drunk had left him slow and feeble.

The horses pawed at the ground, the body of the carriage shook as the driver barged Guido against the door. Guido raised his arms to fend off the man but there was little strength left in them and he got tangled up in his cloak. At the same time he heard a wheezing sound over his shoulder. The other occupant of the carriage, Giuseppe, had remained inside all this time. Now he was reaching through the curtained window-space and seizing Guido by the shoulders. Something flickered before his eyes. Pinned like this from both sides, Guido could not slip away or struggle free.

"What are you doing?" he said.

He tried to speak lightly in the hope that this was all a bit of horseplay. But his voice came out quavering and thin. The carriage-man said nothing in reply but the voice of Giuseppe came to him from across his shoulder.

"You are going to see Dio, Guido," he said. "To see God. You understand, my friend. Don't pretend you don't understand."

Guido opened his mouth to call out, although some part of him knew that there was no one else in this remote spot. In any case no sound emerged from his mouth. Instead Guido experienced a sudden tugging against his windpipe. He tried to jerk his head forward but it seemed to be fastened to the rim of the carriage window. Then the carriage-man was tearing Guido's own cap off and seizing hold of him by the hair so that his head was forced back and his throat exposed. While they'd been tussling, Giuseppe had slipped a cord over Guido's head and was presently drawing the ends of it tighter and tighter from his position inside the carriage.

He was aware of the hot breath and bared teeth of the carriage-man in front of him, of the wheezing of Giuseppe behind and above. Over his head he had glimpses of the full moon above the trees. But mainly he was conscious of the burning in his throat and the rasp of his breath and the blurring of his vision. There was a heaviness in his chest like a sack of lead. He felt wet round his leggings and knew that he'd pissed himself. Great black clouds seemed to be swelling up in the sky, covering the tree-tops and the moon, but these clouds were shot through with red and orange flames. The smoke and flames were making it impossible to breathe. However hard he tried to force air into his lungs, nothing got through. And now the fire had reached his throat.

His last thoughts were of Lisabetta lying warm and unawares in their bed. He even tried to say her name aloud. He wondered if she'd . . . he hoped that she'd . . .

When it was over, when Guido's last kicks and twitches had subsided, the driver stepped away from the figure dangling from the side of the carriage. The man who'd called himself Giuseppe released his hold on the cord which had dug deep into Guido's neck. Unsupported, the body flopped forward on to the earth. The carriage-man stepped back and stood nearby, as if awaiting orders. Suddenly he realized that, at some point in the struggle, he'd lost his cap. With a loud smack he clapped his hand to his head, which looked like a lump of chalk under the moon. A look of real distress passed over his features. He began casting about on the ground. Eventually, a darker puddle in the moonlight revealed itself as the velvet cap. The man sighed with relief. He picked it up and, with stroking gestures, brushed off the dust and dirt before fastening it once more on his bald pate where it hung down like a great purse.

11

Now the carriage door opened and Giuseppe climbed down and stood, panting, in the moonlight. He was a large man. There was a birthmark like a wine stain which clambered up his neck and spread over his left cheek. The dead Guido might have been sceptical about his name but he was indeed called Giuseppe. After all, one can safely entrust such information to a person who will shortly be leaving this world.

"My God, Bruno," he said now, "that fellow nearly did for me. I couldn't have held him up for a moment longer. Did you hear him utter a name? It must have been his sweetheart's name. At least he died happy."

Bruno laughed but said nothing.

Giuseppe clapped Bruno on the shoulder and indicated that he should lead the horses and carriage away from the brink of the quarry. The carriage-man took his team nearer to the margin of the wood where he hobbled the horses. Meanwhile Giuseppe was bending over the fallen body of Guido. Raising the dead man's head, he unpicked the cord from the swollen neck. He ran the silken string through his fingers before returning it to a pocket. The cord was soft as down but strong as steel. Then his eye was caught by a gold clasp glinting in the moonlight. The clasp, with the figure of two joined hands, fastened the dead man's mantle. It looked familiar but Giuseppe couldn't recall where he'd seen it before. Swiftly, he unpinned the clasp and slipped it into the pocket which contained the cord. If he did not sell the token he might give it away, he thought.

The two men lifted Guido's body. Giuseppe noticed that Bruno removed his cap, presumably because he was afraid of losing it while they went about their task. They had halted at this spot near the lip of the quarry because there was a rough path leading downwards. The quarry furnished the materials for the houses and roadways of the city. It had already been worked for many years and was still far from being exhausted. On the floor of the quarry the moon picked out great blocks of stone, together with hoists and cranes, as well as the makeshift tents which sheltered the artisans from sun and rain. The slanting side below Giuseppe and Bruno was in shadow. Down here were the traces of old workings, darker gaps and holes in the night. They shuffled down the steep path, awkwardly manhandling Guido between them. At one point Bruno lost his footing and dropped his end of the body, sending showers of loose stone down the slope. Giuseppe was afraid that any workers sleeping at the site would be alerted, but if there was anybody there they were sleeping soundly.

After they'd descended about a hundred feet, Giuseppe indicated that they should shift sideways on to a slanting ledge of rock. Breathless, they deposited Guido on the ground. On the inner side of the ledge was a low entrance, gaping like a mouth in the rock. Giuseppe had explored it on more than one occasion. In the old days, an excavation must have been halted by a fall of rock and then abandoned altogether as too dangerous. The cave-like entrance remained even though the interior was blocked by a mass of rock and rubble within a dozen paces. But the rock fall had exposed natural holes and fissures on the inside walls of the entrance. These led further into the hill, ending God knows where. Some were scarcely wide enough to take a rat, others could accommodate a man's shoulders, and at least one was wider still.

When they'd recovered their breath, Giuseppe and Bruno once again lifted up Guido. They eased him into the cave, moving as lightly as they could, conscious of the cracked and crumbling roof overhead. Giuseppe had a particular spot in mind. He'd already paced it out. When he judged that they were at the right place, he dropped his end of the body and felt around with his hands. It was pitch black. He found the hole, more by smell than anything else. A draught of dank, fetid air seemed to rise up from the bowels of the earth. He had a sudden fear that he might stumble and fall down the hole.

"It's here," he said, more to himself than Bruno.

For the third time they lifted the body, this time carrying it only a few feet. They eased it towards the edge of the hole, working entirely by feel. Once they had Guido suspended over the hole – holding him by the calves and heels – each man released his grip at a word from Giuseppe. There was a dull thud as the corpse struck some outcrop of rock, then further and more distant bumps as it made its way down the shaft. Finally, the noises ceased. Who knew how far down the body lay? Maybe it was still falling all the way to hell. Yet the smell which climbed up was dank and rotten, not sulphurous.

The men rose from their crouching position and returned to the entrance, guided by the faint grey oval of the mouth. Outside on the rocky ledge, it seemed bright as day although it was not yet midnight. The basin of the quarry, with its tents and cranes, lay undisturbed. Giuseppe and Bruno ascended the rough path. Though they were not carrying a body, the climb seemed to Giuseppe more wearying than the descent. When they reached the top, they paused for several minutes as if in contemplation of what they had done. Again Giuseppe clapped his companion on the shoulder and pointed to Bruno's bare head. Replacing his cap, the carriage-man went to unhobble the horses at the edge of the wood. All this time he spoke no word, although as he was walking to the carriage, he whistled the tune of *Figlia di Mugnaio* to himself.

Giuseppe walked across, clambered inside the carriage and shut the door. The carriage-man resumed his seat and, with one final adjustment to his cap, he urged the horses round so that the carriage was once more pointed back in the direction of the city. He waited for the order to go. A barked '*Via!*' came from within the carriage. Before he urged the horses forward, Bruno glanced up at the moon. Then he shook the traces and the horses started towards the downhill track.

2

It had been a hard journey and it was not quite done yet. But the going was easier now, much easier. The landscape was level, more or less, with a range of hills to his left and low, snow-capped mountains beyond them. The air was soft with the promise of spring. Clouds dotted the blue sky. The meadows were full of wild flowers and in the fields the first of the lenten crops were poking through. The road stretched out like an invitation, gently undulating and wide enough to take several riders abreast. When they'd overtaken people that morning, a cluster of foot-passengers, the occasional lumbering wagon, everyone had exchanged waves or smiles, as if the weather had melted more than the last remnants of winter. Almost for the first time on this long journey Geoffrey Chaucer could appreciate his surroundings rather than huddle inside a sodden cape or wonder when his mount was going to throw a shoe or ask himself whether the next night's accommodation could conceivably be worse than the previous night's.

His three companions ambled along in the same fashion, one up ahead and the other two chattering away to the rear. They were congenial enough fellows, capable and alert, but they spoke little English and Geoffrey's Italian was still of the bookish variety. He could have talked about the poets Dante Alighieri or Francis Petrarch, talked about them with pleasure, but he doubted that his companions would have much use for books or authors even if they could read. And the quick-fire banter of the threesome concerning women or food or each other's personal defects tended to pass over his head, especially when it was delivered in a thick regional tongue.

The four of them had ridden together from Genoa, almost a week's journey by now. He'd been provided with this escort by the Doge's office, partly for company and protection but also because a man travelling alone is always more conspicuous than a group. Chaucer's negotiations in Genoa had been satisfactorily concluded and he was told that it was on the Doge's personal instructions that he was being escorted as far as the city of Florence. There'd been no attempt to worm out of him the reason for this additional journey, it being understood that he was going south on more of the English King's business. The realms of Genoa and Florence were sufficiently distant for each city to attend to herself and her more immediate rivals without bothering much about the other.

Geoffrey Chaucer's dealings in Genoa had proved straight-forward enough. A treaty had been signed between the great port and the English throne more than a year earlier and Chaucer was travelling as Edward's commissioner to the Genoese. He had been accompanied by two gentlemen originating from that city, one of them a naval expert who dwelt in London. Their task was to negotiate the establishment of a special trading centre for Genoese merchants somewhere along the south coast of England. His hosts had taken him to the naval dockyards, which were much larger than anything that Geoffrey had seen in London or Bordeaux. It was the end of February and a bitter wind whipped off the iron-grey waters of the gulf. He was plied with figures: the six-hundred-ton transport vessels which the yard was capable of launching, the tens of thousands of men in their navy. Geoffrey did not have to pretend to be impressed.

Both sides wanted this mutually beneficial arrangement – the Genoese in terms of trade, the English because it is always use-ful to have a powerful ally, especially one who is seaborne.

Chaucer had enough experience of diplomatic manoeuvring to know that even when matters were looking favourable (perhaps especially when they were looking favourable) there was always the possibility of an upset in negotiations. But everything had gone smoothly, if slowly. Within a couple of weeks Jacobo and Johannes, his two companions, set off on the journey to London, leaving it to Geoffrey to take back a series of proposals to present to the English court on his own return. That return, God willing, should be in the late spring.

Before he'd glimpse the apple blossom on the Canterbury road once again, however, he must make this excursion down to Florence. An excursion which, if truth be told, was more significant than his Genoese journey and much less certain of success. It was also more secret. Even though Geoffrey Chaucer had spent many weeks in the company of Jacobo and Johannes – crossing the plains of northern Europe before submitting to the Alpine passes in midwinter – he had not breathed a word of the confidential affair that had now brought him this far south.

From his position high up on horseback he saw a woman carrying a bundle and making her way along the margin of a field. She was several hundred yards distant with her back to him, and Chaucer's sight was not so sharp these days, but something about her brisk movements or perhaps the way she twisted her head round to observe the four riders caused him to think of his wife. He'd said his farewells to Philippa more than three months ago now, at the end of the previous year. Said his farewells not just to her, of course, but to Elizabeth and Thomas and little Lewis.

Geoffrey Chaucer's wife hadn't been altogether happy at his departure, not so much that he was going perhaps as that he should want to go.

"You are happier when you're away from me," said Philippa.

"That's not true. How can you say that?"

"You are aways off about the King's business. Or the Duke of Lancaster's business."

"Just as you are doing the Duke of Lancaster's business in this place," said Geoffrey.

"I do not attend on the Duke but on the Duchess, as you well know," said his wife.

"Anyway, I don't travel for the sake of travelling," said Geoffrey, not wanting to get into an argument about who exactly was his wife's employer. "Why should I be so fond of travelling?"

"Because you can go back to your bachelor's ways on the road."

"Hard beds and stinking food and foul inns, yes."

"That's not what I mean."

Geoffrey wasn't sure what she did mean, precisely, but he chose not to enquire further.

"Where are you going this time?"

"The port of Genoa, and afterwards the city of Florence."

"Oh," she said – as though he was off visiting somewhere a few streets away, in Budge Row or East Cheap perhaps – before adding, "And what a time of year to travel!"

This couldn't be denied. The first sleets of winter had come that week, great swathes of them curtaining the Thames.

"I'd prefer to go in a different month myself," he said, "but it is all arranged . . . I am commissioned by the King to travel with two Genoese. We shall go through Hainault."

She did not respond to the fact that he was to travel through the place where she'd been born and spent her earliest years. Nor did she seem impressed by his reference to the King's commission. Philippa Chaucer was all too familiar with the government, or the court, to be impressed. In fact she was much closer to the heart of things than Geoffrey himself for she was living at the moment with their three children in the palace of Savoy. This great town house, on the banks of the river between the walls of the city and the government at Westminster, belonged to the Duke of Lancaster or John of Gaunt. He was the second son of the King and the most powerful man in the country after Edward the Third (some would say, even including Edward now that the great warrior was in his seventies).

Philippa Chaucer kept company with her younger sister Catherine Swyneford, who was Gaunt's mistress. Chaucer wasn't certain when Catherine had taken this court position – for court position it was. It was perhaps not until after the death of her husband Hugh Swyneford during the campaign in Aquitaine. But, whatever the timing, it was now an open secret. When Gaunt's first wife had died three years ago, he had soon taken himself another one. This was no love match but rather a union of state. No one could deny that Constance, the daughter of Pedro of Castile, was a beautiful woman after her own style but she'd never supplanted Catherine in John's affections. Now, her husband being safely dead, Catherine was installed in the Savoy palace as *magistra* to Gaunt's two daughters; and Chaucer's wife Philippa was there with her sister, as one of the attendants on the new Duchess of Lancaster.

Catherine and Philippa were not that close, but they were bound together by early memories which by their nature were inaccessible to Chaucer. They also knew much more than he would ever know – perhaps more than a mere man could ever know – of what really went on behind the high walls of the Savoy palace, the secret currents of intrigue and speculation that flowed beneath its chambers like the river which ran beyond the terraces and rose gardens. Yet Chaucer counted himself as one of Gaunt's associates, even a friend, inasmuch as one could be a friend with the son of a king . . .

Musing like this, Geoffrey was only half-aware of his surroundings, of the way the road dropped into a wooded valley so that the range of hills and peaks to the north-east fell out of view, of the strips of cultivated land which lay between the road and the trees. The sun was momentarily obscured by clouds and

19

the underlying sharpness of the day was revealed. Whether because of the change of light or because he noticed the single rider in front check his progress slightly and glance across at the wood, Chaucer experienced a sudden unease. There was no one else on the road. The two riders to his back had been gabbling away merrily enough but now, coincidentally or not, they'd fallen silent.

Without making it obvious, Geoffrey examined the woodland to his left. The tree branches were already patched with bright green. Spring came earlier down here. The trunks clustered behind a line of naked scrub and bramble so that the interior of the wood was in shadow. He could see nothing, but that didn't mean that there was nothing to be seen. He spurred on his horse to draw level with Francesco, the leading escort, a man with disconcertingly protuberant eyes. Geoffrey was about to say something but Francesco signalled with a roll of those eyes and a shake of his head that the Englishman should keep quiet.

"*Con calma,*" he said.

Chaucer noticed that he had opened his cloak so that his dagger was on display. They paced on, reaching the lowest point in the shallow valley. The sun came out again. Geoffrey cast occasional glances to his left, knowing that any trouble would most likely come from there. The woodland on the other side was sparser. At one point he caught a movement among the branches but it might have been a bird, no more. There was no sound other than the clinking of the bridles and the creaking of their saddles. Without looking round, Geoffrey sensed that the two riders to their rear – Rini and a third man who went by the nickname of Gufo – had drawn closer. The track began to rise again, a gradual ascent.

At once a shape flashed across Chaucer's vision from the left. He tensed but it was only a deer emerging from the woods. The deer crossed the way ahead of them and – a queer thing, this –

paused at the crest of the track so that its delicate form stood out against the sky. Then it leapt for the cover of the trees on the other side. Something has scared it, he thought, and he felt a hollowing in his guts. The woods crowded closer to the track as it climbed. If anything is going to happen, he thought, then it must happen soon, very soon.

But nothing did happen. And, breasting the rise with the others, Geoffrey saw the landscape spread out before them, the track emerging from the woods and winding down between open fields. This made a less suitable area for an ambush. Ahead of them was another group of riders, but at this distance they were no more than a smudge and it was impossible to tell even the direction in which they were moving. Without being aware of it, he'd been holding his breath for these last few yards. But now they were almost out of the woods.

He relaxed in his saddle. He turned to look at the two riders to the rear, Rini and Gufo. He recalled that Gufo meant 'owl' and it suddenly struck him that this nickname would have been more suitable for Francesco. Chaucer found himself distracted, thinking of nicknames. Perhaps this Gufo didn't care much for company, was a bit of a solitary. Maybe he was a night bird. Or a wise bird. You couldn't always tell with nicknames, for they sometimes obscured a person's character rather than illuminating it. Rambling inwardly like this, Chaucer forgot his surroundings.

This was careless, because from the trees beside the road there now burst a stumbling figure. After a moment's surprise, Chaucer recognized her. It was the woman he'd glimpsed earlier walking along the margin of the field. Then she'd been carrying a bundle but now she carried nothing. Her clothing was dishevelled while her face and arms were scratched and bleeding. Seeing the four men on horseback, she headed for them as if by instinct. Almost falling to the ground, she recovered her balance and then threw herself at the flank of Geoffrey's mount,

which shied and whinnied until he brought it back under control.

Geoffrey found himself clutched by the leg. He looked down at an upturned face, marked by briar scratches. She had great eyes, imploring ones, and a swarthy complexion. A torrent of words, too fast to follow, interspersed with *grazies* and *pregos* poured from her lips. Meantime the three Genoese were gazing towards the woods from where the woman had appeared. Out of the line of trees there emerged a group of armed men on foot. There were perhaps a dozen of them altogether. Seeing Chaucer and the others, they paused but only for a moment before advancing at a diagonal across the tussocky grass which grew between trees and road.

There'd been an instant, no more than an instant as the woman rushed into the open, when Chaucer and his three companions could have ridden on. The events unfolding here were no business of the travellers. They might have spurred on their horses and cantered down the slope, soon to outdistance the cries and prayers of the woman. But it was too late now. Whatever her fate, it was quite likely that the Englishman and the Genoese would have a share in it.

The four of them were easily outnumbered. Fighting would be a last resort. A cool head counted now. His heart beating fast but his senses heightened, Geoffrey observed his companions sitting as tensely in their saddles as he was. The woman had let go of Geoffrey's leg and got herself on the far side so that the riders were between her and the group coming out of the wood. Chaucer's first thought was that these men were bandits. But their appearance counted against that. They were wearing soldiers' outfits of a sort, some of them with iron breastplates which glinted in the sun, others with helmets and chin-guards. They carried a variety of weapons, swords, lances, crossbows. There was a disciplined, steady quality to their movements although they'd emerged piecemeal from the shelter of the trees and the ground was uneven.

Geoffrey Chaucer had some experience of warfare and fighting. Not yet twenty in 1359, he had been part of the retinue of the Duke of Clarence (one of King Edward's sons, now dead) during the King's expedition across the water in pursuit of the French crown. He'd taken part in skirmishes and been present at town sieges before being captured and subsequently ransomed. Geoffrey was familiar enough with the military step, the military smell. This group, now only a few dozen yards away, were soldiers. Or to be more exact, they had been soldiers. Now they were mercenaries, most likely. *Coterels* they were sometimes called, after the coats they wore. England had been spared these wolf-packs of disbanded soldiery but they ran wild across whole stretches of France and Italy, the dross of wars which were officially over but never quite concluded.

In one aspect these men were worse than mere robbers. To be confronted by a raggle-taggle of woodland churls would have been dangerous but they would not have had the fighting skills which (Chaucer trusted) his capable Genoese companions possessed. But from another aspect mercenaries were preferable, in that they might consider it beneath them to rob a quartet of ordinary-seeming travellers. Chaucer and his escort were dressed as plainly as pilgrims – more plainly, if truth be told. Fine clothes don't make much sense on a long journey and, anyway, they had no desire to draw attention to themselves. Neither were they carrying valuables or more money than was required by the exigencies of the road. The one valuable part of Chaucer's luggage was under seal in a cap-case inside his saddlebag. And that was merely paper, being some letters and other documents. Therefore of no interest to thieves or mercenaries, who would not be able to read them. He hoped.

What these men, now drawing closer, were surely interested in was the woman who was standing stiff as a statue on the far side of the riders. After the outburst of crying and entreaty, she'd fallen silent. In a distracted way, Chaucer noticed that she

was attractive enough. Dark hair framed a square face that –
despite the cuts and scratches, despite the peril of their situation
– had a resoluteness about it. Absurdly, Chaucer felt guilty at
having shaken off her handhold. He wasn't sure what it was
about her that had reminded him of Philippa. He could see
nothing of his wife in her now.

Chaucer noted the way in which his three companions were
watching him, as if waiting for the cue for action. Or inaction.

The laws of chivalry demanded that the woman be defended,
to the death if necessary.

Chivalry was for poets and women. The poets write about it
and the women benefit from it. You find it in books, but not so
often in real life.

Common sense said that this business was nothing to do
with Geoffrey Chaucer or the goggle-eyed Francesco or Rini
or the one who went by the nickname of Gufo. They should
leave the woman to her fate and be on their way.

Common sense was . . . well, it was common sense. But
Chaucer's view had always been that common sense was almost
as rare as chivalry.

These thoughts flashed through his mind, some in a hardly
coherent fashion. Meantime the armed men drew nearer, their
steps unhurried but determined. One of them was slightly in
advance of the rest, and that together with the way he carried
himself made Chaucer think that this was their leader. He was
a bearded man of middle height, with eyes close-set in a
weather-beaten face. When he reached a position opposite
Chaucer, he stopped and scrutinized him. Then, with a motion
of his arm, he indicated that the others were to halt.

He began to speak rapidly in Italian, too fast for the Englishman to follow. But it was obvious that he was making some
demand. When he'd finished, Chaucer looked a query at
Francesco.

"E require . . . to 'ave the woman."

Geoffrey glanced at her. She was looking at the ground. Even so, he sensed the fear on her face, in her posture.

"Tell him he can't have her. She is under my protection."

He accompanied the remark with a sweeping gesture, signalling a refusal. Even as he did it he felt foolhardy. No, not foolhardy but plain foolish. Where did these chivalrous impulses come from? Chivalry was dangerous. Chivalry was for knights. Well, the knights could keep it.

There was another exchange between Francesco and the chief of the mercenary band.

"'E say . . . the woman is a . . . *ladra*."

"Thief?"

"*Si, ladra.* 'E want to 'ave 'er."

"Ask him what she's stolen then. She's not carrying anything as far as I can see."

Francesco looked uncertain, as though he didn't understand, and Chaucer was about to rephrase it when he noticed a change in the expression of the leader of the soldiers. In place of a professional scowl there was bafflement. Geoffrey peered more closely at the foremost of the mercenaries. He was not wearing a helmet and an old scar was visible as a jagged white line slanting across his forehead.

"You are English?" the man said, in English, after a pause.

"As English as you are, Thomas," said Chaucer.

"Jesus," said the man. "I thought I recognized you. Geoffrey Chaucer, is it?"

"The very same."

"And then I thought it couldn't be you, because what in the name of Christ would old Chaucer be doing so many miles from home?"

"Why so many miles from home?" said Chaucer. "I could ask you the same question."

"Jesus. And you've put on a bit of weight since I last saw you, Master Geoffrey Chaucer."

25

"On the other hand you've kept your shape, Master Thomas Sparrow."

The man took a couple of steps towards Geoffrey. Some of his followers were standing quite close. It was as if what he had to say next was confidential. When he was within touching distance he said in a serious undertone, "I own to Tom or Thomas or Tomaso. I am not known by the name of Sparrow here but quite another."

Geoffrey clambered off his horse. He was stiff and saddle-sore. He stood about the same height as Sparrow, or whatever his name was now. They hadn't seen each other for, oh, the best part of fifteen years. They shook hands. Then they embraced, awkwardly. Chaucer was conscious of the amazement of the onlookers, both his three Genoese and the line of mercenaries. But Englishmen were expected to behave in odd ways when they encountered each other abroad.

"By Christ, it really is you," said Tom. "The last time I saw you was in that damned town . . . what was it called?"

"Cernay."

"Where some goddam French noble took you off for ransom and you left us in the lurch."

"I didn't have much choice."

"And what was your ransom set at? Tell me."

Chaucer pretended to struggle with his memory before saying, "Sixteen pounds."

"I knew it! Mine was only ten. Even in those days you were well connected, Geoffrey, you were on the way up. How high are you now?"

Geoffrey might have said, *I am on a mission for the King of England.* But he merely shrugged.

"Then tell me, how did you recognize me just now?"

"I thought that scar was familiar," said Chaucer, looking again at the diagonal line on the man's forehead. "I remember the day you got it."

Geoffrey Chaucer and Thomas Sparrow, as he then was, had together been part of the retinue of Lionel, Duke of Clarence, during the foray into France all those years before. Soon after their arrival they were involved in a fight, not with the French enemy, but with the followers of a rival nobleman, Audley's lot. Something to do with the division of spoils and ransom (none of which had yet been won in battle). Sparrow, always eager for a tussle, had got in over his head. There'd been a point when he was set on by three or four of John Audley's men. Their knives were out and it looked as though they would take this disagreement to the ultimate point. Sparrow had already been badly gashed across the forehead and could not see for the blood pouring down over his face. Geoffrey had piled in and retrieved his companion, distracting his attackers so that Sparrow was able to make an escape, and then running away himself. Sparrow had claimed afterwards that he could have dealt with his assailants. But his eyes told a different story to his mouth. His eyes told it, and the still bleeding trench in his forehead. He knew that Chaucer had preserved his life and, knowing that he knew, Geoffrey was content not to enforce the matter further.

"So what do you call yourself in this place, Thomas – if it's not Sparrow?" said Geoffrey.

"My men call me Falcone," he said.

Chaucer was about to say that the step from a sparrow to a falcon was a large one but something about the other's attitude, a kind of touchy pride in his new name, suggested that such a remark would not be well received. Conscious that the longer he could engage his old comrade-in-arms in conversation, the more difficult it would be for him (or his men) to do whatever they'd planned to do to the lone woman, Geoffrey was ransacking his brains for something to say that would not reflect too directly on Sparrow or Falcone's current trade. But the other spoke first.

"So what are you doing so far from England, Geoffrey? You have come from home?"

"Yes," said Chaucer, and there was a short pause, as if both men were pondering the word 'home'.

"Who are these with you?"

"They are from Genoa. We are travelling together to Florence."

Before he could be asked any more questions there was a cry from one of the mercenaries who had taken up position as a lookout. He was waving his arm. Chaucer noticed his Genoese escort tense in expectation. Still on horseback they were able to see further. He remembered the blurred shapes moving along the road in the distance. Evidently it was a group travelling west rather than east, and so coming in their direction. The lookout held up his hand and opened and closed it rapidly several times. A number of riders, a large number, perhaps too many to be taken on by Sparrow's men.

Tom Sparrow didn't hesitate.

"You must come with us now, Geoffrey," he said. "You and your friends from Genoa."

"I fear that my business will not allow of any delay," said Chaucer. He spoke clearly but, even to his own ear, a little too fast. "We have already been on the road for a week. We intend to be in Florence tomorrow. We started first thing this morning."

"That was many hours ago. You must be ready for some food and drink. You can spare us a little time. There is no inn between here and Florence – leastways no inn worth stopping at."

"Then it won't be so different from the ones we've stopped at so far."

Geoffrey looked over his old comrade's shoulder. Sparrow's men stood in a loose semicircle some yards distant. They held their weapons – swords, lances, crossbows – at a half-ready position. The man keeping lookout was peering down the road.

Chaucer glanced over his own shoulder at Francesco and Rini and the one known as Gufo. The mounted escort were watching the two speakers, with curiosity and some apprehension. Francesco's eyes stood out more than ever. Despite his anxiety, Geoffrey couldn't help seeing something comic in this situation. Here they were, hundreds of miles away from home, two Englishmen debating over an invitation to dine, one of them on a mission for the court and the other – well, who knew exactly what the other was about.

"I can see what you're thinking, Geoffrey. But I give you my word that no harm shall befall you or your friends. You shall eat with us and drink with us and we shall pass some cheerful hours together and then you'll go on your way tomorrow. You'll still reach the city in good time. I'll see to it myself."

"You give your word on that, Tom Sparrow," said Chaucer, deliberately not turning the remark into a question.

"Yes, I give you my word. Goddamit! Weren't we brothers-in-arms and is that not a bond which is more enduring than marriage? But listen, no more Sparrows. You are to call me Falcone now or Tomaso if you prefer."

He put his hand on Chaucer's shoulder. The grip was firm, as if he'd brook no argument. Was it worth risking a fight, outnumbered? Chaucer recalled that Sparrow – begging his pardon, Falcone – had that highly developed taste for fighting, something which he personally had lost, if he'd ever properly acquired it in the first place. Even if the Englishman showed reluctance to strike at Chaucer, no such scruple was likely to inhibit his men. Should he play for time until the group advancing up the road reached this point? Could he trust the word of a brother-in-arms? A bond more enduring than marriage, eh? Coming to a decision, Geoffrey turned and nodded to Francesco to indicate, *It's all right. We'll do as he says.* The Genoese looked dubious.

"This gentleman is a friend," said Geoffrey. "*Un amico.*"

"It's a long time since anyone's called me that," said Tomaso Falcone.

"Friend?"

"Gentleman. Ah, but by Christ it is good to see a fellow countryman again, Geoffrey. Come along, it isn't far."

As if there could be no doubt about whether his invitation would be accepted, Falcone said something in Italian and gestured to his men that they should retrace their path into the woods. Chaucer remounted and, together with the others, crossed the strip of open ground. The soldiers seemed to melt into the trees. Falcone directed the riders towards a gap between thorn bushes, just wide enough to take a mounted man. The four entered in single file. Chaucer glanced back at the other side of the track where the woman had been standing, stiff as a statue. But she'd gone.

3

Early in the evening of this same day when Geoffrey Chaucer and his escort had been waylaid on the road to Florence, a young man arrived at the gates of an estate in the open country to the south of the city. The man had a round face given character by a prominent, hooked nose which had earned him the nickname of Aquilino. It was a title which he preferred to his given name. He'd been riding hard to reach his destination before nightfall and, at the exact moment when he reined in his exhausted horse, the last sliver of sun slid over the western horizon.

The watchman recognized him and swung open one of the gates. The rider and his lathered horse proceeded down a tree-lined path that led to the main entrance of a large house. Until a few years before nobody would have ventured to live in a place of this size outside the city walls but with the coming of peace between Florence and Pisa – and a general feeling that the worst of the old, marauding days were done with – a number of wealthy men had started to establish themselves in the near-by hills, either building from new or returning to estates which had been abandoned earlier, as this one had been.

Despite the relatively peaceful times, this house still had something fortress-like about it. The ground-floor doors were thick and secured with multiple bolts and bars. The ground-floor windows were narrow and protected by grilles, and behind them lay the storage rooms or servants' quarters. The living quarters for the family were on the first floor, which was both airy and more secure. Within the house was an open court, containing the well and an external staircase leading to the first floor.

As the hook-nosed man who went by the name of Aquilino reached the front door, he glanced up at the heavy shield which hung above the entrance and on which was depicted the family's arms. The shield was decorated with a strange device, a golden ladder against a pale green field, together with some words which the man could not read. He knew that the ladder signified something about the ascent of the family but at this instant he was not at all concerned with the arms or the motto. He saw a fluttering movement at a window to one side of the great shield and, with a leap of the heart, knew that his arrival was no secret from one person at least. He slipped from his horse and, while waiting for the entrance to be unbarred, he glanced around him.

The walls of the house gave off no heat, as they would in the height of summer, but the air retained a little warmth from the spring day. Martins twittered and flew in great loops before returning to their nesting places under the eaves. The tips of the cypresses which lined the path at his back waved gently in the evening breeze. It would be a fine thing, thought the man, to own a place like this. He had no particular feeling for the beauty of the spot – too many years of living rough had hardened him to the lure of the country life – but even he could understand why its owner referred to it as Paradise. In particular, there was a walled-off area of the garden which the man had never been inside but which he often dreamed of entering.

There was the sound of bolts and bars being withdrawn and the great door opened. The man nodded to the porter, led his horse through the entrance and, on the far side, surrendered the animal to a waiting stable-hand, giving instructions that it should be well cared for. The horse, which was called Fuoco, was the man's most valuable possession, his only valuable possession, in truth. The beginnings of a sneer on the stable-hand's face were wiped away by the pressing of a couple of coins into his hand.

There was a flagged yard inside. The man crossed the yard and mounted the stairs that were set in the far corner. At the top of the stairs he halted once more. A loggia ran parallel to one side of the courtyard. A large, wheezing individual appeared at the far end of it and with a slight bow which, the man felt, had a touch of mockery in it, he gestured to the visitor to proceed. As the man made his way along, the large individual said nothing but contented himself with odd little chuckling sounds. When they were both standing outside a door, the other knocked and a voice told them to enter.

Standing on the threshold, the hook-nosed man struggled to make out the interior of the room. A very little light seeped round the edges of the oiled cloth which hung over the window and there was a faint glimmer from a hearth-fire to one side. The man could see the outline of a figure sitting behind a table with his back to the window.

"You may go now, Giuseppe," said the figure.

"Should I light the candles first, *messere?*"

"Is it necessary?"

"Only as a courtesy to our guest. It is almost dark."

"Very well."

The visitor remained by the door while Giuseppe busied himself with a taper which he lighted at the fire. Within a few moments he had touched the flame to several wall-sconces so that a soft glow filled the chamber together with the sweet odour of beeswax. Once this had been done, Giuseppe withdrew without another word. But before he went he cast his eyes on the top of the table. Among the objects arranged there, was a gold clasp with the design of two joined hands.

Now the individual behind the table said, "Sit down, Aquilino."

The hook-nosed man sat on a stool which was already placed before the table. The reason why the other had asked Giuseppe whether it was necessary to light the candles was immediately apparent. He was blind. He sat forward in his chair resting his folded hands on the table-top. Aquilino had encountered the blind man on several occasions yet he never failed, at first, to be discomfited by the sight of the other's face. The eyes flickered before fixing on corners of the room, apparently at random. Yet the rest of his face was firm to the point of gauntness, with a pointed jaw scarcely covered by the grizzle of a beard. He looked like an ascetic, a man of simple, pious appetites, or perhaps of no appetites at all. But any such conclusion would have been deceptive. Indeed sometimes, Aquilino could have sworn, it was almost as if the blind man knew exactly what he was looking at. For certain, he moved about the chamber and the rest of his household with confidence. He'd once told Aquilino that he knew precisely who was in his neighbourhood by their footfall – a single tread was enough. And everyone carried about their own smell – did Aquilino know that? – a smell which gave them away.

"You've ridden hard," he said now. "I smell sweat."

"I apologise," said Aquilino, wondering whether he should have washed before entering the house.

"Not yours, your horse's," said the blind man.

"I have been riding since this afternoon," said Aquilino.

"You must be thirsty. Help yourself to some wine."

The blind man lifted one of his hands from the table and indicated a flagon and goblets on a cupboard against the wall. Aquilino rose and poured himself a goblet, asking as he did so whether his host wanted one. The other nodded and Aquilino positioned a second drink on the table near him. Unerringly, the blind man raised it to his mouth. He sipped with appreciation.

"It's good, eh?" said the blind man.

"Very good," said Aquilino, regretting that he'd swallowed

most of the red wine so quickly. It was the first liquid he'd touched since setting out several hours earlier. But whatever the circumstances, it was good, much better than anything he was accustomed to in his daily life.

As if intuiting the thoughts of his hook-nosed guest, the blind man said, "You've had a successful season?"

"You must know, *messere*, that winter is a difficult time for – for men like us."

"Times are hard, eh? You need another dose of war and dissension between the cities. So what do you do instead, to get by?"

"There are little towns and villages which will pay us not to trouble them, and religious houses too."

"It's not the same as a full-blooded campaign," said the blind man. "Your Englishman Sparrow must be dying for a full-blooded campaign."

"He prefers to be called Falcone these days."

"Whatever he prefers to be called, fighting is all that the English are good for. You have killed men, I have heard. And you are half English yourself, Aquilino, are you not? Your father was a knight?"

"Yes, *messere*, but my mother was from Lombardy."

"Ah, she accounts for your softer side."

"You would not have said that if you'd known her."

Aquilino paused for an instant with the goblet on its way back to his lips, as if overcome by the memory of his father and mother. The truth was that he had difficulty recalling them in detail now. His father's only legacy was a knowledge of the English tongue, mostly used when he was conversing with Tom Sparrow, while from his mother he had his Italian.

"But you are right about wars and campaigns, *messere*," he said now in that language. "Our commander will have difficulty holding us together if things don't improve."

"Well, this is none of my concern, Aquilino. I like to *hear* news of the world outside but I live the life of a recluse and a scholar away from the haunts of men."

As if to demonstrate his point, the blind man gestured towards a handful of books which lay on the table in front of him.

"I am read to for at least two hours a day. The Latin masters such as Horace and Virgil, as well as those who have succeeded them like our own Dante Alighieri. You can read, Aquilino?"

"Alas no, *messere*."

"The son of a knight and yet you cannot read. That's a pity. I might have asked you to read for me."

Aquilino felt uncomfortable. It was true that he could neither read nor write. However, that didn't trouble him as much as the other part of what the blind man had said. To term his father a "knight" was stretching things just a little. If he had been any kind of knight, it was of the most ragged, broken-down variety. The blind man was about to say something further when there came a tap at the door, which opened before he could reply.

A woman walked into the room. She was young and slender. The blind man smiled to hear her step. She went across to stand behind his chair. He reached out a hand and grasped her by the waist, then stroked it softly. Aquilino felt his heart beating faster and colour come into his face. To cover his confusion, he drank rather quickly.

"My dear Novella," said the blind man. "You know our guest of course?"

"Indeed we have met," said the woman.

She smiled at Aquilino and raised a forefinger to her lips. She tapped them slowly, half in an apparent gesture of secrecy, half in something else.

"And what news from the world?" said the blind man. "You can speak openly before Novella. Husband and wife should have no secrets from each other."

No secrets, thought Aquilino, while the woman for her part seemed seized by a sudden tremor of amusement.

36

"You were talking about the English, *messere*," he said hurriedly. "Well, we have met one of them on the road – this very day. On his way to the city."

At this the blind man brought his hand down from its position by his wife's slender waist and leaned forward slightly. He might have said he was detached from the world – a recluse and all the rest of it – but his manner seemed slightly at odds with the claim.

"One Englishman? By himself?"

"He had other men with him, but they were an escort from Genoa."

"Describe him."

But here Aquilino ran into a difficulty. How to describe the man who'd recognized Tomaso Falcone as some kind of long-lost friend? Aquilino had been standing quite near the pair and had overheard some of the conversation which, naturally, he had been able to understand. He'd had a good look at the Englishman and his escort, noticing in particular a goggle-eyed fellow. But what to say about Falcone's friend?

"He was, well, he was just average. Average height. A bit stout round the middle but not what you'd call fat. Ordinary face too."

"If that is all you could see, Aquilino, then we should change eyes, you and I," said the blind man.

"There was nothing much to see. He looked . . . well . . . he didn't look like anyone important."

"But he must be someone important, to be travelling with an escort from – Genoa, you said? What's his name?"

"Geoffrey Chaucer."

The blind Florentine repeated the name to himself although it did not come as smoothly off his tongue as it had off the half-English Aquilino's. Then he said, "Where is he now?"

"My commander insisted that the Englishman and his escort accompany us back to the place we have requisitioned."

"Seized, you mean."

"At any rate those who used to live there are gone," said Aquilino, risking a quick smile at Novella. All this while, the woman had been standing slightly behind her husband without saying anything. She smiled in return and once again touched a finger to her lips. Perhaps it was a nervous gesture.

"That's where he is now, in your 'requisitioned' place?"

"And where he will be until tomorrow morning, sir. Falcone won't let this Chaucer out of his sight until he's squeezed the last drop of English news out of him. But tomorrow you may expect him to arrive at the city."

"Unless your commander decides to rob and murder him on the spot."

"Falcone has given his word as one English gentleman to another," said Aquilino with a touch of indignation. "Chaucer will be safe."

"Very well, Aquilino, you may go now," said the blind man. "Lodge here tonight. In Paradiso. Novella, will you take our guest to his quarters?"

Aquilino stood up, almost knocking over the stool in his eagerness.

"Thank you, *messere*."

"Speak to Giuseppe. He will give you your soldi."

The woman led the way to the door. Aquilino thought that he heard a sound on the other side of it. As she held the door open for Aquilino to pass through, the man behind the table said, "By the way, what excuse did you give to your Falcone for your absence?"

"I left in pursuit of a woman," said Aquilino. "I did not tell him I was coming here."

The blind man smiled as if this was a sufficient explanation and then motioned with his hand in dismissal.

When Novella and Aquilino were outside in the loggia, he started to speak but she once again indicated silence – this time by placing her hand over his mouth – and drew him away from the door. It was completely dark by now, with the first few stars appearing in the sky. A couple of lamps burned dimly in the courtyard below. When they'd moved to the far end of the arcade by the top of the stairs, she said, "His hearing is very good. I sometimes think that all of his remaining senses are double those of an ordinary man."

"It happens with the blind," said Aquilino, as if he was the one married to the man and not Novella.

"What is this talk about a woman?" said the lady. Under cover of darkness she took his hand and laid it on her breast.

"Oh, she is nothing," said Aquilino, swallowing hard. "There is a woman in the camp who has stolen from us. I said to my commander that I would go looking for her. I knew where she might've gone. Of course all the time I was intending to come here with my news."

"To see me," she whispered, leaning into him.

"Yes, to see you," he said, brushing her lips and reaching down with his other hand. She pulled away.

"Not now, not here."

"But I am lodging here tonight."

"You are lodging with the men. Besides he will expect me back at any moment. He is easily jealous. You saw the way he had hold of me in that room."

"I would be jealous too, Novella, if you were mine."

"I *am* yours, Aquilino. I have been yours ever since you first rode up to this house and I saw you from my window."

"Well then . . . ?"

"It is difficult to get free of him. There are eyes to spare in this household even if he has none. There are – "

She broke off and looked down into the courtyard. A figure was standing by the well, apparently looking down into its depths. Aquilino recognized the rounded shape of Giuseppe. When Novella next spoke it was in louder tones.

"Now, Aquilino, we shall show you to your quarters for the night. Follow me."

She led the way down the stairs, whispering over her shoulder to him, "Don't worry, my dear. I shall arrange matters. You must trust me. You are my knight."

"When will you arrange it?" he hissed.

But it was too late for an answer. By now they were in the court-yard and Giuseppe looked up from his examination of the well.

"My husband says you are to settle matters with our guest," she said. "You should take him to his bed, if you please."

And without another word she turned on her heel and climbed the stairs to the loggia. Aquilino understood she was doing this to demonstrate her public indifference to him, but the display hurt him all the same.

Giuseppe waited until Novella had disappeared up the stairs. Then he said to Aquilino, "Well, what *is* the news?"

"I have already given it. Weren't you listening outside the door?"

"I couldn't hear everything," said the large man. "I need more details about this English visitor. I'll pay you something too, as well as what you're getting from the old Cieco upstairs."

Where was the harm in being paid twice for the same story? While they lingered by the well, Aquilino repeated the substance of what he'd already said in the upstairs chamber. Giuseppe was especially interested in the Englishman's appearance, and once again the other had some difficulty describing that unremarkable man. After Giuseppe had squeezed his informant dry, he put some coins into his hand and then another batch, indicating that he was paying both on behalf of 'old Cieco', as he called the blind man, and on his own account.

Then the large man ushered Aquilino into a low-roofed chamber off the courtyard where some of the household re-tainers lived and slept. A couple of men were playing at dice and Giuseppe seemed almost tempted to join them. Others were eating and drinking. They looked up incuriously when the pair came in. A handful of candles – the cheaper tallow ones, not beeswax – gave off a fitful, smoky light. There were some spare palliasses along one wall and Giuseppe indicated that Aquilino had a free choice of them. Then, telling Aquilino to see him the next morning if he recalled any more information about the Englishman on the road, he left him to it.

Somewhat grudgingly, Aquilino was offered a portion of the communal food. He ate a few mouthfuls without even knowing what it was. By now he'd lost his appetite. His head and other parts were filled with the excitement of seeing Novella once again. He lay down on the uncomfortable palliasse, his mind swimming with her touch, her taste, and thinking not at all of his ostensible reason for being in this place.

Il Cieco, as the blind man was disrespectfully referred to by some, described himself as a recluse, as we've heard. But he still desired to hear news of the outside world, and especially of arrivals in Florence. To this end, he employed Aquilino as his eyes and ears within the band of mercenaries commanded by Tomaso Falcone. The position of Falcone's men on the western fringes of Florence – the principal route into the city – meant that no one of importance travelling in that direction passed unnoticed. When Aquilino had heard Chaucer talking in English on the road earlier that afternoon, his ears pricked up. He judged it to be exactly the kind of information that il Cieco would be interested in, although he couldn't imagine why. In addition, he knew that Giuseppe would pay for such news on his own account. So Aquilino slipped away from his comrades and rode off in the direction of the city, under the pretext that he was going in search of the woman who'd apparently stolen from the soldiers and whom Chaucer and the rest had encountered on the road. The woman had been his, in a manner of speaking, so he had every right to go after her.

Aquilino visited the house called Paradise as frequently as he could find an excuse for doing so, to report on movements on the road and to tell il Cieco of any news from the outlying regions of the city. He would have gone daily to report on the weather if he'd been able to think up a good enough reason for doing so. If he was aware of working for two masters, Tomaso Falcone and il Cieco, the thought didn't trouble him unduly. A mercenary is for hire, after all. And times were bad for soldiers of fortune, although they would doubtless pick up as soon as there was another spat of fighting between the city-states. In any case the real reason for his Paradiso calls was to see Novella, to press his suit with her.

Aquilino and Novella had first encountered each other in this very house in the previous summer. Many years younger than her husband, she was the recent bride of the blind man. This late marriage had very little to do with her wishes and almost everything to do with the impoverished condition of her family, for Novella was the youngest daughter of the house of Arrezo. The fortunes of Novella's family – which were based on the export of carding wool to the west and the import of spices from the east – had started on a steep decline when two of their ships foundered in the straits of Messina. But the parlous condition of the Arrezos could also be laid at the door of the Lipari banking house, which had refused to extend any more loans and had foreclosed on certain properties. One of the consequences of this failure was the marriage between Novella Arrezo and il Cieco, a marriage which by arrangement had wiped out the Arrezo debts. Even so it came too late to save Novella's father from a premature death brought on by the threat of bankruptcy, and it had not preserved her mother from a grudging exile in a cousin's house in Pisa.

Aquilino – that soldier-for-hire who liked to believe that his father was a knight – knew next to nothing of this. If he was even aware that he was paying attention to a member of a once-wealthy clan, he didn't show any signs of it. Perhaps that was part of his attraction for Novella, since she had been transferred

42

between her angry, dying father and her blind husband like a commodity.

Aquilino recalled his first encounter with Novella. The tall woman, seeming scarcely more than a girl by her husband's side, had frankly eyed him up and down in the blind man's presence. Afterwards she'd snatched a few moments in his company in a neighbouring chamber. He'd been amazed at her forwardness, since she was a lady after all. She more than hinted at her dissatisfaction with her husband. Described how he drank spiced wines such as hippocras and gulped down herbal preparations to give him strength and staying power during the act. Told of how he sometimes took her to his secret, walled-off garden to enjoy her under the eye of heaven. In a bower of love up a tree, for God's sake! Told of how his hands roamed across her body in place of his eyes. In the neighbouring chamber she took one of Aquilino's hands and illustrated what she meant, letting him touch her here and here – and then *there*. Aquilino was already aroused by her words. Her movements left him speechless. But in a moment it was over. She said she must return, for she was never permitted to leave her husband for long. Almost all the time she was in his company he kept a hand on her.

And it was the same pattern on Aquilino's subsequent visits to the house in the country, il Paradiso. A few minutes of hurried talk and fumbling with hands, but nothing further. Whenever Aquilino pressed the point, he was told that, yes, she desired his satisfaction as much as she desired her own. After all, was he not her knight and she his lady? But, oh, how difficult it was! The young man could see how she, Novella, had no time to herself apart from these snatched minutes, and even they were dangerous. Suppose that they were seen by a member of the household, suppose word got back to her husband? He'd punish her. He'd shut her up in a cell, he'd strip her of her fine clothes and leave her in rags that barely covered her body. The prospect was terrible, yet even as she was describing it Aquilino was stirred all over again.

He was used enough to the females that he encountered in what you might call his trade. Slatternly wives and the ragged *contadine*, women who gave themselves more or less willingly (usually less willingly) to the band of soldiers under Tomaso Falcone. But Novella was a different order of being. Before long Aquilino began to think himself in love. If he'd been able to read he would have read love lyrics aloud to himself. If he'd been able to write he would have thrust notes into her hand, small notes, secret notes, carefully folded ones. Was she not his lady?

And, as he lay on the thin palliasse in the servants' quarters – nothing very paradise-like in here – he imagined Novella at this very instant, stiff in the arms of il Cieco. Imagined the older man's pinched hands roving over her young flesh, his grizzled face nuzzling against her unblemished skin, his papery voice whispering to her innocent ear. He thought of the man and wife indoors in the marital bed, he thought of them outside, enclosed in the secret garden which he'd never seen, exposing themselves to the eye of heaven. In a love-bower up a tree, for God's sake! These thoughts and images were uncomfortable but not altogether since, with a little effort, he could superimpose his own self on the blind man's shape. Sometimes he worried that Novella was not so reluctant in her husband's grasp as she'd claimed. Yet she had said, *I shall arrange matters. You must trust me.* He'd have to content himself with that.

4

Geoffrey Chaucer too had to content himself with the night's lodging provided by his old comrade-in-arms Tom Sparrow, or Tomaso Falcone as he must now learn to refer to him. Falcone's men had taken control of a farmhouse which, he claimed, had been offered in exchange for some unspecified favours. Chaucer suspected that it had been seized from its rightful occupants. It was on two floors with space for the animals downstairs and humans above. There were no animals now other than a handful of horses but there were humans in every corner. The whole building was in a dilapidated state, with cracked walls and holes in the roof, while the ground around it had long lain fallow. Nevertheless, Falcone welcomed his guest as though they were sitting in a palace and he was the emperor of all the land around.

Chaucer could see that the man, after many years of campaigning and foraging abroad, was hungry to hear about England. He confessed quite readily to being starved of his own tongue. True, there were one or two Englishwomen among the little retinue of female followers who shared their marauding life. But it was evident that Falcone barely counted conversation with a woman as conversation. True too there was one other Englishman – or, to be accurate, half an Englishman – in his company although this particular fellow, Pietro Hodge (but universally known as Aquilino), had never actually set foot in the country and whatever grasp of the language he possessed came from his father who styled himself a knight. His curiosity stirred, Geoffrey Chaucer would have been glad to meet this individual. But, Tomaso Falcone informed him, "Aquilino" had set off in pursuit of the woman, the one on the road.

"What had she done?" said Geoffrey, remembering the imploring, upturned face and the hand gripping his knee.

Tomaso, who did not appear to resent the fact that Chaucer's intervention had permitted the woman to escape, replied without a trace of irony, "She was a thief. She stole from us. We cannot endure that. Discipline must be maintained. But let Aquilino deal with that. It's his business."

Chaucer didn't dispute the statement or ask for any more details. Although he had Tomaso's word that he and his Genoese companions were safe in this place and that they would be permitted to travel on to Florence the next day, he was wary of offending his host. If he hadn't agreed to accompany Falcone to his quarters he suspected that – for all the talk of friendship – force rather than persuasion might have been applied. Geoffrey had been careful to drop hints that he was on the King's business, as a safeguard against a mercenary who was flattered to be called a gentleman. Meantime the Genoese escort were keeping to themselves in another corner of this broken-down building. Their orders were simply to see that Geoffrey reached Florence in one piece.

With the light fading beyond the cloth-covered window, the two Englishmen were sitting in the only chamber of any size on the first floor of the farmhouse and the one which Falcone had taken for his own. They were eating a stew containing gobbets of unidentified meat and hunks of winter vegetable, and they were drinking (unexpectedly good) red wine. They drank from glasses and ate off plates, fine items which were in odd contrast to the dilapidation of their surroundings. Chaucer suspected that the food and drink, like the pieces of furniture in Falcone's chamber, had been scavenged or levied from the local inhabitants. Indeed, it would be surprising if anything in the possession of this band had come to them through honest payment.

Chaucer knew about the great companies that pursued a freebooting existence across great swathes of France and Italy. Why, one of the most famous of them was under the command of the Englishman John Hawkwood, who had been in the pay of the Pisans not so long ago and whose fame had spread as far as his native land. These companies were armies for hire. The best of them followed a chivalric code, at least occasionally, and showed a loyalty to their paymasters that sometimes rose above mere monetary considerations. The worst of them were little better than thieves, though thieves whose experience of warfare and discipline only made them the more fearsome. Geoffrey guessed that Falcone's band – too small to be anything other than an adjunct to a proper company – fell somewhere in between.

Tomaso talked fondly of his time in the retinue of Lionel, Duke of Clarence, and their old campaign in France at the beginning of 1360. He questioned Chaucer about the royal court and seemed surprised to hear that the great figures of his youth were in decay. King Edward was an old man, for all that he was considering further wars. Edward's oldest son – who was still known as the hero of Crécy back in the days when Tomaso had been plain Tom – was by this time prematurely aged and sick with the bloody flux. John of Gaunt, the Duke of Lancaster, was now a power in the land. Tomaso absorbed all this news and then, unprompted, started to talk of how he had been ransomed after the seige of Rheims – "Ten pounds to your sixteen, Geoffrey, Goddamit!" – only to find that his soldier's arts were unwanted once the peace had been concluded at Bretigny.

"It's all very well for you, Geoffrey. You're a man of peace. You've got other strings to your bow, as the longbowmen say these days. And you always were well connected. Tell you the

47

truth, fighting's the only thing I've ever been any good at or wanted to be any good at."

"I remember," said Chaucer. "The set-to with Sir John Audley's men . . ."

"Oh that! A close-run thing! Not that I couldn't have disposed of 'em by myself. But you did me a good turn and I haven't forgotten it even after all these years."

Softened by the memory, Tomaso went on to describe how he'd attached himself to assorted groups of *coterels* fighting in central France and then somehow found himself at the service of various of the city-states which filled northern Italy. Along the way he had sort of married a Frenchwoman and there'd been children, though God alone knew where any of them were now. He had even been a part of the company under John Hawkwood – "A great man, Geoffrey, a perfect knight, I tell you" – during the hostilities between Pisa and Florence. Then peace had broken out once more, the true soldier's bane, and Tomaso Falcone had ended up here on the outskirts of Florence, hiring out himself and his men as and where he could.

"And you, Geoffrey, what about you? You came off unscathed from the wars. You look sleek, for all that you've been on the road. You look like a man who doesn't have to worry about where his next meal is coming from."

"I was ransomed once, remember. I didn't come off altogether unscathed, like whatsisname? . . . like Jack Abbot, for instance."

Both men laughed. Jack Abbot was a well-born young man who had led a charmed life during the French wars. He was the younger son in the family and he used to curse his lack of prospects almost as much as he cursed his older brother. Perhaps it was the fact that he had nothing to lose which made him reckless. If so, he was well rewarded for his daring. Always at the forefront of any attack, always the first into any breach or the last to quit the field, Jack Abbot had sustained not a single injury, not even a scratch.

"And yet," said Geoffrey, "I could tell you a different tale about old Jack." Then, seeing the curiosity on the other's face but thinking better of gossiping, he said, "Another time maybe."

"Remind me again what your business is in Florence," said Tomaso Falcone.

Chaucer shrugged. Some instinct of caution restricted him to the merest outline. "It's dull stuff, fitting for a man of peace. I am to talk to bankers about money."

Falcone snorted with laughter.

"Scratch a Florentine and you will find a banker. Even men like us have their own *banca* these days that lends at special rates. Speaking for myself, I prefer goods that you can carry, not paper contracts and letters of credit. So King Edward needs money for his wars, does he?"

"The King always needs money for his wars. Coins are more necessary than armour for fighting."

Chaucer was diverted by his own words and an image of a knight wearing soldi and florins for chain mail crossed his mind's eye. He didn't hear Falcone's next question and had to ask him to repeat it.

"You have a wife, Geoffrey? A family?"

"Both."

"Happy?"

"No reason to complain."

"Fortunate then?"

"Ask me that when I'm dead, as the saying goes."

"Still the same old Geoffrey, the same old cautious Geoffrey. Goddamit though, it's good to see you once more!"

Later, lying on a makeshift bed in a corner of the room with Falcone sleeping noisily near him, Geoffrey pondered this day's encounter. *Happy?* Tomaso had asked. And then his mind drifted home and he recalled Philippa saying to him, *You are happier away from me.* It was one of those comments which was impossible to answer honestly, because there was a grain of truth in it. Or rather, it was true and not-true.

Just at this instant he'd have given quite a lot to be back in London. Hundreds of miles of plains and rivers and mountain passes separated him from the comforts of his own chamber, with its desk and paper and writing implements, its collection of books, more than twenty of them. He thought of the long, circuitous route he'd taken to reach this far. There was no possibility of travelling through France at the moment because of the dire relations between the two countries. So, of necessity, after crossing the sea separating England from France, he went with the London Genoese through the flatlands which lie around Bruges and Aachen. After Hainault, the travellers took ship at Cologne and sailed upriver before disembarking at Basle. Then there was the long trudge through the winter lands and the slow climb up to the zigzagging paths which led towards the mountains and their terrible ice-sculpted passes. In the relative comfort of his bed, Chaucer shivered at the memory of that crossing.

Yes, hundreds of miles separated him from the comforts of a wife and children. He wondered what Philippa was doing now, at this very moment. Perhaps she was telling stories to the children.

5

Tomaso Falcone was as good as his word and, together with a couple of his men, accompanied Chaucer and the Genoese on the road the next morning. As on the previous day, the sun was out and the riders soon grew warm. After a time Chaucer saw the glint of a river and a cluster of spindly towers lying between hills, and Falcone confirmed that they were indeed looking at the great city of Florence.

Chaucer felt a prickling in his scalp. It wasn't merely the prospect of arrival after many days on the road or the thought of the mission which he was to undertake in this place. It was rather something that he hadn't mentioned to anyone on his journey. For the city that lay before them was the birthplace of the greatest poets and authors, men like Dante and Petrarch, whom Chaucer had delighted to read, albeit in Latin. His collection of their works was by no means complete and he hoped to be able to buy a book or two to carry home. The notion of setting foot in the very streets where these two makers had trod, of breathing the same air that they had breathed, was for Geoffrey Chaucer an adventure that almost outweighed the King's business.

As they drew nearer the road became busier. They passed men and women on foot or steering carts piled with root vegetables. At one point a rider coming in the opposite direction hailed them at a distance and then pulled up to exchange a few words with Falcone. The two talked in a mixture of English sprinkled with Italian and, from that and the fragments of conversation which he overheard while they were reined in, Chaucer gathered that this was the man – Aquilino was his preferred name, wasn't it? – who had set off in pursuit of the woman the day before. Evidently he'd been unsuccessful for Tomaso Falcone dismissed him with an impatient gesture and set off down the road while the other passed them with an uneasy sideways glance. He had no distinguishing features apart from a large, hooked nose. Chaucer, who had a fair memory for faces, thought he recalled seeing him among the crowd of men emerging from the woods on the previous day. He assumed he'd got the name Aquilino from his nose, and – unlike with Gufo – it was easy to see how his beaky profile justified it. This Aquilino person had some English stock for his real name was Pietro Hodge, wasn't it? And Geoffrey felt pleased at this little feat of memory.

As they got closer the city turned from a hazy cluster of diagonals and upright lines to became a place where people lived and worked and died. Chaucer had often tried to identify that moment when the traveller's destination is transformed from a smudge in the distance to a town or city with houses and churches and public buildings. It was a trick that ought to have been easy enough, particularly when arriving by sea, but some-how he'd never been able to pinpoint that precise moment. It was like trying to catch yourself falling asleep.

And, if he was sleeping now, Florence perhaps had the quality of a dream. The heat of the spring day was already mak-ing the air shimmer. Smoke rose in a haze from a thousand ovens and workshops. Closer to, the towers formed a stone forest. For some reason he'd expected them to be the colour of gold, but many were made of tougher stuff, bare stone and mortar. Seen from above, the walls, one inside the other, were great girdles looped carelessly about the place. Geoffrey could only compare the experience to arriving in London, but he was all too familiar with his own town (which was built largely of wood). Besides, London boasted far fewer towers and high buildings and only had a single wall to hold its inhabitants in – or to keep others out. This place was grander, vast and stony and opulent.

There was a scattering of farms and other more imposing buildings outside the walls. The grass in the surrounding meadows seemed to grow greener, the blossom on the orchard trees to be more luxuriant. The sound of bells came to them intermittently on the breeze. Before they reached the outermost gate, Tomaso Falcone drew up.

"This is as far as I go, Geoffrey. I said I'd see you to the city and I have. There is the Porta Brancazio."

They shook hands.

"If you should need help," said Falcone, "go to a place called La Volta in Via Orivolo. Ask there for Michela. She is a friend of ours and will be your friend too."

"An inn?"

"You will see."

Geoffrey thanked him and watched as Tomaso Falcone, with his two men, turned their horses and set off up the road. Then with goggle-eyed Francesco and Rini and the one called Gufo – who, collectively, seemed to have taken a somewhat dim view of his association with this renegade Englishman – he cantered down the last few hundred yards to the Porta Brancazio. They crossed a moat and then rode into the shadow of the forty-foot wall. There was a wide road-bed on the outer side of the wall where trains of carts were drawn up, waiting their turn to be admitted. Chaucer was ready to show one of the letters of commission he'd come equipped with but, in the event, he and the others were waved through by a distracted guard.

It was the busiest time of day, with traders having their goods weighed (and duties imposed) by the town officials whose scales were set up under awnings to the left of the entrance. There was a steady trickle of *contadini*, too poor to afford horse or cart, bringing farm produce for the markets in sacks slung over their shoulders or round their waists. Chaucer was surprised to see that some of them were barefoot. And then there was that cluster of individuals who always gather round town-ports and exits, the same cluster in every town: the blind and the lame, the women with drawn faces who exist somewhere between beggary and whoredom, an anxious merchant awaiting the arrival of a valuable consignment, a well-to-do mother saying farewell to the younger son who is setting out for a month or a year.

Geoffrey Chaucer was relieved that he hadn't had to account for himself or the Genoese at the gate. His affairs weren't exactly secret but a certain discretion was required and there was no saying whether the casual remark of a guard – 'I saw a plump Englishman today, claimed he had business with the Lipari banking house' – wouldn't somehow get back to the wrong ears. Even so, he was conscious of being observed.

They waited while their horses refreshed themselves at one of the water troughs positioned near the gate and tipped a scabby fellow who evidently regarded himself as a guardian of the water. Prompted by Chaucer, Francesco asked directions to a particular street. The fellow picked at one of the scabs which crusted his face while he pondered his answer. Another soldo bought a restoration of his memory and he reeled off a string of names, accompanied by much arm-waving. Francesco, however, nodded in understanding and indicated that they should remount.

The first surprise was that they were now crossing a stretch which felt almost as spacious as the area beyond the walls. It was like a park. Within this outermost part of the city's defences, there were walled orchards and houses several storeys high. There was the scent of orange blossom in the air, which was warmer and somehow denser than the air outside the walls.

Soon they reached the gate in the second, inner wall. This one wasn't guarded at all, and was graced with only a handful of bystanders.

"We leave our 'orses," said Francesco. "Is more simple to walk from 'ere."

There wasn't much doubt about this. The roads ahead were thronged. Francesco chose one of the more reliable-looking fellows by the second gate, who already had charge of a couple of horses tethered to a railing. Some swift negotiations followed, with the usual gesturing. Money changed hands. More money was promised. The understanding was that they'd return to retrieve their mounts later. But the Genoese were careful to take personal items from the bags tied round their saddles and put them in their cap-cases. Geoffrey too removed his cap-case and tucked it inside his doublet. It was a relief to be on foot once more.

Back at the trough near the first gate, the scabby fellow acting as guardian of the water was accosted by someone whom he at first took for one of the casual labourers from the weigh-stations under the awnings. This was a thickset man with a red cap that sat on his head like a great purse. He said nothing but raised his right hand and crooked his forefinger at the man.

"Can't leave my post, master," said the scabby man, nodding towards the water trough as though it was his personal property.

The other held up a coin in his left hand. More to the point, he once more crooked the forefinger of his right in a way that conveyed consequences if the summons wasn't obeyed.

For appearances' sake, the man hesitated for an instant before deserting the trough. He followed the other to an area at one side of the weighing office which was protected from the sun, and from prying eyes, by more awnings made of cloth. Sitting uncomfortably on a stool was another large individual. From his clothes, the scabby man realized that this was not one of the city officials, paid to assess goods and levy duty. He looked round at the red-capped individual, who again held up the coin between meaty fingers.

"You can have that when you've answered a question or two," said the person sitting on the stool. He wheezed as he spoke. "Someone said something to you just now by the water trough?"

"Plenty of people speak to me," said the scabby man. "It's my job."

"These ones weren't from round here," said Giuseppe. It was a statement not a question.

"If you say so, *messere*."

"One of them was English."

The scabby man shrugged, as if England was situated on the moon. The large man grew impatient and shifted on his stool.

"You gave them directions?"

The man appeared to suffer another lapse of memory. His hand flew to his face to resume the job of picking at himself. He looked at the red-capped individual. The coin had disappeared and now only the bare fist hovered menacingly in the air.

"Yes, I told them where to go."

"Where?"

"Via Calmari."

"They said who they were looking for?"

"No, *messere*."

With a nod of the head, Giuseppe indicated that he should be paid. His companion reluctantly unclenched his fist to release the coin and the man took it. He hesitated as if there might be more.

"What are you waiting for? Off with you. *Via!*"

When the scabby-faced individual had gone, Giuseppe said, "You heard that, Bruno? Go after the *Inglese* and his friends. Find out which house they've gone to. If you're quick you might even catch them up. They're unfamiliar with this place and won't be certain of the way there. But be careful, my dear."

Bruno nodded. Moving with a surprising speed given his size, he set off along the road which Chaucer and the others had ridden down only minutes earlier.

Meantime, Geoffrey and his party were making slow progress beyond the inner wall. Inside this second barrier the character of the city changed. The buildings were older and the streets narrow and more crowded the further they went. There was more shadow than sunlight and the sky was sometimes reduced to a strip of blue overhead. Most people were on foot and the way was blocked by knots of talkers and slow-moving carts drawn by mules. After a time they emerged into the clamorous Mercato Vecchio, one of the places named by the scabby individual at the first gate. The market was full and Geoffrey was glad they'd left their horses behind. He would have felt conspicuous sitting several feet above his surroundings, and had no wish to draw attention to himself as a foreigner.

Not that anyone seemed to be paying much attention to them. The air was full of the shouting of the sellers of wool and linen, the clanging of pans and kettles together with the chink of money-changers advertising their services. Underlying everything was the buzz of chat and negotiation, like the sound of insects in a summer glade. Since Lent was recently finished, meat was once again for sale. Geoffrey was surprised to see sheep and calf skins displayed together with the heads next to the piles of flesh, as if the stall-holders had to demonstrate the provenance of their goods. And there were items for sale such as macaroni which he wouldn't have been able to identify a couple of months ago, before arriving in Italy. The air smelt of raw meat and cheese.

They edged their way round the fringe of the market. His companions, Francesco and Rini and the one called Gufo, were evidently delighted to be back in a great city. Geoffrey too felt glad after their time on the road. The Genoese exchanged banter with the stall-holders, they fended off the beggars, they refused offers of a shave from barbers with razors tucked into their belts, they looked with interest at some of the women. No, they looked with interest at all of the women, particularly a knot of yellow-veiled ones under an arcade who were signalling their availability with winks and nods.

Chaucer's attention was divided between the sights of the market and the buildings which surrounded it. Their walls rose in great flanks of stone or brick, pierced by small windows and surmounted by towers which were topped with loggias. He imagined this city in the depths of summer, the baking heat on the ground, the cool air from the hills which would penetrate the uppermost reaches of the towers.

Eventually they threaded a passage through to the far side of the *mercato*. Francesco stopped to ask more directions from a cheese seller who was wearing a particularly low-cut dress. She smiled. She spoke volubly. Her breasts jiggled as she raised her arm to point and Francesco's goggling eyes were split between looking at them and looking at the way she was indicating. They entered a narrower street. The agreeable smells of fresh food were replaced by something more odorous and less pleasant. The dwellings here were smaller with galleries on the upper storeys which extended from either side into the street, so that a person in one of them might almost have stretched out a hand to touch someone from the opposite house. Stone benches ran the length of some of the buildings and, just above head height, songbirds piped up from little cages attached to iron hooks set into the walls.

Francesco, who was leading the way, suddenly halted. The path ahead was blocked by people standing near the entrance to one of the houses. Something had happened. There was scaffolding set against the entrance. From the rope-drawn buckets and the tiles piled on narrow, aerial platforms, it was evident that repairs were in progress to the overhanging roof of the house. But the scaffolding was empty of labourers.

As they squeezed round the edge of the crowd, they caught glimpses of a young man lying on the ground. His cap had fallen off and bright blood was matting round his head. Four or five men were crouched around him. The cause of the accident seemed obvious enough. A ladder with several broken rungs was propped out of the way against a wall. Fragments of rose-coloured tile lay scattered in the road. The crowd was mostly quiet but hands were raised in the air and fingers waggled to show how the tiles had descended on this unfortunate individual who, to judge by his dusty clothing, was one of the labourers. The accident was fresh and other people were joining the onlookers all the time.

For all the warmth of the day, it was shadowed in this thoroughfare and Chaucer suddenly went cold. Like any witness of such a scene, he felt a touch of pity mixed with his curiosity. But it was nothing to do with them. Francesco still in the lead, they edged past the crowd. Further along the street, the occupants of other houses were clustered on their terraces, peering down at the scene. Geoffrey looked up and caught the eye of a monkey-faced individual who was craning forward, his fingers hooked over the stone balustrade. The man furrowed his brow and then called down, tentatively, in English.

"Master Chaucer?"

Geoffrey stopped.

"Signor Bartolomeo Gentile?"

"I am Bartolomeo Gentile, yes."

The Genoese also halted. Chaucer nodded to indicate that they'd reached their destination.

"Wait there and I will come down," said the monkey-faced individual.

He disappeared from the terrace. Chaucer glanced round. If anybody had noticed this exchange they didn't show it. The crowd around the labourer – was he dead or only injured? – was beginning to chatter more noisily. Within a few moments the door in front of them flew open and Bartolomeo Gentile, the man from the terrace, stood in the entrance. He glanced uncertainly at Francesco and the others.

"I was told you would be alone," he said, stepping forward.

"These gentlemen have travelled with me all the way from Genoa," said Chaucer. "They have kept me company."

"Then you are all welcome," said Bartolomeo.

The monkey-like impression of the face – a wide creased brow, the large staring eyes – was reinforced by long arms. Bartolomeo stood to one side to let them enter. Beyond the door there was a groined archway which opened on to an inner court. It was cold and dark beneath the arch. A door was set to one side and beyond it there was a flight of stone steps leading upwards. Bartolomeo gestured that they should go up and then, with a glance in both directions along the street, he shut the outer door.

If he'd observed more closely he would have seen a man taking note of the house. Bruno had followed Chaucer and the Genoese. At the inner gate he had spotted the horses belonging to the four men, tethered to a railing. He recognized the one that the Englishman had been riding. It had a blaze on its nose. Bruno soon caught up with the foursome. He saw their backs as they entered the Mercato Vecchio. He hurried to keep them in sight, conscious that he might easily lose them in the crowd. Fortunately, it was difficult for anyone to make quick progress past the stalls and at one point they stopped to ask directions of a cheese seller. Bruno noticed the woman's breasts, riper than any of her goods. Then he trailed the men into the Via Calmari where something had happened. There was a crowd standing in the roadway. Nothing very significant. Just a workman who'd been struck on the head by some falling tiles.

The four men moved a few yards further on. Someone called down to them from a terrace and words were exchanged in a language which Bruno didn't understand. Pretending to be absorbed by the street accident, he watched out of the corner of his eye as the door to the house was opened and a man emerged. After a brief conversation, the four visitors were ushered inside and the door firmly shut. At that moment a citizen arrived from somewhere bearing a makeshift carrier – which was no more than a sheet of coarse-fibred cloth furled around a couple of poles – and pushed his way through the crowd. It still wasn't clear to Bruno whether the workman was alive or dead, and nor did he much care.

He was on the point of retracing his steps to the Porta Brancazio, where he would report to Giuseppe on what he'd discovered, when an elderly woman on the edge of the crowd turned to him.

"Such a misfortune!"

Bruno nodded. She needed no other encouragement to launch into a monologue. "And such a handsome young man too. I have been watching them at work. What else is an old lady to do, I ask you? We must sit and watch the world go by while others toil. He was climbing the ladder when the rungs gave way and the tiles on the ledge up above tumbled on his handsome head – so."

She clapped her hands to her own head in illustration.

"Misfortune can strike at any time," said another old woman, eager to contribute to the conversation.

"God knows, that's true enough," said the first, stretching her scrawny neck to see what was happening in the middle of the crowd which, having parted to let the man with the carrier through, had closed up once more. She turned towards Bruno as if expecting him to throw in his soldo's worth to the conversation. When he merely smiled, she fell to talking to her companion. Bruno was again about to quit the scene when he heard another useful fragment of talk.

"Did you see Bartolomeo Gentile gawping at the poor young man," said the scrawny-necked woman, gesturing towards the door through which Geoffrey Chaucer and the others had disappeared. She seemed oblivious to the fact that she was as curious about the accident as everybody else, since she went on, "That's typical of a notary, always sniffing after trouble, looking for profit from the misfortunes of good folk. Don't you think so?"

But her question to Bruno went unanswered for he was already pushing his way through the crowd, eager to bring back to Giuseppe what he'd discovered. He already knew the whereabouts of the house into which Chaucer had gone; now he knew that the occupant was a notary. Giuseppe must be informed. Giuseppe would be pleased that he'd discovered so much.

6

Geoffrey Chaucer said goodbye to the three Genoese. Their task, now accomplished, had been to bring him safely to Florence. They would stay a night or so in the city but would not be waiting to escort him back. For one thing, there was no telling how long the Englishman's affairs might occupy him. For another, with the better weather coming, Chaucer would be able to make at least part of the return journey to England by sea instead of going overland. Accordingly, Geoffrey bade farewell to goggle-eyed Francesco and Rini and the one who went by the name of Gufo. The Genoese were not expecting to lodge with the notary Bartolomeo Gentile of the Via Calmari, and seemed more than content to find accommodation elsewhere in the town. Chaucer thought that they probably had an idea or two on how to pass a few hours in a great city. He recalled the way they'd been distracted by the women in the market.

Despite being travelling companions for more than a week, they had exchanged few words with Chaucer. Yet they seemed regretful at parting from him and he was sorry to see them go. Francesco said, "We 'ave a saying in our country, Geoffari. When your journey, it is finished, is when your troubles start. I 'ope is not so with you."

Geoffrey thanked him. They embraced, Geoffrey first with Francesco, then with the other two. Gufo volunteered to get his travelling gear and bring it to the house on the Via Calmari. Chaucer said that they might sell his mount, which he had purchased in Genoa, and keep the profit. All this while Bartolomeo stood in the court of his house looking on with impatient approval. He was evidently eager to have Chaucer to himself.

Bartolomeo Gentile was a notary by profession. He had a partiality for London and its inhabitants, since he'd spent more than a little time there as a child in the company of his merchant father. On account of his expertise with the English tongue, he had long made himself useful to English visitors to the city of Florence, translating for them and acting as an agent, smoothing away any small obstacles that might clutter their path. With his knowledge of law and contracts he was particularly useful to those who visited about commercial matters. Now Gentile was pleased to receive perhaps the most important visitor of all, an emissary from the royal court who'd come – as it was rumoured – to negotiate a loan on behalf of the English King. Yet to look at Geoffrey Chaucer, you wouldn't think that he was an important emissary. No man appears at his best at the end of a long journey, perhaps, but even so . . .

The Englishman, whom he judged to be about his own age, was scarcely any taller than Bartolomeo. Furthermore he had an undistinguished face and no particular gravity of manner. Nevertheless, there was something about him which suggested that it would be a mistake to dismiss him out of hand. And it would be good to talk to someone about London, a place which had assumed a fabled quality in his memory.

Chaucer was shown to his room, a simple but airy chamber on the third floor. There was a curtained bed in the centre and a large carved *cassone* or chest against one wall for storing bed-linen. He looked at the view from the window. He tested the bed. It would be the first time he'd slept alone for many weeks, even months. He removed the documents from the cap-case and put them inside a more convenient wallet or *breve* which he hung round his neck inside his doublet. By this time the rest of his luggage had arrived, and he once more said goodbye to Gufo.

When Geoffrey had washed and refreshed himself, he joined Bartolomeo on the covered terrace overlooking the street. They helped themselves to wine and cake, served by a shrunken, shuffling woman. She was called Bella. Maybe she had been once but the name now looked like a mockery. From her manner – berating Bartolomeo for drinking too much, slapping at his wrist when he reached too soon for a pastry – Chaucer guessed that she had been in his employ for a long time. Either that or she was his mother.

The conversation first turned to Chaucer's home town. The Englishman wondered at Bartolomeo's familiarity with London. In turn the Florentine, once he discovered that his visitor's father had been a vintner, wondered whether his own father had ever done business with Geoffrey's.

"For, you know, Geoffrey, we Florentines are everywhere. Trade follows us or we follow trade, who can say which comes first? Is it not possible that we played together as children by the banks of the shining Thames?"

Chaucer felt certain he would have remembered this fellow as a boy, with his large eyes and his long brow (surely creased even then), but he laughed and nodded and agreed that it was indeed possible that they had met as children. Bartolomeo drank from a goblet. He leaned forward to take a cake from a trencher on the table.

"And is there still skating in Moorfield?" he said, crumbs flecking his lips.

"The marshes hadn't frozen when I left London," said Geoffrey, "and they've most likely thawed again by now, but yes, my older son will go there in a year or two's time – if my wife lets him."

"Ah, I had forgotten the power and the authority of the English wife," said Bartolomeo. "Her *terribilita*."

"You are married, Bartolomeo?"

"Bartolomeo is not married but he has hopes," said the Florentine, disconcertingly referring to himself as if he were a third person. "In fact, my hopes lie with the Lipari family with which, I believe, you plan to have dealings. There is a daughter of that house, a junior member of that noble house. I have been paying her – how is it said in England? – paying *court* to her. Yes, for several years now Bartolomeo has been paying court to this lady. I have even written verses for her."

"I too have written verses," said Geoffrey.

"Verses for a lady?"

"In my youth I did. But yours have been successful, Bartolomeo?"

Bartolomeo Gentile pulled such a gloomy face – his mouth turning down, his brow making a V-shape – that Geoffrey had to look away in case he laughed inappropriately.

"What is success in love? She has not said yes – but she has not said no. Of course, what she thinks does not matter so much. It is the opinion of her father which matters. And I think that he is well disposed towards me."

"Her father is Antonio Lipari? The head of the house?"

"The very same."

"Tell me about him."

"He is hard but he is fair. He does not give much away when you talk to him. He has more than a little English but it is not as good as Bartolomeo's English. He has a queer sense of humour."

Bartolomeo obviously expected to be asked how this queer sense of humour showed itself, so Chaucer obliged.

"Well," said the notary, "for one thing he calls his house Purgatorio – Purgatory. It is humorous but strange. Far from being a place of suffering or discomfort, it boasts every latest luxury you could think of. Why should he do that now?"

"Perhaps he's warding off bad fortune by suggesting that his life on this earth isn't so pleasant after all," said Geoffrey. "He is trying not to rouse the envy of the gods."

Bartolomeo's brow creased while he considered the idea. He took another draught of wine. He might have said something further but there was a sudden outburst of sound from the street. With a practised movement the notary swung round in his seat and craned over the balustrade. Geoffrey joined him and looked down. The body of the workman had been removed at some point during the previous hour but there was still a group of individuals gathered loosely about the spot where he'd been struck down. From their dress they appeared to be labourers, perhaps the very ones who had been working on the neighbouring house.

They were listening to a tall man with a pockmarked face who stood in the centre of the group. He would utter a sentence or two to which they responded with loud groans and cries, then the process was repeated. Since he had crossed into the Italian lowlands Chaucer had become accustomed to the vitality and the extravagant manner of the people of these city-states. Responses which in England would signal an imminent fight or at least an argument – agonized cries, the waving of arms, clenched fists – might mean nothing more over here than heartfelt agreement. So it seemed with this group. Chaucer couldn't understand what was being said, for their speech was too rapid and too local, but Bartolomeo provided some explanation.

"The man who is speaking is called Masetto Cennini. He is a well-known troublemaker. His cry is *Viva il popolo!* Every-where, *Viva il popolo!* He has heard of the accident this morning and comes to make mischief out of it. He is saying something about the shoddy quality of the material which the artisans have to work with. He is saying that they will be charged by their employer for the broken ladder and the broken tiles as well as for wasting time by attending to their fallen comrade. He is saying that this is not fair or just."

Chaucer watched with interest. This was of no real concern to him, although he might have said – had anyone asked his opinion – that a sensible employer ought to forgo the charges for time-wasting even if he fined the men for damage to their materials. But no one was going to ask his opinion. He was an outsider.

Now a handful of men, some armed with halberds, appeared suddenly at the far end of the street where it opened into the market square. From the identical dark serge clothing which they wore, Chaucer assumed they were some kind of official watch. A better dressed commander stood slightly to the fore of the group. The man whom Bartolomeo had identified as Masetto might not have noticed them but some of the labourers did and soon their cries and gestures died down, and they began to turn away from the speaker. Some busied themselves sorting out piles of tile and stone that lay tumbled beneath the scaffolding, others suddenly discovered that they had urgent business elsewhere and sidled away from the knot of watchmen. In the end, Masetto was left surrounded by the empty air. The tall man with the pocky countenance didn't shift his ground but waited until the commander of the watch, satisfied that he had achieved his aim of alarming the band of artisans, ordered his men back in the direction of the square. Then Masetto vanished down a narrow street which led at right angles from the Via Calmari.

"The artisans call themselves the *popolo di Dio*," said Bartolomeo Gentile, when he and Chaucer were sitting down once more. "But I think they will be waiting a long time before God favours them. Let us move to more agreeable matters, Geoffrey. If you write verses too, you surely know that this is a town of poets. Dante Alighieri was born not far from this place."

"I must pay my respects at his door," said Chaucer.

"Then you will do more than this city ever did, for he was driven into exile and died far away from his birthplace. Now we would like to have his bones back from Ravenna so that we can honour them. Once upon a time we would have burned him to death."

"Perhaps poets ought to keep away from affairs of state."

"Yet you are a poet and affairs of state are the reason you are here," said Bartolomeo. Raising his goblet, he looked shrewdly over the rim at his English visitor. "I drink to your success. Tomorrow morning we shall call on Antonio Lipari. Bartolomeo will go with you to interpret."

"I'm glad of that," said Geoffrey, and he meant it.

"And now you must tell me more of London. Are there still swans by the Bridge . . . ?"

The door, Dante Alighieri's door, was quite an ordinary door, the entrance to quite an ordinary house by Florentine standards. It was in an area sometimes occupied by cloth and wool carders and squeezed between the dwellings on either side like an afterthought. Could he be certain he was at the right spot? The house was as Bartolomeo had described it, having a green door and standing almost opposite a small church. Yet there was another house a little further down which also had a green door. Doubtless, one green door was as good as another when you came to it. Geoffrey stood in front of the entrance for a moment, paying homage to the dead poet who'd first seen the light of day here (or further down the street). Then he laughed at himself for his devotions as well as his expectations. Not all great men are born in great houses. True *gentilesse* can emerge from the lowliest or most unpromising of backgrounds. Dante Alighieri himself had made that point. Chaucer looked round to see if anyone had observed his laughter. He had an unsettling sense that he was being watched but there was no one in sight, and he shook the feeling off.

Bartolomeo had directed Geoffrey to this house, which was indeed close to the Via Calmari. Earlier that evening the

Englishman and the Florentine had eaten well. The meal was served by the only visible servant, the shuffling crone, who snarled at Bartolomeo but turned an almost toothless grin on Chaucer. Afterwards, Geoffrey had expressed a wish to look at the town and play the visitor. It was dusk. The air still held a little warmth from the day and the streets were full of people chatting in groups or ambling along side by side. No, not quite ambling, for there was a purposeful, parade-like quality to the way these good citizens filled their own *vias* and *piazzas*, as if they were quite as interested in being seen as in seeing.

Left to his own devices, Chaucer had wandered across squares and down streets and alleys. There wasn't much likelihood of getting lost for, wherever you were in the centre of the old city, you might establish your direction by a glimpse of the great cathedral in the Piazza San Giovanni. This building was nowhere near finished but, even with its uncovered naves and unroofed vaults, the great shell still dwarfed anything in Chaucer's native city. Standing in the *piazza* near to the cathedral he looked up at the great campanile. The fading light on the red and white and green marble made it look edible – no, more than edible, made it into a feast of stone. The upper reaches of the campanile tapered into a twilight sky criss-crossed by swallows. Chaucer had walked round the octagon of San Giovanni with its finely worked bronze doors. He'd passed much smaller domestic doors too – doors half open so as to let in the evening air – through which could be glimpsed the quick passage of a brightly gowned figure or the hands of dicers or a cooking pot being placed four-square on a table. Finally Geoffrey had arrived at the house of the poet.

Once he'd paid his silent obeisance to the spirit of Dante Alighieri, he made to retrace his steps to the Via Calmari. On the way he reflected on what Bartolomeo Gentile had told him about the family of the Lipari, who operated one of the newer banks in Florence. With the bankrupting more than thirty years earlier of some of the older houses, such as the Bardi and the Cianghelli, a fresh generation of financial families was in the ascendant. The Lipari had a reputation for tough but honest dealing. Moreover, they had the resources and the willingness to operate on a large scale.

Chaucer's task was, on one level, straightforward enough. He simply had to convey to Antonio Lipari the documents which, with appropriate flourishes, requested a loan of 160,000 florins to the English exchequer. The preliminary approaches had already been made by earlier envoys. Lipari knew what was going to be asked of him. The documents were a formality, but a necessary one, and the deal would not be concluded until everything was signed. There was a risk to the banking house in lending even to so great a personage as the English King but also the reflected glory of possessing such a grand debtor. If Antonio Lipari agreed he would instruct his agents in London to draw up the appropriate contracts and arrange the necessary letters of credit. No actual gold or money would change hands, nothing so physical or crude.

However, the uses to which the money would be put were purely physical. They were nowhere stated but it didn't take much to work out – as Tomaso Falcone had done immediately – that when a king requires money it is almost always to prosecute a war. In this case it was the continuing struggle against France which had flared up when Edward the Third was a young man and which would most likely see him into his grave, unfinished. This was the same perpetual struggle in which Chaucer and Falcone had played a small part during their early lives. Sometimes Chaucer wondered whether the French war would see him into *his* grave too. Throw all the men and money you could at it, the struggle occasionally seemed like the maw of a monster which could never be satisfied or filled. At other times, he believed that everything was for the best, that fortune and providence ruled over all, even in war. And officially

71

he had no view on the wisdom of the loans and debts which he was now negotiating. They were affairs of state, to be weighed up by more important people than himself. He was a middling civil servant, he was a glorified messenger.

With such thoughts as these, he crossed the square where the market had taken place that morning. The ground was scattered with cheese rinds and nut shells, with fragments of cloth and leather. Judging by the smell emanating from them, a line of stinking barrrels contained offal, which would presumably find its way into the river sooner or later. Dogs and cats slunk in the shadows around the margins of the scene, their raggedness in contrast to the Florentines parading about in all their finery. In contrast also to the city towers which seemed, through some quality of the fading light, to stretch further up into the sky with each passing moment.

Chaucer turned into the Via Calmari. It was quiet here and somehow more chill after the bustle of the square. The birds occupying the little cages on the house fronts were asleep. Scaffolding huddled by the entrance to the house which was close to Bartolomeo Gentile's property. Chaucer paused at the point where the young man had met with the accident. The broken ladder was propped against the wall. There were shards of tile still in the road and stains that might have been his blood. Odd that he didn't know whether the man was dead or alive. Was there a mother or a wife or sweetheart grieving somewhere in Florence this evening? He thought of the tall man with the pockmarked face, Masetto. 'A troublemaker', Bartolomeo had called him. Well, perhaps so.

A draught of air blew down the street and the ropes and buckets hanging from pulleys creaked and swayed. Chaucer glanced up at the scaffolding overhead. It was almost completely dark by now. In among the network of poles he thought he saw a shape which stirred even as he watched. Chaucer blinked. He didn't trust his eyesight, especially in the near dark.

Maybe it was a cat up there. (But the shape was much too large for a cat.) He screwed up his eyes and looked again. The shape had vanished.

He sensed rather than heard someone behind him. He glanced back. A cloaked figure was bearing down on him at street level, arms spread, face hidden by a hood. Instinctively he turned and raised his arms in self-defence. The figure grabbed him by the arm. Geoffrey's foot caught in one of the scaffolding poles and he fell. The violence with which the hooded shape was tugging caused him to hit the ground heavily and to roll several feet into the centre of the roadway. There was a loud thump and a crash close by and he felt a jabbing pain below one eye. He lay, winded and confused, in the middle of the roadway for a minute or longer. He listened and imagined that he could hear feet retreating down the Via Calmari. He raised a hand to his cheek. It was wet and slick. He heard more footsteps, this time coming nearer. He became aware of a figure bending over him. Fearing it was the person in a cloak, he made to scrabble to his feet. A hand pressed down on him.

"Geoffrey," said a voice he recognized. "It is you. Are you all right? No, you are hurt!"

Bartolomeo Gentile was leaning over him, resting a solicitous hand on his shoulder. Chaucer slowly stood up. He felt the blood trickling down his face and tasted it on his lips.

"What happened?" said the notary.

Chaucer looked to the ground. A few feet away a leather bucket lay on its side. The smell of lime and a pale-coloured pool slowly forming by the rim showed what its contents had been. Several shattered tiles lay nearby, freshly shattered ones. No doubt it was a sliver from one of these which had struck Chaucer under the eye. He touched his hand to his face once more. The blood wasn't flowing so fast now.

"I don't know," said Chaucer. "There was . . . "

73

He felt light-headed. He glanced down the street and then up at the framework of scaffolding. No shapes, no cloaked figures.

"Yes? What happened?" said Bartolomeo again. In his voice was a real concern. "Tell me what happened."

"There was . . . another accident," said Geoffrey. "These items fell without warning."

"It is lucky you were not standing right underneath."

But I was standing right underneath, Chaucer might have said. *There was someone crouching in the scaffolding above. If it hadn't been for a man in a dark cloak who pulled me to one side then I would have been struck full force by the bucket and tiles. I might have ended up like that unfortunate young man this morning.*

But he said none of this. Perhaps because he didn't want to trouble Bartolomeo Gentile. Perhaps because he wasn't sure whether he would be believed. Easier to treat this as an accident from which he'd had a lucky escape.

"Let us go indoors," said Bartolomeo.

Still keeping a protective hand on his guest, he walked with him towards his house. Once they were sitting in an upstairs chamber illuminated by oil lamps, he summoned the old woman called Bella. She brought her wizened face close to Geoffrey's and, with the aid of a candle, examined his wound. She tutted and shuffled off. Meanwhile Bartolomeo stood by, wringing his hands and pulling long faces.

"Bartolomeo is sorry, so sorry that this should have happened to a visitor," he said.

"It could have been worse."

"Ah, that is the English phlegm speaking. The phlegm which makes light of trouble and takes things as they come."

He had difficulty with the word and pronounced it 'phleg-em'. Chaucer wondered whether to put him right but a glance at the notary's anxious monkey-face with its creased brow made him feel sorry for Bartolomeo rather than himself. The man was so evidently distressed on Chaucer's behalf and now he gabbled away in his relief that worse had not happened.

"We Florentines are ruled by other humours. We are ruled by blood when we are feeling cheerful, and by choler when we are not. But you English are famous for your phleg-em and do not show your feelings. Let me tell you though, Geoffrey, an angel was watching over you out there."

An angel in a dark cloak, thought Chaucer. Then a disquieting idea occurred. Perhaps the figure who'd rushed out of the darkness had been trying not to save him but to push him further into harm's way. Was this an attack from two quarters? If so, by whom? And for what reason? The idea that he had unknown enemies seemed to justify his reluctance to give Bartolomeo a full account.

Just then the old servant returned bearing several little pots and tubs which she placed on a nearby table. She spoke sharply to Bartolomeo who went to a corner of the room. Chaucer heard liquid being poured and then a goblet was thrust into his hand. He hesitated an instant before drinking. The fiery liquid warmed his gullet before settling pleasantly into his guts. Bartolomeo evidently thought it would be a good idea to fortify himself with drink also. He poured a generous draught, downed it in one and helped himself to another.

Meantime the crone, who was about the same height standing as Chaucer was sitting, bent forward and tilted his head with one hand. With the other she cleaned the blood from the gash below Geoffrey's eye with a rag that was impregnated with something stinging. Then she dipped her fingers into a couple of the little pots on the table and smeared the unguent on his wound. Her withered lips were pursed in concentration while her eyes, squinting in the candlelight, were almost lost in a mesh of wrinkles. He was reminded of his mother attending to his cuts and grazes when, as a child, he'd fallen out of a pear tree. In this old woman's attentions there was a trace of his mother's concern, together with more than a trace of her impatience.

The warmth rising from his belly and the sense of being looked after made him feel calm and sleepy. His eyelids drooped. He saw again the scene in the Via Calmari. The shape in the scaffolding overhead which had almost certainly been responsible for launching the lime bucket and tiles on his head. The cloaked figure who'd darted forward to save him – or to assail him from the other side? The streets of Florence were more dangerous than he'd thought.

But he was safe here, wasn't he, in the house of Bartolomeo Gentile, being treated by this kindly old woman. Wasn't he?

7

Whatever the wizened old crone – or that kindly old servant Bella, as Geoffrey now thought of her – had applied to his face seemed to have done its work because, by the morning, the cut under his eye was already starting to heal. In fact when he first woke in this strange city, with its dazzling light and its clanging bells, it took him more than a moment to recall the events of the previous evening. The shadow crouched in the scaffolding and the hooded figure who'd pushed him to one side seemed like the figments of a dream. And if not a dream, then what had happened was perhaps no more than some accident, not worth fretting over.

He and Bartolomeo Gentile left together the next morning to visit the home of Antonio Lipari, head of the banking family. At the entrance to the neighbouring house which was covered by scaffolding, workmen were already clambering nimbly over the structure. Apart from some darkened stains of blood there was no indication of the mishaps of the day before, no shards of tile, no spilled bucket of lime. As they were walking past, the notary made a queer gesture in the direction of the house. Tucking back his middle and ring finger under his thumb, he extended his other two fingers like a fork. Noticing Chaucer's curious glance, he explained that he was making the *mano cornuto*, a gesture apparently intended to ward off harm or evil, emanating from a place where there'd been two accidents.

"You have similar gestures at home, Geoffrey?"

"Yes – but not so expressive."

"Perhaps the English do not believe in such things? Signs and stars and the like. Perhaps the English do not know about the hidden forces which rule this world."

"What *I* know," said Geoffrey, "is that this is the time of year when the sun is close to entering Taurus and so a good moment to engage in business matters."

"Yes, yes," said Bartolomeo, "since the sign rules over finance."

"That's what they say anyhow. It's a propitious time to be visiting the Lipari house."

"But you, do you *believe* in it? Bartolomeo would appreciate an answer, for you are a man who is *bel erudito*, as we say, Geoffrey."

Bartolomeo did indeed appear eager to discover what Chaucer thought. They were emerging from the Via Calmari into the market square. Chaucer pulled his hat down to shade his eyes and paused for an instant.

"What do I believe?" he said, as if it was a question he'd never asked himself before. "I believe that nothing is lost by trusting in the stars and so on. Men and women need some guide to their actions and the stars are as good as anything else, as long as they don't conflict with conscience. And when things go wrong we can always blame the stars – or blame fortune. She can stand it. She has broad shoulders."

Bartolomeo laughed in appreciation of the remark. They walked on, taking streets that led towards the cathedral in the Piazza San Giovanni and then entering the Via dei Cerretani. The houses were more imposing here, older and taller. Geoffrey and Bartolomeo made to turn in at one of them, the arch of which was crowned by a coat of arms showing a ladder picked out in gold against a background of green. Above it was the Latin phrase *Lente sed certe*. There was an old man sitting outside on a stone bench near the arched entrance. He had only one leg. He gave them a gap-toothed grin and Bartolomeo responded with a wave. A great door sealed the entrance but set into it was a smaller gate or *sportello* and this was open. Beyond was a kind of hut inside which lurked a doorkeeper, a sour-faced fellow who did not stir from his seat. Bartolomeo greeted him as a long-lost friend. But if this was an attempt to show how welcome he was in the Lipari house, it didn't work. The other merely gestured him through wearily.

"Welcome to Purgatory, he might have said," said Bartolomeo.

Beyond the entrance was a courtyard with two separate flights of steps climbing to the first floor. One was of wood and evidently led to the servants' area and probably the kitchens. The other was more elaborate and made of stone. It opened into a flowery arcade. The whole effect was much larger and more elaborate than the lawyer's own house. A girl and a woman were standing talking in the flower-shrouded loggia. The woman had striking red hair partly covered by a pearl-and-ribbon net. The girl had something of the other's looks and hair colouring, with a chin that was a little too prominent. When she saw the new arrivals in the courtyard she waved.

"That is my Philomela," said Bartolomeo, with a slight quaver.

"Who is the other woman?"

"That is her mother. She is Emilia, the wife to Antonio di Lipari."

They climbed the steps and stopped before the women. Bartolomeo Gentile became flustered as he introduced the English guest. Chaucer noticed mild amusement in the mother's eyes, seemingly directed at her daughter's suitor. Philomela smiled, even smiled fondly, at the visitors and said a few words. Then Bartolomeo, as if remembering that they were here on business matters, ushered Geoffrey forward.

At the far end of the loggia they climbed another short flight of stairs and came to a door. Bartolomeo entered without knocking. Inside a large room several scribes were sitting on stools behind desks which were covered with stacks of loose paper and bound ledgers, with quill pens and ink-pots. On this third storey the windows were larger and the light was stronger, no doubt one of the reasons for installing the accounts room up here. Chaucer noticed that many of the sheets of paper were covered with rows of figures, in both Latin and Arabic numerals. Some of the clerks were poring over them, running the forefinger of one hand down the columns and with the other sliding counters on an abacus. They did this by touch, without looking at the counters. Several were transcribing epistles and other documents into large volumes. One or two looked up briefly as Geoffrey and Bartolomeo passed through the room but the attention of most was firmly fixed on their paperwork. It reminded Geoffrey of the office in his father's house in the Vintry ward where all the computations to do with the wine trade were carried out. This place was on a much larger scale but there was the same absorption in the task, the same quietness interrupted only by the muted clacking of the abacuses and the rustling of paper.

There was another door towards the far end of the counting room and this time Bartolomeo did knock. A single word issued from within and the two men entered an even larger chamber which, Chaucer guessed, must run almost the full length of the house on this floor. Instead of thick hangings on the walls, as there would have been in a rich man's room in England, there were pictures painted directly on to the plaster so as to give the effect of tapestry. Chaucer had an indistinct impression of tangled figures and animals, trees and vegetation. A large table in the centre of the room was laden with old bronze lamps and small pottery vessels. The way in which they were laid out suggested that they were for display rather than use. Several marble statues were positioned on plinths on the left side of the chamber. The statues were incomplete, missing heads or hands or arms. The morning sun, streaming through the glassed windows on the opposite side, picked out the pink veining in the marble of the floor.

At the other end of this great chamber were two men. One was leaning forward to whisper into the ear of the other, who was sitting behind a desk. Unlike the cluttered tables of the clerks in the antechamber, the desk was almost empty. The most prominent object on it was an astrolabe. The man who'd been whispering straightened up and the other indicated with a nod of the head that he'd heard and understood. Then the sitting man gestured with his hand and the standing one – a small, reddish-bearded fellow with sharp eyes – bowed slightly before glancing at the visitors with a look of animosity which he barely bothered to conceal. Given his dismissal, he withdrew through a door in the inner wall. The door, like the rest of the wall, was covered with part of a continuously painted scene and was, in effect, a concealed entry. At this end of the room were depicted trees with heavy foliage, and the occasional human shape. Seeing the small man exit through the door gave Chaucer the impression that he was slipping into the middle of a dark wood, an impression reinforced by the fact that the image of a figure, its back to the viewer, was painted on the door itself.

The man behind the desk half rose in acknowledgement of Geoffrey and Bartolomeo's arrival. The notary spoke in Italian, with a flourish of his long arms, introducing Antonio Lipari – *nostro illustrissimo banchiere* – to Geoffrey Chaucer – *nostro eminente visitatore inglese*. And then the introductions seemed to be made the other way round, with more arm flourishes and differently phrased descriptions of host and guest. Geoffrey grasped the extended hand of Antonio Lipari. It was a firm, powerful grasp but a warm one.

"*Il mio piacere*," said the banker. "Please, to seat yourself."

He indicated a couple of chairs which were already positioned in front of the desk and rang a little handbell. Almost immediately, as if she'd been waiting on the far side, a servant-woman came through the same painted door. Lipari said something too rapid for Chaucer to follow. While the banker was speaking, he took the opportunity to study the man's face. Antonio Lipari was clean-shaven and jowly. A fringe of hair, rather like a monk's tonsure, accentuated the massiveness of his head, which seemed to bear down on his shoulders like a ball of stone. There was a bull-like quality about the way he turned when he was listening or talking to someone at his side. Chaucer wondered whether he had indeed been born under Taurus, the birth sign which would have been fitting for a banker. Lipari's brown-eyed gaze was steady, contemplative.

Geoffrey gazed about the room. He had been inside many rich, highly decorated chambers but never one quite like this. Antonio Lipari saw him looking and said, "Please, *messere*. Regard."

Accompanied by Bartolomeo, Chaucer got up and went a few paces down the room. He looked first at the ancient statues which were dotted about the place. Every one was damaged, as if they had been involved in fighting each other. The second or third he examined was a particularly impressive example, for all that it had no head and was missing part of an arm. Despite its headless condition, and leaving aside the low marble plinth it stood on, the statue reared taller than any mere human. It was a marble figure in antique dress, wearing a close-fitting breast-plate above a tunic and a kind of armoured skirt that reached only as far as the kneecaps. The limbs were flexed in a fighting posture, most of the figure's weight being braced on the right leg. One of the bare arms, the left one, was broken off above the elbow but the other held aloft a short sword. The sinews in the neck and arms stood out like cords or rope. It was the sculptor's skill which suggested that the warrior was about to bring the sword down in a single skull-splitting stroke.

Chaucer reached out a hand and touched the place where the head had been severed from the neck. The break was clean and the marble was worn smooth. It was cold to the touch and, with alarm, he noted that the figure shifted very slightly under his fingers, as if wanting only a touch to set it in motion. Or so it seemed to him. He felt the skin on the back of his neck prickling. Even if it was meant to represent an emperor or some great Caesar of the past, there was something inhuman about the antique shape. Bartolomeo agreed apparently, for Chaucer heard him draw in his breath. Accustomed to the warm stone of church effigies in England, Chaucer wondered how old this piece was. It seemed to come from a different world, a colder world of gods and giants. He turned away, wanting to get out of range of that short sword.

Now Geoffrey, followed by Bartolomeo Gentile, went on to examine the wall painting. Closer to, he saw that it was a scene of war, at least in this section. Against the background of a barren plain, there were men on horseback who'd joined battle, their lances at all angles like porcupine quills. Others were on foot, wielding swords and battle-axes and flails. Yet others were on the ground, writhing in agony and with blood gushing from their wounds, while a handful lay in the stiffness of death. Atop a nearby hill there stood a temple made of steel, not stone, with a single narrow entrance and no windows. Above the door was incised the word *Marte*. The painter was very skilled. Geoffrey had seen his share of fighting and the depiction reminded him, unpleasantly, of the heat and terror and the mad exultation of battle.

He sensed rather than saw the bullish bulk of Antonio Lipari right behind him.

"You say Mars in your tongue?" said the banker.

"Yes. Mars, the god of war. Is that also the god of war . . . ?"

Chaucer indicated the headless statue, the one with the raised sword.

Lipari pouted and shrugged, a surprisingly delicate gesture.

"I cannot tell you," he said. "'E is my *commendatore*. My knight, you would say. I 'ave bought him not long since but already 'e give me good fortune."

He reached out a hand and touched the figure gently. The breastplate was illuminated by a bolt of sunlight. Geoffrey waited to see if the statue stirred but he could detect no movement.

"He has great power," said Chaucer. "And Mars too, he has power in this painting of yours."

"Ah, 'e is not the only force of power in our lives. Also there is this one."

Lipari grasped at Chaucer's arm and led him back down the room to where Bartolomeo was already studying the wall. Here the barren plain turned to a background of mountain and forest and sea. A naked woman emerged from green, glassy waters which covered her to the navel. She wore a garland of roses. Doves flickered above her head, while a winged boy wearing a blindfold and holding bow and arrows hovered in attendance.

"*Ecco Venere*," said Bartolomeo, "and her naughty little *ragazzo*. He strikes where he will, that one, and no one can help himself."

The notary accompanied this remark by miming an archer pulling a miniature bow and then clapping a hand over his heart. Chaucer wondered whether he was making some oblique reference to himself and his feelings for – what was the daughter's name? – Philomela. If so, it seemed to pass Antonio Lipari by, to judge by his next words.

"But all is not – 'ow you say? – *dolcezza* in this place. See."

He pointed to other pictures beyond Venus's shore. Chaucer looked more closely. It did not surprise him that there was almost as much misfortune and misery here as in the scene presided over by the temple of Mars. He was beginning to get the measure of Antonio Lipari's taste, the sardonic humour of a man who would call his comfortable town house by the name of Purgatory.

On this section of wall there was a series of scenes. A herd of swine with the faces of men were overseen by the half-dressed witch Circe, a smile of satisfaction on her seductive features. There were women who had suffered for love: Cleopatra leaping into a pit full of snakes, naked except for her crown; Queen Dido sacrificing herself on a funeral pyre as her beloved Aeneas sailed away with the Trojan fleet. There were anonymous figures: a female wearing a yellow garland and holding a cuckoo in her hand; an old hag exposing a withered breast and leering hideously at a pair of half-interested young men. One couple were lying in a green bower and engaged in the act of love but they were framed by all this suffering. Over the door itself was the ambiguous figure, running and half turning her head round as if she was being pursued. There was no pleasure in her expression. Or was it *his* expression? Chaucer peered more closely and could not tell whether he was looking at a man or a woman.

Antonio Lipari was watching Geoffrey for his reaction.

"You call this place Purgatory, do you not, Signor Lipari? Your grand house, I mean. And these paintings show much . . . unease. Agitation. Discomfort."

By the smile on Lipari's face, Chaucer knew that he had responded appropriately.

"'Ere is the 'istory of women, no."

"The legend of good women," said Chaucer, indicating Dido of Carthage.

"But this one is – 'ow is it said? – a witch, and this one, she is *ingannatrice*," said Lipari, waving his arm first at Circe then at Cleopatra.

"A deceiver," said Bartolomeo.

"*Così fan tutte*," said Lipari.

The concealed door opened and the servant-woman returned

with a salver on which was a flask of wine, a trio of goblets and a plate of cakes. They went back to their seats. Lipari established himself behind his desk, while the wine was poured and the cakes handed round before the servant was given the order to leave. The wine was pale gold and sweet-tasting while the cakes were delicious, ginger and another taste which Chaucer couldn't pin down. He sipped appreciatively.

"*Vernaccia*," said Antonio Lipari. "Is from our region."

"My father was a vintner," said Chaucer. "I grew up with the vine. The grape was our table-talk."

Lipari looked puzzled at the words and Bartolomeo swiftly supplied a translation. The banker nodded in understanding. Chaucer had been wondering whether Gentile's presence was necessary in these negotiations, for the Florentine appeared to have a fair grasp of English, but he realized now that the notary could explain any subtleties or complicated phrases which might otherwise slip past the banker.

"*Allora*," said Antonio Lipari. "Let us commence our business, Signor Chaucer."

He held out a broad palm. It was the moment Chaucer had been waiting for and he extracted a package of documents from the *breve* or wallet inside his doublet and passed them over with a sense of relief. He'd been carrying them for nearly four months across seas, over plains and mountains. This was where his responsibility ended, surely.

Using a slim knife which lay on the desk, Lipari slit the seals on a couple of the documents and unfolded the paper. He replaced the knife on the desk. He scanned the sheets with a practised eye. Chaucer had been given them himself by the secretary to the King's exchequer. They included a personal letter dictated by the King. He didn't know what the documents said, or even whether they were penned in Italian or French or English, or some mixture of all three. But in any case Antonio Lipari already knew what was being requested of him. Money speaks with a universal tongue.

After a few moments Lipari put the papers down. He looked at Chaucer with his large, contemplative brown eyes.

"Is secret, yes?" he said.

Chaucer wasn't absolutely sure what he meant but he nodded and said, "No one in Florence knows about my business – apart from you, sir, and Bartolomeo Gentile here."

"Good, good," said the banker. "*Affare di tutti, affare di nessuno.*"

Geoffrey got the general sense of this – that everybody's business was nobody's business – but then Antonio Lipari launched into a stream of Italian which he had difficulty in following. When the other had finished speaking, Chaucer looked a query at Bartolomeo.

The notary explained: "Signor Lipari says that other banks in Florence have advanced money to the English King in the past but with unfortunate results. He has only to mention the great names of the Salvini and the Cianghalli – to say nothing of the even greater house of Bardi. Some have even gone bankrupt as a result of making imprudent loans . . ."

Chaucer felt uncomfortable. Was he expected to defend the spending habits of Edward the Third? Or to account for the King's unconquerable taste for waging war?

"May I respectfully say that that was a long time ago – in the time of our fathers – "

" . . . but," continued Bartolomeo, "Messere Lipari says that it is not every day that one receives a missive from the court of the English King. And that he is prepared to consider a request from such an elevated source."

Lipari stuck out an emphatic forefinger and said something else, as if he wanted to underline what had just been said. Perhaps his English was better than Bartolomeo had claimed. Now the notary translated the qualification, "Only to *consider* this request, mark you . . ."

Then Chaucer understood that this was all part of the lender's game. It was the same on those rare occasions when he'd been compelled to borrow money in London, as he had before his marriage to Philippa for example. He might have been sipping wine in a fine chamber in a *palazzo* in the Via dei Cerretani but the experience wasn't essentially different from going to one of those little business houses north of East Cheap. Few usurers could resist the temptation to show that they held the whip-hand. They liked to make things just a little tricky for the borrower. Everyone knew that loans had to be paid for, not only in money but with deferential smiles and nods of gratitude. So it was that Geoffrey Chaucer now found himself nodding and smiling on behalf of his distant master, Edward the Third of England.

" . . . and finally," concluded Bartolomeo, "Signor Lipari says that he will give you his answer in three days' time, on the evening of which day you are bidden – we are both bidden – to do him the honour of eating and drinking with him and his family. In the meantime you are to enjoy yourself as a visitor to the greatest city in the world."

Antonio Lipari rose slightly in his seat to indicate that the interview was finished.

"The honour is mine – or ours, I should say," said Geoffrey. He stood and bowed slightly in the direction of the banker. "Thank you for receiving us, sir, and showing us the treasures of your fine chamber."

They shook hands. Before the two visitors could turn away, the concealed door opened once more, the one situated at what Chaucer now thought of as the 'Venus' end of the room. It was the red-bearded man, the one who'd been whispering in Lipari's ear when they first arrived. Again glancing with a scarcely concealed hostility at the others, he went across to his master and once more bent towards his ear. Chaucer suspected he had a taste for conducting all his conversations in this manner, since it showed his importance by excluding others.

Geoffrey and Bartolomeo walked down the long chamber, passing the Venus and Mars wall paintings and the curiously incomplete statues, and skirting the table covered with brass and pottery gewgaws. They went through the long ante-chamber, full of clerks poring silently over their accounts and clicking their abacuses. Down to the loggia and then out into the courtyard. There was no sign of Lipari's flame-haired wife Emilia or his daughter, and the sour-eyed doorkeeper ignored them as they passed, but the one-legged man sitting on the stone bench outside the *palazzo* gave them the same cheerful, gap-toothed grin. Chaucer had never seen so many people simply sitting or lounging about the streets as he had in this city. Something to do with the weather, he supposed, thinking of the cold draughts which could sweep through London even in the middle of summer. But it was also to do with the temper of the Florentines. They liked acting out their lives in public. It was as if they had nothing to hide.

Meanwhile Bartolomeo Gentile was saying something to him.

"What did you make of our illustrious banker, Geoffrey?"

"A man of power."

"Of course."

"Someone who respects the past but wants to make it serve his purpose. All those antique figures and paintings reflect his standing in this town."

"Of course, again," said Bartolomeo. "But Antonio Lipari is also a modern man even if he collects old items. Did you see the glass in his windows? You won't find that in every wealthy house. Some of our older citizens consider that glass is the height of decadence. It has even been blamed for the floods that afflict our city, and the terrible pestilence which I remember from my childhood."

"We will blame the stars when we don't know the causes of things – or the glass in rich men's windows," said Chaucer.

"Ah, we are back to the stars."

They strolled in silence for a time through the streets. The air was like a tepid bath.

"You noticed his arms?" said Bartolomeo. "The *scudo* above the entrance?"

"The golden ladder against the green, and the Latin?"

"*Lente sed certe*. Slowly but surely. Signifying that the Lipari family have risen by their own efforts, which is true I suppose. They may have risen slowly but surely they have risen. They weren't born at the top of the ladder."

"Those who are born at the top have nowhere to go," said Chaucer. "Tell me, who was that in Signor Lipari's chamber when we entered and again when we left? Small, with the reddish beard."

"A gentleman by the name of Peruzzi," said Bartolomeo in a grudging way. "He is a kind of secretary to our banker, I suppose."

"You don't like him? He certainly didn't seem to like us."

"Are Bartolomeo's feelings so obvious?" said the notary, referring to himself in that odd, detached fashion. "I suppose my voice gives me away. Yes, it's true, Geoffrey, I do not care for Matteo Peruzzi. I don't trust him. He has his master's ear yet the advice he gives serves his own purposes. And I believe that he has designs on my Philomela. He would like to cement his position in the Lipari family by marriage."

"But that's exactly what *you* want to do, Bartolomeo."

"I am motivated by love and love only. If Philomela was the daughter of a humble *contadino* I would still feel just the same towards her. I was struck by Cupid's dart the first moment I saw her. That naughty *ragazzo* with his bow and arrow. But did you see the way she smiled at me? Wouldn't you say that there was warmth and promise there? And in her mother's gaze too."

Chaucer recalled only a gentle amusement in the mother's eyes but he agreed with Bartolomeo that, yes, both mother and daughter had looked quite fondly on him. This didn't seem to be enough for Gentile, however. He sighed.

"And yet, Master Geoffrey, I do not consider that my suit advances as fast as it might."

"Love never runs smooth, my friend."

"Sometimes you sound middle-aged."

His light tone robbed the remark of any offence. In any case, Geoffrey was not offended. Middle-aged, eh? He had sometimes thought of himself in the same light. But Bartolomeo wasn't finished.

"It must be the English phleg-em in you. But listen, you could help your friend Bartolomeo in this matter of Philomela!"

"If I can. But I must tell you one thing. That word you are so fond of is pronounced phlegm. The 'g' is silent."

"Phlegm," said Bartolomeo experimentally. "*Phlegm*. See, already you are helping me. You have written verses to ladies, Geoffrey? Maybe you could advise me on what to write in my verses to Philomela."

Why not? thought Chaucer.

"Why not?" he said.

After all, he was only here to negotiate a loan on behalf of the English King so that Edward could prosecute another of his wars against the French. Suddenly, it seemed more important to him to help this love-lorn notary in his affairs of the heart than to raise cash so that more men might lose their lives on the battlefield. No, not more important but much more congenial. Antonio Lipari's decision was a matter for him alone. The banker would be swayed by business considerations, and perhaps by the royal missive. Chaucer was no more than a messenger, now relieved of his burden. But when it came to writing love lyrics, Geoffrey believed himself to have a certain skill. Why shouldn't this be put at the service of the amiable Gentile?

"Show me what you have written," he said. "We'll see whether we can't improve on it."

While Geoffrey and Bartolomeo were having this conversation in the street, the banker Antonio Lipari was talking to his secretary Matteo Peruzzi in the long chamber decorated with the statues and all the benevolent works of Venus and Mars. Peruzzi had been in the employ of Lipari for only a few years. He had served an apprenticeship with the other clerks in the counting house where he'd shown himself remarkably quick with figures, capable of holding large numbers in his head and doing mental calculations with a speed that appeared almost magical. Very soon he had risen in favour, and Lipari fell into the habit of consulting him about almost every commercial decision. Lipari sometimes referred to him as *mio volpacchiotto* – my little fox cub – on account of his red beard and general sharpness. Peruzzi's origins were obscure. His family had, like so many citizens of Florence, died in the terrible outbreak of plague to which Bartolomeo had referred, but it was his abilities which spoke for him and not his background. In the old days he might not have advanced so quickly, but things were more fluid now.

In fact, Antonio Lipari himself came from a family that had made its fortunes comparatively recently, and his house had climbed to its current prominence after those same bankruptcies of the 1340s which he had mentioned to Geoffrey Chaucer. The failures of the Bardi family as well as the Salvini and the Cianghalli and others had been the rungs on his own ladder. Accordingly, the banker was perhaps more inclined to trust classless newcomers who weren't hampered by old beliefs and practices. His respect for the past was confined to statues and other objects that came to light when the ground was being broken for the new villas and *palazzi* which were springing up everywhere on the outskirts of the city. He collected antiquities and paid a high price for them, but when it came to commercial matters he was thoroughly modern.

So Antonio Lipari had no business secrets from Matteo Peruzzi and trusted him absolutely. Now they were discussing the matter of the loan to the English King. Peruzzi had just made the very point which Lipari had touched on with Chaucer: that such 'royal' loans were often a prelude to disaster even though they might look good on paper and could enhance the reputation of a house. Disaster had happened before; it could happen again. Lipari was amused to hear his own opinion being echoed back to him. But where his words had been spoken for form's sake – as Chaucer guessed, it was part of the dance between borrower and lender – there was real force behind Peruzzi's objections. In fact, had Antonio Lipari but known it, Peruzzi had already gone rather further than mere words in order to thwart Chaucer's mission.

"So cautious, Matteo?" he said now.

"I am only thinking of the best interests of your house, sir."

"But such a request as this . . . "

Lipari gestured at the documents which still lay on his desk. The Lipari house had advanced money to several princes and dukes of the city-states but not yet to a foreign monarch. Antonio Lipari would never have admitted it but he was prepared to be a little impressed by the royal seal.

"A king may default on a loan more readily than other men," said Peruzzi. "Who is to hold him to account?"

"The world, since it will know him for a defaulter, a cheater."

"Puh," said Peruzzi with an explosive detonation of his lips. "What would a king care about that, especially the English one? All the English care about is fighting and brawling. Their skulls are too thick to contain anything else. You may lend them money and all the repayment you will get is a blow on the head."

"Master Chaucer, the man who visited today, he doesn't look like a fighter," said Lipari.

"It's the exception proves the rule, sir. Your brother always says that the English are good for nothing but fighting."

A shadow passed over Lipari's face at the mention of his brother and Peruzzi realized he'd said the wrong thing. Almost any mention of Lipari's *fratello* was unwise. The banker and his brother, who was blind, were at daggers drawn although they could generally put on a display of fraternal friendship in public. Peruzzi went no further in this direction. He was always very careful not to show open opposition to his master. He offered exactly the right amount of criticism or qualification to make him appear an independent thinker, even a robust one, knowing that Lipari respected such men. But in this case he genuinely considered any loan to the English crown to be an unacceptable risk. Why, it could easily lead to the house of Lipari being ruined. And if the house of Lipari was ruined, so were all his hopes and plans . . .

"So, sir, you will turn down this request?" he said.

"You think I should turn it down, *mio volpacchiotto*?"

"I would if I were sitting in that chair."

Before the words were out of his mouth, Matteo Peruzzi realized that once again he'd blundered, and more seriously this time. For all his influence with Lipari, he was still an employee. Even to hint at the possibility of what he might do if ensconced in the considerably more comfortable chair on the other side of the desk was to reveal too much of the ambition which he harboured.

"But you do not sit here, Matteo," said Lipari. "I, Antonio Lipari, occupy this place. And the decision whether to look with favour on any request from the English King is mine and mine alone. I will think about this matter and give my answer tomorrow night."

"Of course, sir. Forgive me if I have spoken out of turn. It's merely the interests of the house that concern me."

8

It had taken Lisabetta Greco some time to pluck up the courage to go in search of the individual known as Giuseppe. Her man Guido had vanished nearly a fortnight earlier. He had simply slipped away from their room late one evening, saying that he had some business to attend to and that she should sleep sound and not worry about him.

Guido Greco had been behaving oddly before his disappearance. Behaving oddly or unwisely. He paid too much attention to that fiery speaker Masetto, who was always attempting to provoke the workers into protest. Following Masetto's lead, he muttered about the injustice that was the daily lot of artisans like him, labourers who were too lowly to be part of a guild. It was all very well for Masetto to say such things. He came from a good family, and people like that were forgiven if they occasionally spoke out of turn.

But it was different with Guido. If he drew attention to himself he would not be forgiven, yet he forgot his station in life and persisted in making extravagant claims. For example, he said that the times were changing, and that a moment was coming when the rich would be pulled down from their seats and the humble exalted in their place. Lisabetta shushed him when he proclaimed these things in the privacy of their bed, usually after a drink too many (but almost any drink was a drink too many for Guido). She pleaded with him not to make such comments in public, whether he was with the other day-labourers or with his associates in the tavern. You never knew who was watching and listening. The city authorities were always on the lookout for dissent, and they paid informers to bring them tittle-tattle. But Guido was, by nature, an open man. His favourite expression was *'per dire il vero.'* He was also careless by nature. Sooner or later, she'd often warned him, his oh-so-honest, truth-telling tongue would get him into trouble, deep trouble which he wouldn't be able to talk his way out of.

Was that what had happened to him, deep trouble?

It must have been. What other explanation was there for his disappearance?

At first when Guido didn't return, she thought he must be lying in a doorway or a ditch somewhere, sleeping off the night before. She cursed him for his weak head and his weaker will. Then, as the hours went by and the next night came down, she grew anxious. Perhaps he was injured or worse than injured. By the time the following day dawned, she was sure he was dead. Her initial reaction was anger. They hadn't been married long, only a matter of months, and she was convinced that, in what had been almost their last time together, he had left her pregnant. There was no evidence of this – it was far too soon for any signs – but somehow she *knew*.

It even crossed Lisabetta's mind in the midst of her anxiety that, if Guido really was no more, then she should catch herself a new husband. If she acted straightaway, any child could easily be passed off as the next man's. It wouldn't be too hard for her to lay her hands on someone. She might be short but she had nice, full breasts and a wandering eye that had occasionally landed her in trouble in the past. She rebuked herself for having thoughts of another husband – so soon, so soon. On the other hand, didn't they say that a mouse with only one hole to go to was poorly provided for? Then she rebuked herself for having that thought as well.

Nevertheless, whatever she might do in the future, her first duty was to try to establish what had happened to Guido.

Lisabetta put aside work for a couple of days although she couldn't really afford to do so. She took in washing and performed small repairs on torn and frayed clothing for neighbours. They said she was a miracle with a needle, and indeed she possessed a pair of small but powerful hands. Now she had no choice but to forgo her earnings until she'd discovered Guido's fate.

First of all she visited the Santa Maria *ospedale* which lay on the Via Egidia just outside the old city wall, in case her husband had fallen sick in the street and been put in the care of the nuns there. Then she called on other hospices and *lazaretti* that dealt with the poor. But no young man answering to Guido's description had been admitted recently. She examined the lists posted in the Signoria, among which was a record of those whose bodies had lately been recovered from the waters of the Arno. Lisabetta could not read but she would have recognized the general shape of Guido's name, had it appeared on the list and had he been identified. Equally, there was no report of an anonymous and youthful male corpse being fished from the waters. (This she discovered through questioning a male passer-by who could read and was only too happy to assist Lisabetta.) Therefore if Guido *was* dead – and she tried to think calmly about this – it would appear that he had not ended up in the hands of any official institution.

There were other possibilities, of course. Her husband might have been robbed and casually killed. This was not likely though. He was a simple labourer. He never had more than a few soldi to rub together, and they usually vanished quick enough when he was in the neighbourhood of a tavern. Would anyone rob and kill a man for a few soldi? Yes, they would. The world was a wicked place, Lisabetta knew. There were those who'd kill even for a single soldo. But Guido's remains would surely have been discovered by now if that had happened.

Another possibility was that he'd left the confines of Florence of his own accord. This didn't seem very likely either. If he left, where would he go? He'd been brought up on a farm just outside the city walls, but he looked down on anybody who wasn't a true-born Florentine as a proper provincial. And to leave the city Guido would have had to pass through one of the principal gates and, as an ordinary artisan, he might have had to account for himself – at least if he'd journeyed by night. Anyway, how was she to find out? There were, she thought, at least fifteen gates in this city, maybe more. It was one thing to question the nuns and almoners at the hospices, some of whom had responded to her questions in a kindly fashion. It would be quite another to tour the gates and exchange banter with the guards who, almost certainly, could tell her nothing.

Lisabetta was baffled and, as she pursued her course through the city, increasingly despondent and exhausted. At night, alone in bed, the different possibilities tumbled through her mind. Had Guido run out on her? The bastard – if he had! Did he suspect that she was with child, something of which Lisabetta was growing more and more convinced? Did he have some other piece on the side in a different *borgo* but in the same city? Was he even now squeezing another woman's tits? It was at this point that Lisabetta cried herself to sleep. Then, that very same night, she dreamed of her man. Guido's face swam before her mind's eye, curiously swollen and appealing soundlessly for her to help. His mouth flapped like a fish's mouth and he wore a kind of thin scarf around his neck. She woke with a start, sitting upright in the hard bed which she had until so recently shared with him. She waited while her heart slowed and then lay down again and, as calmly as she could, tried to examine whatever it was the dream had been telling her.

But the dream seemed to tell her very little. There was poor Guido's face, discoloured and swollen, his mouth opening and shutting. It was night-time, but with a dead white light. Beyond him was a line of trees with a moon hanging above them and on the other side a gaping hole in the ground – like a grave large enough for the whole world. She shivered. Well, that dream gave her next to nothing! Except that Guido must have been murdered, for the purpose of the thin scarf buried in his neck suddenly became clear to Lisabetta as well as explaining his open-mouthed expression. Tears filled her eyes once more. He had been throttled, *murdered*. Not in some back alley but in the open air under a line of trees.

What should she do now? Go to the office of the *gonfalonier*, who was responsible for the administration of justice in the city? But a poor working woman would not be listened to, especially without any evidence. The dream didn't count as evidence. She was hardly sure that she believed in it herself.

While she was lying in her bed, divided between grief and fear, a memory came to her of the last time she'd seen him. That final evening when Guido had unexpectedly quit their room in the crowded tenement. It was already late.

"What are you doing?" she'd said. "Where are you going?"

"Going about my own affairs," he'd said. "Go back to sleep. Don't worry."

Then, muttering to himself about the cold outside, he struck a light and fumbled for the cloak which she'd only recently darned for him and wrapped it around himself. He whistled as he did so and mouthed a few words, unaware of what he was doing. It was *Figlia di Mugnaio*, a song doing the rounds at the moment.

What was going on? Lisabetta asked herself, watching her husband through half-closed lids and hearing his humming and feeling troubled. He noticed her looking and said again, "Don't worry, for alle Grazie will take care of me. Sleep sound."

With that he blew out the candle, closed the door and slipped out of her life. She was tired – tired from bending over other people's garments all day in the poor light of the little room, tired from plying the needle with her capable hands – and she fell asleep almost at once, thinking that the 'affairs' Guido was engaged on most probably involved a visit to a tavern where he'd join in some sozzled singing of *Figlia di Mugnaio*, the ballad about a miller's daughter who took men into her bed about as often as the wheel of her father's mill spun round. With each chorus the men would swing their arms in imitation of the wheel.

But it was only now, after she'd searched fruitlessly for Guido, that Lisabetta remembered those other departing words of his, *Don't worry, alle Grazie will take care of me.*

Lisabetta had assumed that he was simply talking about our Lady and how She would be watching over him, even while he drank himself silly and spouted nonsense in between singing coarse songs! But suppose that he was referring to the actual place known as alle Grazie, the chapel dedicated to the Madonna which stood at the end of the Ponte Rubaconte.

The little chapel was very new but it had already won a place in the hearts of some Florentines who, she'd heard, believed it was the place to pray when they wished for divine intercession in matters of love. Had that been the reason why Guido was visiting alle Grazie, to pray for success with some fresh woman? No, Lisabetta thought, for why should he do so in the cold of a spring evening when he could make his devotions in the warmth of day? Besides, she could almost reject the idea that Guido was two-timing her because he had not been furtive enough. He might have been keeping secrets when he departed but he seemed resolute rather than stealthy. Now, recalling his words, she became convinced that the 'affairs' he'd mentioned had something to do with the chapel or with the Ponte Rubaconte. Perhaps he had planned to meet someone there and had taken the cloak to keep warm while he waited.

It wasn't much to go on but it was all she had. Early the next morning, Lisabetta Greco made her way to the Ponte Ruba-conte. There were other chapels near the bridge, three of them to be precise, but she entered the one known as Madonna alle Grazie. She knelt down before the votive light in front of the image of the Blessed Virgin and Child. At this time of day, the only other company was a couple of old women. Not very likely that they would be asking for intercession in affairs of the heart! She prayed that she might discover what had happened to Guido and, if he had suffered wrong, that she might be given the strength to do . . . to do she wasn't sure what.

She emerged from the chapel, blinking in the brightness. Sun glittered along the waters of the Arno. The bridge was already quite busy, mostly with people crossing over from the Oltrarno into the main part of the city. On each side of the Ponte Rubaconte were tiny house-like structures spaced at intervals. These cells were occupied by ladies of distinction who had planned to give themselves up to convent life, but, scandalized by the loose morals which they found in the religious houses, chose instead to immure themselves in these little buildings so as to lead purer lives. They received their food and water through grilled windows, and were known as the *romite*.

Such a way of life was incomprehensible to Lisabetta, even though she knew there was no fathoming the odd tastes of wealthy and distinguished young ladies. As it happened, she knew one of these *romite*. Several years before, while working in the laundry-room of a *palazzo* on the Via de Neri, she had become the confidante of Maria, one of the daughters of the house. Maria was a shy, nervous girl who'd been destined for convent-life from her earliest days. She'd taken a liking to Lisabetta – both girls were in their mid-teens – and talked much of her imminent marriage to Christ. At about the time Lisabetta had left the house, Maria had become a novice. Subsequently, or so Lisabetta had heard, she had discovered that a nun's existence was not unworldly enough after all. So, under the guidance of a lady known as Monna Apollonia, Maria had decided to live out her life as an anchoress in this half-public, half-secluded fashion on the Ponte Rubaconte.

Feeling that she was on a ridiculous errand, Lisabetta Greco made her way along the bridge, pausing by each of the grilled apertures through which the hermit women received alms and sustenance. Some of them still had curtains drawn across for the

101

sake of privacy. Each of the structures had a little door set low in a side wall, for the occupants were free to leave if they wished. And indeed, it struck Lisabetta that there was something strange about being a hermit in the middle of a great press of people. If she hadn't known any better she might have supposed that the occupants of these cells were more concerned to be known for their piety than they were to pursue their religious vocation. Most Florentines had grown used to the presence of the *romite*, and strode or ambled past them without a second glance. But there were always travellers curious to examine the women in their cells, as well as devout passers-by eager to show their approval by giving food and drink to those who had chosen such a self-denying existence.

In the end it was less difficult than she'd expected. She'd made her way down the west side of the Ponte Rubaconte, with a growing sense of her own foolishness, and was now walking back on the eastern, more shadowed side of the bridge. As she was passing the third or fourth cell – truly they were like little prison-houses – she saw a familiar face actually looking at her through the grille. She stopped and then moved a couple of paces into the shade thrown by the building.

"Donna Maria, is it?"

The woman on the other side of the bars did not look so different from the girl Lisabetta had known in the Via de Neri. She still had the same pinched, anxious face. Her complexion was whiter than that of the average fashionable lady while her dark hair hung loose and unkempt. The *romite* deliberately avoided the starched and elaborate wimples of the nuns. The woman seemed to recognize Lisabetta straightaway and smiled slightly.

"Lisa! *La mia lavandaia!*"

They touched hands through the grille. Lisabetta was obscurely pleased to be acknowleged as a laundress – *my* laundress, no less – and had a moment's pang for those days on the Via de Neri before she'd known men and the struggle to earn an independent living. That was at least three years ago.

"You are not among my usual visitors," said Maria.

"I don't come this way very often," said Lisabetta. "But now I have."

"All the world passes our door eventually," said Maria. "Not that we are of the world."

Lisabetta couldn't shake off the impression that she was talking to someone in a prison. As her eyes grew more used to the gloom, she struggled to make out the interior of Donna Maria's cell. She could see a stool and a straw mattress but not much else. Even her and Guido's tiny room was better furnished!

"You think I live poorly?"

"I remember your old chamber, Donna Maria, in the *palazzo* on the Via de Neri."

"Memories are the thorns which we suffer to prick us, Lisa," said Maria. "I have only one object to remind me of the vanity of those days. Here."

She held up a blue cap so that Lisabetta could see it through the window. Lisabetta almost laughed aloud, so out of place did this item seem in the colourless austerity of the cell, but she turned the laugh into a smile. At this, Maria stroked the material of the cap as if she was by no means as convinced of its vanity as she had claimed. Then her rather doleful expression brightened and she went on, "But you, *mia lavandaia*, what has happened to you? You have a husband, you have children by now? You used to talk of a husband and children."

"Did I?"

Lisabetta Greco couldn't remember talking of *that*. But then she felt tears beginning to run down her face and, again, Maria reached her hand through the grille, and what Lisabetta did remember now was how she'd always liked this pinch-faced girl. Maria had spoken to her more kindly than the other members of the household. Why, she'd even given her a gift when she left the place. Underneath the pious remarks and tendency to lecture, there had lain a warm heart and it was there still.

So Lisabetta found herself saying that, yes, she was married and that she hoped for children one day. (She said nothing of her suspicion that she was expecting at this very moment.) But things were not going well. Her husband, a good man called Guido Greco, had been missing for many days and she was searching for him. Briefly she explained about the night he'd left and her reasons for thinking that he might have been meeting someone here on the Ponte Rubaconte.

"And you think I might have seen him, *mia povera Lisa*?" said Maria.

"Well, I hoped . . ."

"But I don't even know what he looks like."

"Of course you don't know. How could you know?" said Lisabetta, the futility of her hopes striking her more forcibly than ever. Was it even worth attempting to describe Guido? She half turned away in embarrassment. What had she expected to achieve by coming here? She must go now. It had been enough to see Donna Maria once more.

"Just a minute," said the other. "What night did you say this was – the night of the full moon? Last month?"

"Yes, it was."

"But I *did* see something that night, Lisabetta. The light was good and the moon was shining right through this opening. I couldn't sleep. Often I cannot sleep. I heard a noise and I looked out."

"What sort of noise?"

"Someone whistling." Here Maria seemed to turn coy and a faint colour rose to her white cheeks. "It was the tune to a song which I am ashamed to say I recognize. About a miller and his daughter . . . and how she, you know . . . does things with men . . . as often as her father's wheel turns round . . . up to fifteen times, no less!"

"*Figlia di Mugnaio!*" said Lisabatta. "It is very popular in the town right now – so I've heard. But how do *you* know it, Donna Maria?"

"The world passes our door, Lisa. I have often heard it sung or whistled by those who cross the bridge."

Lisabetta had been momentarily distracted by the thought of this hermit girl being familiar with the words to a bawdy ballad. But now she got back to the matter in hand.

"What did you see when you looked out, Donna Maria?"

"There was a man standing just along the Rubaconte on the other side. He was coming out of the shadows by Our Lady alle Grazie. But I couldn't see much because he was wearing a cloak."

Lisabetta's heart beat faster. The alle Grazie chapel! A man wearing a cloak! Was it the cloak that Guido had been searching for even as he tunelessly hummed *Figlia di Mugnaio*? Was the man in the shadows her husband Guido?

"And it was he who was whistling?" she said.

"Why no, that was the man on the cart."

"Oh, please tell me everything, Donna Maria."

So Maria described how she'd witnessed this man emerging from the shadows. The cart – more of a carriage since it plainly belonged to a wealthy family – had just drawn up, she thought. The carriage-man whistled the *Mugnaio* tune and the mantled man appeared as if the tune was a signal. The driver took off his cap and his bald head gleamed in the moonlight. Then the man must have got into the carriage, for Maria saw it swaying and even heard the sound of a door clicking shut. After that she observed the carriage-man urge the horses forward across the bridge. The carriage passed outside within a few feet of where Lisabetta was standing at this very moment. Maria heard rather than saw it moving into the distance for she ducked down below the grille, having an aversion to being seen. Perhaps she was frightened too. In any case the view from her little window was restricted.

"So the carriage was going towards the Oltrarno?"

"Nothing else lies in that direction," said Maria. "You think it was your husband waiting on the bridge, your Guido?"

"It might have been," said Lisabetta. "But what was he doing? Whose carriage was he in?"

"I can't tell you that," said Maria. "But the driver I could recognize by his baldness. I remember him from the Via de Neri. His name is Bruno. He has sometimes worked for the noble families."

"Such people come from a different world to mine. What was my Guido doing getting into a fine carriage?"

"There is a man who may be able to tell you more. His name is Giuseppe Orioli. He is a man with many masters and yet with none. In serving all, he serves himself. He is a friend to this Bruno. But be careful if you go asking questions of him."

"How do you know all of this?" said Lisabetta. "You say you live out of the world yet you know much more than I do."

"I remember one of the employers of this man Giuseppe clearly, my Lisa. For he was blind, you see, and he had to be helped out of the carriage when he came to visit my father. Helped by the bald-headed carriage-man Bruno and by Giuseppe Orioli."

"A blind man?"

"Il Cieco, as he is known. He has one of those new estates outside the city walls. He calls it Paradise – the ignorance of these worldlings to suppose that they will ever find heaven on earth! I did not like him although I hardly knew him. I might have pitied his blindness but he seemed to sense what was around him better than many a man who can see."

Lisabetta felt confused by this talk of blind men and wealthy estates. More than that, she felt as though she'd trodden on a paving stone to find it give way and plunge her into some dark, dangerous waters below. Almost breathless with all the information she'd gained, she leaned against the wall by the grille.

"One more thing," said Maria. "You might recognize this Giuseppe by a mark which he has on his cheek . . . so." She touched her own bloodless cheek in illustration. "He must have had it from birth. It is the colour of spilled wine."

106

"Spilled wine," repeated Lisabetta.

"Are you all right?" said Maria.

"Yes, yes. But I must go now."

"To look for Giuseppe Orioli?"

"I – I suppose so."

"Then I say again, be careful."

"I will pay you another visit, I promise."

Lisabetta turned away from Maria's cell. There were plenty more people on the bridge by now. A few of the men glanced at Lisabetta with a passing interest but their eyes scarcely took in the pale-faced figure behind the grille.

"You are happy here, Donna Maria?" said Lisabetta, who was suddenly reluctant to leave the other woman.

"Happy, *la mia lavandaia*? Why yes. It is like heaven, this place. I can look out at the world even though I am no part of it."

But as Lisabetta walked away she couldn't help thinking she detected a wistful note in Maria's voice. She too would be wistful if she spent her life in voluntary confinement on the Ponte Rubaconte. She resolved to be as good as her word and to see Maria again soon, to tell her of her progress.

She returned to her lodging in the tenement and considered everything which she'd learned. That Guido Greco had been the man on the Ponte Rubaconte during the night of the full moon, there seemed to her little doubt. She had no proof but several details pointed to this conclusion. Why Guido had climbed into the fine carriage she couldn't imagine. All she knew was that something bad had happened to him afterwards. It was her dream which was telling her this but, more certainly, there was her instinct. Even so she had too little evidence to go to the *gonfalonier*. Whatever she did next, it would have to be done by herself. And it would have to be carefully done, for the chances were that this Giuseppe Orioli was somehow involved in Guido's disappearance. She could not ask him direct questions but would have to go the roundabout route. And first of all, she had to find him.

107

The next step, like the reunion with Maria, proved less difficult than she'd expected. She asked around among her tenement neighbours, who were mostly men and women like herself and Guido, casual workers who were too lowly or unskilled to be attached to any of the grand guilds. A number of them had, also like Lisabetta, held menial positions in the great houses of the city and were familiar with their occupants and hangers-on. She asked whether any of them had heard of the bald-headed Bruno or a man called Giuseppe with the purple birthmark on his face.

Yes, she soon discovered from two or three sources, we know the men you're talking about. They are good friends, it is rumoured, although Bruno has never been heard to utter a word to Giuseppe. Digging a little deeper, she found out the places that Bruno and Giuseppe frequented in the city, for although Florence was then a great place containing many tens of thousands of inhabitants it also had something of the character of a village in which no man's business was completely his own. Bald Bruno sometimes visited a house of ill fame, a *bordello* near the outermost wall. That was no good for her purposes, thought Lisabetta, since she could not simply visit a brothel. But she had more luck with Giuseppe Orioli's off-duty tastes. The man was an inveterate gambler, it seemed.

Unlike some other Italian cities, Florence did not provide public gambling houses. Gaming was, officially, a vice. But it didn't exactly discourage the offence either, since money could be made out of fining those who committed it. Games were played both in the open and in private houses – or *baratterie* – which were often to be found near the churches by the Baptistery. This was convenient if you wanted to get absolution before making a vow to the Blessed Virgin never to play again (a vow usually made only once you'd lost). However, the establishment favoured by Giuseppe was, Lisabetta discovered, close to the market square.

On the evening of the day after the meeting with Maria, she

retrieved from the chest in the corner of her room the one good item of wear which she possessed. It was an off-white linen dress but shot through with golden threads which drew the eye. It had been given her by Maria when she left service in the Via de Neri. Although the dress was not the kind of thing which Maria would ever have worn – it was too low-cut for that – the gesture had pleased Lisabetta more than the gift itself. Lisabetta had thickened a little round the middle since those days but that simply meant that the dress fitted more snugly and gave her breasts an extra prominence. She slipped it on, feeling better than at any time since Guido's departure. In fact she felt like one of those women in stories and legends, women who were both tough and cunning.

Weaving through the warm evening streets, she made her way to the address, a fairly modest one, which she'd been told was Giuseppe's preferred *baratteria*. She knew she'd come to the right place by the steady trickle of people who entered and left. In fact, so careless was the proprietor and so frequent the traffic, that the door was left half open and Lisabetta could hear from within the sound of numbers being called out and the occasional whoop of delight or groan of disbelief and despair. The playing was evidently taking place in a shuttered ground-floor room. Lisabetta recognized the dice game of *zara* when she heard it. If it hadn't been for the shouted numbers, she might have imagined that she was standing in the neighbourhood of a *bordello* since most of the visitors were male and furthermore they were of all types, merchants and soldiers as well as monks and friars. The sight of the religious entering this house, without so much as a furtive glance to see if they were being observed, made her think of her friend on the Ponte Rubaconte and Maria's discovery that life in a convent wasn't so unworldly after all.

Lisabetta didn't have the money to play but that wouldn't necessarily be a bar to her going inside. Though the majority were male, there were a few women visitors even if they were obviously higher-born or at least more expensively dressed than she was. Nevertheless, she loitered in the street near this *baratteria* without quite nerving herself to enter. She scanned the arriving and departing men for one who was large and had a purple birthmark across his cheek. There were plenty of large persons but not one them had the right mark on his cheek.

Because she was peering at men in the street and because she was – there was no other word for it – loitering outside a gambling house, she was approached several times by men who were leaving the place, even though she was not wearing the yellow veil which was the badge of the *meretrice*. One of those who accosted her to demand whether she was available was a friar! Each time she shook her head with as much anger as she could muster and stalked off down the street, only to return when the man had gone. From their generally crestfallen or grim expressions she guessed that the gamblers were going away with empty purses. She observed that they generally arrived in twos or threes but left singly. Since they had lost their money, how would they have paid her? Still, she thought, if my fortunes become really desperate there is at least one hole for me to go to . . .

After an hour or so she grew afraid that she might attract too much attention by staying, even though there were a fair number of casual passers-by almost all of whom strolled past with that kind of parading air which Geoffrey Chaucer had noticed on his first evening in the city. Her earlier optimism draining away, Lisabetta Greco went back to her room and wondered whether she was wasting her time. Perhaps she'd been given the wrong piece of gossip and Giuseppe was no gambler after all, or perhaps he frequented a different *baratteria*. She returned the next evening and with the same lack of success. She was on the point of giving up. Only her obstinacy, together with the fact that she couldn't think of any other course of action, caused to her to go back once more.

And it was on the third evening that she struck lucky.

9

On the afternoon of the same day as Lisabetta struck lucky in her search for Giuseppe, the mercenary soldier known as Aquilino (on account of his beaky nose) also struck lucky in his transactions with the lady Novella, wife to il Cieco or – to give him his proper name – Lorenzo Lipari. Aquilino had just now ridden across to the country estate on the pretext of reporting something new from the road.

Although the blind man was a jealous husband, he could not have Novella always in his presence. Occasionally he needed to discuss matters with one of his stewards in her absence. Although she read Italian to him she had no understanding of Latin or Greek and sometimes he had to call on the services of Giuseppe Orioli or even of his brother's secretary Matteo Peruzzi for the task. Neither man was employed by il Cieco but each was a more than occasional visitor to Paradiso since, however bad relations between the brothers, there was always a requirement to transact family business. At such times Novella was free. And then there were, inevitably, other periods when husband and wife were in separate chambers of the house or different corners of the estate.

So Novella Lipari's life wasn't quite so constricted as she'd sometimes claimed to Aquilino. It suited her, however, if the mercenary believed that she possessed a murderously jealous husband. It gave her a pretext for fending Aquilino off.

But this afternoon she was not fending him off. This afternoon she had seized Aquilino by the hand and led him into this secret place, to his amazement and delight. Now he was getting somewhere, Aquilino thought. Now *they* were getting somewhere! He and Novella were crammed into a tiny room, more of a storage space, in the servants' quarter of the country house called Paradise while, at this very moment, Novella's husband was being read to in Latin or Greek. She didn't know which nor did she care. The main thing was that Lorenzo was occupied.

Novella and Aquilino were lying in the near darkness on a tumble of blankets and curtains. A sliver of light was admitted through a vent high in the wall. He was fumbling with her dress, and she was gasping and writhing underneath him. There was scarcely room to stretch out in this tiny area and their feet banged against the door. But it didn't matter, nothing mattered. Aquilino's head was full of buzzing bees while his loins were on fire. Truly, he was almost in paradise.

They only had moments. Novella had come pantingly to him, saying that she had managed to slip the company of her husband. Hurry, they must consummate their love now, this instant! And she'd dragged him off to this secret space, a tiny room situated at the junction of two passages. Aquilino had just got his hand between her legs, and she had her hand on his thing, when there was a rapping on the door. Then it rattled as someone tried to open it. Luckily, Novella hadn't been in so great a hurry as not to remember, firstly, to obtain the key from somewhere or other and, secondly, to lock the door from the inside.

"What's going on in there? Come on out!"

It was a woman's voice, a strident woman's voice. Novella's hand flew away from Aquilino's thing and covered her mouth instead.

"I know that must be you, Agnola. I bet you're in there with that no-good stable-boy."

The door rattled again. Aquilino and Novella lay hunched in the near darkness, hardly daring to breathe. After more rattling, they heard footsteps retreating outside.

"That was the mother of Agnola," said Novella. "They're both servants here, mother and daughter. She's got it into her head that one of the stable lads is trying to get off with her Agnola. She'll be back. She will probably try and break down the door."

"Then we've just got time to finish the job," said Aquilino, reaching out with his hand once more. His thing had hardly wilted during the door-rattling, so ardent was he to possess his Novella. But any corresponding fire in the wife of Lorenzo Lipari seemed to have been fatally dampened by the disturbance from outside.

"No, no, my love. Not here, not now. We do not deserve this. We must enjoy ourselves at leisure."

With any other woman, Aquilino might have disregarded her objections and taken what he wanted by force. But, with Novella, it was different. He was on fire but he was also in love. So he listened to her even while he was stricken with the pangs of lust.

"You are my knight, you are my Aquilino," she said, stroking his face.

"I am your knight. And you – you are my lady, Novella."

Aquilino's voice sounded thick to his own ears. The blood pounded in his head. He suddenly realised how hot and stuffy it was in this little cupboard.

"Furthermore you know, my Aqui, that a knight has to perform certain . . . tasks to earn his lady's favour."

"Yes, yes," said Aquilino. "But, Novella, shouldn't we be leaving this dark hole? In case that woman comes back and tries to break down the door, like you said?"

"Shush, shush, this is my husband's house, I can face down any servant."

Aquilino couldn't understand the lack of urgency in Novella's tone. If they had time to talk, then surely they had time for the other matter . . .

"What tasks?" he said.

"Tell me, Aquilino, what would you do to prove your love to me so that I might give myself to you without reserve? After all, I am running a risk by doing this. Is it not fair that you should run a risk too?"

"I would do anything for you," he said.

"Would you – for the sake of your Novella – kill a man?"

Aquilino was surprised but not altogether shocked at the suggestion. He surely knew that Novella was passionate and hot-blooded. And the idea of killing a man did not repel or frighten him. Novella must be referring to her blind husband. He was aware that she hated her husband, that she loathed his jealousy, his insane possessiveness, his hot breath and his dry hands, which scarcely left off clasping her sweet body for a single hour out of the twenty-four. So she said.

"It is your husband you mean?"

"Why no," she said. "Not him but another man."

"Explain, explain," he ordered.

So she did. She explained who was to die and the reasons why. Her account was brief but compelling. She promised on everything which she held sacred that if Aquilino performed this task for her she would give herself to him in every and any way that he chose. They would be united forever.

Would he do it?

Aquilino barely hesitated. He would do it. Oh yes, he would do it. If it meant she became his, he would do it.

She gave him a lingering kiss and his manhood, which had drooped slightly at the complications of a premeditated murder, began to stir once again. But Novella rose and smoothed down her clothes and, more by touch than sight, turned the key in the lock of the store-room.

She gave a quick glance up and down the passageways before blowing a last kiss to Aquilino (who was struggling to his feet in the dark recesses of the cupboard) and indicating with a motion of her head that he should take the opposite path to hers. Then she strode off. Aquilino exited the room more cautiously. He half expected to encounter the fearsome-sounding woman, mother to Agnola, demanding to know what he'd done with her daughter. But there was no one in sight and he slunk back to the servants' quarters.

If he'd followed his lady Novella down the other passage, which led to the internal stairs mounting to the family area of the house, he might have been taken aback to see her encounter the servant-woman who'd beaten her fist against the door of the linen-room. This woman was indeed mother to Agnola, and both were servants in Paradise. But, if the stable-boy genuinely had the itch for the young servant-girl, the mother would hardly have known – or cared. As Novella passed the woman, the mistress of the house winked at her and nodded her head slightly as if to say, *It worked!*

It was but one person less, thought Aquilino as he was riding away from Paradise on his horse Fuoco. It was but one person less in this busy world. He had killed in his time, both in battle and during ambushes and other operations. Killing was in Aquilino's blood. His Lombardo mother had fallen, dagger in hand, against the men who were trying to violate her, and later his English father had killed the men who'd assailed her. At least, that was the story told by Aquilino's father when he was in his cups. Aquilino couldn't remember any of it. He was too young at the time. He could scarcely remember his father at all now, his only legacy the English tongue which he still used when talking with Tomaso Falcone – or Master Sparrow.

So the act of killing did not trouble Aquilino unduly. He would not lose much sleep over it. And Novella had given good reasons why she wanted this particular individual dead. Not that Aquilino was unduly bothered about reasons either. It was simply one body less in this busy old world. And to dream of what he would gain if he did this deed! To receive another body in exchange but a living one, Novella's, warm and white and supple. *I will give myself to you in every and any way that you choose*, she'd said. The memory of her words caused Aquilino to grow heated once more. He had to wrench his imagination away and instead think of how he might bring about the death that Novella had commanded. It would require a certain amount of planning. But, in Aquilino's experience, the key requirements would be nerve and resolution when it came to the moment – and he knew that he possessed those attributes.

10

Lisabetta was waiting for a third night outside the gambling house near the old market. The usual trickle of visitors passed through the door. She recognized a few from the previous evenings but still there was no sign of the man known as Giuseppe. She was on the point of giving up and going home. She paced up and down the street, humming to herself under her breath and gazing at the ground, almost unaware of her surroundings.

Suddenly she was conscious of someone standing at her elbow.

"Excuse me, madam, but can you tell me the tune that you were humming?"

She looked up. The evening was well advanced and the light was poor. Even so, she could see that this was the man she'd been searching for. He was large and his breath came heavily. And the left side of his face was covered with a mark like a dark wine-stain.

"I – I – was I humming, *messere?*"

"You were humming," he said. "Was it *Figlia di Mugnaio?* It sounded like it."

Had it been? It must have been. The song, so very popular in certain quarters in the town, had been on her mind lately. It was the same tune which had supposedly been whistled on the Ponte Rubaconte on the night her Guido had disappeared into that carriage . . . Had this man, if it was Giuseppe, discovered her

117

identity? Did he know her purpose in hanging about outside the *baratteria*? At once she felt uncomfortably warm – and a little fearful. For all that, the man's next request was an odd one.

"Will you sing me the refrain to that song?" he said, holding out a couple of soldi.

She'd been asked to do odder things in her time. Lisabetta cleared her throat and in a clear voice sang out:

'The miller's daughter lays on the ground,
Every time her dad's wheel spins round,
He grinds the corn, she grinds her mound,
She grinds the men, she grinds between,
She grinds 'em fifteen times fifteen.
Oh, fifteen times fifteen.'

Lisabetta didn't mind the bawdiness of the song. However, she didn't accompany the last line with the arm-swinging or the other, more suggestive gestures which any male singer in a tavern would have done. But the man seemed pleased. He handed her the coins.

"Fifteen," said the man. "Why not? It could be a sign."

"A sign of what, sir?"

"Why are you here?" he said, answering the question with one of his own. Then, taking in her low-cut dress and casting his eyes up and down her plumpish figure, he said, "You want company?"

Despite the question, and though she couldn't have said how, Lisabetta knew that he was not interested in her in *that* way.

"What do you take me for, sir?"

"Then you are waiting for someone?"

"Waiting for a – a friend."

"Well, you have found a friend. What is your name?"

"Lisabetta."

"Then come with me, Lisabetta. Who knows but you'll bring me luck."

Taking her arm, he directed her towards the door of the gaming house. Lisabetta allowed herself to be guided. Inside the door, there was an old woman standing behind a *leggio* or reading desk. It was ornately carved and reminded Lisabetta of similar items in a church. But the woman, ornately painted herself, was not dressed for church. Lisabetta wondered for a moment whether she had indeed entered a *bordello*. The woman noted something in a book that was open on top of the *leggio* and she leered at the man before greeting him by name.

"Well, Giuseppe, wonders will never cease. You and a lady. And who is this young thing?"

"This is the lady who will bring me fortune."

They passed into a ground floor from which the shouts and cries were issuing. A group of men were standing around a cloth-covered table on which were scattered piles of coin. As Lisabetta and Giuseppe stood at the entrance, one of the men shook his fist and simultaneously shouted out a number. Three dice flew from his hand, and then there was a flurry of shouting and peering at the dice-faces before more coins were added to the various piles. Lisabetta had never understood gaming, and the speed and concentration of the gamblers who played in the streets had always amazed her. The caster now threw another handful of dice. More shouts followed and coins were scooped up or redistributed to different piles.

A new game was about to begin. Holding Lisabetta by the arm, Giuseppe drew her towards the gaming table. Now he too joined in the betting on the throws. Lisabetta noticed that he consistently used the number fifteen, hoping to match the total on the three dice put together. At first he wasn't successful but his fortunes changed sharply on the third game and soon he had amassed quite a pile of coin. For herself, she was confused by the press of people crowded about the table, mostly men but with a few women in attendance.

Giuseppe drew a leather flask from a pocket. He offered it

to Lisabetta. This was courteous, this was generous of him, to offer it to her before taking a swig himself. Automatically she tilted the flask to her lips and drank. Although she used to nag poor Guido about his drinking, she wasn't averse to a draught or two herself. The fiery liquid burned her gullet and she gasped. But then it settled down into her belly where it cast a nice, warm glow. The candlelit room seemed to waver before her eyes and the actions of the dice-caster and the gamblers to slow down as if these individuals were moving through a vat of oil or honey. Particular gestures caught her eye and were invested with great significance: a hand reaching out to position a coin with fussy precision on the gaming table; a woman turning her head to look up at the man beside whom she was standing. Lisabetta took another drink. She made to return the flask to Giuseppe but he shook his head, so absorbed was he in the game of *zara*.

The next she knew, Giuseppe was gathering up several piles of coin and pulling her away from the table. He'd won, he'd won! She had brought him good fortune! That might be useful in . . . in whatever she was planning to discover from this man with the wine-stained cheek. She couldn't remember exactly what it was at the moment. There were comments, protests even, from the other gamesters that he should be quitting like this, without giving them the chance to make good their losses, but Giuseppe ignored them and ushered her out of the *baratteria*. They passed the woman behind the desk. Lisabetta saw the woman winking at Giuseppe. It was a strange wink. Lisabetta had never before realized how odd was the action of winking: the slow descent of the eyelid, the crinkle which formed on the old woman's cheek and which seemed to crack the very plaster she'd coated it with.

The next thing she knew they were sitting on a bench inside some tavern further down the street. It was crowded and noisy. So many people! Giuseppe impatiently waved away a drawer who'd come to take his order. To her surprise Lisabetta found that she was still clutching the leather flask. There wasn't much liquor left in it. Anyway she'd had enough of this drink, whatever it was. The pleasant effects of the first few draughts had been replaced by a queasy feeling. Her senses seemed, curiously, to be at once dulled and sharper. Or rather, things stood out more clearly but mattered less. She returned the flask to Giuseppe who tucked it away inside his doublet, without troubling to help himself to the last few drops. She gazed at the red mark on the side of his face. It was fortunate that she wasn't an imaginative woman, she thought, for she might otherwise have mistaken it for a bloodstain. In fact, perhaps it was a bloodstain.

"You have brought me luck, Lisabetta," he said, "though it's not many gamesters who know the right moment to stop. Most of the fellows in there will go on until their purses are drained. But your song about the miller's daughter was a sign of the number to bet on. *She grinds 'em fifteen times fifteen. Oh, fifteen times fifteen.*"

And, in a good mood, he started to hum that familiar tune. Lisabetta shivered.

"What is it, my dear?"

"It's nothing. Just that my . . . a friend of mine is very fond of that song."

These were the first words she'd spoken since they'd left the *baratteria*. Her voice sounded unfamiliar in her own ears.

"Well now, my Lisa," said Giuseppe, leaning close to her and wheezing slightly, "tell me who it is that you were expecting outside the gaming house."

Lisabetta struggled to recall exactly what she'd said earlier. Eventually she came out with, "It was only . . . a friend I was searching for. The same friend who likes the miller's daughter."

"Not Guido by any chance?"

How did this person know his name? A prickle of alarm

stirred somewhere within her. Despite this she said, "Yes, that's it. He is my husband."

"Your husband must be a gamester – since you were standing outside the *baratteria*?"

"Why no. Guido has many faults but he does not gamble."

"Then he has run away?"

"Why do you say so?"

"Because you are searching for him. That was what you said just now."

Had she said that? She wasn't sure.

"Tell me what happened to him," said Giuseppe, leaning still closer so that the wine-stain filled her vision.

"I don't know. But I fear that some harm has befallen him. I had a dream which told me so."

"Oh, is that all? You had a dream," said Giuseppe, easing his large bulk back on the tavern bench. "Well, dreams aren't always what they appear to be. When did you last see him in the flesh, so to speak?"

And suddenly Lisabetta came out with the whole story. It must have been the effect of the drink, she thought afterwards. Now she told how Guido had left their little room one night a few weeks earlier and never reappeared. Of how she'd gone to the Santa Maria *ospedale* and the other hospices and *lazaretti* in case he'd met with an accident. Of how she believed that he had kept an appointment with someone on the Ponte Rubaconte on the very night he had left her asleep in their bed.

At the mention of the Ponte Rubaconte a change seemed to come over Giuseppe's features.

"How do you know this? Was this in your dream too? Or did he tell you he was meeting someone at the bridge?"

"No. Guido told me nothing. But he was seen there by a friend."

"A friend? You have so many friends, Lisabetta. Who was this one?"

122

"It was . . ."

Lisabetta paused. She'd been about to mention Donna Maria but something made her reluctant to come out with the name.

" . . . it was one of the *romite*. The hermit women who live on the bridge."

"I understand," said Giuseppe.

The tavern drawer returned and this time Giuseppe ordered wine for himself. Lisabetta shook her head. She still felt muzzy. They sat in silence for a time. Lisabetta wanted to leave but she couldn't summon the energy to rise from the bench. When the drawer brought the drink, Giuseppe swallowed it in a single gulp.

"Tell me," he said, "if something had happened to your Guido, and if you found those who were responsible, what would you do? Would you go to the justices, to the *gonfalonier*?"

"Justice is not for poor people like us," said Lisabetta. "That's what my Guido used to say and I see now that he is right."

"He is right," said Giuseppe. "This is a hard city. You know what they say about it? They say, even men's hearts are warmer than her stones."

Something about the remark seemed to amuse him. He went on, "So you would take the law into your own hands?"

"We make our living with our hands, why shouldn't we make our laws with them too?"

Giuseppe examined the goblet he was holding, as if to detect any final drops of wine.

"I think that I may be able to help you, Lisabetta," he said finally.

11

A conversation about sudden death was taking place between two men on horseback approaching the country villa known as Paradise. It was between Giuseppe Orioli and Matteo Peruzzi.

Orioli was a man of several occupations, most of them beyond the law. When Lisabetta's friend Maria had described him as having both many masters and none she was correct. Above all, Giuseppe enjoyed mischief. He liked setting people against each other, sowing discord, provoking trouble. He operated, unofficially, on behalf of a group of wealthy Florentines who were concerned to protect their position from the encroachment of the lower orders. These people looked back with distaste on the period a couple of decades earlier when shopkeepers and artisans had briefly been permitted to participate in the government of the city. This was an experiment not to be repeated. Above all, their desire was to avoid a *romor* or insurrection. To this end, it was necessary from time to time to deal with some representative member of the Ciompi such as Guido Greco. The Ciompi – or *il popolo di Dio* as they called themselves – were the labourers who were not members of any guild, they were individuals without power or standing in the city. Possessing next to nothing, they had nothing to lose. Occasionally they needed cutting down like weeds that grow too tall. This not only disposed of potential troublemakers but served as a warning to others.

Giuseppe Orioli was happy to undertake the cutting down of weeds. In this labour, delicate and ruthless, he worked alongside his friend Bruno who, he knew, would never betray him. But Giuseppe had other, more innocuous tasks, one of which was to run messages between the Lipari brothers. Today he was on his way to Paradise to invite il Cieco, Lorenzo Lipari, to dine with his brother in Purgatory in a few days' time. The ostensible reason for the dinner was to welcome and celebrate the arrival of an emissary from England, one Geoffrey Chaucer.

Antonio Lipari's secretary, Matteo Peruzzi, had taken the opportunity of visiting Paradise at the same time. He'd claimed to his master that a double visitation would make the request for Lorenzo's presence seem more pressing. The blind man was genuinely reluctant to venture into the city, frequently describing himself as a recluse (and scholar) who was happiest away from the haunts of men. Particularly he was reluctant to consort with his brother.

But the real reason why Peruzzi wished to accompany Giuseppe was in order that the latter could report on the failure of the scheme to dispose of the English emissary, Geoffrey Chaucer. Peruzzi had taken his opposition to the English loan beyond mere words. Knowing that Chaucer was arriving in Florence, he realized that the simplest way to thwart the loan – which he believed would ruin the Liparis and destroy his own plans and prospects – was to prevent the Englishman ever reaching the *palazzo* in the Via dei Cerretani. Peruzzi had approached Giuseppe, knowing of the undercover work he carried out on behalf of some of the wealthy families of the city.

Taking Giuseppe into his confidence, Peruzzi explained that any measures to frustrate the loan would be justified. The trouble was, said Matteo, that Antonio Lipari would be inclined to listen to a royal request. Like all men whose fortunes were recent – and here Peruzzi had gestured in a lordly way as if he himself did not want to be just such a man – Lipari was easily

126

impressed by titles. He'd pretend to haggle and make terms but he'd be falling over himself to throw the bank's gold into the bottomless English coffers. So said Matteo Peruzzi. They had to prevent the English emissary from reaching Lipari. He had left the method up to Giuseppe. In fact, he did not want to hear any details.

But now he was compelled to listen as Giuseppe Orioli described what had gone wrong. For safety's sake, and out of some superstitious desire to avoid being overheard, the two men waited until they were riding in the open country beyond the city walls before they broached the subject of the "accident".

"It was intended to look like a mishap – following your instructions, Matteo."

Just as well to lay the responsibility for that at the right door, thought Giuseppe.

"We didn't want an enquiry about a dead Englishman, an Englishman unlawfully killed," said Matteo. "That is why I suggested it be turned to an accident. But you failed, evidently."

Giuseppe might have replied that it was Bruno who had failed. But he would never have blamed his friend. Instead he sought for something positive to say.

"The plan was a good one. Chaucer was to be struck on the head by tiles from a roof under repair."

"Tiles? Tiles! Puh! Surely you could have found a better means to . . . to deal with him?"

"I told Bruno to use whatever was to hand. There'd already been an artisan killed at the same spot earlier in the day."

"Then another accident would have been doubly suspicious, wouldn't it? Did that occur to you, my dear Giuseppe?"

"In any case, it's all immaterial, my dear Matteo," said Giuseppe, imitating the other's patronizing tone, "since Chaucer was saved at the last moment. According to Bruno, at the very point when his skull would have been crushed, a passer-by saved him. Pushed him to the ground out of the way."

"A passer-by?"

"A figure in a cloak."

"Figure? Cloak? Is this a story, Giuseppe? It sounds like a story. What did Bruno say exactly – oh, I forgot, he can't say anything, can he. The poor fellow is dumb."

The two men were riding side by side. They were pacing slowly so as to talk more easily. Giuseppe turned to look at Matteo, and the secretary quickly looked elsewhere. He knew that it was dangerous to make such remarks about Bruno in Giuseppe's company, but his disdain and irritation had got the better of him. Anyway, it was the plain and simple truth, Bruno was dumb. He could make meaningless sounds and even whistle but Matteo had never heard him utter a word.

"I can understand Bruno as well as I can understand you, Matteo. Better in fact. He didn't get a clear look at the person who saved this Chaucer. Whoever it was rushed off down the street and by then it was too late for my man to have another go at the Englishman – if it was to appear like an accident."

"And now it's too late for any accident. The Englishman has already delivered his message to Antonio Lipari. The whole intention was to prevent that happening."

"Perhaps Messere Antonio will reject the English request. He has you to guide him after all."

"Not in this matter. Whatever I say makes no difference. Antonio will take his own decision. He is a gambler like you, Giuseppe. Prepared to risk the fortunes of the Lipari house on a single throw."

"A single throw? Not me. I've always regarded myself as a cautious gambler."

"There is no such thing as a cautious gambler," said Peruzzi. "No more than there is a chaste whore."

Giuseppe rode on in silence. They had failed, there was no doubt about it.

128

"I shall have to have another talk with Antonio. Persuade him to change his mind. Do whatever is necessary."

"There is one further thing, Matteo," said Giuseppe Orioli. "I've met a woman . . ."

Despite himself, Peruzzi smiled, slightly.

"You? A woman? Congratulations, my Giuseppe."

"I think she could be useful to us."

"How?"

"She is married – she *was* married, I should say – to a man called Guido Greco. You remember that one . . .?"

"I'm not sure."

"Yes you are," said Giuseppe. "This woman has followed a trail which links Guido's, ah, disappearance to a meeting on a certain night on the Ponte Rubaconte."

Matteo Perruzi shifted in his saddle. Realizing it was no use to claim ignorance, he said, "You were seen, you and Bruno? Yet you assured me you were not seen."

Giuseppe had told Matteo of the silencing of Guido Greco, in outline. Matteo wasn't sure whether the man had told him so as to establish his own lack of scruple or whether it was to bind the secretary closer by making him an accessory to a crime. Not that he knew it to be a crime, of course, for Matteo had quickly shushed Giuseppe when he sensed where that earlier conversation was headed. As far as Peruzzi was concerned, a potentially troublesome member of the Ciompi had simply taken it into his head to disappear one day. The truth was that Giuseppe had told Matteo because he wanted to see the expression on the little secretary's face. For the same reason – mischief-making, pleasure in another's discomfiture – he had said a few things to Lisabetta in the tavern on the previous evening.

"*I* was not seen on the Ponte Rubaconte," continued Giuseppe now, "for it was the woman herself who confided in me. But she has found out about Bruno's presence, since he was out in the open driving the carriage. She is friendly with one of the *romite* on the bridge and that holy woman witnessed – ”

Peruzzi lifted a hand from the reins to cut Giuseppe off.

“Then you will have to deal with that yourself, my Giuseppe. The less I know the better.”

“I am taking steps to deal with it,” said Giuseppe. “But listen. This Lisabetta woman believes that Antonio Lipari had a hand in the disappearance of her man. I have persuaded her of this. She is looking for . . . satisfaction. We might be able to use her and solve the problem of the English loan at the same time.”

“I don’t know, Giuseppe, I don’t know. Let me try my hand at persuasion once more.”

12

Night was about to fall and Donna Maria was preparing to lie down on the mattress in her cell-like room on the Ponte Rubaconte. The mattress was as plain and bare as the handful of other items in this space. It was scarcely more comfortable than the cold flags of the floor, on which were laid no rushes or herbs. But Maria was so used to her various discomforts that she scarcely noticed them any longer. If she had thought of them, she would have welcomed them as the necessary and desirable price to be paid for her life as an anchoress. In the same way she welcomed the icicles which sometimes formed at her window in winter and the biting cold which the curtain hung there for privacy could not keep out. She welcomed the stifling heat of summer or the flea-bites on her arms and legs, just as she accepted the occasional bawdy comment lobbed through the grille by a male passer-by.

It was only when a visitor from the outside world, such as her laundry-girl Lisabetta, seemed to be surprised by them that Maria became aware once more of her surroundings. The low stool and the tiny table on which presently lay a book of prayers and devotions, together with a tin trencher and a knife and spoon; the scratchy mattress for sleeping or sitting on; a bucket containing water and another bucket for her physical necessities (emptied out through a small drain in the floor and, thence via a stone channel, straight into the Arno below). Yet even these sparse objects weren't the property of Donna Maria but belonged to Monna Apollonia, who was the unofficial head of this unofficial order of *romite* on the Rubaconte bridge. The true hermit should not only be without possessions but also live with nothing, thought Maria. She recalled the story of the philosopher Diogenes who had thrown away even his drinking cup since a man could hold all the water he needed in the palm of his hand.

She took one last glimpse at the evening sky, streaked with pink beyond the western side of the bridge, and at the pitched roofs of the houses of her fellow *romite*. It was strange to think that there were a dozen or more women like her living on the Ponte Rubaconte, and that none of them was in communion with any of the others. She pulled the thin curtain across the window-space. Even to admire the beauty of the sky for too long might be regarded as a sinful act, for it pleased the sense of sight with the surface of things and caused one to forget their God-given essence. She lay down on the mattress. She was just drifting off to sleep, lulled by the distant sound of the river flowing many feet below, when she heard a scrabbling at the low door which was set to one side of the cell. Startled, she sat up. There was a little light still remaining and she saw a white scrap of paper being pushed under the door. There were more scrabbling noises, as if someone was trying to catch her attention by scratching at the wooden door.

Maria reached over and picked up the paper. It was a note with her name on it. She unfolded it and took it closer to the window. She was accustomed to receive occasional messages in this fashion. People who were too shy to approach her directly sometimes asked her to intercede in her prayers either for themselves or for those they loved. No doubt the other anchoresses received similar requests. Once Maria had received an obscene communication which she screwed into a ball and discarded with the other waste. It had tainted her for days afterwards and required many hours of prayer and devotion, asking God that she should not be the cause of lustful thoughts in others.

But this message was different. It was hard for her to decipher in the dim light but eventually she made out the words: *I have news of your friend Lisabetta, please let me enter. I cannot be seen outside.* It could not, of course, be from Lisabetta herself since her laundry-girl was unable to read or write. What surprised Maria was that anyone connected to her laundry-girl could write either. Perhaps it was to do with the disappearance of Lisabetta's man, Guido. Maria recalled that night of the full moon, the whistled tune, the mantled figure entering the coach. A draught of air stirred the paper-thin curtain and she shivered. At the same moment there were renewed sounds at the door, an insistent tapping.

The only visitor Maria received inside the cell was her confessor, a wrinkled old priest personally selected by Monna Apollonia who came at regular intervals to shrive the *romite*. Nevertheless there was no reason in principle why she shouldn't open the door to visitors. No reason, in fact, why she shouldn't have gone through the door herself and re-entered the world outside, since there was nothing confining the hermit women to their cells but their own will-power and their obligation to God. Maria and the other women were not prisoners. There was a bolt which fastened the door on the inner side but no means of securing it from the exterior.

"Who is it?" said Maria, crouching down and speaking to whoever was outside the cell. The door was low, so low that anybody using it almost had to proceed on hands and knees, a prompt to humility. There was no answer but a renewal of the tapping.

Maria reached for the bolt then hesitated. Suppose that the person on the far side was a . . . an enemy? Then she rebuked herself for her fearful response. Who could be an enemy to an anchoress, one who was without property, ambition or

133

influence? Such thinking was worldly thinking. No, it was undoubtedly someone with news of Lisabetta, private news which for some reason they did not wish to communicate through the barred window. She would make a compromise with her caution, however. She would see whoever it was on the outside but she would not permit that person to enter her cell.

Maria slid back the bolt. It was stiff and she had to use both hands. As she tugged at the door so that it swung inwards, she opened her mouth to tell the visitor to remain on the outside, they could talk like this.

But she never had the opportunity to speak. She had the impression of a crouched black shape filling the entire door space. The next instant the figure had leapt into the cell and smothered her with its bulk. A great hand was clamped over her mouth and nostrils. Her face was buffeted by his hot, angry breath. With the instinct of survival she thrashed about on the stone floor, knocking over the stool and table. Among the items dislodged from the table was the knife that she used for cutting up her food. It clattered on the ground. Again more by instinct than intention, she fumbled for the knife, grasped it and lashed out at the muffled face of the figure overhanging her. She struck her attacker somewhere about the cheek, which roused him to greater fury. He seized her close by the hair – which she wore long and unkempt as a lesson against vanity – and repeatedly beat the back of her head against the flagstones.

Eventually, when Maria was lying unmoving with the blood pooling out from beneath her hair, the man lifted himself from her body. He was panting hard and he stood bent over, hands on knees, regaining his breath. Who'd have thought that the holy woman had so much fight in her? The man wore a dagger on his belt – wore it out of sight in a special sheath that snugged in the small of his back – but he hadn't even troubled to unsheathe it, so confident was he that he could deal with the anchoress with his bare hands. And yet it had been she who had attempted to use a knife on him! He wiped his hand down his face and felt it grow slick with blood. But he knew from experience that this was a superficial wound, quick to heal.

As his breathing calmed, he listened in case anyone had been alerted by the sounds of struggle. He'd been instructed to visit Maria at the end of the day when the Ponte Rubaconte was likely to be empty. The entrance to this queer little room was in any case tucked away round the side of the edifice, and the casual passer-by probably wouldn't have observed a shadowy shape tapping at the low-set door.

He cast his eyes round the rapidly darkening room. The curtain was still drawn over the window. He saw the sheet of paper with the writing on it. Not being able to read, the man did not know exactly what it said but the words had been sufficient to get the anchoress to open her little door. He tore the paper into pieces and allowed them to flutter through the drain-hole in the floor. Then he righted the stool and the table before replacing the prayer book and other items. He rolled Maria's body until it was lying on the mattress against a wall. He emptied the bucket of water over the blood on the stone floor and heard it gurgle down the drain. He looked around for something to take with him, as proof or keepsake of the deed. But of course there was nothing to take. He was about to give up when his eye lighted on a cap of some kind. He stuffed it in a pocket. Then he slipped out of the cell, almost on his knees, and pulled the door shut behind him. There was no way of securing it but there was no reason, either, for anyone to enter Maria's cell. Not, that is, until the smell got so high that passers-by became aware of it or of the congregation of flies crowding into this chamber. That would happen soon enough but not as soon as it would have done in the summer. He had a few hours' grace.

Lisabetta had had a night and a day and then another night to think of what the man called Giuseppe Orioli had told her.

Sitting in that tavern near the gaming house, she'd felt the heaviness afflicting her head and limbs drop away as Giuseppe explained that he might be able to give her information about Guido Greco's fate. First of all, he told her to prepare herself for the worst: he very much feared that her man was dead. She gasped and felt her eyes brimming, but inside she knew it for the truth, had known it almost from the instant she set out in search of her husband.

The fact was that Guido had made some powerful enemies, he said. Enemies? Lisabetta couldn't understand *that*. Giuseppe pressed Lisabetta to be frank now – after all, he was on her side. Was it not the case that Guido was associated with the Ciompi, the artisans who weren't affiliated to any guild and were regarded as the lowest of the low? Wasn't he the confederate of one Masetto Cennini, a firebrand who wished to diminish the power of all the nobles and merchants and bankers in Florence? She'd heard something of this, said Lisabetta, but it was just so much talk. What did men do but talk? It was more than talk, said Giuseppe. Guido had incurred the enmity in particular of a banking family, the house of Lipari. He, Giuseppe, sometimes worked for Lorenzo Lipari who was a good man, living out his life in a country estate which he called Paradise, and keeping out of harm's way. But Lorenzo's brother, Antonio Lipari, whose house within the city walls was known as Purgatory, was an unscrupulous money-man. Giuseppe believed that it was Antonio himself who might have given the orders for Guido's death. But why? said Lisabetta. This time the tears flowed uninterrupted down her cheeks. My husband may have said foolish things from time to time, but it would have only been under the influence of drink. He never really meant them. Someone took him seriously though, said Giuseppe, and decided to deal with him as a warning to the other Ciompi. Lisabetta shook her head, not so much because she found the ruthlessness of the wealthy hard to credit as because she could not think of Guido as posing a danger to anyone. She said as much. Yet it was so, Giuseppe assured her, it was so . . .

She pondered the information during that night and the following day. She could not do much by herself, yet any notion of going to the authorities seemed out of the question, especially since the individual who'd apparently given the order for Guido's disposal came from the same class of men as those very authorities. In the tavern she'd talked in a high-flown way about making the law with her own hands. But, by the cooler light of dawn, she realized how powerless she was. From the neighbouring rooms in her tenement came the cries of babies and the sounds of men and women and children preparing for another working day. She stroked her belly and wondered if there was indeed the seed of a new life in there.

That same day, under the pressing awareness that if she didn't earn a few soldi soon, she wouldn't have enough to pay her rent, she took up her needle once more and resumed her repairs. There was a pile of mending to be done. As she plied her needle, she observed her small, powerful hands with detachment. She recalled the conversation with Giuseppe. Why should she not take the law into her own hands? She'd said to him that the law was not for poor people like her, and she believed this to be so. She had an aunt who worked for a man of law, she remembered, but it scarcely crossed her mind to ask advice from him.

Before she lay down to sleep that night she determined to visit her friend Donna Maria once more and ask for her advice. Although the hermit woman had lived out of the world for so long, Maria seemed almost uncannily aware of what was happening in it. She was a good woman, with a warm heart beating beneath that white, pinched exterior. In truth, Lisabetta already knew what Maria's advice would be. She'd be told to put all thoughts of vengeance behind her. She'd be told that this story of Giuseppe's was just that, a story, one without proof. The best course of action for her, Lisabetta Greco, would be to observe a period of mourning for her Guido if she truly believed him to be no more. Then she should resume her life. She was young. She was not unattractive. Though poor, she had many advantages. Lisabetta could almost hear her friend uttering these very words, for they were similiar to the advice she would have given to herself.

So for the second time by the light of an early morning, Lisabetta went to the Ponte Rubaconte. Once again she stopped at the chapel of the Madonna alle Grazie and knelt before the votive light, in the company of a pair of ancient women, perhaps the same two as on her previous visit. Then she made her way directly to Maria's cell on the bridge. The curtain was drawn across the grille, yet through a gap to one side Lisabetta could make out a table with a handful of objects neatly arranged on it. She called out Maria's name, softly at first and then more firmly. The air on the open bridge was still fresh, without the oppressive heat that would blanket every quarter of the city in high summer. Despite this, Lisabetta scented a disagreeable smell under the spring breezes. Goose bumps broke out on her arms. An inner voice told her to turn away now and go back to her tiny room and pick up her repairs and resume her life as needlewoman and laundress. Have nothing more to do with this affair, said the voice.

But a different voice told her that it was too late. She was already knee-deep in this affair. She slipped round the flank of the stone cell. She bent down by the wooden door and once more called out for Maria. Now she was not expecting an answer and so was unsurprised when none came. She reached out to tap at the door and it opened a fraction under her hand. Not locked or bolted. This did not surprise her either. Drawing a deep breath, she pushed at the low door and scrabbled inside in a single movement. The dimness of the interior after the morning sun was a blessing. A blessing because she did not have to look too clearly at the body of Maria where it lay on the mattress on the other side of the cell or look at the buzzing flies that were gathering in the region of her friend's head. A blessing because she did not have to examine the dark staining on the floor, and the insects that were already crawling over it.

Her gorge rising, Lisabetta backed out of the little cell. She had enough presence of mind to pull the door to. Then, scarcely aware of what she was doing, she walked stiffly across the bridge towards the Oltrarno. She turned left into the Via de Bardi and then took one of the several smaller lanes which came together at a town gate. Shoving against the stream of people entering the town, she followed a path which led towards the stone quarry that lay beyond this area. Lisabetta pushed ferociously against the slope as though she was battling against an adversary. The houses and smallholdings petered out and she emerged into the open, out of breath and with her throat burning. She almost wished that she, and not Maria, was lying on the floor of a cell on the Ponte Rubaconte.

She was standing on the upper side of the quarry. The tawny ground gaped in front of her, as though a giant had taken a bite out of the hillside. The cutters were already at work down below, small dark figures among rectangular blocks of stone. Lisabetta clung on to an olive tree that stood near the quarry-edge. She recovered her breath. The image of what she'd seen in the cell on the Rubaconte was more real than the scene in front of her eyes. The fly-infested stains on the floor, the shrunken body of her friend Maria on the mattress. Yes, Maria her friend. Not merely her one-time mistress but her friend, who had given her a gift of a linen dress woven through with gold threads. Her friend, who had tried to help her in her quest for Guido.

Lisabetta wiped at her eyes but they were dry. No tears would come. Her face burnt. Who could doubt now that Guido had come to a bad end or that the same person who commanded his death had also dealt with Maria? Someone will pay for this, thought Lisabetta. Someone will pay or there is no justice, anywhere.

Another individual with death on his mind was Matteo Peruzzi, secretary to Antonio Lipari. It was the morning of the day on which the banker was due to give his decision concerning the King's loan. Peruzzi knew that his master was going to agree to it, which was why he had already attempted to frustrate such an agreement by dealing with Geoffrey Chaucer, using the unscrupulous Giuseppe Orioli.

He and Antonio Lipari had discussed the English loan yet again and Peruzzi came as close as he dared to outright opposition. It made no difference. The banker was set on this fatal course. With an 'ordinary' loan, adequate security would be provided and the proper terms agreed before a single florin changed hands. Yet the King of England was offering nothing by way of collateral, except a few tracts of land somewhere on the margin of his kingdom, most likely uninhabitable bog or steep mountainside. And when it came to the proposed terms and conditions in the contract – the times for the repayment both of interest and of principal, the penalties for defaulting, and so on – there was a perfunctory quality to the documents which Master Chaucer had brought with him. Obviously it was considered that any mere Florentine banker should bow and scrape for the privilege of advancing gold to the English throne. Yet Antonio Lipari seemed eager to grab this privilege for himself and, by doing so, to endanger the future of his house.

Matteo Peruzzi knew that Antonio's blind brother was as hostile to the idea of the loan as he was. Lorenzo Lipari was not quite as detached from the business of the world as he liked to pretend. In fact, Peruzzi had ventured so far as to discuss it with Lorenzo Lipari a few weeks earlier on one of his visits, all the time feeling uncomfortable under that sightless gaze. Yet the animosity between the Lipari brothers was such that, if one of them was aware the other was thinking or acting in a certain direction, he would be sure to do the precise opposite. Of little use, then, to enlist Lorenzo to speak for him . . .

If he was looking for a lever to shift the banker's stubbornness, it would be equally futile to approach Lipari's wife Emilia or his daughter Philomela. The wife seemed to have little interest in financial matters and, even if asked for her opinion, would always have deferred to her husband. As for Philomela – whose hand Peruzzi planned sooner or later to seek as a means of confirming his position in the banking house – she was merely a daughter. If she had an opinion, it would hardly be worth discovering.

Something had to be done to stop Antonio Lipari embarking on this disastrous course. A thunderbolt that would strike him dumb. A palsy that would seize his hands and prevent his signing any agreement or letter of intent. A suspect helping of shellfish which would confine him to his bed for many days and render him weak, feverish and incapable. Even his . . . yes, Peruzzi could contemplate this . . . even his death, for was it not better that one man should perish rather than that the whole house should collapse through his imprudence?

Bartolomeo Gentile, careful lawyer that he was, was unused to making a move without considering all the possible consequences. So he was surprised to find himself about to make a direct approach to Antonio Lipari in pursuit of the man's daughter, without having the slightest idea of how the banker was going to respond.

His determination to do this was fired by a discussion with Geoffrey Chaucer. As promised, the Englishman had tried to give him some hints on writing love verses. He'd had the time. Chaucer had played the visitor, as Antonio Lipari had directed him. He had seen many of the city sights and tried to forget that he was here on business.

141

Now Bartolomeo produced a little sheaf of the poems which he had sent to Philomela Lipari. Placing them on the table, he explained that they were fair copies – for it was a sensible, lawyerly habit to make a note of one's correspondence. The verse was, of course, penned in Italian but Chaucer's understanding of the written word was good, and anyway Gentile was on hand to translate. The Florentine complained that, although Philomela had read his verses with apparent approval (or at least without sending them back unopened), she had not been swayed by them.

"But, my friend," said Chaucer, "surely you don't believe that poetry is like a magic charm? That the right words are a spell to soften the lady's heart or smooth the path to her bed?"

"What is the point of it all then?"

"To relieve the sufferer's heart, perhaps. Or it may be a mere exercise, of course."

"How can you write without feeling? I could never write without feeling."

"The truest poetry may be the most feigning," said Geoffrey.

"This is all too deep for Bartolomeo," said Bartolomeo. "Why don't you just look at my verses instead, Master Geoffrey, and tell me where I am going astray."

Geoffrey soon saw what the trouble might be. Bartolomeo was extravagant enough in his claims of what he might do as proof of love for Philomela – he would ride as far as Inde in search of diamonds, he would dive to the bottom of the sea to retrieve the richest pearl, and all the rest of it – but there was one thing wrong. He wasn't abject enough. He suggested that he would be able to go on living without his beloved.

"The lady must feel that she holds your life in the palm of her hand," said Chaucer. "Throw yourself on her mercy. It is up to her whether you live or die. I am sure that's the way you really feel. You have only to say it."

"Is that how you approached your wife, Geoffrey?" said Bartolomeo doubtfully.

"No, I did not. She isn't very susceptible to poetry."

"Then you spoke to her father?"

"No, both her parents were dead. My marriage was more direct, Bartolomeo. It was somewhere between an arranged match and a personal preference which each of us had for the other."

"A personal preference – ah, you are so English and measured! Where is all your talk of dying without your lady then?"

"Who said that love poetry had anything to do with real life?"

Bartolomeo didn't seem very satisfied with this. He sat silent for a moment before saying, "You think I ought to try the more direct approach? Speak straight to Philomela. Or her father."

"What have you got to lose?"

"I do not think I could bear a refusal, Master Geoffrey. I might resort to desperate measures."

"Spoken like a true lover," said Chaucer.

13

Aquilino did not attempt to make himself inconspicuous. Why should he? He felt confident. He walked down the middle of the street, passing an old, one-legged fellow who was sitting on a bench in the cool of the evening. Aquilino carried a wooden tray on his shoulder, supporting one side with his right hand and with the other side wedged into his neck. A trio of trout – not the freshest-looking fish, to be honest, nor the sweetest-smelling – were nestled in straw on the tray.

Aquilino turned in at the entrance to the house of Antonio Lipari. The large gate was open. There was no immediate sign of the doorkeeper in his little hut and for an instant Aquilino thought his efforts had been wasted. He was almost disappointed. He was about to pass through the arched entrance into the courtyard when a voice called out.

"Where d'you think you're going?"

It was the sour-eyed doorkeeper emerging from the obscurity of his hut. (Aquilino recognized the man's function because he had prepared himself for this task by observing the Lipari *palazzo* from a distance during the day. Also, Novella had told him as much about the household as she knew.)

"Where d'you think I'm going?" said Aquilino, turning his head and squinting at the speaker over the fish on the tray. "You got a dinner on tonight. Kitchen delivery."

"You shouldn't come to this entrance. Deliveries round the side."

"Well, I'm here now, friend. So tell me where I can put these."

The doorkeeper came closer. The light was poor in the archway and, from his squinting, he did not see well. There was nothing wrong with the doorkeeper's nose, however. It wrinkled at the high-smelling fish. This wasn't surprising since Aquilino had bought them for a couple of soldi at the end of the day from a trader who intended, most likely, to chuck his unsold stock into a gutter.

"Christ, mate. I know where you ought to put 'em. What you trying to do? Kill the guests?"

"There's no accounting for tastes, especially rich people's," said Aquilino. "Just tell me where the kitchen is."

The doorkeeper directed him to the back part of the house, somewhere on the first floor. Aquilino nodded and the tray of stinking fish wobbled under his chin. But he was scarcely listening. All that was necessary was that he should get into this large house without arousing suspicion. This Aquilino seemed to have achieved for, once he'd finished giving directions, the doorkeeper went back to his little hut without further comment.

Aquilino entered the courtyard. There were three or four liveried servants lounging about but they paid little attention to him. Ragged strains of music came from an open window somewhere overhead. If he'd been quite unobserved, he would have abandoned the tray of fish there and then. After the doorkeeper's comments, he'd suddenly become conscious of just how rank they did smell. But Aquilino had to go on with the pretence now. There was a flight of stone steps up to a flower-entwined arcade, which was obviously the entrance to the family or business area of the house. And, set against the opposite wall, there was a less substantial flight of wooden steps to the servants' quarters. That was the one he ought to be taking. Instead, he quickly looked round to check that none of the liveried servants was observing him, then climbed the stone stairs.

The tray of fish almost overbalanced but he caught it and reached the loggia with his stinking cargo unspilt. He paused and then strode forward. If stopped and questioned, he intended to say that he'd lost his way. But the loggia was deserted. All the fine ladies and gentlemen of the house were getting ready for dinner, he supposed. The strains of music continued on the other side of the courtyard. He arrived at the door to the counting house and knocked on it. No answer. Opening the door, he slipped through. The room was empty. As he'd expected, it was too late in the day and the natural light too poor for the clerks to be at work. Not that Aquilino was familiar with the shadowy items in this room. Ledgers and abacuses, pens and ink-pots, they were as alien to him as a sword or crossbow would have been to the clerk or scholar, more alien perhaps. He simply registered the fact that the counting house was deserted, and thanked his lucky stars for it.

Before going a single step further, however, he had to dispose of his smelly burden. He found a chest against a wall, opened the lid and up-ended the tray so that its fishy contents slid inside. He dropped the tray inside the chest as an afterthought. Then, with relief, he closed the lid. Aquilino stood in the middle of the counting house and took stock. He allowed his eyes to become used to the gloom. He remembered the instructions that Novella had given him.

To the left of the main entrance, she'd said, there is a small door. Go through it and into a passageway. Turn right. That will take you to another door, almost a concealed one, which leads into the long chamber of Antonio Lipari. There are spy-holes set in each door, for my brother-in-law likes to be able to observe the clerks in his counting house, and he also sometimes watches the guests who are shown into his private chamber, watches them when they are unawares.

Everything unfolded as Novella had described. He slipped through the counting-house door and found himself in a dark passage. A little light came through a few slits in the stonework to his left which formed part of the outer wall of the house. More by touch than sight, Aquilino groped his way along the passage until he felt the outlines of a second door. Two small holes pierced the door at eye-level. Aquilino pressed his face to them. Whoever was accustomed to stand behind here must be of about his height. Even though it appeared at first to be unoccupied, the chamber on the other side was brightly illuminated by candles – these rich folk knew nothing of waste.

All at once Aquilino's view through the eye-holes was obscured, as if a curtain had been drawn across the door. The sound of footsteps and conversation made him realize what had happened. There were two men, at least, in the room and one of them was standing with his back to this very door. The man's head must have been positioned at almost exactly the place where the eye-holes had been bored into the door. Now Aquilino pressed his ear to the wood. He heard the voice of Lorenzo Lipari, il Cieco, the blind husband of Novella. Aquilino couldn't catch the words since it was Lorenzo himself who was standing against the concealed door, but he sounded tetchy, in his dry way. The answering voice was just as irritated, and had an oddly similar ring to it. Aquilino guessed that he was listening to Antonio Lipari, brother to Lorenzo and the man he had come to kill.

After a moment the figure moved from the door and Aquilino resumed his spying. There were three individuals in the chamber, he now saw. Giuseppe, the gentleman with the wine-stain on his face, was hovering in attendance on the sightless Lorenzo while the blind man settled himself down into a chair on one side of a desk. On the other side of the desk sat Antonio, a stocky, bull-headed individual. Good relations must have been restored for now Aquilino saw Lorenzo pass some small object across to his brother. The word 'friendship' was uttered. The banker examined the object, almost with pleasure it seemed, before placing it on his desk. This was the first time Aquilino had seen Antonio Lipari in the flesh, and he assessed his victim.

The banker was larger than Aquilino, if not more powerful, but the mercenary would have the advantage of speed and surprise. Aquilino fingered the handle of the dagger which was snugged into his belt. He became lost in thoughts of how – and when – he would dispose of Antonio and only attended from time to time to fragments of the conversation which penetrated his hiding place. They were talking of things which Aquilino didn't really understand anyway: loans, *creditori*, *malleverie*. Sums of money were mentioned but Aquilino was sure he wasn't hearing right because the sums seemed too large even for this plush company. All of the conversation was between the brothers, although very occasionally Giuseppe would be invited to throw in a comment.

So Aquilino considered how he would kill Antonio Lipari. Creep up on him from behind and plunge the dagger between his shoulder-blades? Approach him from the front and, with one swift jerk under the ribs, pierce his heart? Or were there other, more subtle means of killing?

He had been surprised when Novella had given him the task – the knightly mission – of killing her brother-in-law. If Aquilino was going to be requested to kill anyone, he might have expected it to be the husband. But no, Novella desired the death of Antonio Lipari. For, she said, it was the banker who had ended her father's life by refusing to extend loans and foreclosing on family properties. Her father had died prematurely aged while her mother led a miserable existence in the house of a cousin in Pisa, the old enemy of Florence. Novella had more or less been traded with the Lipari brothers in exchange for the cancellation of the remaining debts. Even Aquilino saw something wrong with this. If the debt was between Novella's father and Antonio Lipari, then why had Lorenzo been the lucky one,

149

the one to lay his hands on her in marriage? "I believe," said Novella, "that Antonio saw I could be the ruin of Lorenzo. He thought I could make him run mad with jealousy. I was not a gift of love but a gift of hate. Besides Antonio Lipari was already married."

This was all a bit too deep for Aquilino but he took Novella at her word. Hadn't she promised him herself, in any and every way he wished to have her? For that prize, even murder was a trifling thing.

So now he had ended up in a secret passageway, hand on dagger-hilt, watching over the husband of the woman whom he loved and lusted after (oh, how he lusted!) and another man who would die at the request of that same woman. This was a long way distant from the simplicities of open battle and even of ambushes. But he was resolute. Was he – Pietro Hodge, also known as Aquilino – not the devoted knight and lover of the lady Novella? Had she not requested him to avenge a dishonour done to her and her family by this bull-necked banker, Antonio Lipari?

At this moment a fourth character emerged into Aquilino's field of vision. This one was a slight man, with a neat red beard. He brought in some documents and placed them on the desk in front of Antonio Lipari in an over-demonstrative manner. Aquilino thought there was a certain reluctance in the gesture, which was accompanied by a wary glance at Lorenzo Lipari and a nod in the direction of Giuseppe Orioli. But the banker looked at the red-bearded man, looked at him more warmly than he had at his brother or Giuseppe. Then he raised his head and snuffed the air.

"Have you been eating fish, *mio volpacchiotto*? Or selling them, by chance?"

The other looked baffled and shook his head. Aquilino too, in his hiding place, did not understand the reference until he remembered the tray of fish which he'd deposited in the chest in the counting house. Then he had to stifle a giggle. He still couldn't understand, however, why one grown man would call another his 'little fox cub'.

Lisabetta Greco gained access to the house in a more straight-forward fashion than Aquilino. A woman in her tenement was a sister to one of the Lipari servants. Lisabetta knew her name and she called at the house using a side entrance, unlike Aquilino, and pretended that she wanted to speak to the woman. There was always plenty of coming and going on the servants' side, especially during such an evening as this when guests were expected and there were last-minute errands to be run. By the time her neighbour's sister appeared, Lisabetta had slipped inside and was searching for a place where she might spend an unobtrusive hour or three.

What happened to her after that, she didn't much care. Her sole aim in coming to Purgatory was to confront Antonio Lipari and . . . deal with him. There was a cold rage in her heart. To the disappearance (and murder) of her Guido had been added the brutal killing of the harmless anchoress, Donna Maria. Someone should pay, and it would be the head of a house known as Purgatory.

She had not known that the house would be so full of people. She almost thought of creeping back to her lodgings. But her resolve was stronger than her fear. She would wait until this place called Purgatory was less busy, say during the middle of the night, and then she would somehow find the chamber of Antonio Lipari – find it by instinct, if necessary – and after-wards she would plunge the bodkin which she was carrying into his black heart.

In the meantime she had to keep out of the way. By trial and error, Lisabetta found a flight of stairs that led to the uppermost reaches of the house. Several times she passed people going in the other direction but each time she kept her head down and moved purposefully upward. Eventually she emerged on to an upper terrace protected by an overhanging roof. The sun was setting, casting a bloody glow over the spires and towers of the city. This was the place where blankets were aired or garments dried, but the clothes-lines were empty and Lisabetta knew that the laundry-girls had already collected the last items before the night chills came down. In high summer the ladies of the house might have gathered up here in the hope of bleaching their hair by exposing it to the stronger rays of the sun, but there was not much risk of being disturbed now. Beneath her was the bustle of a household preparing for visitors. The sounds of music rose up. She sat down in an angle of the wall and waited.

14

Antonio Lipari was about to discuss marriage with his daughter Philomela. Although named for the girl in the old story who'd been turned by the gods into a nightingale, there was nothing particularly sweet or bird-like about her in either voice or appearance. She did not say a great deal but in so far as her father respected any woman's opinions, he respected hers. That was the reason he was consulting her now. They were sitting in the long chamber. It might have been an audience between the banker and a client, for husband and daughter were sitting on opposite sides of the desk. But there was almost a hint of softness in Lipari's features which was never evident during business affairs.

"My dear," he began, "Bartolomeo Gentile has expressed a wish to see me later on this evening. He wants a confidential discussion. You can probably guess what it's about."

"Yes. He sends me poems, father."

Lipari already knew this but he raised his eyebrows, as if in mild surprise, and said, "You do not return them then, but read them instead?"

"Out of courtesy – and curiosity."

"Are they good?"

"If I wasn't the recipient, I might consider them . . . passable."

Philomela knew that she wouldn't get anywhere with her father by a display of enthusiasm. A dry, sardonic style suited him best. She had a taste for it too. For the same reason she kept aloof in front of Bartolomeo Gentile, of whom she was actually rather fond.

"Then, from your tone, you won't be too disappointed by what I intend to say to him."

"I don't know what he intends to ask you yet, father."

"You do, my dear."

"Very well," Philomela conceded. Both of them were oddly reluctant to specify exactly what it was that Bartolomeo intended to ask. "*I* may not be disappointed. But if you are telling Messere Gentile to wait, *he* will be disappointed."

"You care for his feelings?"

"I would not see him hurt."

"Hurt is unavoidable in this life," said Lipari. "It's not a question of telling him to wait."

Philomela said nothing. She glanced down at the objects on her father's desk. The astrolabe whose hoops and curves caught the candlelight, the small handbell, the dagger which he wielded for slitting the seals on his correspondence. And a little fastener made of gold. It depicted two hands joining in a wrist-clasp. She thought of hands joining in marriage. She thought: my father does not intend to tell Bartolomeo Gentile to wait for, say, a few months or a year. Nor does he intend to accept Gentile on my behalf straightaway. That must mean he has other plans. She grew hotter in the face. Her prominent jaw set firmer.

"I have other plans for you, Philomela," he said now, echoing her thoughts so precisely that she almost started from her seat.

"I am listening, father."

"I have a high opinion of Matteo Peruzzi – "

"Matteo Peruzzi!"

She couldn't restrain herself this time. She'd never liked her father's secretary. He crept about the place, he whispered in his master's ear, he was devouringly ambitious. Couldn't her father see that?

Antonio Lipari looked taken aback at Philomela's reaction. He attempted to lighten the mood with a trifling joke.

"You cannot dislike him, my dear. Why, he has the same shade of hair as you have – and your mother!"

"How can you compare us?" said Philomela. She didn't know whether to laugh or grow indignant at her father's observation. "His is earth-coloured. Ours is like flame. Where did this come from?"

She picked up the gold clasp with the joined hands from where it lay in front of her.

"That is a gift from your uncle. He says that it shows friendship."

"Friendship? I'm not so sure."

When she looked more closely, Philomela thought that the two hands were gripping each other very fiercely. The clasp was finely worked so that tendons seemed to stand out on the backs of the hands. She was frightened of her uncle. Perhaps that coloured her opinion of his gift. She replaced the clasp on the desk and sighed.

"To return to Signor Peruzzi," said her father.

"I don't like him, father. I dislike him."

"Love can grow from dislike, even from hate."

"You do not propose that I should . . ."

Once again she was reluctant to finish her thought aloud . . . that I should marry *him*? And, seeing her resistance, even Antonio Lipari drew back. One thing at a time. He gestured expansively. He reassured her. "No, no. At the moment I am merely telling you what I intend to say to Bartolomeo Gentile – *if* he makes the request which I expect."

"You mean to say no? If he asks for my hand."

"Why, yes," said Antonio Lipari, growing impatient with the conversation now. What was the point of listening to women, after all? They were all the same. *Cosi fan tutte*. "I shall say no."

"He says he will see Bartolomeo for a few minutes after the meal," said Bartolomeo to Chaucer. The little lawyer was all eagerness, as if achieving a short audience with Antonio Lipari rather than obtaining the hand of Philomela was actually the summit of his dreams.

"Don't forget why we're really here," said Geoffrey.

155

"To secure a wife."

"While I am securing a loan on behalf of my king."

"A thousand pardons, Master Geoffrey, I had almost forgotten. Messere Lipari says that he will see you afterwards as well, to give you a formal answer to take back to England. The letters are ready."

"Then let us hope we are both successful," said Geoffrey.

"Now everything is on the – how did you describe it? – on the shoulders of Fortune, no? So we might as well eat and drink and enjoy ourselves while we can," said the other, waving a long arm about the dining chamber. The guests were assembling as liveried servants scurried about holding basins of scented water and with little towels draped over their arms for hand-washing before the meal. Others were pouring out goblets of wine. Geoffrey recognized the taste of the *vernaccia* he'd enjoyed on his previous visit. In a corner of the room, a group of musicians were tuning up.

There was a stir by the main door as Antonio Lipari entered accompanied by his secretary Matteo Peruzzi. Slightly behind them was a trio of figures, none of whom Chaucer had seen before. One of them was a man, thin and reedy where Antonio was bull-like, but having some intangible similarity to the banker. He could not see, Chaucer understood straightaway, for he faced the world with that curiously level-headed posture of the blind. But Geoffrey already knew this man's identity for Bartolomeo had told him something of Antonio's blind brother, explaining how the condition was quite common in Florence, with some blaming the cold winds that blew down from the Apennine passes in spring and others the dazzling light of summer. However, in Lorenzo Lipari's case, it was an accident which had deprived him of sight. Though no child, he had tumbled from a tree and landed on his head.

To Lorenzo's left side there was a large fellow keeping him company, whose cheek was overspread with a purplish stain. This one was whispering something in the blind man's ear and at the same time steering him gently by the upper arm. On the man's other side was a striking young woman, tall and slender. She wore a veil over her face but it was made of such fine material that nothing was hidden, but rather was her beauty enhanced. Just as the large fellow had his hand on the blind man, so did the blind man have his hand on the young woman's arm. They came through the door together, one leading the other, as if they were executing a complicated dance.

"That is Lorenzo Lipari," said Bartolomeo, "and his wife Novella. He is a jealous man. He cannot let her out of his sight for long – but since he has no eyes to see with, instead he keeps a hand very often on her. Sleeping and waking, they say."

"And the man at his other side . . .?"

"Ah, that is Giuseppe. I seem to remember, Geoffrey, that you have an expression in your country about using a long spoon to sup with the devil. You might say that Giuseppe Orioli is Lorenzo's long spoon."

Chaucer did not have a chance to ask Bartolomeo to explain what he meant for his attention was distracted by the next individual into the dining room, a face both recognizable and unexpected. It was the tall man with the pocky features whom Chaucer had observed from the terrace of Bartolomeo's house on his first day in Florence. His name . . .? Chaucer had it after a moment. He was called Masetto. What was this man doing in the wealthy Lipari household when he'd been stirring up the artisans after the fatal accident under the scaffolding?

Bartolomeo must have guessed Chaucer's unspoken question for he said, "Ah, you have recognized him too. That one comes from a wealthy family so he is not out of place in houses such as these. Yet he is a younger son and they often have a touch of the rebel. He is friends with the labourers and the common people because he says that God shaped us all from the same cloth."

The pocky man went across to the blind man and his wife. He bowed slightly in front of them. Giuseppe, standing to one side, inclined his head and Chaucer could have sworn that some signal passed between them, some tacit acknowledgement that lay beyond the usual niceties. He looked to Bartolomeo for enlightenment but the notary was staring fixedly at the newest arrivals, love in his gaze. The elegant Emilia, wife to Antonio, was framed in the doorway. Next to her stood Philomela. The girl was finely dressed, her blue gown figured with white lilies, yet she looked ill at ease.

"See where she comes," said Bartolomeo. "The face and figure of an angel. Have you ever seen anything more beautiful?"

Truly, reflected Geoffrey, love is blind. At the same time he was touched by the little notary's infatuation, and regretted that he would never see with such eyes again. Had he, actually, ever seen with them?

These speculations were interrupted when Antonio Lipari ushered over his brother, holding him by the upper arm. Lorenzo drew his wife after him so that, once again, there was that impression of a strange dance. She had drawn her veil aside. She looked nervous. When it came to Lorenzo Lipari, Chaucer saw a study in how two members of the same family may nevertheless be as divergent as branches on the opposite sides of a tree. Antonio Lipari was stocky where Lorenzo was gaunt. The bull-neck of one proclaimed force and power; the pinched face of the other indicated a life of introspection. Chaucer noticed that, for all that, he kept a firm grip on Novella's arm.

Antonio Lipari said, "'Ere is my *fratello* Lorenzo, Signor Chaucer. And 'is wife, Novella."

The woman smiled slightly while the blind man inclined his head and said, "*Con piacere.*" His voice, dry and dusty, held no trace of pleasure. Releasing his wife, he extended both hands. He gripped Chaucer's right hand for a long moment. His palms and fingers were as arid as his voice. Geoffrey had the odd sensation that he was being 'seen' through the blind man's grasp.

"My brother does not like the city," said Antonio. "For 'im to come 'ere is like going to 'ell. *All'inferno.*"

"*E vero*," said Lorenzo. His mouth cracked into a smile, of sorts.

Chaucer said, "I saw the house of the great Dante Alighieri recently."

Bartolomeo translated and again Lorenzo Lipari nodded, before making some remark to the effect that Dante was the only poet who could begin to compare with the great masters of the Roman age such as Virgil and Horace. His speech was measured and clear so that Geoffrey was able to follow most of what he said.

"Ah, Signor Geoffrey," said Antonio, as if reminded by his brother's words, "I 'ave a gift for you."

He snapped his fingers and a hovering servant brought across a leather-bound book and presented it to Chaucer. Antonio watched attentively as Chaucer opened the parchment pages. It was a copy of that very *Inferno* by Dante which they had just been mentioning.

Sensing something happening, Lorenzo said, "*Lasciate ogni speranza voi ch'entrata*," and gave another mirthless grin. Geoffrey's heart swelled with gratitude, and he thanked Antonio in a mixture of English and Italian. For a moment, it hardly mattered to him whether he returned home with the royal loan or not. This book, this leather-bound volume, would be the most precious item in his baggage. It was a propitious moment altogether for Antonio pressed a heavy hand on Geoffrey's shoulder and said, "*La commedia e finita*. Letters are signed and sealed. Come after supper."

"Let-ters," said Lorenzo, picking up the word and repeating it as if it tasted disagreeable. His brother turned towards the blind man and, now clutching at his shoulder, whispered in his ear. Chaucer noticed that Lorenzo did not look gratified but perhaps he merely disliked Antonio's closeness.

Then they were summoned to the table and the liveried servants began to bring in wine in metal goblets together with the bread for dipping. Geoffrey tucked the *Inferno* inside his doublet. He would not touch it again until his hands were clean after eating. The news that Antonio Lipari had agreed to the loan, which was presumably what he meant by the reference to signed and sealed letters, sharpened his appetite for the meal.

The feast was a reflection of the standing of Antonio Lipari and the banking house. Whether they were eating calf or carp, pork or pike, all the meat and fish was covered with a paste made of egg and saffron so it appeared to be gilded. Some of the dishes were set off with gold leaf. And golden streams of *vernaccia* flowed too, so that the buzz of talk soon took on the intensity of bees in a hive and almost drowned out the noise of the musicians.

Several private conversations took place in the course of the feast or shortly afterwards. Among them was a short dialogue between Antonio Lipari and his sister-in-law, Novella, who was seated between the two brothers. 'Dialogue' is perhaps not the right term, since Novella said almost nothing. Indeed an observer who was sober – as most of the company were not by this time – would have said that she was apprehensive, even frightened. She seemed to be leaning away from Antonio as if she wanted nothing to do with him. At the same time she was beseiged from the other side since Lorenzo's left hand would, when not occupied with eating, reach out to grasp a hand, a thigh, a shoulder, as if to remind himself of his wife's presence. On Lorenzo's right hand sat Philomela, his niece. To her fell the task of indicating what was on Lorenzo's plate and occasionally guiding his knife so that it speared a gobbet of food from the trencher. Philomela might have been fearful of her uncle but she did her duty patiently and tried to make small talk.

There was also an encounter between Giuseppe Orioli, the man who had no master or many masters (depending on how you looked at it), and Masetto, whose master was . . . the common people.

As Bartolomeo Gentile had informed Geoffrey Chaucer, Masetto came from a wealthy family – the Cennini, to be precise. Early in life he'd discovered that he was a persuasive speaker. He had also developed early on an aversion to the idea of change, specifically any change which threatened the position of the Cennini and their wealth. Masetto's family was part of that unofficial group which had taken it upon themselves to nip trouble in the bud, trouble from the Ciompi, for instance.

Masetto ran with the hare and hunted with the hounds. He gave verbal encouragement to the lowest of the workers – the wool-washers, the casual builders – at the same time as reporting back to the authorities on any likely troublemakers in their ranks. He enjoyed flourishing his heretical morality, claiming that all men were like stone hewn from the same quarry and that they differed only in the uses to which they were put. He enjoyed his double game. At least he had been enjoying it until this point. Now Giuseppe was giving him some unwelcome news.

"Our mutual friend Guido Greco, he had a wife," said Giuseppe.

"I know her," said Masetto. "A pretty little thing. Not that you'd be interested, Giuseppe."

"Now this wife has been searching for her husband."

"She won't find him though?"

"Not unless she digs deep," said Giuseppe.

"Well then?" said Masetto, who was like Matteo Peruzzi in that he did not wish to hear too many details of unlawful actions.

"We were seen on the night when Guido was met on the Rubaconte."

"*We?* I wasn't there," said Masetto. "Who saw you?"

"It doesn't matter," said Giuseppe. "It is taken care of."

But Masetto's quickness in distancing himself from the sticky side of this business irritated him, and Giuseppe was reluctant to let him off so easily. After all, it had been Masetto who had first ensnared Guido Greco, by setting up the false meeting and so on.

"You have recently lost a clasp, I believe. A gold piece which shows two hands having hold of each other like this."

In demonstration, Giuseppe crossed his hands so that each was holding the other by the wrist. Masetto looked startled. The pocky marks on his face stood out like holes on a wall. He'd given the clasp to Guido when he wanted to show himself as that young man's friend. Also, to allay the other's suspicions. How did Giuseppe know about it?

"You've found it?" he said.

"Not exactly. But it has come into the possession of . . . a certain gentleman . . . by a roundabout route. I wondered whether you wished to get it back."

"How can I get it back if I don't know where it is?" said Masetto.

"It's in this house," said Giuseppe. "In fact, it is at the moment in the long chamber of Antonio Lipari, our host. It came into the hands of Lorenzo Lipari and he has given it to his brother – out of friendship, you understand. Maybe you ought to go and ask him for it back."

Giuseppe said this in a spirit of malice and was gratified to see the discomfort on Masetto's pocky face. He had no particular interest in the clasp but he now saw the opportunity to make trouble. Once he'd removed the clasp from the body of Guido, he remembered where he had seen it before. It was Masetto's. *Bene.* So once upon a time it was Masetto's, then it was Giuseppe's. He had given it to Lorenzo, watching the blind man's thin fingers trace out the design, and taking pleasure in the fact that – unknown to Lorenzo – it was the transferred property of a dead man. Then Giuseppe went one further and suggested to Lorenzo that it might be an appropriate present for Antonio, a symbol of 'fraternity'. So Lorenzo had duly passed it to his brother earlier that evening. Now, considered Giuseppe, it would be fitting if its owner stole it back all over again. He left him to think it over.

15

Hearing the tread of Antonio Lipari outside the door, the figure took shelter behind the nearest object of any size. It was an instinctive reaction. Someone is coming . . . hide! The nearest object was the great statue which stood on a pedestal to one side of the long chamber, the marble statue with the raised sword-arm and no head. Large areas of the room were in near darkness. There was no more than a cluster of candles at one end and a couple of wall-sconces still burning on the other side of the chamber. Very faintly could be seen the outline of human shapes on the wall painting, the warriors at the service of Mars, the lovers and others in thrall to Venus. Yet the individual behind the statue was aware of none of this. Instead, he – or perhaps she (since it's too dark to see whether a man or woman is in hiding here) – concentrated on the sound of the door opening, the sound of Lipari's footsteps advancing down the great chamber.

It was a very assured tread, a ponderous tread, not unexpected in a man who was secure in his own private quarters, secure with his place in the world. A man who believed that he was alone. The would-be murderer fingered the haft of the weapon tucked under his (or her) garments before withdrawing it. In the darkness, the figure grinned, an involuntary movement and no sign of pleasure. The smiler with the knife. The banker was off his guard and all the advantage of surprise lay with the watcher, who reached out with the hand that wasn't holding the dagger to touch the headless shape in the small of its back. Only to snatch the hand away, for the cold marble had moved slightly. Or seemed to.

Antonio Lipari had reached the end of the room and was standing by his desk, a great dark shadow with hands extended, ruffling through a sheaf of papers by the sound of it. The figure behind the statue could just see the outline of the banker out of the corner of an eye but was wary of turning his (or her) head in case Lipari was alerted to the hidden presence by a tiny movement in the corner of *his* eye. The only other sound was the thudding of the watcher's heart and a roaring in the ears. It was like the preparation for battle, when expectation is tightened to an almost unbearable pitch so that action – any action – comes as immediate relief.

And now Antonio Lipari replaced the papers and lit a couple more candles at the far end of the room in the region of his desk, as if he had further business to conduct. The room was so large that the light seemed curiously localized. He started to move back down the long chamber in the direction of the main door. The watcher couldn't understand why. It didn't matter, though. Within a few seconds Lipari would be within striking distance. The hider behind the statue faced a choice: to leap out from this hiding place, accost Antonio from the front and, with one swift jerk under the ribs, pierce his heart. Or to creep up on him from behind while he was passing and plunge the dagger between his shoulder-blades. This choice presented itself not in words but as two distinct sequences of images, and the decision was made. Safer, perhaps, to stab the man in the back. So better to wait until Antonio had moved a pace or two beyond this great marble statue and then . . .

And then the footsteps halted directly in front of the headless statue. Clutching the knife more tightly, the would-be murderer sensed rather than saw Lipari standing on the far side. The banker was saying some words which sounded like: "*Mio commendatore.*" The phrase was repeated, almost in loving tones. "*Mio commendatore.*"

But Antonio Lipari's tone changed when he said, "You may come out of hiding now."

It was almost a relief to be found. Time, which had been wound taut, slackened slightly. It gave the would-be murderer a moment's pause to reflect. You had to admire his courage (this was the thought in the murderer's mind), you had to give him that. Lipari was afraid of no man - or woman. Then (without thought) the murderer dropped the dagger. It clattered on the floor. Plans change. Instinct takes charge. At the same instant as the dagger struck the floor, the murderer thrust with out-stretched arms at the headless statue. It teetered on its pedestal and began to topple forward.

On the other side of the marble figure Antonio Lipari stood expectantly, waiting for whoever was concealed behind it to emerge. The light was uncertain and the marble figure seemed to swell in front of his eyes. Its breastplate billowed like a sail and the sword-arm began a downwards sweep. Lipari blinked as if his eyes were deceiving him. Then he realized that the figure was moving in his direction. Another second and he might have leapt back. But Lipari was a large, ponderous man. Although he'd become aware that there was a person lurking in the shadows of his chamber, he had not considered himself to be in any real danger. He had been absent for only a few moments. (In a privy in another wing of the house, if you wish to know.) During that time, someone had crept in. It was probably one of the guests from the feast, come to make a private request out of earshot of the others. He was used to people making private requests. He dismissed the idea that it was Geoffrey Chaucer. The Englishman would not sneak in unannounced. Possibly it was that little lawyer Bartolomeo Gentile returning to press his suit for Philomela's hand. If it was, then he'd get the rough end of his tongue. No more courtesy and temporizing.

165

At any rate, there was no one who could be a threat to him, Antonio Lipari. Who would dare to assail him in his private quarters?

Consequently, when he'd strolled down the chamber, he felt at ease, capable of dealing with this intruder, whoever it might be. And now it was too late. The full weight of the antique marble figure fell on Lipari, pinning him to the floor. The statue's sword-arm, unbroken by the fall, reared up above the banker's shoulder. The headless neck struck him on the temple. But Lipari was already dying, he was almost dead. His head had struck the marble floor with a crack that was only masked by the crash of the falling statue. Very soon blood started to pool out from beneath the ancient figure. If a detached observer had been watching he might have thought that the marble was, miraculously, shedding blood, an illusion which was enhanced by the dim, flickering light from the sconces.

But there was no observer with the leisure to think this. The murderer paused only to ensure that the task was complete. Antonio Lipari was dead. Not by a thrust from a dagger but killed by one of his own weighty possessions, you might say. Not what was intended. But plans change and instinct takes charge.

Pausing only to pick up the fallen dagger, the murderer slipped from the room.

"Geoffrey, Geoffrey!"

The notary was out of breath. His brow was more furrowed than ever. His cheeks were hectic as if he'd been drinking more than usual. But then all of the guests at the dinner had drunk well. The musicians were still playing, the sweetmeats being picked over, the last dregs of wine poured, while the diners had grown noisy or confidential or somnolent. Some had wandered away from the dining chamber altogether.

"What is it, Bartolomeo?"

"Messere Lipari, he will see you now. He is in the long chamber."

What was the matter with Gentile? Why did he look so hectic? Then Geoffrey remembered to ask the right question.

"Did you succeed?"

"Succeed?"

"In your quest for the hand of Philomela."

"Ah, I see what you mean. Yes and no . . . he said he would think about it."

Which means he's already made up his mind, thought Chaucer. Perhaps Lipari did not wish to disappoint his daughter's suitor by an outright refusal. Or perhaps he wanted to keep Bartolomeo sweet for as long as the man had a part to play in negotiating the English loan.

"Are you coming with me, Bartolomeo, to see Lipari once more?" said Geoffrey. "To get his answer to *my* request."

Gentile looked even more uncomfortable.

"Why, I do not think so, Master Geoffrey. To you he will say yes, I am sure. He has enough English for that. I am not needed to translate his yesses."

"Very well."

Understanding that Bartolomeo was reluctant to encounter the banker again, Geoffrey left the dining chamber by himself. He was becoming familiar with the general layout of the *palazzo*. He passed through the silent counting house, illuminated by a pair of lonely sconces. Strangely, there was the faint odour of fish here. He reached the door to the long chamber. It was ajar. Chaucer raised hs hand to knock at the door but some impulse made him pause.

He stood, undecided, on the threshold. What was holding him back? Was he apprehensive about Antonio Lipari's answer? Suppose that the 'signed and sealed letters' contained a refusal so that Chaucer had to return with his mission unachieved. Yes, he was no more than the messenger. But it is often the messenger who takes the blame for the bad news he bears . . .

Chaucer rapped lightly on the door before pushing it all the way open. In front of him stretched the long chamber. There was a cluster of candles which drew the eye to the desk at the far end where Lipari was accustomed to preside, and some lesser lights on the right-hand wall between the windows. The marble floor lay as smooth as a frozen lake. The great central table was crowded with the bronze and pottery artefacts. The statues were arrayed down the left-hand side of the room and at their backs were the painted images of fighters and lovers.

Everything seemed as it should be, yet Geoffrey's senses told him that something was wrong. There was a stony silence in the chamber. Without moving from the doorway, he called out for Lipari by name. No response. And indeed he couldn't see anybody at the other end of the room. Then Chaucer looked more carefully at the marble slabs on the floor. God's bones! There was a body lying there, an elongated shape half in the shadow of the table of antiquities.

He squinted at the body and then breathed a sigh of relief. It was no corpse after all, but one of the marble statues which had toppled from its perch. It must have come down with a thunderous crash, enough to wake the dead. But the rest of the house had been occupied with their feasting and merry-making. No surprise that it had gone unheard. From a distance, the statue appeared to be the headless figure with the upraised sword-arm, the one that Antonio Lipari had referred to as his knight, his *commendatore*.

And, come to think of it, where was Lipari exactly? Hadn't Bartolomeo said only moments ago that the banker was ready to see Chaucer? Maybe he had been distressed at the fall of his favourite figure and was summoning servants to retrieve the situation. It would take ropes and pulleys to haul the figure upright, assuming he wasn't damaged beyond repair. 'He'? Why was he thinking of that lump of stone as a person? Geoffrey started to walk, reluctantly, down the chamber.

He hadn't gone far when he observed that there was a more disturbing aspect to the scene. The fallen figure was not resting directly on the ground but on a bulky shape that lay between it and the stone floor. Chaucer observed a curious mirroring of limbs on the near side, the sword-arm made of marble and a human arm outflung below it. When he was closer he saw a pool of blood in the area where the statue's head should have been. Geoffrey squatted on his hams. It was perhaps fortunate that the light was dim. Crushed under the fallen figure he recognized what was surely the outline of Antonio Lipari and the bloodied oval of the man's face. The banker's head was slightly averted, as if he'd turned aside at the last moment from his descending fate. The other statues ranged along the room looked out impassively.

Chaucer rose from his crouch. He stood over the statue for a time, not knowing exactly what he felt. Or what to do next. He ought to have called for help. But he did not move, as if turned to stone himself. Then he shook his head to rid himself of the queer notion that the marble figure had come to life in order to attack Lipari. The queer notion that the two men – one of stone, one of flesh – had been engaged in some deadly struggle which could have only one outcome. He looked down at the decapitated shape, larger and more terrible now that it was lying prone, the inhuman shoulders, the mighty forearm and the giant hand gripping a sword. Supposing the statue were to shift now . . . supposing it clambered to its knees . . .

With an effort, Geoffrey turned his mind back to the victim of this event. He was no friend to Antonio Lipari. Yet, in a couple of meetings with the man, he had admired the other's force and confidence. He was grateful for the copy of the *Inferno*, which even now nestled in an inside pocket.

There was something grotesque about the way in which the Florentine banker had met his end. Chaucer recalled his and Bartolomeo's first visit to this room. He remembered examining this very statue, the cold marble under his fingertips. The slight motion of the statue as he'd touched it. Obviously it was not secure on its pedestal. Hadn't Lipari said that it was a recent acquisition? Chaucer could visualize how the accident had occurred. Lipari had been alone in the chamber, inspecting his collection of objects and figures. He had reached out to touch the marble giant – as a mark of respect or a token of good fortune? Had unbalanced the figure from its unsafe lodging place. The warrior was already facing forward, with one leg slightly in advance of the other, in fighting stance. And, before he could shift himself, Antonio Lipari had been pinned down and crushed. It must have happened quickly, between Bartolomeo Gentile's departure from the long chamber and Chaucer's arrival.

A very strange death. Chaucer could not remember hearing of anything similar.

And a very inconvenient death for him, Geoffrey Chaucer.

What was to become of his diplomatic mission now?

Geoffrey skirted the two figures on the floor, taking care to avoid the pool of congealing blood, and walked the length of the chamber. He was conscious that he should by now have raised the alarm, but there was one small item to make certain of first. He examined the desk at the far end. This was the best-lit area of the room, the burning candles a sign that Lipari hadn't concluded his business for the evening. Chaucer was searching for those letters, those statements of intent. There were several documents lying on the desk but nothing Chaucer could identify as relating to his mission. For a proper look, he'd have needed more time and a better knowledge of Italian and its commercial phrases. He could not postpone alerting the household for more than a few minutes longer. It crossed his mind that he might be held to account if he didn't act soon. Nevertheless he continued to scan the surface of the desk. Besides the paper, there was the astrolabe and a little handbell.

He also noticed that there was some object missing . . . something which had been on the desk the other day. What was it?

It occurred to him that Lipari might have been carrying the items which he was searching for. He visualized the Florentine walking down his chamber, ready to greet his English guest with a letter of intent or some other material connected to the English loan in his hand. This was a remote possibility but Chaucer took up one of the lighted candlesticks from the desk and returned to where Lipari was lying beneath the statue of the warrior.

For the second time he crouched down and peered at the banker and the fallen statue. On this side the figure's marble arm was broken off above the elbow. Presumably the arm would have been holding a shield, or perhaps a dagger to complement the sword. Disconcertingly, Lipari's right arm was flung outwards in such a way that the human limb appeared to a be a thinner, more frail continuation of the interrupted stone one. From here Lipari's face was not visible but only the back of his head beneath the torso of the statue, resting on a lake of blood. There was no sign of any document. Raising his own arm, Chaucer swung the candle from side to side. As he did so, the light reflected on a glinting object which lay on the far side of the empty pedestal.

Still at a crouch, he moved round to examine the object. It was a curious ornament, a clasp intended to fasten a garment, with a design of two interlinked hands. There were no marks on the clasp, no blood. What was it doing here? Had it been dropped by Lipari? Or by someone else? Almost without thinking, he picked up the clasp.

Then Chaucer placed the candlestick on the floor and looked more carefully at the area between the rear of the statue and the painted wall. What he saw caused him to get right down on his hands and knees so that he had a spider's-eye view of the floor between the empty pedestal and the wall. He was squinting at

171

a patch of floor about six feet square. Chaucer wondered how often the bare marble was swept. More often, no doubt, than the covering of rushes and herbs would have been changed even in the finest London house. Nevertheless there was still a thin layer of dust down here. From this angle, there were footmarks visible in the dust. Scuffed, smeared footmarks passing to and fro, from people who had strolled up and down this side of the chamber, perhaps stopping occasionally to admire some feature of the Mars-and-Venus wall painting. He'd left footmarks himself as he shuffled round to pick up the clasp.

But what drew Chaucer's eye was a pair of footprints positioned directly behind the now vacant pedestal. He drew the candle nearer and bent down so that the side of his head was almost touching the pink-veined marble. Unlike the other markings, these prints were more distinct and complete. Someone had been standing in this spot with the painted wall behind him and right up against the rear of the statue. Had been standing here recently, because otherwise these impressions too would be scuffed and blurred. Perhaps he – or she? – was admiring the sculpted figure from either side, front and back. Perhaps . . .

Chaucer's gaze returned to the elegant clasp which he was still holding in his own hand. Whose was it? Had there been someone else in the long chamber when the statue tumbled on to Antonio Lipari, pinning him down and crushing him to death?

Bartolomeo Gentile had been here recently, of course. Maybe he'd seen something. Chaucer resisted the next thought, that Gentile might have done more than see . . . He wanted to trust the notary. Nevertheless, to the shock and dismay of discovering Lipari's body was added a deeper sense of disquiet.

Uncertain what to do next, he returned to the far end of the chamber. He must summon help. No, it was far too late for help, but he had the responsibility of alerting the household to this dreadful event. Better that than be caught in the presence of the dead body. One of the household servants would surely come soon to see whether the master required anything. Or Matteo Peruzzi would appear for some confidential exchange. How long had he been here with the dead man for company? Ten minutes at least.

Geoffrey glanced up at the painted wall. At this end of the chamber were the figures of men and women under the spell of Venus, all entangled in the dark wood of desire. The goddess herself emerged nearby and naked from glassy green waters, as if to supervise her kingdom. Set in the wall and close to Lipari's desk was the concealed door. Not really concealed, because if you looked carefully you could see a door handle among the painted foliage and branches. What caught Chaucer's eye was the image of a figure vanishing into the forest, head half turned as if listening or watching for pursuit. Unlike most of the men and women in the forest, this one was clothed. The figure was painted so that, if you were aware of the door, it might appear to be leaving the room – the painter's little joke, no doubt.

Geoffrey went to peer more closely. Was it a man or a woman? When he'd first glimpsed it, he had assumed it was a woman. But closer examination made it more difficult to say. The face, which was partly turned so that a beardless cheek and a fearful eye were visible, was curiously sexless. Hanks of nondescript hair stuck out from beneath a cap while the person's back was clothed in some reddish garment. His (or her) leggings were obscured by undergrowth. The only thing that was certain was that the figure was running away.

Chaucer tried the door handle. To his surprise it turned and he pulled the door open. He peered into a dark passageway. There were sconces on the wall, unlit. He wrinkled his nose. The air was slightly fresher here, indicating some ventilation. But there was an underlying smell, a fishy smell. This passage must connect to other areas of the house since, on his and

Bartolomeo's previous visit, the entrance had been used by Lipari's secretary Peruzzi as well as by the serving-woman bringing wine and cakes. Presumably Antonio Lipari required access to the long chamber not only via the counting house, which was somewhat public, but also through this more discreet entrance.

Geoffrey went into the passageway and closed the door behind him. It was dark in here, but not absolutely dark. Threads of candlelight from the large room penetrated through what he assumed were knot-holes in the wood of the door. But there were only two of them, and they were regularly spaced at about eye-level. Chaucer had to stand at full stretch to see through them. When he did, he had a good view of this end of the long chamber. Well, the existence of these spy-holes proved nothing very much. Possibly Antonio Lipari liked to observe any guests to his inner quarters, to note their behaviour before he made an appearance. Or Matteo Peruzzi could have kept watch on his master's business through these eye-holes. And servants might have been instructed to wait on the other side until some visual signal came from their master.

What Chaucer couldn't account for was the faintly dis- agreeable odour of fish in this place. Food brought from the kitchen? No, because this was the smell of raw fish, not cooked. Anyway, the feasting had all taken place in the dining chamber. There'd have been no call to bring a dish of fish along here this evening.

Geoffrey was about to slip back through the door in the wall when he heard a voice calling out. Then, almost at once, two or three voices came clamouring together. A stream of sound, excited and high-pitched, issued from the area of the long chamber where Lipari lay under the fallen figure. Too late now for him to call for help. Help had arrived, itself too late.

Geoffrey Chaucer turned away from the hidden door. Instinct told him that, if he was suddenly to materialize through the wall, he might be blamed for the scene, as though he'd had a hand in Lipari's death. Nonsense, of course. It was an accident, a freakish accident. He hadn't even been the last person to see Antonio Lipari alive. (But he was the first to see him dead, wasn't he?) Then he thought of the ghostly footmarks and the clasp. He was still holding the clasp tight in his left hand. He'd forgotten about it. Now he slipped it into a pocket.

All this while Chaucer was making his way along the dark passageway which ran parallel to the inner wall of Lipari's office. He did it by touch, running his left hand along the rough plaster of the wall. On the other side were occasional slits in the stonework which admitted the night air and which, during the day, would provide some glimpses of light. There were also a couple of wall-sconces. Geoffrey reasoned that there were other exits from this passage, or at least one exit connecting it to the servants' quarter of the house. In fact, he came sooner than he'd expected to a second door on the left-hand side. This was also provided with a pair of peep-holes. Through them, Chaucer saw the desks and ledgers of the accounts room. From here the banker could keep an eye on his clerks. There was some illumination in this room and the sound of raised voices came from off to his left, that is from the area of Antonio Lipari's long chamber.

Chaucer cautiously turned the handle and opened the door a fraction. He saw the backs of a couple of people disappearing through Lipari's door but there was no one in the counting house itself. Swiftly, he slipped through to the other side. Pausing only to check his clothing – not too much in disarray, no marks of blood or tell-tale patches of dust – he walked resolutely towards the same doorway.

A shifting cluster of men and women had gathered in the area of the statue. Several were holding candles which swung or dipped in agitation. Some people were crouched on the floor, others were clutching at each other or had their hands over their faces. He recognized Bartolomeo Gentile and Lorenzo and Novella Lipari and Giuseppe Orioli among others. The air was filled with a mixture of cries and groans and exclamations. From a distance it might have seemed they were lamenting the fall of the antique figure.

There wasn't anybody watching him but Geoffrey drew a deep breath and squared his shoulders. He stroked his beard. When he'd achieved some sense of calm, he walked to the nearest group of onlookers. From here he couldn't see Antonio Lipari's body but only the marble back of the statue. "What happened?" he said to no one in particular.

"What happened?" said Geoffrey Chaucer to Bartolomeo Gentile. "When you saw Signor Lipari, I mean. You must have been . . . one of the last people to see him alive."

Bartolomeo looked ill at ease. But, reflected Chaucer, he probably looked uneasy himself. The whole household was distracted or distressed or worse. The two men were in the dining chamber, keeping out of the way while Antonio Lipari's body was being retrieved from beneath the weighty statue. Chaucer reckoned that this was a task best left to members of the household. There was enough confusion and distress in the long chamber already. He had taken advantage of it to have another rapid search for the letters supposedly authorizing the English loan, but without success. Now Geoffrey and Bartolomeo were by themselves. The forlorn remains of the feast, like the guttering candles, were a reminder of the cheerful spirit of the evening. A dead calm ruled over the *palazzo*.

"What happened?" repeated Bartolomeo. "I told you what happened. Messere Lipari and I spoke together, before this terrible accident."

"And he did not agree to your request – for his daughter's hand?"

"He did not turn me down either."

176

The notary sounded prickly and defensive at the same time. He would not meet Chaucer's eye. In fact, the interview with the banker was still fresh and painful in Bartolomeo's mind. When he claimed that he had not been turned down, he was correct, but only in a literal sense.

Antonio Lipari had responded to the notary's request with a snort of laughter. In his eyes, Gentile was a decent enough fellow but he lacked the drive and ambition which would have made him a suitable match for his Philomela. As he'd indicated to his daughter, he had other plans for her. But Lipari saw the hurt in the lawyer's expressive face and, in a rare mood, hastened to mollify him. Antonio Lipari did not want to quarrel with life at this moment. The evening had gone well, he had given out appropriate little gifts at the feast, he was on the verge of making a substantial loan to the English crown (a decision that could only reinforce his growing status in Florence). So instead of an outright refusal, he gave some temporizing answer to Bartolomeo.

But the other man wasn't so easily fooled and he went away with a bitter heart. Although, when first questioned by Chaucer, he had implied that there was hope, Bartolomeo was quite capable of reading the truth in the eyes of the father. What they said to him was, *You are a little, jumped-up man of law. If it wasn't so amusing, this wish of yours to marry Philomela Lipari, I might become angry about it.*

"What was Signor Lipari doing when you left him?" said Geoffrey, breaking in on Gentile's thoughts.

"He was alive."

"Of course he was alive."

"In fact, he was preparing to see you, Geoffrey. I told you as much in this very room."

"But what was he *doing*? Was he sitting? Was he standing? Looking at his wall paintings? Strolling among his marble figures?"

Bartolomeo didn't answer the question but said: "His death was an accident."

"I never said it wasn't."

"If it comes to that, Master Geoffrey, how did you find him? *Sitting? Standing?* Oh no, I remember, you arrived in the long chamber after me, didn't you, for I looked round and suddenly I saw you. I might ask you why it took you such a time to get there since I, Bartolomeo, witnessed you leave this dining room many, many minutes earlier. Did you get lost in this great *palazzo?*"

"No," said Geoffrey. "I made my way straight to the long chamber."

Now it was Bartolomeo's turn to wait for an explanation. Even as he was speaking, Chaucer was weighing up in his mind whether to pass on the things which he had discovered. He harboured some suspicions about Lipari's death, suspicions to do with the hand-clasp he'd found on the floor and, more significantly, the footmarks behind the fallen statue. These details aside, it seemed the banker's death could be viewed as an accident and no murder. If it was generally accepted as such, why should Chaucer get involved?

But by admitting to Bartolomeo Gentile that he'd gone directly from the feast to the long chamber, Geoffrey had trapped himself into accounting for his delayed arrival. Intuition told him that Bartolomeo had no hand in Lipari's death, that he could be trusted. Chaucer was about to find out whether his intuition was right.

In a few words he explained how he had reached Lipari's office to find the man himself crushed beneath the giant statue. Uncertain what to do next (which was true enough), he had entered the passage behind the painted door at the far end of the room. Perhaps he was searching for help (this was less true). While he was inside there, the first alarm had been raised. Some reluctance to appear at that moment caused Chaucer to grope his way along the passage and emerge into the counting room.

From there he had re-entered the long chamber to find a gaggle of people surrounding the banker's corpse.

It was a curious relief to come out with this. Geoffrey felt no guilt about Lipari's death – whether that death was accident or murder – but he did feel uneasy about his actions since. Gentile regarded him shrewdly.

"There is more that you have not said, Geoffrey. You saw something else which you have not mentioned to Bartolomeo. Otherwise you would have declared yourself openly, not gone creeping down passageways."

"You're right. There are a couple of items which say that the death of Antonio Lipari might have been deliberately caused."

And Chaucer described the discarded clasp, the ghostly footprints on the marble floor. Bartolomeo listened intently.

"Wait!" he said. "I saw that clasp. It was lying on the desk. I particularly noticed it for the joined hands made me think of . . . marriage. It seemed a good omen that Messere Lipari had it on his desk."

"What was it doing by the fallen statue?"

"How often have you risen from your desk, pen or paper in hand," said Bartolomeo, "to attend to something on the other side of the room? One forgets what one is holding."

"True enough."

"As for the footprints which you saw, there are people coming and going all the time in the long chamber. You yourself were examining that figure the other day."

"We both were."

"And any marks near the statue would have been wiped away now by all the activity in the long chamber."

"They would."

"So have I convinced you that this was an accident and no murder?"

"You have convinced yourself, Bartolomeo. I shouldn't have raised the subject. But, tell me, did you smell fish in that room?"

Bartolomeo looked at Chaucer as though he'd gone off his head.

"A fishmonger killed the banker?"

"No. It's odd though . . . I could have sworn I smelt fish about the place."

"Listen to Bartolomeo. He says that matters are already complicated enough."

"Bartolomeo is right," said Geoffrey.

But, inwardly, this conversation with the notary hadn't settled his mind. Geoffrey remained convinced that things were not as they should be with the death of Antonio Lipari, even if Bartolomeo seemed to have no doubts.

16

B ut by the next day everything had changed. Geoffrey Chaucer had woken up that morning, hardly refreshed by the night. Brief snatches of sleep had been haunted by the image of Antonio Lipari crushed beneath the giant marble figure. And, for the rest of the time while he was lying awake, he contemplated the failure of his mission to the Lipari house. With the banker dead and no apparent way of establishing what his ultimate wishes were in the matter of the English loan, Chaucer considered that he had little choice but to return home. He assumed that control of the financial business would eventually pass to the widow or, more likely, to the blind brother, possibly aided by Matteo Peruzzi. He didn't know what Emilia Lipari's views were but he suspected that Lorenzo Lipari and Peruzzi would not be as amenable to negotiation as the dead man. Or that, if they were prepared to deal, it would take many more months of to-ing and fro-ing, further exchanges of letters and diplomatic approaches. At the least Chaucer would have to return to London for fresh instructions.

In truth he was ready to return. Florence was a beautiful city and her people were hospitable and engaging, for the most part. But it was springtime in England now. The blossom would be out on the Dover road and in the Savoy gardens. His youngest child, little Lewis, would have grown and changed even in the few months during which he'd been absent. Doubtless his wife was managing perfectly well without him. Geoffrey recalled a frosty exchange before his departure. But there was a small pang even in the thought that she – as well as Thomas and Elizabeth – would be doing well without him.

When he rose from his bed in Bartolomeo Gentile's house, it was to find that his host had gone out. Or, more precisely, according to what he could discover from old Bella, Bartolomeo had been taken away by officials working for the *gonfalonier*, who was responsible for the administering of justice in the city. Gentile had not been arrested, it appeared, but summoned to a hearing. This was as much as Chaucer could glean from the wrinkled Bella. The agitation in the woman's face and gestures showed her real fondness for her master. Geoffrey too felt agitated, and not only on Gentile's behalf. He was a material witness to the death of Antonio Lipari, he had been first on the scene. No one knew of this except the notary. Suppose he should let it slip while he was being questioned. Chaucer might be blamed for not raising the alarm in the first place. He enjoyed a certain immunity as an English visitor, one who was on the King's business, but the Florentine authorities could inconvenience him, perhaps worse than inconvenience.

Chaucer passed an uneasy stretch of time before Bartolomeo reappeared. He tried to read the Dante which the dead man had given him, but his mind wouldn't settle and he could not lose himself in the circles of the *Inferno*. The morning was hot and sticky and he thought again of the spring breezes shaking the blossom back home. When Gentile eventually returned he was in a state. However, if Bartolomeo was still nervous at being summoned for questioning, it was well covered by indignation.

"What do you think, Master Geoffrey?"

"I don't know, Bartolomeo. You haven't told me what has happened yet."

"I am roused from my bed at some unearthly hour by the *ufficiali*, the justice's men, and escorted like a common criminal to the Signoria. There I am kept waiting before being questioned by a fellow I remember well from my university days. He's a lawyer like me. His name is Marco Sandro. He and I never got on. You see, even all those years ago he was never –"

"But today – tell me what happened *today*, Bartolomeo."

"Has he been talking to you, Geoffrey, my 'friend' Marco? You see, he was speaking to me as if Antonio Lipari's death was not an accident but murder. Just as you thought!"

Chaucer started. He assured Bartolomeo that he had said nothing of his doubts about Lipari's death. In fact, after their conversation the previous night, Geoffrey had accepted that his suspicions were groundless – or at least that they were unprovable. Now it was Bartolomeo's turn to reassure Chaucer.

"Do not worry, my friend. I said nothing about *you*. Furthermore I know exactly who it is who has been pointing the finger at Bartolomeo Gentile. It is that secretary Peruzzi. I've never liked him and he has never liked me. He plans to have the hand of my Philomela, but she has too much sense and taste, God be thanked!"

"So Peruzzi has accused you of . . .?"

"Oh, the gentleman has accused me of nothing yet, I expect. He is too subtle for the downright lie. But he is aware that I was the last person to see his master alive. He knows of my feelings for Philomela since his own miserable carcass harbours a pale shadow of them. And he has no doubt hinted to the justices that I might have been driven to some desperate act by Messere Lipari's refusal."

"How would he have known what passed between you and Lipari?"

"Peruzzi is a sneaking spy, he sees and hears too much."

"Anyway Lipari did *not* refuse you, according to your account."

"No, he did not refuse Bartolomeo. Not exactly refuse," said Bartolomeo.

"Well then?"

183

"There is no telling how some unscrupulous fellows will try to twist things," said Bartolomeo, accompanying the remark with much hand and arm twisting of his own. "Peruzzi can say this, Peruzzi can say that, and Bartolomeo comes out covered in pitch."

"Be cheerful," said Chaucer, realizing that Gentile needed to be calmed. "Whatever Peruzzi said it cannot have had much effect on the justices, for here you are come home again!"

"I have been released, you mean? How merciful of my old 'friend' Marco Sandro! But listen to me, Geoffrey, I am afraid that there is more to come. If Peruzzi is allowed to go on pouring poison into the ears of the *ufficiali*, they will throw poor Bartolomeo into jail. It might have happened today except that the whole Signoria is distracted by the murder of one of the *romite* on the Rubaconte."

Murder? *Romite*? Rubaconte? What was he talking about?

Bartolomeo soon explained. It seemed that there was a strange Florentine sect of women, mostly from good families, who lived as hermits on the Ponte Rubaconte. They occupied the little stone houses that were set along either side of the bridge. Perhaps Geoffrey had seen them in his perambulations about the city? Anyway, one of these women had been attacked the previous day. At least that was when her body had been discovered. Her assailant had been most brutal, repeatedly striking her head on the stone flags of her cell. This terrible deed must have occurred during the hours of darkness when the Rubaconte was deserted. No one could understand why a harmless and devout young woman should have been put to death in such a fashion. What could she have done to warrant it? She had no possessions to steal, she posed no threat to anyone.

Chaucer listened attentively. Though no concern of his or Bartolomeo's, the murder of this religious was an unfortunate omen. Together with the demise of Antonio Lipari, it suggested

184

that, like the turbid Arno, there were muddy currents of death and disorder at work beneath the sunny surface of this place. But now Bartolomeo had finished with the outrage on the Rubaconte and was speaking of something else.

"I said, will you help me, Master Geoffrey?"

"Of course, if I can. But what exactly . . .?"

"It is apparent that the authorities at the Signoria are inclined to look on the death of Messere Lipari as a case of murder, which was your thinking too as I recall. Peruzzi is determined to ensnare me in this business so that he can have me out of the way and have Philomela all to himself. This I know! This I feel inside! So we must discover the truth for ourselves, Master Geoffrey, we must discover what really happened last night in the long chamber. You were there first. You have sharp eyes and a sharper head."

Chaucer noted the 'we' and the way in which Gentile was reminding him of his early presence on the scene. It made him feel more uneasy. He protested that, as a matter of fact, his eyes weren't particularly sharp – and that the trouble with having a sharp head was that its owner frequently cut himself with it. But Bartolomeo was having none of this. He was convinced of the Englishman's deductive powers. Hadn't he shown those very qualities after his discovery of Lipari's body?

There was more still. The indignation on Bartolomeo's face was replaced by a touch of triumph. The man of law had been doing a little investigation on his own behalf. He had not been detained at the Signoria during all this time but had busied himself asking questions in and around the Lipari house. He'd unearthed something. It was all to do with fish. When Geoffrey asked on the previous evening whether he'd noticed a fishy smell in the long chamber, he, Bartolomeo, had thought that his friend was going a little soft in the head, perhaps unsettled by Lipari's death. But it was true! And furthermore it was proof of the sharpness of all Geoffrey's senses, physical and mental, for some rotting fish had been smelt out in a chest in the counting house. They were trout, three of them, old trout. It was as if they had been put in the chest for storage or disposal. Odder and odder!

So then Bartolomeo asked some more questions and found out from the doorkeeper – the sour-faced fellow – perhaps Geoffrey remembered the sour-faced fellow? – that he had let pass through the gate on the previous evening a man delivering a pile of odorous fish to the kitchen. When the lawyer pressed for a description, the doorkeeper couldn't or wouldn't say anything further.

"But," said Bartolomeo, "Bartolomeo did not stop there, no, no. I have found a witness to all this. I have brought him here, hopping all the way. I have promised him a reward if he repeats his story. He is downstairs. He finds it difficult to climb stairs. Come, my friend."

Geoffrey thought that if anyone was going soft in the head it was the little Florentine. But he followed Gentile to the ground floor. There was a man sitting in the cool of the lobby. He possessed only one leg: hence the references to hopping and stair-climbing. A stick lay on the ground beside him. When he opened his mouth in a gap-toothed grin, Chaucer recognized the individual he'd seen on a couple of occasions outside the Lipari house in the Via dei Cerretani, watching the world go by. Bartolomeo spoke a couple of sentences and the man replied with a volley of almost incomprehensible Italian. After a time, Bartolomeo held up his hand for silence and turned to Chaucer with an expression that said, See what I mean? But it was no good, Geoffrey was unable to understand more than a handful of the words. So the notary had to explain.

The gist of it was this: the one-legged man, whom Bartolomeo referred to as the *viecchio*, had been outside Messere Lipari's house the previous night – had observed the individual bringing fish to the door – knew straight off that he wasn't a genuine fish delivery-man, he didn't have the proper walk or manner – instead he moved with the swagger of a soldier – and this *viecchio* should know, he'd seen his share of soldier's service, which was how he'd lost his leg – so this false fish-carrier had slipped inside the Lipari house – and then an hour or three had gone by with the *viecchio* still sitting on his stone bench, and aware that rich people were arriving for a feast and hoping perhaps to pick up some alms – when he'd observed this same fish-man running past at a fair old rate – running down the street as if he was being pursued or had committed some crime or both – running until he disappeared around the corner.

And so what did Master Geoffrey Chaucer think of all this? said Bartolomeo in his own person as he slipped some coins to the old man.

Chaucer didn't think a great deal of it, in truth. There'd been many people in the Lipari house the previous night. Almost any one of them might have been the agent of Antonio's death, if it was indeed a murder. Why should the act have been perpetrated by a supposed soldier in the guise of a fishmonger?

"Ask him what the man looked like, his facial features," said Geoffrey.

Another exchange followed. Bartolomeo held his hand to his own face and said, "He had a great nose, a fine nose."

"Oh, the nose is always a distinguishing feature," said Chaucer, half in mockery. "And a soldier? There must be many soldiers in Florence and quite a few with big noses."

"None of our own soldiers now," said Bartolomeo with a touch of pride. "Not since the days of the *viecchio* here. You know what we Florentines say? When men discovered they had more brains than oxen, they put them to plough. And when we Florentines discovered we had more brains than other men, we set them to fight on our behalf. We employ mercenaries."

"Mercenaries," said Geoffrey. Then he paused because he re-called the mercenary in Falcone's company, the one he'd encountered when they were riding into Florence. Aquilino, so called for his nose, although his actual name was a yoking together of England and Italy . . . Pietro Hodge.

"You have an idea, Master Geoffrey?"

"Probably not. But you can direct me to an inn called La Volta – in, let me see, Via Orivolo? You know it?"

"Yes, but it is not a respectable place and you should not go there alone. I would not call it an 'inn'."

"Even so," said Geoffrey without asking Bartolomeo what name he would have given it instead.

17

At this very moment in a private, first-floor room in the unrespectable 'inn' on the Via Orivolo, the would-be lovers Aquilino and Novella Lipari were meeting. It was a chamber set aside for what – if you were romantically inclined – you might have termed trysts. But a colder eye would have observed the scabby walls and the bed which provided the only furniture and which, from its age and condition, might have played host to Adam and Eve (after the Fall). Even the sun's rays poking through the rents in the dirty cloth covering the window were turned to a dirty gold. From a neighbouring room, also private, came a shriek, whether of pleasure or pain it was impossible to tell.

Aquilino was ready and eager to claim his prize for the killing of Antonio Lipari. True, things hadn't exactly gone according to plan – and, if he had been really pressed under interrogation, he would have denied the killing altogether – but he saw no need to tell Novella any of the details. It was enough that the banker was dead, according to their arrangement. Now Lorenzo's wife must fulfil her side of the contract. But, yet again, the woman was making difficulties!

"I tell you, my dearest Aquilino, my dearest knight, that I have no more than a few moments to spare. I have only escaped from my husband because of the great turmoil in the house in the Via dei Cerretani – "

" – which was what you desired, my lady. Antonio Lipari is

189

no more. The man who brought ruin to the Arrezo family is dead."

"Dead at your hand?"

Aquilino nodded but said nothing.

"How did you do it? I mean, I know it wasn't done with this." She fondled the dagger at his belt. "I also know that they found my brother-in-law pinned beneath a great statue . . ."

"It did not fall by chance."

"I did not think so!"

"Then it is better you know nothing else besides."

"I came looking for you," she said. "In the house last night I came after you. I might have changed my mind about the deed."

He looked uneasy. "You didn't find me though. Just as well. There was too much happening."

"I know," said Novella. "They are asking questions at the Signoria."

Aquilino looked more uneasy still. Novella kissed him but in a distracted rather than a passionate way. Now Aquilino's anger began to grow hand in hand with his confusion. He would have pushed her on to the bed there and then but her reference to the Signoria had unnerved him. At the same time Novella, as if sensing his intention, wrinkled her nose – her nose, so delicate in comparison to his! – and said, "There is a fishy tinct in here."

Aquilino grasped her roughly by the shoulders but she said, "Not here, not now. Listen!"

Aquilino listened but all he could hear were low moans from one of the adjacent chambers (sounds of misery? of content? who knew or cared?) and the persistent scrabbling of vermin behind the walls of the room.

"I had rather take a vow and become a religious than do it here," she said.

"You have taken a vow," Aquilino reminded her. "A vow to be mine when Antonio Lipari is dead. He is dead and you are not mine."

190

Aquilino was proud of the clarity and good sense of his words.

"You are right," said Novella. "Oh how right you are. But, my Aqui, we had much better be surrounded by birdsong and the soughing of the wind among the boughs."

Aquilino didn't know what she was talking about, but every time she spoke in such a poetic fashion he was reminded that he was in the presence of a lady. If his anger didn't exactly abate, it was clouded by admiration – and more confusion still. Now she produced from the folds of her dress a little gilded key. She held it up before Aquilino's eyes.

"This is the key to the garden where Lorenzo takes me when he wants to, you know . . ."

She giggled a little.

"How – how did you come by it?"

"Better you should know nothing now," she said, echoing his words of a moment earlier. "It is enough that I have it, and that my husband does not know I have it. And tomorrow you *will* come to the house called Paradise, and then, my dearest knight, you *will* enter into your true paradise. There is a well in the corner of the garden whose waters run deep and which you may plumb to your heart's content. You may pick the finest flowers from my husband's garden, you may ravish his most secret blossom."

Deep wells, fine flowers and secret blossom! The mixture of lust and poetry was enough to make Aquilino's senses swim. No one could use words like his lady! Novella gave him a final kiss and said, "You must bathe yourself before tomorrow, my love."

Then she left the room.

As she felt her way down the rickety stairs to the dark, odorous lobby, her expression changed. Not that the two men who were politely waiting at the bottom for her to pass noticed this. She, in return, scarcely glanced at them, let alone recognized them as fellow dinner guests of Antonio Lipari.

191

As she swept past them and out of the door, eager to get away from this squalid hole, Bartolomeo Gentile nudged Geoffrey Chaucer.

"I know," he said. "Novella, the wife of Lorenzo Lipari. I thought her husband was so jealous that he would never let go his hold of her."

"Even Lorenzo must have been distracted by the death of his brother," said Bartolomeo. "They are staying at the Via dei Cerretani after the death. He forgets his young wife for a moment. But I am very surprised to see her in this place."

"We might be able to use that fact," said Geoffrey.

On the way to the Via Orivolo, Geoffrey had explained to the notary why they were visiting this place. Tomaso Falcone had told him to go to La Volta if he needed help, that its proprietor was a friend to his mercenary band. Chaucer reasoned that if it really had been the fellow known as Aquilino inside the Lipari house the night before, then there was a chance that the owner might know his current whereabouts. The chance was remote, what an English bowman would call a 'long shot', but what else did they have to go on?

In turn, Bartolomeo had explained that the Volta 'inn' was nothing more than a house of ill fame, with a drinking area on the ground floor and a mouldy honeycomb of rooms on the upper levels. The place was popular with the rougher type of customer such as the mercenaries.

The madam of the house, who dwelt in a lair near the entrance, assumed they were regular patrons but when Chaucer – using Bartolomeo as interpreter – gave the name of Tomaso Falcone, Donna Michela's well-worn smile of welcome changed to something more genuine. The woman had a leathery look and small eyes. These, combined with the high collar which encased her neck, somehow made Geoffrey think of a tortoise, a creature old and beyond any surprise.

She declared that she'd always had a soft spot for Englishmen. When the English left behind their foggy island and travelled to warmer climes, she said, their appetites swelled in the sun and they knew no bounds. She hinted that a distinguished visitor such as Chaucer, and his Florentine friend of course, might benefit from a discount in her establishment. Geoffrey thanked her but explained that they were searching for another Englishman – or, to be precise, half an Englishman – one Pietro Hodge, generally referred to as Aquilino. Did the good lady know his whereabouts? Why, they were in luck, declared Donna Michela. She did not know any 'Odge, as she pronounced the name, but she was familiar with Aquilino. The gentleman they were looking for was upstairs at this very moment. With a lady. A real lady. Though not one of hers. Not that her ladies weren't real ladies. But couples sometimes rented her chambers when they were in urgent need of a private *conversazione*, and she always looked favourably on anyone from Tomaso Falcone's company. So while they were waiting for the pair to finish their conversation, wouldn't her visitors like to take advantage of the wares . . .

Hearing feminine but unfamiliar footsteps descending the stairs, she broke off and went to the door of her lair. She stuck out her leathery neck. She beckoned to Chaucer and Gentile with a beringed hand. "That's her coming down now," she said softly. "You may go up. Take the first door on the left."

Once they'd waited for Novella Lipari to pass, the two men hesitated at the bottom of the stairs, absorbing this new twist in the situation. Then they groped their way up the stairs. There was a small area at the top off which several doors could be dimly discerned, as well as another flight of stairs going further upward. One of the doors was slightly ajar while the others were shut fast. Sounds of activity came from behind these and a solitary groan from the partly open one.

Chaucer drew a deep breath of stale air, knocked on the door and, without waiting for a reply, pushed it fully open. There was a man on the bed. When he heard the door open, he turned his head expectantly. Seeing two strangers he sprang to his feet. Despite the poor light, Chaucer recognized him as the man he'd glimpsed twice before, once on his initial meeting with Falcone's men and then on that second occasion as they were approaching the gates of Florence.

The first thought that went through Aquilino's head was that the men were customers who'd wandered into the wrong room. When it became apparent that they were scrutinizing him instead of turning on their heels, his next thought was that Lorenzo Lipari had somehow discovered his and Novella's trysting place. Guilt caused him to conclude that these men were two of il Cieco's agents, intent on mischief! But they did not look heavy and brutish enough for the task. Though he was sure he'd glimpsed one of the men, the plumper of the two, somewhere before.

"I hope we find you well, Master Hodge," said the plumpish individual. In English.

And all at once Aquilino remembered where he'd seen this man. On the road to Florence, twice on the road in fact and that very recently, in the company of his commander Falcone. He was an English traveller. He'd reported his arrival to Lorenzo Lipari. Though God alone knew who the little fellow with the long arms was. And then, on a closer look, he recognized him too. Well, well, interesting . . .

"*Che vuoi da me?*" he said, then in less practised English, "What do you want?"

"I want a talk," said Chaucer. "*Una conversazione* as the lady downstairs calls it."

"*Chi me lo dice?*"

"My name is Geoffrey Chaucer. I have come from England on business. This is my friend, Bartolomeo Gentile. He is a notary of this city."

Aquilino sized the pair up. They were blocking the doorway. Neither of them looked to be in fighting trim. He could probably put his head down and barge right through them. But why should he? He had more right to be here than they did. He'd paid good soldi for the use of this chamber. Immediately after Novella's departure it had crossed his mind to use one of the regular women in the Volta. A straightforward transaction would be a relief from Novella's teasing delays. But, judging by the surrounding sounds, they were all in the throes of activity. So he'd lain back on the age-old bed and thought of his forthcoming encounter with Novella Lipari. How he must bathe beforehand. That fishy tinct! He'd give her smells and tincts! But nevertheless, fresh and perfumed, he knew he'd go to Paradise tomorrow and gain entrance to her husband's secret garden. To which she held her husband's secret gilded key. And if she did not give way to him tomorrow, he would do . . . terrible things. He groaned with frustration, and at that moment the door flew open to admit two strangers and he leapt from the bed.

After Chaucer had identified himself and his companion, Aquilino decided to play for time.

"*Non capisco*," he said.

"I know that you have English blood in you, Pietro Hodge, so let's talk in English," said Geoffrey. "That way we'll all understand ourselves much better."

Aquilino grunted. He recognized in the tones of the plump man someone who was used to being listened to, probably to being obeyed. He retreated to a corner of the grimy room and slouched against the wall.

"One thing before you start your talking, you will be pleased to call me Aquilino."

"Very well, Aquilino," said Chaucer, privately wondering at the fondness of these soldierly types for their nicknames. As his eyes adjusted to the gloom of the chamber he saw its grime and bareness, somehow intensified by the uncongenial bed. "We heard that you were entertaining a lady just now. We even had the pleasure of seeing her as she descended."

"This is a place for entertaining the ladies. Maybe you didn't know."

"I did not know that the wife of Lorenzo Lipari was a *puttana*," said Bartolomeo.

The man with the large nose looked startled, and then indignant.

"She is no *puttana* but a lady."

"Whatever else she may be, she's still Lorenzo Lipari's wife," said Bartolomeo.

Now Aquilino looked a touch fearful. He'd just been tricked into an admission that he knew Novella Lipari. Geoffrey might not have let out the information so soon but he admired Bartolomeo's deftness. The mercenary's expression showed that he was afraid of the blind man. Chaucer could understand why this might be.

"Does her husband know she was in this *bordello*?" he said.

"What do you think, Master . . .?"

"Chaucer. Don't bother to answer that question, Aquilino. Of course Messere Lipari is not aware that his wife was here. I've seen for myself that he is a jealous man, so jealous that – had he eyes – he would not let her out of his sight. But, having no eyes, he must keep his hands on her. So I say to you that her presence here is doubly surprising, both because she is a lady and because her husband is very vigilant over her. I wonder what he would do if he found out that you had been meeting her for . . ."

" . . . *un appuntamento d'amore*," said Bartolomeo, looking disdainfully round the room.

"Are you a lawyer too?" said Aquilino sullenly, ignoring Gentile and addressing himself to Chaucer. He was pushing himself against the corner as though the walls might open up and let him in.

"Never mind what I am. We know that you were in the house of Antonio Lipari last night . . ." He paused for a second, to allow Aquilino to deny it but the other said nothing. "And furthermore we know that you were in the very chamber where Signor Lipari met his death. We have evidence which we will take to the Signoria."

This time Geoffrey waited a little longer. Still no denials came.

"You pretended to be delivering fish to the kitchens, Peter Hodge. Then you discarded the fish in the counting house, and hid yourself inside Antonio Lipari's office, the long chamber. And there you waited for your victim to appear . . . there you toppled the marble figure on to him . . . there you killed him . . ."

"It's not true!" said Aquilino. He pushed himself off the wall. "I wasn't the only one there. It's all lies. *Sono tutte menzogne*. And don't call me Peter Hodge."

"The fish say otherwise, the fish say you were there," said Bartolomeo. "You cannot conceal the smell of the old trout. Your nose above all should tell you so."

Aquilino then did something odd. He barked with laughter.

"Very well," he said. "I admit those fish were a mistake. They've got me into all sorts of trouble. I'll tell you what really happened. But not up here, for Jesus' sake. Let's go down and get ourselves a drink in Donna Michela's even if all she sells is piss. And let us talk, man to man."

The story that Pietro Hodge told was odd enough. In Geoffrey Chaucer's experience, oddness in a tale was often the guarantee of its truth. But not in this case, necessarily. He had the impression that Aquilino was holding back on more than he was revealing. They sat over a bottle of vinegary *vino di sotto* in a dingy back room of Donna Michela's establishment, Chaucer and Gentile perching side by side on a bench and facing Aquilino across a rickety table. Other men, waiting for their own *appuntamenti d'amore* upstairs or with their business concluded, came and went, ordered and drank, keeping to themselves. The three of them were undisturbed.

Before he started, Aquilino said that he was speaking in confidence, one Englishman to another. Master Chaucer was on his honour not to pass on what he was about to say – and he must guarantee that his Florentine friend did likewise. Chaucer wondered what it was about mercenaries and their honour, for he recalled Tomaso Falcone making similar references. Nevertheless he agreed, provided that Aquilino had committed no crime.

Only the crime of love, said the hooked-nose man.

He admitted that he had indeed entered the Lipari *palazzo* the previous evening for an assignation with Novella Lipari. Man to man, he hoped that the two of them would understand his reasons. For Jesus' sake, they had glimpsed the woman and her beauty! But, as they well knew, the husband was almost insane with jealousy. Therefore he was relying on their honour to keep quiet. In return he would tell them the truth, the whole truth of what had occurred . . .

There were many passages and corners in the *palazzo* called Purgatory. The Signora Novella was familiar with the layout of the house from previous visits to her brother-in-law. In particular there was a passage that connected the counting house and the long chamber or the banker's office. This would be a good place to meet, she'd suggested, and she gave him directions on finding it. He, Aquilino, needed a pretext to get into the house and in a moment of inspiration had disguised himself as a deliverer of fish. Now he realized that this wasn't such a good idea, since he had evidently left a trail wherever he went. Anyway he had got rid of the fish and hidden himself away in the passage behind the long chamber. The arrangement with Novella Lipari was that she would come to him when the rest of the household was busy with their feasting.

"I thought that her husband could not bear her absence," said Chaucer. "How was she to get free of him?"

Aquilino thought for an instant as though the problem had

only just occurred to him and said, "There are moments when nature calls and everyone has to be alone, especially a lady. Or else she would pretend that something she'd eaten at the feast had made her feel sick, and so she had to quit the table."

"Which is what happened?"

"No. She never came."

"But you waited?"

"I waited in the passage and watched the comings and goings in Lipari's office."

"How could you watch them if you were the other side of the wall?" said Geoffrey, though he already knew the answer.

"That Florentine was a cunning man, Master Chaucer. There are eye-holes in the door which give a good view on to the long chamber."

"I see."

"So did I see. I saw. Oh, I saw many things."

"Tell us about them, Aquilino."

The man took a deep draught of wine and wiped his lips. It appeared to Chaucer that he was calculating how much he could safely say.

"First of all, I observed the banker and his blind brother and other men. There was one of them who has a birthmark on his face, like spilled wine. He is called Giuseppe Orioli. And then there was a fourth, a red-bearded one."

"His name?"

"I do not know everything, Master Chaucer. But Antonio called him *mio volpacchiotto*."

"My little fox cub," said Bartolomeo. "It was Antonio Lipari's term for Matteo Peruzzi, the secretary. It was a term of affection."

"What were they doing, these four?" said Chaucer.

"Talking and arguing a little," said Aquilino. "I couldn't hear everything but it was over my head anyway. All about *creditori*, about money and *malleverie*."

"Then what happened?"

"They left, I suppose. After a time Messere Lipari returned to where I could see him, the banker not il Cieco. There was a woman with him, his daughter, it was."

Bartolomeo shifted on the bench. Aquilino observed the notary's unease. Sensing an advantage he continued, "They talked as well. This time I *could* understand it. They talked of marriage."

Bartolomeo Gentile lifted his goblet and swigged as if he'd like to bury his face in the cup. Aquilino grinned. He knew he'd recognized the little, long-armed fellow earlier. Well, that one would be sorry for the high-handed way he'd spoken to him. If he was squirming now, he'd be wishing he was dead in a moment.

"Don't you want to know what they said?"

"Not right now," said Chaucer.

"Father and daughter didn't see eye to eye in *their* little talk either."

"Say you so?" said Bartolomeo.

"Lipari's daughter was the last visitor to the long chamber?" said Chaucer quickly.

"No, no," said Aquilino, leaning against the wall to his back. He was beginning to enjoy himself. Who said that a simple soldier couldn't put one over on a Florentine lawyer and a gent from England? "There's plenty more to come. The next person to enter with a suit to Antonio Lipari was . . . what is your name again, *messere?*"

"It's no secret that I was there," said Gentile, half to Chaucer, half to Aquilino. "I visited Antonio Lipari with – a particular request."

"I heard the request. I heard him laugh too, from my position on the other side of the door."

"He was joking," said Bartolomeo. "We were enjoying a joke together."

Geoffrey felt for Bartolomeo. The poor lover's pretensions were being cruelly exposed. As he'd suspected, his friend had got a dusty reception from Lipari the previous night. And shortly afterwards the banker was found dead. Bartolomeo looked very uncomfortable now – but there was a large gap, Chaucer reflected, between embarrassment and guilt.

"And after Bartolomeo Gentile left, what happened next?"

"Bartolomeo Gentile. Of course, that's your name, *messere*. How could I forget? Well, Antonio Lipari went after you – or at least he disappeared from my view."

"And all the time the lady you were expecting did not come, so that Messere Gentile was not the only disappointed man."

"That's as may be," said Aquilino. "If I'm going to tell you any more, Chaucer, you're going to have to buy me another bottle of this piss."

When they had bought a second bottle, Aquilino took his time over filling his goblet and drinking it off in one gulp. Then he resumed his story.

"So there I was, stood in the dark and looking out at the long chamber. Candles had been left burning on the table. That's the thing about these rich folk – they have money to burn. And they blame a poor soldier for taking what he can where he can when he can!"

"Never mind that," said Chaucer. "Give us the rest of it. We're still able to report you to the Signoria, remember, word of honour or not."

"Then you'll have to report a whole crowd of us," said Aquilino. "The next person who came in was not Antonio Lipari, but someone who walked over to the table and looked at the things lying on it. Then he started to handle some of them as though they were his own property."

"Who was it?"

"Don't know. I've seen him around, though. He was a tall fellow with a pocky face."

Bartolomeo leaned across and whispered 'Masetto Cennini' in Geoffrey's ear.

"You know him too, eh? Well, whoever it was, he was an outright thief!"

"Explain."

"He picked up an object from Signor Lipari's table and held it to the light and then he shoved it in a pocket."

"Object?"

"Something small. It gleamed in the candlelight. A brooch or clasp, maybe."

"Then this . . . person left the long chamber afterwards?"

"I could only see what I could see, gentlemen. He moved away from the table with his treasure. He wasn't visible to me any more."

Once again Aquilino paused to refill his goblet and glug down its contents.

"That wasn't the end of it, neither. There was another caller. A woman this time."

"A woman?" said Bartolomeo, tensing on the bench.

"Yes, master lawyer. You're familiar with women, you know what they look like, don't you? But this was not the one you call 'your' woman, so don't worry."

"And it can't have been the one you were waiting for either," said Geoffrey, hastening to prevent his friend lashing out at Aquilino and coming off the worse in any scrap.

"No, it was not my lady, no," said Aquilino. His eyes looked vacant for a moment. Chaucer saw that, whatever else you might claim about Pietro Hodge, he did believe himself in love with Novella Lipari.

"You didn't recognize the woman in the room?"

"Now I'm supposed to know every man, woman and child in this city? No, I haven't the slightest idea who she was. But she was short and she was pretty enough. And she had a nice pair of tits on her."

Aquilino let go of his drink and cupped his hands in demonstration.

"And *she* was a thief too, believe it or not! Like everyone else, she was hanging round the table belonging to Signor Lipari. In the end she picked up a little knife – not a proper knife but one of those toy daggers that rich folk use for slitting seals and opening letters and such. You can do damage with them too, mind. Then she does something really odd, this woman. She puts this little knife side by side with a bodkin, the kind of thing a needlewoman has. She looks from knife to bodkin and back again, as if deciding which one she wants to use . . ."

"Yes, that's right," said Geoffrey. Prompted by Aquilino's account he'd suddenly remembered what was missing from Lipari's desk. It was the knife for opening letters. All this gave credence to the mercenary's words.

"What happened next?"

"Alas, master, I couldn't see. She turned her back on me. A pity because I was enjoying looking at her titties more than I was interested in the little things she was holding in her hands. Maybe she put the paper-knife back on the table, maybe she took it with her, I don't know. She quivered. Her back shook. She sighed a great sigh, I know that much."

He paused as if tired by all his talking. Geoffrey glanced over his shoulder. They'd been sitting in this back room in the *bordello* for the best part of an hour. There were other men in here, wearing slightly furtive or carefully nonchalant expressions. He caught the eye of an individual who removed his cap and scratched at a bare head. He had a wound on his cheek. Chaucer supposed he was another mercenary, used to the rough life. This gent gave a smile as though in wry acknowledgement of the fact that, however the visitors to this place passed their time in drinking and talking, they were really here for one purpose only, to visit the women upstairs.

"We must be at an end, Aquilino," said Bartolomeo. "There

can't have been any more visitors to the long chamber of Antonio Lipari, for God's sake."

"Oh, there was one other, *messere*. There must have been one at least."

"Why?"

"Because I saw them. Saw him, I mean."

"Him?"

"Or her. It might have been a her. I couldn't tell."

"It was Novella Lipari?"

"Why no, not that one. You think I would not recognize my lady?"

Chaucer noted the surprise on the other's face at the suggestion that he might have met Novella. Yet hadn't the mercenary claimed that this was the reason he was waiting in the first place? He said, "You had better finish your tale in the proper form, Aquilino. You're talking in riddles."

"It's a riddle to me too. I'd seen so much through these little peep-holes that in the end I grew tired of looking. I sat myself down in this dark passage and I thought of all the rich folk feasting. From time to time I heard the sounds of laughter and revelry coming from far off."

"We know about all that because we were there," said Bartolomeo. "Get on with it."

"I must've fallen asleep because I suddenly woke up to an almighty crash. The floor shook. I thought the house had been struck by a thunderbolt. Didn't know where I was at first. Then I realized the sound had come from the other side of the wall in the long chamber. I looked through the peep-holes. Everything was the same. Candles burning on the table but no one in sight. Slowly, I opened the door, just a crack, and gazed down the room to where the noise had come from. Couldn't see much at first, just a great white form lying flat on the floor. Not human but a statue. No harm done, only a pile of old marble. Even so I sensed something bad had happened. And beyond the

204

statue I saw the door of the long chamber opening . . . and a figure slipping through it. Only caught the glimpse of his back – or her back, like I said. Now I was sure that a bad thing had happened. I crept down the chamber to where the statue lay and there was red coming out from underneath as if the marble itself was bleeding. So I knew some poor soul was crushed beneath all that weight."

"You must have known it was Antonio Lipari."

"*Must* have known? I knew nothing, Chaucer."

"It was an accident, the statue falling on to the man?"

Aquilino shrugged. "Maybe it was. But I don't believe so. Why did it fall? Who was the person slinking out of the chamber? I tell you that a great fear seized hold of me and I turned away from the fallen statue and the blood seeping from underneath it, and I left that place as fast as I could. I went through the hidden door and down the passage and then through the counting house and so out by the way I had come in. It was dark by now. I was not seen."

"You *were* seen – running down the street."

"That shows I'm telling the truth," said Aquilino.

"A soldier and run away?"

"It's a wise soldier who knows when to run. Death on the field is one thing, an honest ambush in the open air is another. But this did not smell like an honest death to me. A dark deed rather."

"Nothing you've said so far, Aquilino, says that you couldn't have done this dark deed yourself."

The mercenary stroked his outsized nose and paused before replying. Instead of indignation he spoke with consideration. "There you are in the wrong, sir. If I had done this I would not have been so open with you. I have told the truth, that I was waiting to meet Novella Lipari and that instead of her I saw many people visiting the chamber of Antonio Lipari. I have told you all I know. And, consider this, if I was going to kill any man

. . . then it would surely have been *her* husband Lorenzo and not his brother."

Chaucer nodded. Whatever the accuracy of the detail of Aquilino's story, there was a ring of truth to the whole account. Maybe there was an element of cunning in his last admission – since he'd conceded that the idea of killing was a possibility – but it was surely as he'd said, that if he was going to do away with anyone it would be Lorenzo. How would killing the brother-in-law to his lover advance his cause?

So it seemed as though the fishy trail which Pietro Hodge had started was turning out to be a red herring.

18

The warmth of the city could be oppressive even on a spring afternoon. Doors were closed fast and windows were shuttered against it, although people still sat in the shade, talking or sleeping. Few were on the move. There was a timeless pause between the bustle of the morning and the parade of the evening. Geoffrey Chaucer imagined what it must be like in midsummer or during the dog-days of August when the stone of the buildings would store up heat like a furnace. He felt a sudden desire to get away from the place, to see trees and fields again, to escape from these enclosing walls and great towers, and the suspicions of murder.

He remembered the words of Francesco as they parted. *When your journey, it is finished, is when your troubles start.* The Genoese had been proved right. Chaucer had been in this town only a few days and nothing had gone to plan. The Lipari affair was turning out to be as maze-like as the little back streets down which he found himself wandering.

After the *bordello* encounter with Aquilino, Bartolomeo had returned to the Signoria to see if he could pick up any more information about the investigation into the banker's death. Geoffrey and the notary had agreed to say nothing at present about Aquilino's story. For one thing, the two of them had been sworn to secrecy. And for another the mercenary's account of an unknown figure slipping away from the long chamber after the fall of the statue hadn't really clarified things much.

Geoffrey asked himself what his responsibilities were in this matter. He was a visitor from England, it was not his proper concern. Already he'd overstepped the mark by tracking down one of the witnesses to the 'crime', if that's what it was.

Chaucer had been pacing, head down and thoughtful. Now he came into a more open area and saw that he had arrived at the Piazza San Giovanni, the heart of the city. The unfinished cathedral dominated the square but Geoffrey's eye was caught by the stone confection that was the campanile. Its layers of coloured marble glowed in the afternoon sun and the large windows on the upper floors gave it an airy feel as though it was cut from some material less substantial than stone. Well, if he couldn't leave the bounds of the city, then he might rise above them and enjoy some fresh air that way. He skirted the beggars who were clustered round the entrance and stood for a moment in the cool shade of the interior. A gaggle of Dominicans stood gossiping here, like great birds in their black mantles and white tunics. A flight of stone steps opened off to one side. A party of well-dressed men and women emerged at the bottom of the steps. If Chaucer had been uncertain where the steps led, he was enlightened by an overheard comment about the *bella vista*.

He started on the ascent. The staircase wound round and round in slow segments. He passed other people coming down, laughing and chattering. He began to count but gave up once he'd reached a hundred and fifty. The first part of the climb was in near darkness but after a time he reached one of the great arched windows from where one might admire the expanding view. He paused to get his breath. Already he was above the surrounding roofs and on a level with the upper reaches of the nearby cathedral. His legs began to ache and his breath to come quicker and shorter. He'd never climbed so high a building in his life.

Then, just as he was beginning to regret he'd ever undertaken this feat, Geoffrey Chaucer emerged through a door on to a wide stone platform that lay beneath the great bells. The sun was in his face. There was a precipitous flight of steps which must give access to an even higher level but he felt no obligation to continue. This was far enough. No one else was up here. His legs a little unsteady after the climb, Chaucer walked across to the nearest arched opening and gazed out. He was on the river side. The Arno glittered, without visible motion. He could see the outer limits of the city, the whole set like a jewel in the green of the surrounding hills. A breeze came from the south and bathed his face, more refreshing at this height but with a hint of the terrible hot days to come. He breathed deeply and looked down. The streets which he'd been walking through for the last few days were reduced to a finger's width. The houses seemed to huddle under their diminutive roofs and the handful of people moving about were as tiny and purposeful as ants. The base of the campanile was impossibly small to support this great edifice. It seemed to him that the tower was shivering slightly in the breeze. Or that he was shivering from the height.

He'd heard no one when he was on the stairs but now there were gentle footsteps on the stones behind him and he turned his head to look. A large figure was already heading for the opposite side of the viewing platform. The man must possess enviable reserves of wind because, even after all those stairs, he began whistling to himself. Chaucer recognized the tune. He'd been hearing it around the streets of Florence. Then the whistling stopped as the man leaned over the opposite parapet and admired the prospect. Chaucer reflected that this was a platform for solitary communing, even for prayer since one was several hundred feet closer to heaven. There weren't many places in Florence where a man could get away from other men, could get away from himself perhaps. Indoors or out, life was lived in public. Yet even up here you could never be alone for long. He heard the distant sound of feet and voices as another party ascended the stairs.

Grasping the parapet, he took one final look at the golden coil of the river and the network of streets and squares. Then he turned to go. It was the shift of position which most likely saved his life. Almost filling his vision was the shape of the man whose back he'd glimpsed moments before. The man moved lightly on his feet, as some large men do. He was coming at Chaucer with his arms extended, like someone rushing to meet a friend. He was wearing a hat and the lower half of his face was muffled with some kind of scarf but Chaucer could see in his eyes a blank indifference.

Instinctively he ducked, then stumbled and rolled to one side on the ground. The man must have been reckoning on Chaucer to check his onward rush before coming to grips with him. Instead he collided with the stone parapet, braking his motion with his arms. His cap sailed off to reveal a bald head before floating out into the emptiness.

The man stood looking out after the cap for an instant. Absurdly, Geoffrey sensed something of his distress. The man gave a grunt of anger and then swivelled round and threw himself on top of Chaucer. His expression had changed. Now he was furious at the loss of his headgear. His weight drove the Englishman's breath out of his body. Geoffrey received the other's panting breath full on his face, a mixture of cheap wine and garlic and something fouler. Even as he floundered beneath his attacker, some small segment of Geoffrey's mind registered it was the man he'd caught sight of in the *bordello*. The bald-headed individual who'd acknowledged him from the far side of the room even as they were both sipping the same vinegary piss.

The rest of Geoffrey's head wasn't occupied with such deductions but was wrestling with the problem of staying alive. Chaucer wasn't exactly fit – the long climb up the campanile steps had shown that – but he had been hardened by several months on the road. It was many years since he'd been in battle and quite a few years too since he'd last become embroiled in a real street tussle, but some reduced part of him was a fighter still. The trouble was that his assailant was better prepared and stronger. While he struggled to hold Geoffrey down with one arm, he fumbled behind his back with the other. As if he was hovering above the scene and looking down on his own demise, Chaucer understood that the man was groping for a knife which he must keep in a sheath somewhere in the small of his back. The man's efforts were frustrated and the weapon he was tugging at refused to come free. It was tangled up in his garments or wedged into his belt at an awkward slant.

Chaucer got his hand under the other's chin but his hand kept slipping on the serge scarf which still covered it. With his other arm he tried to lever off the weight on top of him at the same time as he bucked violently with his whole body. Just when he sensed that he might manage to escape from beneath his attacker, the bald-headed man succeeded in freeing his knife. In a single movement he brought it out into the open. The steel blade caught the declining sun. It was a small blade but good enough for the job in hand. The man held it aloft for a second, as if to allow Chaucer to see his own fate or to give himself a better angle to strike from. Geoffrey put out his left arm to ward off the blow. He wished that he was wearing thicker clothes or gloves since the man would inevitably slash at his hand or arm before moving in for a deeper thrust.

This took only a second but it lasted forever. Geoffrey had time to think that he was nearer heaven up here. He wondered who his opponent was, and what lay behind this attack. But the man was holding still. Why was he waiting? Just then the sound of footsteps and panting voices grew louder. Of course, the group that was on its way to the top of the campanile! The eyes of his attacker flickered sideways. The momentary distraction was enough. Chaucer jerked upwards with his whole body and at the same instant swept his left arm out so that it deflected

211

the attacker's knife-hand. Then he rolled out from beneath the other man.

By this stage, a gaggle of men and women had emerged on to the platform. Because of the brightness up here they would have been blinded for an instant. Chaucer's assailant might still have carried through the murderous task but his victim's temporary escape and the unexpected presence of witnesses gave him pause. He scrambled to his feet and, within seconds, had vanished through the doorway at the top of the stairs, knocking aside a couple of the visitors. There were gasps and cries of *bruto!* and *buffone!* as they gazed at the retreating figure. Chaucer took advantage of their confusion to get to his feet. He didn't want to have to explain himself. He couldn't have spoken much sense anyway.

Geoffrey leaned against the parapet, his back to the sunlit vista, his vision blurred and his chest heaving. The shock of the attack hadn't hit home yet. He forced himself away from the reassuring solidity of the stone and moved towards the doorway. The men and women looked curiously at him but he walked past with lowered eyes and reached the semi-darkness and safety of the stairs. Halfway down to the ground level, he stopped and slumped against the cool stone of the inner wall. He was shaking too much to go on. He took deep breaths and sat down on one of the wide steps. He dabbed at his face, feeling for damage. The back of his head was beginning to throb, at the spot where it must have struck the stone flags. Eventually the worst of the tremors subsided.

If Chaucer had required any proof that he'd sailed into deep waters, then the proof was here. There was no doubt that the muffled man had intended to take him unawares and, using main force, pitch him from the top of the campanile. He could have achieved it too. He had strength and surprise on his side. At the instant of his attack there'd been no one to see. It would have looked like an accident or suicide. With a renewed bout of shaking, Geoffrey visualized himself tumbling through the golden air, tumbling down towards those tiny roofs and ant-like people until his bones snapped and his brain-box split open on the stones of the street.

His survival had rested on two lucky circumstances: that he'd turned from the parapet just in time to see his assailant and that, when the other was brandishing his knife before plunging it in, the group of sightseers had arrived on the platform. Was the attack connected to the first one in the Via Calmari, when he'd been set upon in the dark? Or was it connected to the death of Antonio Lipari? How could it not be? Yet what did it mean? Why should a visiting Englishman become an assassin's target? Was it by chance that the bald-headed man had been drinking in Donna Michela's house of ill fame, where he recognized Chaucer and determined to do away with him? Or had it been Bartolomeo Gentile that he recognized? Or was it rather that the bald-headed one had followed the two to the *bordello* and, seeing them talking to Aquilino, decided to take action? In that case, shouldn't the mercenary be warned?

These questions spun round Chaucer's throbbing head, without producing any answers. Now he heard the sound of the group who'd, in effect, preserved his life beginning their own descent of the tower. He clambered to his feet and returned thankfully to the firm ground. When he'd left the lobby of the campanile and emerged once more into the afternoon glare of the Piazza San Giovanni, he was almost taken aback to see life proceeding normally, knots of people talking in the shade or wandering across the square. So easily might they have been crowding about his own corpse in horror or concern or, for the more hardened, in a spirit of curiosity. His bones shattered, his life-blood filling the crevices between the stones. And his own heart began to flutter again as he glimpsed what he at first took to be some ghostly image of just such a piece of harm. A puddle of dark red lay on the ground in front of him. He blinked and rubbed his eyes.

Drawing closer, he saw that it was a discarded hat or cap. He stooped and retrieved it. The velvet was a deep red, almost purple. It was soft and warm to the touch. There was nothing to identify the owner. Even so, he'd seen this item of wear hundreds of feet up and very recently, on the head of his attacker and then floating out into the empty air when the man collided with the parapet. It was a tiny revenge for Chaucer that he'd found an item that was obviously valuable to its owner. A tiny revenge that his attacker would have to purchase another cap to keep the sun off his bald pate. Looking round as if he were fearful of being seen, Geoffrey rolled up the cap and bundled it into a pocket. He'd show it to Bartolomeo Gentile. Maybe the lawyer would have something to say about it.

19

B ut the notary did not have much to say about the cap.
Bartolomeo returned from the Signoria with a tale of his
own to tell, and was not ready to to be diverted from it until
Geoffrey said that he'd almost been murdered during the course
of the afternoon. The Englishman waited before describing the
attack until Bella – who'd been serving them wine and tutting
over Geoffrey's fresh wound – had left the room. Once he'd
heard the outline of the story, Bartolomeo's brows furrowed as
if they were going to fold over on themselves and he wrung his
hands with real distress. First the attack in the Via Calmari
outside the very house where they were sitting now. Then the
business with Antonio Lipari. And now this assault on the
summit of one of the most noble edifices in Florence! Whatever
would Geoffrey think of his fellow Florentines? They were not
all murderers and thieves, he should know! He must tell the
people of London that they were not all murderers!

Swiftly Chaucer passed across the cap, partly so as to stop the
other's incessant hand-wringing. Bartolomeo turned it over and
over with his long fingers. If Chaucer had been hoping that this
might have been evidence of some kind, however, he was to be
disappointed. The cap was no peasant's for it was made of good
material, but the style and visible wear on it did not suggest that
its owner was exactly prosperous. That was about all that
Bartolomeo could say, and more or less what Chaucer was able
to see for himself. Then Gentile began to talk about how clothes

were no guide to the wearer anyway because the sumptuary laws, which once prescribed what the various classes in Florence were permitted to wear, had broken down, so that people these days were always dressing above their station -

Chaucer interrupted him to say that he had recognized his attacker from Donna Michela's *bordello*. Surely Bartolomeo had observed the man sitting at another table as they were talking to Aquilino? With a bald head and a wound on his cheek? He must have been watching them the whole time. But Bartolomeo hadn't noticed anyone in particular in the brothel.

"And he was whistling," said Geoffrey, suddenly remembering and at the same time wondering why he was mentioning this. "When he reached the top of the campanile, he was whistling a tune after climbing all those stairs. I've heard it before. It went like this, I think . . ."

Uncertainly he strung together a few sounds, half humming, half whistling. Bartolomeo laughed but not with much pleasure.

"You know it?" said Geoffrey.

"Every Florentine knows it. It is *Figlia di Mugnaio*, about the daughter of a naughty miller. No, I have that wrong. It is the daughter who is the naughty one. But listen, Geoffrey, I have a strange story for you, and the *Figlia di Mugnaio* is a stranger part of it. You recall how that soldier told us he saw a woman from his hiding place behind the wall in Purgatorio. The one with large – how did he say it in English?"

"Tits."

"In my country we would say *cioccie* . . . it is still a little rude but more poetic, I think."

"Yours is a poetic tongue, Bartolomeo. I'd never deny it."

"Thank you, Geoffrey. Well, I know who she is!"

"Who?"

"The woman in the long chamber."

This story was another odd one, like Aquilino's. Bartolomeo jerked a thumb in the direction that Bella had just taken out of

216

the room. It transpired that the crone had a young niece whom Bartolomeo had met on occasion when she'd called at the house on the Calmari. ("It is correct to say that she does have fine *cioccie*. Any man would have noticed, even a dry notary.") Well, he'd encountered the girl again when he visited the Signoria this afternoon. She herself had just been questioned about a murder, that of the *romite* woman on the Ponte Rubaconte. Someone claimed to have seen her in the vicinity of the cell where the poor recluse had been beaten to death. Geoffrey Chaucer remembered all of this? He did remember, but he also wondered where all of this was leading. What had the death of a female hermit to do with Antonio Lipari?

Wait, said Bartolomeo. Wait.

The woman, whose name was Lisabetta Greco, had been relieved to see a familiar face. She was badly shaken by the questioning though she'd stoutly maintained that she had nothing whatsoever to do with the murder of her poor friend Maria. Yes, it was true that she'd recently renewed their acquaintance after a long gap. There was nothing suspicious in this. In her younger days she used to work in the house of Maria's parents on the Via de Neri, and the shy young girl, who even then had seemed destined for a religious life, was the only one to show her any kindness. What more natural than that she should stop for a few minutes' chat with her old employer when she was crossing the Rubaconte?

So much had she told the magistrate, with many tears and protestations of innocence. And the magistrate – not the severe young one who'd questioned Bartolomeo but an older fellow (who was perhaps impressed too by Lisabetta's fine *cioccie*) – was inclined to believe her. After all, the brutality of the attack on Maria did not point to a woman's hand. So Lisabetta had been allowed to leave the Signoria and, outside, she'd run into Bartolomeo Gentile in whose house her good old aunt Bella lived and worked.

Soon Bartolomeo discovered the reason for her continuing distress. Like the old magistrate, he assumed Lisabetta's innocence. But all his comments to that effect were greeted with a fresh outpouring of tears. And what she had not been able to confess to in the strict confines of the Signoria, she now confessed in the presence of her aunt's employer. She needed to tell the truth to someone. Self-preservation had kept her quiet in front of the magistrate but now the truth came out, like water which must find an outlet. She and Bartolomeo were sitting in a quiet corner of a church, at about the same time that Chaucer was having his adventure up the campanile.

According to Lisabetta, she had indeed known of Maria's death before word of it spread through the town. She had been the one to discover the body of the recluse early on the previous morning. It was a complicated story but she was in search of her husband Guido Greco, whom she feared murdered too. And, through the information provided by another man (whom she wasn't prepared to name), she believed that Antonio Lipari was behind both Guido's death and that of Maria as well. Some thread, which again Bartolomeo didn't properly understand, was provided by the tune of *Figlia di Mugnaio*.

Seeing the sceptical expression on Chaucer's face, the notary raised an appeasing hand.

"Yes, I know, Geoffrey. I would not have believed her either except for what we heard from that man Aquilino. Listen . . ."

Lisabetta Greco was determined on vengeance against Antonio Lipari. Somehow she gained access to the *palazzo* on the previous evening during the feast. There was rage and loathing in her heart, and she fully intended to stab the man who'd been responsible for the deaths of Guido and Maria. It was the only way. After all, there was no such thing as justice for poor people like herself, and anyway who would have believed her if she'd denounced the banker? In preparation for the killing she equipped herself with a bodkin, one of the tools of her trade as

218

laundress and needlewoman. She found a secluded place in the top of the house while the preparations for the feast were going forward, then when she judged the time was right she crept down to the long chamber.

"Just a moment," said Geoffrey. "How did she know where to go in the *palazzo*, if she'd never visited it before?"

"By instinct, she says. It was as if she was guided by a divine hand to the place where she might confront Antonio Lipari."

"A divine hand? To go and murder someone? The devil's hand surely?"

"It was not murder, but vengeance in her view."

"You believed her?"

"She swore that she was telling the truth to Bartolomeo Gentile," said Bartolomeo. "Swore on her mother's bones and by the sacred stones of the church where we were sitting. But I haven't finished yet, Geoffrey . . ."

When she'd found herself, by instinct or otherwise, within the private office of Messere Lipari, Lisabetta had examined the chamber. She wandered across to his desk, and picked up the paper-knife. Under the candlelight she held it side by side with the bodkin which she was carrying. It was as if the divine hand had not merely brought her to this place but was also showing her a choice of weapons. She wondered which implement to use. She had no doubt that Antonio Lipari would be delivered up to her to exact vengeance. When he arrived in the room she would kill him in cold fury.

This story would stretch belief, said Bartolomeo, if they hadn't already had confirmation of it from the hidden witness, Aquilino. The mercenary, in his position behind the spy-holes, had indeed seen Lisabetta by the desk, had seen her pick up the knife and compare it with the bodkin.

"So far, so true," said Geoffrey. "But he didn't see what happened next."

"No, he didn't," said Bartolomeo. "I have only her word for

the rest. She tells me that while she was weighing up the two weapons – the paper-knife and the bodkin – the dreadfulness of what she was about to do overcame her. She started to shake with terror. Aquilino said that she – how did he say? – she quivered and sighed a great sigh, you remember. So she put the bodkin back under her clothing and she crept out of the long chamber and out of the *palazzo* and went back into the common streets."

"What did she do with the knife from Lipari's desk?"

"She took that too," said Bartolomeo, slightly irritated to have the flow of his narrative broken. "She did not kill the man but she took his little knife. Then she returned to her lowly residence and slept the sleep of one who has obeyed her conscience. When she was summoned for questioning at the Signoria today she thought it was to do with the death of Antonio Lipari, and that some witness had glimpsed her in his house. But it was the murder of Maria on the Ponte Rubaconte they wished to talk about."

"Where is she now, this Lisabetta?"

"I left her praying in the church where we talked. She thinks that she is guilty of murderous thoughts and will never be forgiven."

"Few of us will be forgiven if that is the case," said Chaucer. "But, Bartolomeo, consider this. The woman may have done the deed, for all her protestations. Perhaps she did have a fit of conscience and was overcome with great fear, as she claims. But she might have recovered her wits and remained in the long chamber or gone back later. Then, when Lipari entered the room, there she was concealed behind the statue which she toppled down on top of him. All her tears and grief could be the marks of real guilt."

Bartolomeo shrugged before saying, "I believe her. After all, Geoffrey, there were many others in that long chamber who could have done this thing."

"Including you, Bartolomeo. To say nothing of Antonio Lipari's daughter, Philomela."

Chaucer said this mostly to see the other's response. It was predictable. Gentile half rose from his chair and spilled some of his wine.

"You do not suggest that my Philomela would have . . . had a hand in her father's death."

"If we're to believe Aquilino about one matter then we should credit him in others. He said that father and daughter were arguing beforehand. And she looked displeased at the feast. Perhaps *she* was the one who returned to the long chamber later."

"*Impossibile! Assurdo!*"

"Very well."

"What about Masetto Cennini?" said Bartolomeo. "He was in the long chamber. And he stole something from the desk – a brooch or clasp, Aquilino said."

Chaucer nodded. He felt uncomfortable. He hadn't told Bartolomeo that he had picked up the 'two-handed' clasp from the floor near Antonio Lipari. He had not added this detail to his earlier account and now the moment seemed to have passed. Yet the clasp, which was tucked inside his cap-case, was surely evidence that this Masetto Cennini had been in the room, exactly as Aquilino had described? He must have dropped it on the way out. Or had he too lingered in the long chamber and been surprised there by Antonio Lipari?

"Then there is Novella Lipari," said Bartolomeo. "I heard her husband berating her for her absence towards the end of the meal."

"Why would she want to see her brother-in-law dead?" said Geoffrey. But he remembered the lady's visible unease while she was sitting next to Antonio.

"And then there is that secretary, Matteo Peruzzi," said Bartolomeo, eager to widen the circle of suspects.

"Why should *he* want to see his master dead?"

"Because he thought that the English loan was a bad risk and yet knew that Lipari was going to proceed with it . . . Forgive me, Master Geoffrey, but many Florentine bankers would not be willing to lend to you English, however illustrious the debtor."

"Maybe Peruzzi is right," said Chaucer. "Our King Edward is profligate, at least when it comes to fighting wars. I don't know what's going to happen now about the loan. Perhaps I should approach the blind Lorenzo. We spoke to him last night. We share an interest in Dante Alighieri, you remember."

As he said this, a memory indeed snagged at Geoffrey's mind. What was it? Something Lorenzo had done, something he'd said? He reached out to grasp it, but the fact – or the phrase – slipped away, elusive.

"You shall speak to him indeed," said Bartolomeo. "I have received a letter which he has dictated. He invites both of us to visit him tomorrow morning to discuss any business which has been left unconcluded by his brother's sudden death."

"Have you got the letter?"

"Why yes," said Bartolomeo. He got up and rummaged among some papers on a nearby table. He passed it to Chaucer. "Why do you want it?"

"I am curious to test my knowledge of Italian."

The letter was written in a firm hand, no doubt dictated to a steward of Lorenzo's household. Geoffrey found it easy enough to understand.

"This is all very graceful," he said. "He is inviting us to Paradise and telling us we may escape the hell of the city, with its many circles – *fuggire dalla citta – inferno – circoli – il settimo, per esempio –* "

"He has always hated the city," said Bartolomeo.

"So it seems," said Geoffrey. "And tomorrow we shall see Paradise. It is not every day that one receives such an invitation."

The discussion with Bartolomeo preoccupied him that night after he'd retired to his chamber. It seemed as though there was no shortage of individuals who might have wished harm to Antonio Lipari. There must be many whom Geoffrey wasn't even aware of, since any man who has reached a powerful position is likely to have used others as rungs on his ladder upwards, his golden ladder. Then, apart from those unknown people, there were the ones he did know or at least could enumerate in his head.

To begin with, there was the mercenary Aquilino himself, whose presence in the house was apparently explained by his assignation with Novella Lipari but who might have been caught skulking in the long chamber by the banker. He was no stranger to death and killing. He'd been on the scene, though in hiding. He claimed to have seen an anonymous figure slipping from the chamber after the fall of the statue, but suppose that his truth-telling was a blind?

The woman called Lisabetta Greco had gone to the *palazzo* with the express purpose of killing Lipari, but had apparently been called away by her conscience before she could do the deed. Then there was Antonio's daughter Philomela – she had quarrelled with him before the feast. And even Bartolomeo Gentile, who'd been mocked and dismissed by the wealthy man, should not be forgotten. Laughter can make a man murderous. Geoffrey remembered the hectic look on Bartolomeo's face after the feast when he'd said that Lipari was ready to see him.

Geoffrey recalled also Bartolomeo's comments about Matteo Peruzzi, the red-bearded secretary. He was implacably opposed to the English loan – that seemed obvious from the way he'd looked at Chaucer – so was it conceivable that during an argument he had killed his master, by accident or design? There was Novella Lipari herself. She'd apparently been away from her husband towards the end of the feast. Finally there was the rabble-rouser Masetto Cennini, who had been seen taking an object from Lipari's desk, the very clasp presently in Chaucer's possession. This theft was baffling in a different way, since why should a man who came of a wealthy family steal a clasp that wasn't of great value? But, whatever Masetto's motive, you could suppose that Antonio Lipari had encountered him as he was sneaking from the room . . . and that, in the confusion which ensued, a struggle had taken place leading to Antonio's death.

Bartolomeo the notary, Hodge or Aquilino the mercenary, Peruzzi the secretary, Masetto the rabble-rouser, the daughter Philomela, the sister-in-law Novella, and Lisabetta Greco the needlewoman. The parade of figures passed across Geoffrey's mind's eye like a line of pilgrims.

Were any of these individuals capable of murder? Any person, Geoffrey told himself, is capable of the deed. But there are greater and lesser likelihoods. Of the two of whom he had direct experience – Bartolomeo Gentile and Pietro Hodge – the soldier was the more plausible villain. Aquilino had been frank with them, but Chaucer knew that there was sometimes nothing more deceptive than a display of frankness.

Besides the more than half a dozen people he'd identified as being present in the long chamber at some point during the evening, there were others who might have passed through unseen. The bald-headed individual who'd attacked him in the campanile was surely involved in the business. Who was to say that it wasn't he who had concealed himself behind the statue and waited for the right moment to bring it down on Antonio Lipari? And, if that was so, then only God knew *his* motives.

The tangles and shadows of the business were proving too much for Geoffrey. He couldn't even begin to work out how the violent death of a hermit woman on a Florentine bridge fitted into the picture, if it did. He tried to distract himself by reading but the words of Dante's *Inferno* floated before his eyes and he soon extinguished the single candle. The back of his head throbbed, where he had struck the stone floor of the campanile.

He fell into a troubled sleep, filled with flitting shapes and marble statues, all trapped in the circles of hell, blown about by the winds of passion, rolling weights backwards and forwards at each other, until it seemed as if he himself had been struck down and that there was a dark figure looming over him.

He opened his eyes to see that there was a figure standing by the bed. It had parted the bed-curtains and stood, a darker shape against the pale walls. Chaucer sat bolt upright and pushed violently with his hands. He lashed out at something yielding and there was a squeal, a feminine squeal. The figure fell backwards and crashed to the floor. His heart thudding, he reached for the flint and struck a light with shaking hands.

A woman was huddled on the ground, almost entirely concealed by a cloak. For a moment he assumed it was Bella but the ankle which protruded from beneath the cloak was no old woman's. She wasn't moving her limbs but the rapid rise and fall of the cloak showed she was still living and breathing.

Geoffrey bent down and placed the candle on the floor. Then, none too gently, he pulled the cloak from her face. He was tired of all this mystery and subterfuge, tired of being followed and assailed by unknown individuals. He tensed in case she had a hidden weapon (like Lisabetta Greco and her bodkin). But the woman lay on the ground, staring up at him with great eyes. He was framing a question in Italian – "Who are you?" – but it died on his lips when he recognized the large eyes and the swarthy face surrounded by a tangle of dark hair.

It was the woman he'd encountered on the road into Florence, the one being pursued by Tomaso Falcone and his men for some infringement of their code. The one who'd clung to his leg and pleaded. She was wearing a similar expression of entreaty now.

He raised his own eyes in bewilderment. And was more bewildered still when he noticed the great chest or *cassone* which stood against one wall and which was used to store bed-linen. The lid was open. Was this woman trying to steal Bartolomeo's blankets? Seeing the direction of his gaze, and seeming to understand his unspoken question, she shook her head and then curled herself up in a mime of sleep. Meaning that she had been hidden inside it! When he'd first glanced at the chest, he'd considered it large enough to contain a man. Well, it had contained a woman instead. Geoffrey wondered how long she'd been hidden inside. Why was she hiding? He could think of only two reasons why a woman would conceal herself in a man's chamber. One involved robbery, while the other was . . . well, the other. It was almost beyond belief, like an incident in some old-fashioned romance.

He stood up. It was his duty to rouse the household, to alert Bartolomeo Gentile. It was his house. The lawyer would know the procedure for dealing with intruders. Geoffrey made to go to the door to call out, but halfway there he stopped and turned on his heel.

"*Che vuoi da me?*" he said softly, repeating Aquilino's question in the brothel.

"I saved your life," she said, just as softly. "You saved mine."

Her English was like Aquilino's, she spoke as if the words were a little rusty but they still belonged to her own tongue. He helped her to her feet. It seemed most natural that they should go and sit side by side on the bed. There was nowhere else to sit in any comfort. He drew the bed-curtains right back. The single candle cast a dim glow across her features. The briar-scratches were still on her hands and face.

"I did not save your life . . . mistress . . .?"

"Joanna is my name. You did protect me and you get my thanks. You defended me on the road according to the laws of chivalry."

"Oh that!" said Geoffrey, thinking it better to say nothing of the tussle he'd had with himself over whether to speak up for the woman at all. "How is it you speak English and know the laws of chivalry?"

"I speak English 'cause I come from Essex, the county of John 'Awkwood," said Joanna, as if that answered both parts of the question.

"Hawkwood the *coterel*? Hawkwood the *brigante*?"

"Sir John 'Awkwood, knight of the realm. Tomaso Falcone 'imself served under 'im. When 'e left the service, I did too. Which was my mistake."

As Chaucer already knew, the woman was a camp-follower. Such women talked of 'service' as though they were the veterans of many campaigns – which, in a way, they were.

"Why were Falcone's men after you on the Florence road?"

"I done nothing, I swear. There was a fellow in the company used to be sweet on me. But ever since 'e started sniffing round richer game, 'e's been trying to get rid of me. So 'e and his mates accused me of nicking things, all trumped up of course. Said I was keeping back a portion for myself."

"What would they have done to you?"

"Give me a good beating, worse than a good beating maybe." She shrugged. "Yeah, worse for sure. I seen the look in their eyes when they started off after me. Then I got to the road and there was you and your friends like a godsend . . . the rest you know. While they was distracted I took the chance to slip off. 'Say 'e can't have 'er. She is under my protection.'"

Chaucer recognized the last words as his own on the road. The woman, Joanna, placed a hand on his thigh as she repeated the defiant phrases. As gently as possible, he removed her hand. To distract her and himself, Geoffrey said, "The man in Falcone's company, the one who was sweet on you, can you describe him?"

"Not much to say about 'im," said Joanna, "'cept he has this great bent conk which give 'im the nickname of Aquilino. And you know what they say, large conk, large you-know-what."

She laughed and Chaucer shushed her. He felt uneasy. He didn't want Bartolomeo or old Bella bursting in on them.

Joanna recovered herself and said, "Not much else to say about old Pietro at all. Aquilino, begging 'is pardon."

"And the rich woman he was going after? You know who she is?"

"Search me. She lives somewhere outside the city. 'E was always finding excuses to go off and visit 'er. Why are you so interested, Master . . .? I don't know your name, do I?"

"Later. Tell me what you meant by saving my life."

"When I left Falcone's company – run away from it, more like – I saw there was better pickings for me inside the city instead of stuck with a bunch of mercenaries beyond the walls, specially if they was going to accuse me of thieving. I can tell my peas from my paternoster, as they say 'ere. There are a few places I can rest my bones in this city. But I 'adn't forgotten I was obligated to you, Master . . . Master . . .? You ashamed of your name?"

"Call me Geoffrey."

"Call me Geoffrey. Well, Geoffrey . . . The evening after I got 'ere, who should I see but Master Geoffrey looking at a door in a street, as if 'e wanted to lick the paint off it."

"The house of Dante Alighieri."

"If you say so. I sort of followed you, Geoffrey, because I was a bit shy, a bit reluctant to push myself forward and give thanks. So I followed you at a distance and back to this very 'ouse in the Calmari."

"But before we got here you saw someone up in the scaffolding along the street."

"That's it. 'E was about to throw something down on top of you and without a second's thought I leapt forward and I pushed you to one side. There was this great crash of buckets and tiles. I looked back and saw that you hadn't been 'urt. Leastways, not 'urt too bad. Is that it?"

Gently she touched the tip of a finger to the cut under Geoffrey's eye. He nodded.

"Then a fellow come out of this 'ouse where we are now and rushed up to you, all troubled and talking, and I guessed 'e'd look after you better than I could."

"You didn't see the person on the scaffolding, the one trying to kill me?"

"Just a shape to me. But a man, I'd say. So we're quits, you and me. You rescued me on the road while I saved you in the street."

"We are quits, Joanna. But that doesn't explain how you got in here."

"There are windows and ladders, Master Geoffrey. There are builders down the street."

Chaucer remembered shutting the window against the night air when he entered his chamber. No doubt if he'd looked out he would have seen a ladder propped close by. The woman certainly had daring. But then she was used to living on her wits.

"Knew this was your room," she said. "Recognized your kit. Didn't want you to throw me out straightaway so I looked for somewhere warm and secret to wait for you. Must've dropped off. I've slept in worse places than a trunk. I came 'cause I wanted to thank you, Master Geoffrey. You know, *thank* you."

Joanna had a kind of earthy attractiveness. He couldn't deny it. Her hand had landed, innocent as a bird, on his thigh again. A warm smell emanated from her, a smell of the clean linen which she had been nestling in, and of something sharper and more rank beneath. He was wearing a nightshirt. Beneath the cloak, which was crumpled on the floor, Joanna was attired in her day clothes, the same ones she'd been wearing when Chaucer encountered her on the road. Her dress might have been cut from cheap material but it was cut low and the swell of her breasts glowed darkly in the candlelight.

"The owner of this house is a notary. He could make trouble for you, Joanna. I'm surprised he hasn't woken up already and come to see what's happening. You should go and lay your bones somewhere else."

"I can't," she said. "I was somewhere else . . . 'ouse in the Via Orivolo . . . then I had to leave it, didn't I. Saw someone I didn't want to see."

Geoffrey blinked and nodded. The only house in the Via Orivolo which he knew was Donna Michela's, La Volta. A soldi to a florin it was the place which Joanna was referring to. He wondered if she'd left – or been told to leave – because Aquilino was there. The someone she didn't want to see must surely have been Aquilino. If the mercenary had pursued her on the road then he might make trouble for her if he found her in La Volta.

It was odd how all these strands seemed to twine together. The woman on the bed beside him sensed Geoffrey's surprise.

"Familiar with the 'ouse in the Orivolo, Master Geoffrey, are you? So that's how you've been passing your time in the city?"

"You're wrong about me and that house, Joanna, but it doesn't matter. I say again you should go. Messere Gentile could cause trouble for you."

"But 'e won't, will 'e, Master Geoffrey, 'cause you'll protect Joanna. Laws of chivalry."

Geoffrey wondered again, as he had in Falcone's encampment, at the odd understanding these people had of chivalrous rules. It was as if, the more lawless and rapacious their way of existence, the more they deceived themselves that they were living according to some ancient code. And then he thought that such thoughts were just a little . . . beside the point. Here was this woman, who was by now leaning against him as if he were her last prop on earth. Here was he, Geoffrey Chaucer, diplomat and versifier, a stranger in a strange city, far from home and wife and family . . .

What should he do?

Send her packing? Invite her to to stay?

What *did* he do?

He did what you would have done.

20

B runo reported to Giuseppe Orioli on the second un-successful attempt to dispose of the Englishman. On the first occasion, when he had hidden in the scaffolding on the Via Calmari, he had been following Giuseppe's instructions. But the second time he acted on his own initiative after seeing Chaucer and the other man in Donna Michela's questioning the soldier Aquilino. Bruno was a frequent visitor to the *bordello*. After a session upstairs he was in the habit of taking a drink or two in the dingy back room. Nobody bothered him, he bothered nobody.

But this time he recognized the Englishman and the little Florentine from the house on the Calmari. He could overhear some of their words but they might as well have been in Greek to him, since the three were conversing in English. Neverthe-less, he realized that they were interfering in matters which were no business of theirs. Without any clear plan in mind he'd tailed Chaucer once they'd left the *bordello*. When the foreigner wandered into the Piazza San Giovanni and then entered the campanile, Bruno had pursued him inside – on the off-chance that he might be able to take him unawares. And so it had proved, almost. If only the fellow hadn't turned his head at the last moment! Within the next second he would have been over the parapet, gone fishing in the empty air. And if it hadn't been for the interruption by those sightseers to the tower, then he, Bruno, would have completed the job with his knife.

What distressed Bruno almost as much as the Englishman's escape was the loss of his red velvet cap. He kept clasping his hand to his bald head and gesturing to demonstrate how the cap had sailed off into the air. It must have fallen down somewhere in the *piazza*. He should go back and search for it. Giuseppe could have sworn that there was a little water in his friend's eyes as he told the story in his own way. Never mind, Giuseppe hastened to say, it's only a hat. This was the wrong thing to say. Sometimes dealing with Bruno was like dealing with a child. Giuseppe put on a firmer voice. Do not go back to the *piazza* and look for your hat. It won't be there. This is a dishonest world, someone will have picked it up and taken it away. We'll get you another one. In fact you have another one, don't you, the one you took from that woman's cell on the Ponte Rubaconte. You remember you showed it to me the other day? And Bruno seemed a little mollified at the memory.

Nevertheless, he was displeased because he sensed Giuseppe's disappointment. Bruno wasn't accustomed to failure. When he did a job well, with Giuseppe or under Giuseppe's instructions, he revelled in his friend's praise. The murder of Guido Greco had been just such a case of job well executed (until it turned out that there'd been a witness, and then *she* had had to be dealt with in turn). Why it was necessary for an ordinary labourer like Guido to die had not occurred to Bruno. It was sufficient that Giuseppe had arranged it. Bruno did not ask questions.

Bruno could not ask questions for he was a mute. He was capable of making grunting noises and even of whistling (especially popular tunes such as *Figlia di Mugnaio*) but he had never been able to talk. Giuseppe, however, knew him so well that he could understand him better than he could many people who were in full possession of their tongues. When he had said this to Matteo Peruzzi, he was speaking no less than the truth. Giuseppe had, for example, fully understood Bruno's account of the first failed attempt on Chaucer's life. This was conveyed through gestures, a little mime, with Giuseppe supplying the words on cue. But there was more to it than this. It sometimes seemed to Giuseppe that he could see into Bruno's mind and watch the pictures unfurling there.

This understanding, this friendship, between the two men went back to boyhood. Giuseppe Orioli, now a large, even portly individual, had been a shrivelled child, lucky to survive his first few years. In fact he never would have survived them at all had not Bruno – already a silent, hulking fellow at the age of ten or eleven – intervened to prevent Giuseppe being thrown into the Arno while the river was running high during one gusty day in March. It was Giuseppe's friends who intended to throw him in the river where he would, most likely, have drowned. They said they were going to wash the birthmark off his neck and cheek. Why Bruno came to his aid and gave to the other boys bloody noses and bruised ribs, Giuseppe didn't know. The mute hulk couldn't explain. But it was enough for Giuseppe that he had a protector. In return he would look after Bruno.

The two – first as boys and now, many years on, as men – were almost inseparable, although Bruno did not share Giuseppe's inclination for his own sex. (In fact he was a regular visitor to establishments like Donna Michela's.) They had taken part in many enterprises together, Giuseppe supplying the brains and Bruno the brawn. But the portly Florentine knew that his lumbering companion wasn't without a wit of his own, for all that he was unable to put it into words.

Now he reassured Bruno that he had done the right thing – the good thing – in attempting to rid the world of Messere Geoffrey Chaucer. At this critical point in the affairs of the Banca Lipari, they did not require the further interference of some Englishman. Giuseppe felt fully entitled to act on his own initiative here. The indication from Matteo Peruzzi that Chaucer should not leave Florence alive was still in force, as far as Giuseppe was concerned.

When the first attempt on Chaucer's life had failed, it seemed that more direct methods would be needed. Then it appeared that the death of Antonio Lipari had put a stop to negotiations. But there was no saying how brother Lorenzo would respond. The blind man had hitherto taken no great interest in the day-to-day running of the Banca Lipari. He was engrossed by his country estate and even more by his young wife, as slippery as a lamprey, in Giuseppe's view. As an example of that, she had disappeared at the banquet on the night of Antonio's death in Via dei Cerretani and Giuseppe had been dispatched in search of her, all to satisfy the jealous whim of Lorenzo. But then jealousy was an all-consuming pattern of life for him.

How the blind brother might react to a new approach from Chaucer was a question that Giuseppe had discussed briefly with Matteo Peruzzi. It was made more urgent by the discovery that the Englishman intended to make a call at Paradise on the next day, ostensibly to offer his condolences and to take his farewells. There was a risk, though, that Chaucer would try to reopen the question of the loan and that Lorenzo would think he should honour his brother's arrangement – though, if Giuseppe knew anything about it, he was most likely to take the opposite course to Antonio. Still, one couldn't know how the death of the banker had altered things. Therefore the Englishman should be dealt with once and for all.

Briefly Giuseppe explained to Bruno what they were going to do on the following morning in order to prevent Chaucer's reaching Paradise – or perhaps to speed up his arrival there in a different sense! Giuseppe was gratified by Bruno's appreciation of the jest. People assumed that Bruno was slow and stupid, but they were wrong. Indeed it sometimes seemed to Giuseppe as though nature had atoned for depriving his friend of his tongue by giving him such a quick understanding. And that thought – of nature's compensating powers – led him to consider Lorenzo Lipari, and the blind man's extraordinary sensitivity to what was happening around him, surely finer than many a sighted man's.

Of course, it was true that Lorenzo had not been blind from birth but had lost his sight suddenly, one summer's day. Having known the brothers for a long time, Giuseppe was familiar with the story.

In their late youth Antonio and Lorenzo Lipari had been in competition for the same girl. They had even fought over her. The fight - more of a battle – had taken place in the secluded garden at the country house which was now known as Paradise. No one had witnessed the battle. No one had known anything about it until Antonio staggered into the house, clothes torn and bloodstained, to say that his brother had fallen and injured himself. The household rushed out. Young Lorenzo had tumbled from an old pear tree in which was fixed a kind of wooden platform where the brothers, when children, had played childish games. Lorenzo had fallen on his head. It soon emerged that the fall was no accident but the concluding point of a fight up the tree. And worse was to come. The bruised and bloodied Lorenzo was unconscious. Several anxious days passed before he re-entered the world. Miraculously, he seemed at first to have escaped serious injury, although he could see only glimmers and hazy outlines. Then, just as everyone believed him to be recovering, his sight went altogether. It was presumed that the fall had deprived him of his vision. Yet the helplessness of Lorenzo did not last long for he soon adjusted to his new condition, even seeming to take a perverse pride in it.

Antonio, as the one responsible for this disaster, was beaten to within an inch of his life, for the younger Lorenzo had always been the favourite of both their parents. Lorenzo bore his loss with dignity, and this only served to increase the guilt and shame of Antonio. The brothers never quarrelled again. The girl they'd been fighting over was forgotten. But you might say that, many years afterwards, Antonio had repaid Lorenzo by giving Novella Arezzo to him, almost as if in settlement of a debt.

This was the story which Giuseppe knew. It was true in its outline at least. He'd heard it from two or three sources, and all were agreed on the principal facts. That Antonio and Lorenzo had tussled up a tree in a garden, that Lorenzo had fallen and been deprived of his sight, and that the paths of the brothers' lives had diverged after that, Antonio being a worldly man of affairs who had built up the family banking business and preferred living in the city while Lorenzo became a near-recluse who took pleasure in his country estate and in his beautiful wife, even if she was as slippery as a lamprey.

Sometimes the story of the brothers was told as if there was a lesson in it, like a parable or the tale of Cain and Abel. But for Giuseppe there was no lesson at all, except that the bonds of family (of which he knew next to nothing) were as treacherous as ropes of straw. Much better to have a friend and companion one could trust with one's life – like Bruno!

21

In a state of high old excitement, Aquilino nevertheless had the presence of mind not to give his horse Fuoco to the stable-hand. He might need to make a quick exit from Paradise. While he'd been riding down the cypress-lined drive, he had glimpsed Novella disappearing round the side of the house. She was wearing a red dress which blared out in the morning like a cock crow. She was alone, and had the casual air of someone setting out for a morning stroll. Clever her! She must have glimpsed him from her upstairs window. She was heading in the direction of the walled garden. She held up a hand, as if in greeting. Aquilino thought he saw a glinting object in it. It must be the key. She was being as good as her word.

As Aquilino ambled on horseback away from the house – giving the impression that he too was simply taking the air on this fine morning – it occurred to him that his lady was finding it easier these days to slip out of her jealous husband's grasp. But perhaps that was natural enough, given all the turmoil in the Lipari family. Lorenzo must be busy planning how to take advantage of his brother's death. Aquilino had little interest in the demise of Antonio. It was simply the lever which he could use to get Novella to himself. And now the moment had come!

Or was about to come. The very turf under his horse's hoofs seemed to have an extra spring to it. The birdsong was clamorous. The trees were unsheathing their green. The whole earth was groaning with expectation. Aquilino himself didn't know

237

whether to groan or to whistle, so he did both. Fragments of that popular tune about the miller's daughter escaped from his lips.

He'd been up since first light, in the room he was renting at Donna Michela's. He scrubbed himself as best he could in a bucket in a communal courtyard. He washed his shirt and purchased a new doublet. He placed a jaunty cap on his young head. His small savings were almost exhausted, and soon he'd have to return to Tomaso Falcone's camp on the outskirts of the city. He'd likely be in trouble with his commander, who did not look kindly on unofficial absences and parroted remarks about the maintaining of discipline. As if they were knights of the Round Table! Aquilino might even be dismissed from the service of the mercenaries. If so, he didn't care much. He didn't care much if the world ended once he had had Novella Lipari. No, all things considered, he'd prefer the world to continue . . . but only so long as he might have Novella again and again.

Ahead of him was a stone wall which closed off an area of the larger estate. This was the secret garden. The stones of the wall looked older than those in the larger walls which it abutted. There was a small wooden door set into the wall. Aquilino dismounted. He tethered Fuoco to a rusty ring which might have been set into the wall for this very purpose. He approached the door. Next to the latch was a delicate-looking keyhole. Looking round to see that he was unobserved, Aquilino reached out and lifted the latch. The door creaked open and his heart leapt with it. His lady had passed this way very recently. He slipped through and closed the door behind him. In front of his eyes stretched haphazard rows of fruit trees. The grass underfoot was tussocky and uneven. He felt like a trespasser. It was as if he was the first man to enter the garden for many years.

The blossom swayed in the gentle breeze. The sun shone out of a cloudless sky. But where was Novella? He stepped uncertainly away from the wall and wandered down the nearest alley. There was no sign of her. Softly he called her name and a

238

cuckoo replied, but no lady. At random he turned down another path which was lined with pear trees in blossom. The grass, still heavy with dew in the places that were shaded, brushed at his leggings. Some of the trees here were old, their branches sagging and gnarled. He called again, more loudly. No response, not even a bird this time.

Aquilino's mood darkened suddenly. By heaven, if she was playing another game with him, he'd -

"Aqui! Aqui!"

He jumped. The voice seemed to have come from over his head. It was her voice, though, and her private name for him. Then came her laugh, half mocking, half fond. He looked up.

Novella's face was framed among the pale blossom. She extended an arm and crooked a finger. Aquilino had no time to be amazed. He grasped one of the lower branches and then one above that. The pear tree seemed to have disposed itself for climbing, with branches and handholds at easy intervals. Nimbly, he rose to her level, shaking off gouts of blossom as he ascended. She grasped his hand to guide him to her.

Novella was kneeling on a wooden platform that had been wedged across several branches. It was lashed to the tree with ropes. There was no room to stand up, at least not fully, but space enough to accommodate the two of them in other positions. The platform felt surprisingly secure, although it trembled and groaned as Aquilino climbed aboard and knelt beside his lady. In her other hand she was holding a bottle. Aquilino smelt the wine on her breath. He had never smelt anything more delicious, her breath and the wine fumes mingled together.

And at once the mercenary realized that this was where Lorenzo Lipari brought his wife for their private business. There were silk cushions scattered on the rough wood of the platform, and a tarpaulin overhead that no doubt protected them from the worst of the elements. But how did Lorenzo get up here? The man was blind.

"How does he – ?" he began, curiosity for an instant getting the better of any other desire.

She understood at once. "There is a little ladder beneath the tree. I guide him up."

"Ladder?"

"I've hidden it in the long grass, so we shan't be disturbed. He knows this place well, does my husband. It was where he played with his brother when they were little children."

Yes, it was true, this 'place' did have something of childhood about it. But now they were going to play at adults, he and Novella. As if she could sense his purpose – and of course she could, it was the reason they were here up the blossomy pear tree – she took a swig from the bottle and placed it carefully to one side. Then she lay back on the cushioned wood, pulling up her dress. She wore no undergarments.

"Come and collect your debt," she said.

Aquilino needed no further encouragement. If his senses hadn't been swimming, if his mind had retained a particle of sense, he might have thought that there was something a little, well, perfunctory, about Novella's approach. Nor, in other circumstances, might he have enjoyed being reminded of the murder of Antonio Lipari, the 'debt' which Novella Lipari had incurred and which – at last! – she was about to repay. But, naturally, he didn't think like this. He didn't think at all. Instead he threw himself on top of her.

22

Geoffrey Chaucer and Bartolomeo Gentile also set out early that morning. Like Aquilino they were on their way to visit the place called Paradise. The invitation from Lorenzo had come as a formality. Geoffrey intended to offer condolences on the death of Antonio Lipari. He would also, if the chance arose, broach the subject of the English loan again although he wasn't optimistic of success. Privately, he was curious to see the country retreat belonging to the blind brother. After that his diplomatic business in Florence would be done. The most he could hope to return home with would be a promise to continue negotiations. Overall, though, he'd failed . . .

The two men had hired horses for the day in the Oltrarno, a pair of sturdy cobs. They paced slowly up the streets which led away from the river and towards the edge of the town and the green slopes beyond. They passed through the gate. The day was fair, yet Chaucer's mood was clouded. Riding side by side, he and Bartolomeo now emerged into a more open area, with a scatter of artisans' dwellings and smallholdings where dogs were scratching themselves and chickens fussing in the sun.

Geoffrey observed a cock, its comb like a red battlement, parading in the dusty yard of a hovel with several hens in attendance. A sunburnt old woman stood in the sagging doorway of the hut, watching her birds. She looked at the passing riders incuriously. The cock paid the humans no attention at all. The patch of dirt was its only realm. From its regal air, the male bird and not the wizened woman in the doorway might have been the possessor of the hut and yard. If the bird could speak, it would undoubtedly claim as much, and think itself the lord of a wealthy kingdom.

Do we humans on our little squares of earth know any better? thought Chaucer. An idea occurred to him, for transferring human passions to a farmyard, giving animals the power of speech, making them as vain and fallible and as ingenious as human beings. Some kind of story to be told in verse, the sort of thing which children would like as much as adults. The idea caught his imagination. He had not written anything for a long time. When Bartolomeo next spoke he was unprepared.

"You have been sleeping well in my house?" said the lawyer.

"Why yes," said Geoffrey, surprised at the question. "Why do you ask?"

"Bartolomeo has seen you giving the yawns on this fine morning. So you are tired?"

Had he been yawning? He must have been. The suggestion was enough to set Chaucer off on a fresh bout.

"Bad dreams?" said Bartolomeo.

"A man died suspiciously the other night. I suppose that has troubled my dreams since."

"Bella heard you talking last night in your chamber."

"Bella? She has sharp ears, that one."

"We have a saying over here, Geoffrey. White only on the top of the head, green elsewhere. *Testa bianca, verde per il resto.* The saying comes from the trees in blossom. Is better in my tongue, I think. It means – "

"I can understand the words, my friend, whether they're in English or your own tongue."

Chaucer's response came out more sharply than he intended. For his part Bartolomeo sounded faintly uncomfortable, as if he was looking for reassurance or an easy excuse of what the

242

servant had overheard. Geoffrey felt he owed some explanation to the notary.

"I must have been talking in my sleep, I suppose."

"It's all right, Geoffrey, I will enquire no further. I was concerned only for your well-being."

"You are a good host, Bartolomeo."

Chaucer gently urged his horse forward so as to put an end to the conversation without appearing to do so. Exactly what had old Bella listened to last night? What conversation had she heard which she couldn't have understood, what sounds which she could? Had she grinned to herself in the dark?

The mercenary's woman, Joanna, had departed as the sky began to lighten in the east and the birds started to sing. She had made her exit from Geoffrey's chamber as surreptitiously as she had arrived there, using the window and that convenient builders' ladder. He didn't ask where she was going. She was much more familiar with the city of Florence than he was. She had her bolt-holes, he hoped, besides Donna Michela's. She could look after herself, couldn't she? Yet even as he repeated these things to himself, he was aware that they were convenient words for him.

By this time the two riders had left most of the houses and huts behind. They were skirting the upper edge of a quarry, a great basin carved out of the hillside. The descent on this side was steep. Olive trees and tufts of grass clung to the rim. The sounds of chipping and sawing ascended through the air. Down below, tiny figures were visible among swirls of dust and powder, while mules waited between the shafts of carts laden with blocks of stone.

"Our city, she comes from here, from the ribs of the earth," said Bartolomeo, gesturing at the scene. "Such labour there has been in these recent years of peace! Such new things built on old foundations!"

They had ridden only a few paces further when Bartolomeo drew up his hired horse and looked around uncertainly.

243

"You know the way to Paradise?" said Chaucer.

"Of course I do," said Bartolomeo, but from his tone he wasn't so sure. Eventually he chose one of several tracks that led away from the quarry. Soon the sounds of work faded and they entered a patch of woodland and then a kind of gully, so narrow that the two men could scarcely ride abreast. Grassy banks, dotted with spring flowers and overhung with trees, reared up on either side. There was the scent of wild garlic, earlier by a good month than it would have come to England. And Geoffrey thought once again of the blossom on the Canterbury road, the road home from Dover. He thought of Philippa and his children in Gaunt's palace of Savoy. Their distance from him – and his from them – did not seem entirely one of miles.

All at once he shivered. It was unexpectedly cold down in this gully. The air was dank and sunless, for all the flowers that grew here. The horses' hoofs were muffled by a thick mush of fallen leaves. Chaucer had pulled slightly ahead and now he glanced back. He should let the other go first since only Bartolomeo had an idea of their direction. But the notary was peering beyond Geoffrey with a look of alarm. At the same moment there was the rustle of branches from the front and Chaucer looked forward to see a large figure half running, half slipping down the bank. The man came to an undignified halt in the middle of the path. Geoffrey's cob shied at the sight. By the time he had his mount under control again, the man had recovered his balance and was standing directly in their way. Chaucer recognized the individual who'd accompanied Lorenzo Lipari to the house of his brother. The wine-coloured stain on his face wasn't so evident in the gloom of this place but there could be no doubt that this was -

"Signor Giuseppe!" said Bartolomeo.

Still on horseback, the notary brushed past Chaucer and approached the portly man as if he was an old friend. The man said something to him. Bartolomeo dismounted. Chaucer glanced over his shoulder again. The path behind him was empty, so it was two against one. Nevertheless, he felt uneasy. The conversation between this Giuseppe and Bartolomeo seemed amicable enough. There was even some laughter. A chance meeting? Somehow he didn't think so. He felt under his cloak for the knife at his belt.

"What is it?" he called out in English. "What's wrong?"

"Eh? Nothing is wrong," Bartolomeo said, half over his shoulder. "Giuseppe has heard that we are visiting Paradise today and has come to guide us. He knows of a quicker route."

Was it a helpful offer, particularly since Gentile didn't seem to be absolutely sure of the direction? Again, Geoffrey didn't think so. He might have objected but Bartolomeo wasn't listening. By now, Giuseppe was offering him a flask to drink from. The riders had taken some ale before setting off that morning but Bartolomeo, never averse to another drink or two, now tilted back his head and took a swig from Giuseppe's flask.

"Where's his horse then?" said Geoffrey. "If he's here to guide us, where's his horse?"

He was perhaps ten yards from the two Florentines. He noticed the attentive manner in which Giuseppe watched Bartolomeo swallowing the contents of the flask. Chaucer's cob snickered and shifted restlessly under him. The Englishman heard nothing but he sensed the presence of someone to his back. Slowly, almost casually, he turned his head to see another figure standing in the gully and blocking their retreat. This one was further off.

He recognized the second man as well. More by his stance and outline than from any facial features. The man was wearing a cap – a blue cap this time and one that was too small for his head – but Geoffrey Chaucer had no doubt that, if he were to take his headgear off, a bald pate would be revealed. The same bald pate that he'd seen during the fight on top of the campanile.

This was no casual meeting, but an ambush.

His guts tightened and his mouth felt dry. He breathed deeply. He was frightened but at the same time curiously relieved. The skirmishing and the deception were over. He knew what they were facing. The trick would be to get out of here alive. It would be difficult but not impossible. The two ambushers, Giuseppe and the bald-head, had chosen their place carefully. A narrow gully, whose exits could easily be blocked. A secluded place in the woods where they were unlikely to be disturbed by other travellers. Chaucer had the advantage of being on horseback. If only Bartolomeo had not dismounted! Even so, he should be able to jump back on his horse if Chaucer shouted a warning.

Unless, of course, this was a trap into which the notary had directed him, and the exchange with Giuseppe was all a piece of play-acting.

These thoughts and fears shot through Chaucer's mind with the speed of an arrow, almost in the time it took him to turn round and face the front again. Yet he moved slowly, to give himself time to think, to avoid giving the impression that he was panicked.

If he'd been fearful that Gentile had betrayed him, then what he saw next should have been reassuring.

Reassuring in one way but deeply troubling in another. Bartolomeo Gentile would not have been capable of remounting his horse with any speed, and possibly not at all. Instead he was holding on to the cob's bridle with one hand and leaning against the animal's flank like a man exhausted after a race. From the fingers of the other hand dangled the flask out of which he'd been drinking. Chaucer saw Giuseppe reach out and retrieve the flask. He prised it from Bartolomeo's nerveless fingers and tucked it neatly under his cloak. No doubt he'd be using the adulterated drink again. Whatever Bartolomeo had swallowed hadn't killed him, but it had rendered him as good as useless.

God's bones, what to do now?

With a fair helping of luck, Geoffrey might have spurred the cob forward and shoved his way past Giuseppe. But the path was so narrow and the distance between man and rider so short that he would not be moving very fast, certainly not fast enough to swing out of reach of the dagger which Giuseppe, having deposited his flask safely, now withdrew from under his mantle. And this would be an attack from two directions. Geoffrey didn't have to glance over his shoulder to know that the bald-headed individual was even now advancing towards him across the floor of fallen leaves, his own dagger drawn. The very dagger with which he had attempted to kill him on top of the campanile. The hairs on the back of Chaucer's neck told him as much. And then, more eerily, the other began to whistle as he drew closer. Only a few bars but Geoffrey was familiar by now with *Figlia di Mugnaio*, all too familiar.

Chaucer had a couple of seconds to respond. Could he rescue Bartolomeo? Probably not. But if he managed to get away he might distract the two men into making a pursuit and so save the notary – at the risk of his own life. But his life would be forfeit altogether if he delayed. He could have dug his heels into his mount and run for it in the direction they were already travelling. But the path ahead was blocked not only by Giuseppe but by the other cob, to whose bridle Bartolomeo clung with the air of a man half-dead on his feet. If Chaucer spurred forward, very likely he and his horse would go down together. He'd be thrown and, even if uninjured, at more of a disadvantage.

He jerked at the cob's reins to twist its head and struck at its flanks with his heels. Despite the narrowness of the gully he succeeded in turning the horse so that they were both facing toward the whistling man. As Geoffrey had expected, he was moving steadily forward, dagger drawn. When he saw what Chaucer was doing, the whistling ceased but no surprise registered on the broad face.

Giuseppe shouted out something, a barked command which Chaucer couldn't understand even though its general meaning was clear enough, for his associate halted and stationed himself in the very centre of the path. He stood with legs braced and at a slight crouch, his dagger-arm extended. Chaucer's horse, already badly unnerved, might bolt at any moment or throw his rider. The whistling man, however, showed no fear but stood four-square in the track. Come to me, his stance said, come to me. I am ready to receive you. Mounted or on foot, it makes no difference.

Chaucer's hand, hovering above his own dagger, flew instead to another pocket and drew from it an object which was more friendly than the handle of a knife. He brandished it over his head so that it was clearly visible. The eyes of the man on the path flickered, then fastened on the object. His gaze narrowed and a look of delighted recognition filled his face. Any man would be gratified to be reunited with his lost cap of red velvet, after all. Chaucer could almost have been pleased for him, if he'd had the time. But at the back of his mind was the grunt of anger which the attacker had given at the top of the bell-tower, and the look of baffled fury on his face at the loss of his precious headgear.

Geoffrey pivoted the cap on his index finger, whirled it round a few times and sent it spinning into the air in the direction of his assailant. The man on the path watched as it flew over his head and landed near the top of the bank to one side of the gully. A perfect shot! A second shout came from behind Chaucer, undoubtedly a command from Giuseppe that the other should stand his ground and leave the cap lying where it had fallen. But it was too late. Already the man had abandoned his position on the track and was climbing up in pursuit of his property, which showed like a gout of blood among the pale spring flowers on the top of the bank.

Now the path was empty. Chaucer yelled and banged at his horse's flanks. The cob leapt forward and moved off down the gully. Geoffrey felt a moment of elation. He'd do it! The man called Giuseppe was behind him, and on foot. He'd never be able to catch up. The other ambusher was scrabbling for his discarded cap, all thoughts of attack forgotten. Chaucer might draw the two of them away, get out into the open spaces above the quarry, and so give Bartolomeo time to recover his wits.

These thoughts, in garbled form, passed through his mind in the time it took his mount to cover a few yards. But Chaucer's optimism was short-lived. The man on the bank grabbed for his lost cap, seized it in a single sweep of his arm and almost fell back down the slope just before Chaucer drew level with him. The horse jinked to one side. Geoffrey's cob was no battle-hardened steed but a hired jade, used to plodding down city streets or along peaceful country paths. It reared up as the man, off-balance but no less dangerous, lashed out with the dagger which he was still holding. The dagger connected only with air, but the damage was done. A better horseman might have kept his seat but Geoffrey had never been truly at home in the saddle. He was flung from his position. His fall would have been worse if he hadn't landed on the sloping bank of the opposite side of the gully.

Winded, he was aware of his cob trotting off, leisurely and unencumbered now. The man with the cap regained his balance and was ready to finish the task of disposing of the Englishman. He even took the time to fold his recovered hat and tuck it neatly away. Chaucer reached for his dagger. Out of the corner of his eye he saw Giuseppe approaching from the other side. The wine-dark stain on his face stood out like an omen of the blood to be spilt.

He was done for. These men were bigger – and stronger – than him. There was nowhere for him to run, with the steep bank to his back and both ends of the gully closed off. Anyway the two could outrun him, most likely. Worst of all, they were used to killing. He might have been able to hold off one of the fellows for a time but with two there was no hope.

Chaucer rose to a crouch on the bank where he'd fallen. Instinctively, his feet sought for a firmer hold on the grass and mud. His knife was slippery in his grasp. He glanced down and saw blood on his hand. It didn't matter where it came from. There'd soon be worse.

Geoffrey Chaucer stood like an animal at bay, moving his knife-arm from side to side. He could do no more. As an Englishman, he would give a good account of himself. He would make a good end to things here, in this wooded gully outside the city of Florence, many miles from home. He might get in a swipe at the bald-headed man or the one called Giuseppe, he might inflict some damage before they overpowered him. His assailants were moving cautiously but with confidence. They knew they would prevail but wanted to do so with the least risk to themselves.

All at once Chaucer determined not to wait for the attack but to launch himself at one of them. Why should he perish on their terms? He glanced at Giuseppe to the left, only a couple of yards away, then threw himself in the opposite direction, towards the second man.

He was counting on surprise. From the gaping expression on the other's face, surprise was what he produced. He collided with the bald-headed man. Instead of resisting Chaucer or attempting to counter-attack, this one gasped, threw out his arms and buckled at the knees. His cap – the blue cap – flew off, just as the red one had atop the campanile. Chaucer lost his own balance and tumbled on top of his opponent. He felt something prick at his chest and immediately rolled away before the other could wield his knife more effectively. He was fearful too of Giuseppe attacking him from the rear. He couldn't understand why the second man was being so slow to respond.

From his position flat on his back, Chaucer raised his knife-arm, ready for the final attack to begin. But Giuseppe wasn't moving any closer. Rather, he was looking intently not at the two figures on the ground but at something above his head and further away. Chaucer glanced aside at the second man, the one who had lost his cap. On his broad face was an expression of outrage. He hadn't risen to his feet. He would never rise to his feet again. The reason was apparent in the conical shape protruding from his chest. It was the tip of the arrow which Chaucer had mistaken for a knife-point a moment before. Even as he'd been preparing to fling himself at the bald-head, the man's chest had been pierced by an arrow. Or not precisely an arrow, since Chaucer's eye told him that this was the tip of a quarrel fired by a crossbow. That explained how it had driven right through his assailant's body.

At a half crouch, Chaucer swivelled round to look in the direction that Giuseppe was gazing. On top of the bank a handful of men stood among the trees. One of them was aiming a crossbow over Chaucer's shoulder, at Giuseppe. The others were holding drawn swords or knives. The crossbowman was an expert. Not merely because he'd struck the bald-head fair and square in the back – which was a fine shot, executed in poor light and from an awkward angle – but because he'd reloaded his weapon within a few seconds.

Chaucer turned back to look at Giuseppe but that one was already running in the opposite direction down the gully. He was uttering strange, whooping noises as he went. He brushed past Bartolomeo Gentile, who was walking unsteadily down the path towards the scene. Geoffrey saw the crossbowman shift his aim slightly.

"No!" he shouted. "He is a friend. *Amice!*"

The crossbowman lowered his weapon and looked over his shoulder. From out of the shadow of the trees emerged a figure whom Geoffrey recognized. Somehow he wasn't surprised.

Tomaso Falcone – Tom Sparrow, as ever was – slithered down the bank until he was on the same level as Geoffrey Chaucer.

"By God, Geoffrey, another second and your bones would have been laid to rest on foreign soil."

251

For an instant Chaucer couldn't speak. There was a roaring in his ears and his legs almost gave way beneath him. He had come within a hair's-breadth of death. Now one assailant lay dead on the ground while the other was fleeing through the woods, and his life was saved. Even so, he knew from experience that the full shock of this incident wouldn't hit him for hours yet, maybe days.

"You're hurt, Geoffrey," said Tomaso as he drew nearer.

Absently, Chaucer glanced at his right hand. He was still holding the knife. The haft was sticky and blood was seeping through his clenched fingers. He replaced the knife in the sheath on his belt and examined the hand as if it belonged to someone else. There was a gash across the palm. He'd no idea how he'd come by it.

"It's nothing," he said.

Falcone produced a piece of dirty, stained cloth from somewhere and Geoffrey tied it round his hand, pulling at the knot with his teeth. Now the hand started to throb. He hoped that he would not be required to wield a knife again that day. By this time Bartolomeo had arrived. He stood swaying like a drunk. With glazed eyes and a profoundly furrowed brow, he regarded the body of the bald-headed fellow on the ground. Then he looked with alarm at the armed men who were sliding down the grassy bank. The man who'd fired the bolt from the crossbow also drew near. He glanced down at the body he'd created and then gave a little, ironic bow in Geoffrey's direction.

"*Ruggiero, a tua disposizione,*" he said.

"*Mille grazie,*" said Geoffrey, and then, "It's all right, Bartolomeo. These are friends of mine. They have saved our lives."

"Then an old debt is repaid," said Falcone.

Chaucer didn't know what he was talking about. Then he recalled the incident involving Sir John Audley's men all those years ago at the siege of Rheims. Well, Tom Sparrow had never thanked him for saving his life at the time. But neither had he forgotten. Chaucer felt a sudden outpouring of warmth towards this rough Englishman, and clasped him round the shoulder. In truth, he was also a little unsteady on his legs and needed the support.

"There was something in that drink," said Bartolomeo, referring to the flask which Giuseppe Orioli had given him. "Why was there something in the drink? What is happening? *Non comprendo.*"

"I don't understand either," said Geoffrey, releasing his hold on Falcone and standing unsupported. A muscle in his left calf was twitching uncontrollably. "All I know is that the man who's run off was in the company of the Lipari brothers and that the one lying down dead is the individual who tried to kill me yesterday."

"The Lipari brothers?" said Falcone.

"Why yes."

Chaucer looked sideways at Tomaso. Falcone shrugged, as if there was no more to explain.

"How do you come to be here, Tom Sparrow – your pardon, Tomaso Falcone?"

It was chance and good fortune together, said Falcone, ignoring Geoffrey's slip over his name. He and his band had been engaged on some business of their own on the edge of town. One of their number – in fact, that excellent crossbowman Ruggiero (who was presently crouched over the corpse which he'd felled, either in gratification at his own handiwork or in the hope of pickings from the dead man's pockets) – had spied two individuals preparing to lay an ambush for travellers through this wooded gully. It was a natural spot, secluded and easily blocked on either side. But this pair were not professionals. They were unaware that they themselves were being watched and stalked. Falcone thought it would be good sport to wait on events.

Imagine his amazement when one of the travellers turned out to be his old friend and comrade-in-arms, Geoffrey Chaucer! Less surprising to Tomaso Falcone was Geoffrey's skill under attack. He'd admired the way Geoffrey had spun the red cap to distract his attacker, and his determination when – unseated from his horse – he'd faced up to the two of them together. By God, it took an Englishman to show these foreigners what real grit and fighting spirit meant! It reminded him of the days of tournaments and jousting in Edward's court. The moment had arrived, however, when it was clear that Chaucer was about to face a final attack, and so he had given the command to Ruggiero to shoot.

"For, you know, Geoffrey," said Falcone, "I do not think that you would have prevailed. We are all slower and heavier than we were."

Falcone was lean and hardy still, but the description was certainly fitting for Geoffrey Chaucer. By this time, Ruggiero had finished examining the corpse of the fallen man. He held aloft the two caps, one red and the other blue, and tapped at his own head. He did not need them for he was already wearing a battered leather helmet. They were small trophies, the coloured caps. The other members of Falcone's band were wandering up and down the path, waiting for orders. So Falcone now gave an order, instructing a couple of his men to remove the body from the path and give it a hasty burial in the woods.

"Which is more than they would have done for you and your friend, Geoffrey. They would have left you lying here or they would have tossed your corpses aside like so much carrion. But that is not our way. We bury our foes."

This was most likely true. But despite Tomaso's words about their 'way' and its implied superiority, Chaucer couldn't help wondering whether the mercenaries' plan had been to ambush the ambushers, and take whatever pickings they could, stealing at second hand. If so, they'd been unlucky with two caps as prize.

"We should not have let that other fellow get away, though," said Falcone. "If he'd fallen into our hands he'd have informed us of his dark purposes soon enough. He was working for the Liparis, you say?"

"Not on this occasion, I hope. His name is Giuseppe Orioli. You know that one of the brothers is dead?"

"By God, I have heard as much," said Falcone. "And my business now is in the place called Paradise where the other one lives . . ."

"Lorenzo Lipari? We are on our way to Paradise now, Bartolomeo and I."

"Then we should continue our visit together. It will be safer that way. Don't worry, Geoffrey, I won't poke my fingers into your affairs. It is not Lorenzo Lipari I want to see but a certain individual who I believe is sheltering under his roof. One of my own. He is absent without leave. I will not have deserters. Discipline must be maintained."

Chaucer was almost certain that Falcone was referring to Pietro Hodge or Aquilino but he said nothing. One can show oneself too well informed.

At this point the men who'd been detailed to dispose of the body returned. Considering the length of time they'd been absent, the corpse must be resting in a very shallow grave indeed. Another of Falcone's men came back leading Chaucer's cob. He had found it grazing on the patches of grass at the edge of the quarry. Not all of Tomaso's men were mounted and he now instructed several of them to scour the woods in search of Giuseppe while he and a handful of others rode off towards Paradise in company with Chaucer and Bartolomeo Gentile.

Chaucer was glad of the escort. For one thing, Giuseppe remained at large and might try to attack again. For another, Bartolomeo was not recovered from the effects of the drugged

255

drink. He had to be helped on to his horse, and one of the mercenaries rode alongside to ensure that he didn't tumble off. Geoffrey did not know why an ambush had been laid for him and Gentile – but he could guess. Robbery was surely not the motive. Rather, this was the latest in a succession of attempts to frustrate his mission to negotiate a loan for the English crown. Was that the reason why Antonio Lipari had died? But, if so, why persist with the attacks when Antonio was dead? Were they trying to prevent his reaching Lorenzo Lipari even now? How dare they interfere so murderously in his lawful business! A sudden gust of anger swept through Chaucer. He almost wished that, knife in hand, he was confronting Giuseppe and the bald-head again. Fury alone might have enabled him to prevail, one against two.

Geoffrey felt his injured hand throbbing on the reins of the cob. He breathed deeply. *Con calma*, he said to himself, *con calma*. You will get nowhere like this. There are too many questions still unanswered. A cool head is necessary to see the matter through.

And he wondered whether the answer to any of these questions lay in the place called Paradise.

23

For his part, Aquilino was already in Paradise, in at least a double sense. Half-naked, he lay with his love, the lady Novella, on the platform up the pear tree in the secret garden which belonged to her husband Lorenzo. Aquilino was dressed only in his shirt, with his doublet and leggings thrown carelessly to one side and his jaunty cap rolled into a corner. Novella lay with her dress hoisted up round her waist and her breasts exposed.

Passion spent for an instant, Aquilino stroked one of her breasts while her hand nestled in his groin. From time to time Novella whispered satisfying endearments or suggestive ones.

Had he ever been so . . . so full? He did not believe it. There had been occasions during his long wooing of the lady when he doubted whether he was destined to achieve his aim. Whether she would ever take pity on him and show true *gentilesse* (as he believed the poets called it) by relieving his suffering. How unworthy those doubts seemed as they lay now, intertwined, up the pear tree! The pear tree was their bower, the branches their screen against prying eyes. The wooden boards beneath them were as soft as a meadow in heaven and the pear blossom strewed their bodies like manna.

Gazing up through half-open eyes, Aquilino thought that he had never seen a sky this blue. The breeze – what was Novella's word? – soughed, yes, the breeze soughed (*sussurrava*) in the branches of the orchard trees. Birds sang. Sweet scents wafted over their bare legs and mixed with the earthier tones of their own bodies, which smelt just as sweet after their own fashion. It was enough to make a man learn to read in order that he might understand verse, and even compose it.

As he was enjoying these thoughts, Novella burped.

She had just taken a swig from the wine bottle. Now she offered it to Aquilino. While he was tilting it to his lips, she tickled him down below and he jerked the bottle and wine ran everywhere, down his chin, over his clean shirt (which was no longer so clean). With anybody else, such an action would have roused him to fury. Now he laughed, and smeared her with red, so that her bare breasts matched her bunched dress for colour. But Novella did not see the joke. She sat up and shifted away from him. The wooden platform groaned and swayed, perhaps unaccustomed to all the strenuous activity it had played host to in the last hour or so.

"Fool, Aquilino!" said Novella. "I shall have to clean myself up before I go indoors."

"But your husband cannot see you, my love."

"He is not the only one in the household. There are other eyes and they can see."

"Do they matter?"

"Of course they matter. What do you think I am? Some common *contadina* without a position to keep up?"

Aquilino was startled by the irritation in her voice. Where were the soft tones of a moment ago? Better still, where was the urgency of several moments earlier? Wasn't it time that they recaptured their first rapture up the pear tree? He reached up, more forcefully this time, to pull her down again. She resisted, but only for an instant. Then she was lying on top of him. Yet barely had they started once more than Novella raised her head and clapped her hand over his mouth, not in excitement but in alarm.

"Wha – wha – " he gurgled under her hand.

"Listen!" she hissed.

He listened but was aware of nothing apart from the soughing of the breeze and the birdsong. He was about to protest more loudly when he heard a creaking sound in the distance. He'd heard that sound before, and recently too. Someone had just opened the door to the secret garden. Or was closing it after slipping inside.

24

Giuseppe Orioli was mad with rage and grief. After the failure of the ambush, he had stumbled down the gully in the woods, unaware that even as he went he was uttering strange cries of woe. He fled from the scene when he recognized the strength of Chaucer's rescuers. Also he had known straightaway that Bruno was dead, and that there was nothing more he could do for his mute friend. He veered off the path and into the trees. Eventually some small part of his brain told him that he was behaving foolishly by exhausting himself to no purpose and, by his loud progress through the underbrush, drawing attention to his presence. He halted, his portly frame covered in sweat and his entire face the colour of the wine-stain on his cheek. When he'd recovered his wind and when his blurred vision had begun to clear, Giuseppe took stock of his surroundings. To his surprise he'd moved in a circle. He was on the fringe of the woods, at a place where the trees thinned out above the stone quarry.

Wheezing, he sat down with his back against an olive tree. It was a hot morning – still morning after all that had happened! – and he was glad of the shade. He looked round to ensure that he was alone and then stared across the quarry at the gleaming walls of the city which contained the campanile, the tower of the Palazzo del Podesta, the half-built cathedral. But, after the first few moments, Giuseppe saw none of these things nor did he hear the workaday sounds of cutting and sawing ascending from the quarry. In his mind's eye he was witnessing again the moment when his mute friend Bruno had been felled by a bolt fired by the wicked crossbowman. He saw that evil object protruding from his friend's chest and the look of surprise on his friend's face. Giuseppe felt water leaking from his eyes. He could not remember when he had last cried. Perhaps he had never truly cried before.

Giuseppe was baffled by the arrival of the men-at-arms, and the reason for their intervention. The bowman was dressed in the style of one of the mercenaries who infested the Florentine region like vermin, but he could not understand why they should interfere with an honest ambush laid by himself and his dear, dead friend Bruno. Now he vowed that he would track down Bruno's killer, and kill him in turn, even though he had no idea at the moment who he was. He would ask a few questions of that fellow Aquilino who was always sniffing round Paradise in quest of Novella Lipari. Aquilino was a mercenary. Aquilino would help him. If he didn't, Giuseppe would make trouble for him . . .

Giuseppe loosened his doublet and thought about killing Bruno's killer. He drew out his knife. He had no memory of putting it back in its sheath but must have done so as he was fleeing through the wood. He turned the blade so that it caught the sun and tested the edge with the ball of his thumb. The steel had been deprived of one victim this morning. It would soon be satisfied with a fresh offering. He visualized the tip entering the extended throat of that bowman.

Yet, Giuseppe mused on this bright spring morning, perhaps strangling was to be preferred to stabbing. He put the knife to one side and drew out the red silken thread which he carried with him always, the very one with which he had strangled Guido at the beginning of this story. That young man Guido Greco who was, even now, going about his eternal rest somewhere in the quarry below. Giuseppe remembered how he and

Bruno had carried the corpse down the rough path and deposited it in the old, abandoned working. He almost wept once more, not in grief for Guido, but because Bruno would never again be his partner in such an enterprise.

Now, sitting against the olive tree, he ran the cord through his fingers. It was soft as down and strong as steel, and had disposed of more than one man. But even the red cord wasn't right. Though he was greatly looking forward to killing the crossbowman when he tracked him down, this instrument did not seem . . . appropriate. Giuseppe required something more personal for the individual who had robbed him of his Bruno. Therefore he would strangle the bowman with his bare hands. It was decided. With a satisfied sigh, his grief momentarily forgotten, Giuseppe closed his eyes and tried to make himself comfortable against the contours of the olive tree to his back.

He must have slept, if only for a moment. He jerked awake and felt something bite into his neck. Automatically his hand flew up to investigate. A thin cord was pressing into the ample flesh below his chin. He couldn't see it but he knew instinctively that it must be his own cord. He cursed himself for not having replaced it in the inner pocket of his doublet. He would cut himself free with the knife which – let me see – the knife which he had returned to its sheath, no, not to the sheath – the knife which he had put down in the grass close at hand. He was unable to lower his head far but he felt about among the tussocks of grass on his side, without encountering the welcome touch of steel.

It was only then that the truth of his predicament struck home. It may seem strange that it had taken an intelligent man like Giuseppe even a few seconds to grasp the simple fact but it was so. Perhaps he was still half asleep, perhaps he had taken a swig from his own drugged flask. After all, it was no magic which had tethered him by the neck to the olive tree. The simple fact was that an enemy had crept up on him while he slept and secured him to the tree so that he was scarcely able to move his head. They had stolen his cord, looped it over his neck and round the olive tree, and fastened it tight. But they'd left his arms and legs free. That was their mistake. They'd soon learn what it was to interfere with Giuseppe Orioli.

He reached behind him with his hands, fumbling for the knot which must secure the cord. Fortunately the tree trunk was slender enough for him to encircle with his arms in reverse. But it wasn't as easy as he expected. Whoever had tied him up had judged the tightness in the cord to a nicety. Not tight enough to throttle him outright but not so loose as to allow him to move his arms and shoulders without the thread pressing painfully against his windpipe. He could not even slip a finger between the silken thread and his puffy flesh. For an instant he thought he'd laid hands on the knot but it was only an irregular bump in the tree-bark. In frustration and fury, Giuseppe attempted to tear himself free using his hands, but the cord was strong – strong as steel – and all he succeeded in doing was making himself breathless and scratching his hands on the bark. The sun had moved round so that he was no longer sitting in the shade. Sweat ran down his face.

Slowly he lowered his arms. This situation required more careful consideration. It struck him that his enemy might still be in the vicinity. He, Giuseppe, would surely have woken at the very instant of the cord tightening at the base of his throat. Therefore the man might not be far away. Was he even now lurking behind Giuseppe on the other side of the olive tree, or had he fled the scene? Once Giuseppe got himself free, it would be as well for his unknown enemy if he had fled! Whoever secured the cord possessed agile fingers, to have tied the knot so fast. Agile fingers and a cool head. Giuseppe gazed at the blue sky, cloudless, as if it might answer the question of who had done this. The crossbowman who'd murdered Bruno? No, that individual would have used his weapon. The Englishman by the name of Chaucer? No, it would not be him either. So who . . .?

At that instant a shape came between him and the sun.

Not a man but a woman. At first he thought she'd come to rescue him – until he recognized her.

It was Lisabetta Greco, Guido's woman. She was holding his own knife. She stood just out of his reach. He remembered that she was a needlewoman, possessed of agile fingers. Used to tying knots. Used to wielding a bodkin too. Despite this, he experienced a moment's relief. Only a woman, only this woman. Of little account. Easy to pull the wool over her eyes, as he'd done before in the gaming house and the tavern.

"Don't be foolish," he said before she could speak. "Let me go free and no harm will come to you."

"You will not be free until you give me the truth. Antonio Lipari did not kill my Guido."

So she was still after revenge.

"Maybe not," he said, "but it was you killed *him.*"

"I did not," said Lisabetta. "I swear on the grave of my mother that I did not kill him. My conscience got the better of me and I thank God for it."

She has a conscience, thought Giuseppe. She is in the habit of thanking God. This will not be so hard.

As if discerning his thoughts, Lisabetta said, "But I have put my conscience back in its hole where God cannot see it. It will not stop me doing what I want to do now. I ask you again, Giuseppe, why did you tell me that Signor Lipari killed Guido?"

"I gave you that news in good faith."

"You gave me nothing in good faith."

Lisabetta darted forward and jabbed him in the thigh with his own knife. He shouted, more in surprise than pain. But there was pain too. With difficulty, because of his tethered position, Giuseppe looked downwards as blood began to seep through his leggings. For the first time he felt a trickle of real fear. As if ashamed of what she'd done, Lisabetta moved away and gazed into the quarry which lay beneath her feet. Giuseppe reached behind with his hands. He thought he could feel the knot in the cord on the other side of the trunk. But then Lisabetta turned round again, a fresh resolve on her face, and he swiftly brought his arms down.

"How did you find me?" he said, to distract her.

"I have been following you. I saw you lay an ambush for that good notary, Signor Gentile, and his friend who is English. I talked to the notary yesterday, and he treated me with real kindness. Then I began to wonder about you, Giuseppe, and whether you had tricked me, a simple laundrywoman. I began to consider all the things you said and then the things which happened. I have been on your heels since early this morning. I tracked you into the woods here."

She gestured towards the trees that lay behind the bound Giuseppe. Despite himself, he was impressed by the woman's persistence – and her cunning.

"I saw you *and* I heard you," she went on. "Then I saw how those soldiers gathered and how you were unaware of them. I saw the ambush on the riders and then how you were surprised by those men-at-arms. All the time I kept very quiet and waited."

"The whole world was waiting in the wood," he said. "But this does not signify. We were set upon by the mercenaries just like those two gentlemen you mention."

"You killed Donna Maria," said Lisabetta, changing the subject but still hovering over him with the knife.

"What are you talking about?"

"You killed a good and religious woman, you killed a *romita* on the Ponte Rubaconte."

"I have heard of this deed," said Giuseppe, "and a terrible deed it was too. I swear that I had no hand in that murder. I swear it on the grave of my mother."

Again Lisabetta's arm darted out. Giuseppe felt another stabbing pain in his thigh. More by instinct than intention, he lashed out with his uninjured leg but she had already skipped out of reach. The tugging at his throat was very uncomfortable now.

"Liar, Giuseppe! You are a liar!"

"I swear on the – "

"Oh no, Giuseppe, do not swear. I saw your friend wearing the little blue cap that belonged to my friend, Donna Maria. I heard him whistle that tune which the murderers of my Guido were whistling."

Cap? Tune? What did the woman mean? he might have protested. But Giuseppe knew what she meant. The little blue cap had indeed been snatched by Bruno from the anchoress's cell on the Rubaconte. The mute had brought it to him as some sort of proof that he had committed the 'terrible deed' of murder before appropriating the cap once he'd lost his scarlet one. Giuseppe might deny having a direct hand in the murder – hence his oath – but he was otherwise as guilty as Bruno since he had arranged matters, even down to writing the note which was slipped under her door. When it came to the 'tune', Giuseppe could only suppose Lisabetta was referring to the popular piece about the miller's daughter that he'd paid her to sing outside the gaming house. He had no idea how this linked the pair of them to the death of Guido, but it was evident that the woman was convinced by her own words. There was a frightening fixity to her face. He was in genuine peril of his life. Giuseppe made a decision.

"Very well," he said. "There are . . . some matters of which I can speak. But, lady, one thing first. I am finding it difficult to talk with this cord around my neck. If you would only loosen the cord I would find it easier to say what you want to hear."

For answer, Lisabetta squatted on her haunches and pricked him delicately in the thigh, the other one this time. He yelped.

She skipped back out of reach. She was beginning to enjoy this, he realized. He didn't blame her. He would have enjoyed it, had their positions been reversed. But her pleasure made his situation even more precarious.

"I will tell you what happened to Guido Greco," he said at once. "You must promise to leave me alone though."

"If you tell the truth."

"It is true that your man was . . . unlawfully killed."

"Say murdered."

"Murdered then."

"Why? Why was he murdered?"

"What I told you in the tavern was true. There are powerful men in this city who would do anything to stop the rise of the Ciompi. Your man was their chosen victim."

"But you were their agent, Giuseppe. You and your friend with the blue cap."

"Him, yes. Bruno was his name," said Giuseppe, considering that to blame Bruno hardly mattered now. "He did it."

"I do not care what his name was." Then she checked herself. "He *is* dead then. That soldier killed him?"

"He is dead."

"Then only you are alive to pay for it, Giuseppe."

Lisabetta, who had been pacing backwards and forwards like a sentry, stopped and stared at the bound Giuseppe. She advanced on him once more with his own dagger. So far she had given him surface wounds. Was she going to cut him more deeply and leave him to bleed to death like a slaughtered animal? She could not do it, surely. But she could do it. The bleeding wounds in his legs, the ferocious look in her eyes told him so.

"If you believe I had anything to do with the death of Guido, then go to the justices, go to the *gonfalonier*," he said. He was finding it hard to breathe, either in his fear or because the cord was pressing too tight against his throat.

"Justice is not for poor people like me, Giuseppe. You agreed with me on that."

"Very well, very well. But don't you want to know where Guido is buried?"

That made her stop.

"He is lying beneath your feet, Lisabetta."

She almost jumped, as if the husband might stretch up a hand from the earth to claim his wife.

"Where? What do you mean?"

"I mean that his body is resting down there in the quarry, in one of the abandoned workings."

"You could not even give him burial like a Christian. I am bearing his child."

"A prayer was said."

It hadn't been, of course, but Giuseppe was making up for it now by praying fervently.

The knowledge was too much for Lisabetta. Her face contorted with pain. She fell to her knees. Giuseppe had his eye on the knife. He hoped she might let it drop, but she kept clutching it even as she covered her face with her hands and sobbed. Then she dropped the knife in the grass and scraped at her face until the blood started to come. While she was distracted like this Giuseppe reached behind the tree once more. His heart leapt when he felt the knot of the cord under his fingers. He was in a most awkward position, every movement increasing the constriction on his throat. Normally his awkward fingers would not have been able to unpick the knot. But panic made him supple. He knew that if he did not free himself in the next few moments his life would be forfeit.

Then he saw that Lisabetta was looking at him. But her gaze was so tear-streaked she didn't understand what he was doing.

"It's true," he croaked. "Your Guido is buried in the quarry. Down there. Go and see."

As if prompted by his suggestion, Lisabetta clambered to her feet and moved towards the lip of the quarry. There, turning her back on him, she sank to her knees once more and, like a pilgrim approaching a shrine, shuffled towards the edge. Perhaps she'll fling herself off in despair, thought Giuseppe. Her shoulders were shaking as she sobbed. All the time his fingers were working at the knot. The cord burned into his exposed throat. At last the knot began to loosen. *Keep her distracted for a moment longer*, he prayed, *keep the good woman weeping for her dead man*. He was oblivious to the tearing of his fingernails and the deep scratches on his hands and wrists. He didn't feel the pain in his contorted shoulders or the tightness at his windpipe. Some small part of him was aware of Lisabetta, now doubled up at the cliff-edge, but all the rest of Giuseppe's self was concentrated on getting himself loose from the silken cord.

It was done! He pulled for a final time at the loop in the knot and the cord slackened. The pressure against his throat eased. He drew in air in great wheezing gasps but he did not move from his position against the tree. The advantage was his again. He was free to move, with his arms and legs unencumbered. The woman was still sunk in her grief, her back to Giuseppe. But he no longer dismissed her as of little account. She was dangerous and must be disposed of. That she was bearing a dead man's child might, in normal circumstances, have given him pause. But these weren't normal circumstances. It was him – or it was her.

First he had to get close to her, whether he was going to employ his hands or the red cord which she had used against him. His knife was in the grass, nearer her than him. She'd use it, he didn't doubt that now. She'd kill him if she had the chance.

Pushing himself up with his arms, Giuseppe rose to his feet. Moving quickly, before Lisabetta might turn and see him coming, he covered the few yards between the tree and the kneeling figure. For all his weight, Giuseppe could move quickly and quietly if he had to. He'd abandoned any plan of grappling with her or strangling her or seizing back his knife to stab her. She was poised so near the edge of the quarry that a single shove should send her spinning into the air.

At the last instant, though, as he was about to throw himself at her, Giuseppe's weakened leg – the one which Lisabetta had twice pierced with the knife – gave way and he lurched sideways. Alerted by the rush of air or by some sixth sense, Lisabetta did turn and, by instinct, huddled lower on the earth as his shape closed on her. Giuseppe stumbled over her prone body. She was very close to the rim of the quarry. There was an overhang of turf and then a clean drop of dozens of feet. It was Giuseppe who flailed his way into the empty air. Lisabetta heard the sound of his body striking the rock below, and then a distant cascade of stones as he tumbled further down towards the more level ground.

Her whole body shaking, she inched across to the brim. She clung to the tufts of grass and peered over. Far below lay the body, the size of a beetle. It showed unnaturally black against the pale stone and dust which covered the basin of the quarry and which was hovering in a cloud above Giuseppe. The sounds and sight of the fall had halted work, and several of the men were running towards the spot. Others were crossing themselves or shielding their eyes and looking upwards, pointing to the place where Lisabetta lay. She shrunk back, in case she should be seen.

But no one came to investigate. Lisabetta, too exhausted and shaken to move, listened to the babble of voices from below. The next time she looked down, Giuseppe's corpse was being unceremoniously dumped in one of the quarry carts. The muleteer whipped his beast and the makeshift bier trundled off in the direction of the Oltrarno. The quarrymen must have assumed that Giuseppe had fallen by accident, or flung himself off deliberately. Which was true, in a way.

After a time, the sounds of chipping and sawing resumed. After a longer time, Lisabetta got to her feet. She brushed off the worst of the dirt and earth from her clothes. She scraped her hand over her face. Her eyes were quite dry. She did not think she would ever cry again. Her enemy was dead, the man who had killed Guido Greco was dead. Chance had brought about what she might never have accomplished by herself. But she was still alive. The baby, which she was more convinced than ever was growing in her belly, was alive too.

By the position of the sun in the sky she knew it was soon after midday. Suddenly the rest of the day stretched in front of her. There was work to be done, laundry work, needlework, there was a living to be made. She noticed the dead man's knife glinting in the grass. She bent down and picked it up. When she straightened, she found herself looking into the eyes of a man who had appeared from nowhere, from out of the trees. He was staring at her. His face was torn and bruised as if he'd recently escaped from a fight. In terror she jumped back and almost followed Giuseppe to the bottom of the quarry.

"It's all right," said the man, instinctively stretching out his arm and catching her by the shoulder. "I won't harm you. There has already been trouble enough for one day."

He continued to stare, even harder, before releasing his hold. His eyes flickered to the knife which she held, poised, in one hand before alighting on her scratched face.

"I know you," he said.

Lisabetta screamed.

25

Some time before any of this occurred – that is, before Lisabetta Greco had crept up on the sleeping Giuseppe and started a train of events which ended with his death-fall – before all this, Geoffrey Chaucer was riding towards Paradise with Tomaso Falcone and a ragged escort of mercenaries, Bartolomeo to the rear. They had cleared the woods and were travelling through more open country. The sun shone, and every now and then there was a glimpse of a secluded estate tucked between a fold of the hills or on some rise of the ground.

Falcone was curious about the ambush. He was speaking no less than the truth when he said that Ruggiero had spotted the two men by chance, but he suspected that Chaucer knew more than he was letting on.

"You said one of the ambushers had already tried to kill you."

"More than once," he said. "I've been attacked three times in almost as many days by the same man. Once in the street at night and then yesterday, in the campanile, and now this morning in the wood. Is this a Florentine welcome?"

"By God, you said you were here about dull business, Geoffrey. How could your business provoke a man to kill you? Had you eyed his wife?"

"I swear not," said Geoffrey.

"They are a jealous lot, the Florentines. Though lax also."

"You might be talking of Londoners or almost any towns-people."

"There is no Londoner as jealous as Lorenzo Lipari. God's bones, he keeps his hands on his young wife all the time – or so I've heard."

"That's more or less right," said Geoffrey. "Though she seems to get free at times."

"She's worth keeping hands on, and more than hands – or so I've heard."

"Yes, she is."

"If you're blind like Lorenzo Lipari I suppose your other senses are heightened – your touch and taste and feel, they're all stronger and sharper – or so I've heard."

"He's not," said Chaucer.

"Eh, you've lost me, Geoffrey. Who's not? Not what?"

"Lorenzo Lipari. He's not blind."

It was definitely the creaking of the garden gate. The two lovers on the platform up the pear tree tensed. They listened for more sounds but none came.

"Why didn't you lock it?" said Novella into her lover's ear.

"You've still got the key," said Aquilino. "Is there someone there? Who is it?"

"My husband, it cannot be anyone else. No one else would dare to come here."

Even as Aquilino's ardour died, his mind started to work again.

"Then we're all right. As long as we keep quiet. He doesn't know we're here. He can't see us, can he?"

"His other senses are sharp," said Novella, "especially his ears. You should know that by now. Shh."

They strained their own ears to hear the the rustle of steps in the grass or the squawk of a bird suddenly alarmed into flight. But the garden noises continued exactly as before, the breeze in the trees and all the rest of it. Perhaps they'd imagined the creaking of the garden gate, Aquilino thought to himself. Or hoped. Provided they stayed still, there was no reason why

Lorenzo Lipari should discover them in their roost. Anyway, how could one be afraid of a blind man? But Aquilino was afraid of him, and not merely because he was serving the blind man's wife.

Scarcely daring to breathe, Novella and Aquilino waited. After several minutes which seemed the equivalent of hours but during which no further sounds came, Novella once again perched herself on top of Aquilino, and soon they were muttering and groaning. At some point she said, "It must have been – the wind blowing at the door – oh, Aquilino, *o mio cavaliere* – oh, we are safe."

But before the words were quite out of her mouth, there came a bellowing shout from down below.

"Novella! Wife!"

In her surprise Novella threw herself off Aquilino with such force that the wooden platform quivered. Together the couple turned their heads in the direction of the shout. It was Lorenzo all right. They could see him through the branches. Again he shouted, "Novella!"

Among other things, Aquilino was taken aback by the power of the blind man's voice. When he'd heard Lorenzo speak it had always been in a dry, papery rustle, so that he found it natural to believe that the other's reedy frame was incapable of producing anything above a whisper. Now Lorenzo's mouth was wide open as he shouted her name to the skies. Then the cuckolded husband moved a pace or two nearer the couple as they peered, heads together, down at him. He, in turn, looked up at them. Why, if you hadn't known better, you might have sworn that he had the faculty of sight! Although the bower of love was largely hidden by the leaves and blossom of the pear-tree branches, there were gaps through which a sharp-eyed observer on the ground might have detected figures or movement. Therefore it was a great relief to know that Lorenzo Lipari did not have the faculty of sight.

273

As long as we hold still, Aquilino told himself, as long as we don't -

"Wife," said Lorenzo, speaking less loudly but fixing his wide stare directly on the spot where Novella's head peeped from among the pear blossom, "what are you doing up our pear tree with a young man?"

"With a man?" declared Novella. "There is no man, young or old, with me, husband. This is *our* private place. The morning was so clear and the skies so unclouded that I decided to climb up to our bower and relive the many happy hours which we have spent here together. Relive them in my mind and my senses."

Aquilino admired the steadiness in her voice nearly as much as he admired her quick wits. Even now he believed that Novella might save their skins.

Sensing her husband's doubt, she said, "If you do not believe me, Lorenzo my dearest one, then give me permission to descend so that I may get the ladder and help you climb up to Paradise. Then we may enjoy ourselves all the livelong day. Who is to call Novella and Lorenzo Lipari to account?"

"Very well," said the husband.

Novella made urgent gestures to Aquilino. He hardly needed her arm-waving to understand what she meant. While she was getting down one side of the tree, he would use the noise of her descent to make his own exit. Aquilino edged over to the far side of the platform.

But it was too late now for the young man to make his getaway. Lorenzo Lipari had accepted his wife's kind invitation to join her in the bower. However, rather than waiting for her to climb down and retrieve the ladder, he was already grasping the lower branches of the tree. He was already hauling himself up to their level. He had no need of any ladder. Aquilino and Novella didn't even have the time to wonder how it was that a blind man was so sure of his footing or where to place his hands, before his head and shoulders appeared above the edge of the platform. He clung there like a man about to board a boat. Before him lay his wife and the mercenary in a tangle, their clothes disordered or cast aside. Novella had not thought to tuck her swinging breasts, still wine-stained, back into her red dress. Aquilino's shirt didn't cover his privates, while his doublet and hose were thrown nearby. Anybody with the faculty of sight could have had no doubt about what had been going on up the pear tree.

Lorenzo Lipari turned his narrow head from side to side. His eyes, which usually flickered aimlessly from quarter to quarter, now appeared to take in their flushed faces, their bare limbs. It was Novella who first realized the truth.

"You can see, husband!"

But there was not as much wonder or disbelief in her tone as you might have expected.

"I can see," he said. "It is a miracle."

Lorenzo's voice had reverted to its customary dryness. Novella seized on his last word.

"Yes, it is a miracle! I give thanks to God and all his saints that your sight has been restored, Lorenzo. But one word of advice . . . the man who has not used his eyes for many years cannot be sure of what he sees when – the heavens be praised! – his vision is restored. Many delusions and mirages will appear to disturb his brain."

"Delusions and mirages that you are not alone here, my dear?" said Lorenzo.

"Just so."

Aquilino didn't know what to do so he stayed as still as a statue although he couldn't stop his legs trembling. Lorenzo Lipari raised himself a little higher up the tree. He must have found a secure foothold among the lower branches. All the time, his eyes moved across the scene, like a sleeper newly awakened to strange surroundings. Dimly, Aquilino's ears heard what Novella was saying and, dimly, some part of his brain registered her great cleverness. If Lorenzo had truly regained his vision, then their only hope lay in tricking him that he was seeing things imperfectly.

But Lorenzo was having none of it.

"So that is not Aquilino the mercenary I see with you but a mirage."

Almost as alarming as the fact that Lorenzo could see him and knew who he was, was the calm tone in which the cuckold spoke. Ever since he'd first met Novella, stories of Lorenzo's outrageous jealousy had been drummed into Aquilino. It was why she'd denied him relief for so long. Yet now, the cheated husband stood halfway up a pear tree gazing on the disrobed lovers and speaking to them in accents of sweet reason.

"I can explain that too, husband," said Novella, simultaneously scooping up her breasts and slipping them inside her dress, as if she'd suddenly recalled her half-naked state.

"Perhaps it is Aquilino who would like to do the explaining," said Lorenzo, with ominous calm.

Aquilino opened his mouth but no words came out apart from "I . . . um . . . I . . . you . . . she . . . I . . ."

"This is not our bargain, my dear," said Lorenzo.

"Bargain?" said Novella, but once again she did not sound so surprised.

"You think I did not know how you hated my brother as much as I did? You think that I was ignorant of what you were urging Aquilino to do? Why else do you suppose I tolerated the frequent visits of a stupid and brutish mercenary to Paradise but that I saw the way your mind was tending. To use him to get rid of the man we both hated."

"Then it worked, it worked!" said Novella. "For Antonio is dead, and we are both satisfied."

"At the hands of this man?" said Lorenzo. "So Aquilino killed Antonio, did he?"

This was the direct question which Novella had so far avoided putting to Aquilino. Now husband and wife turned to

276

look at the hapless mercenary, who huddled awkwardly, hoseless and hatless, on the far side of the platform. Suddenly, the truth became apparent to him. What he had perceived as a union of himself and Novella against Lorenzo Lipari was, in reality, an alliance of husband and wife against him, poor old Pietro Hodge. But he'd done what they wanted, hadn't he . . . or rather *he* had not done it but someone else. The result was the same though. Antonio Lipari was dead. Perhaps confessing to a murder now would get him off the hook of adultery.

"Yes, I did it," said Aquilino. "I killed the man you both hate."

Novella turned to her husband, who was still perched on the lower branches of the tree. Daringly she reached out and grasped him. "You see, my dear. And . . . as for this thing now . . . you surely cannot begrudge Aquilino his small reward. He has had me for a few moments and in return your brother has gone for an eternity. You talk of a bargain. This is a fair exchange surely. And – wonders will never cease – you have recovered your sight. We should rejoice."

She released her hold on Lorenzo's shoulder. The thin mouth split into a smile and for a moment, a moment only, Aquilino thought that they might get away with it.

"If I believed any of that, wife, then I would truly be blind – not outwardly blind but in my mind."

"It is so, husband," said Novella. "What I have said is so."

"Your friend is a liar," said Lorenzo. "He did not kill Antonio."

"I did! I did!"

"No," said Lorenzo, his voice so low that it was hardly audible above the rustling of the leaves. "I did the act. I grew tired of waiting for your mercenary to show his colours. Not only did I hate Antonio, I also had to prevent him concluding his business with the English. You see, Novella, if Aquilino had committed the deed which you were enticing him towards, I might have forgiven you this transgression. But it is a lopsided bargain, where one man goes away empty-handed."

277

Her husband peered at her and her lover. There was colour in his usually wan cheeks. The eyes, which for so long had shown the vacant stare of the blind, now burned with a frightening intensity. He levered himself up on to the platform which shifted slightly with the additional weight. Aquilino clutched at the edge like a man on a sinking ship. There was scarcely space up here for the three of them. Novella scrambled away from Lorenzo.

"Save me!" she shouted to Aquilino.

But Aquilino was still bare from the waist down, and by now Lorenzo had drawn a dagger from within the folds of his clothes. Aquilino was more concerned to protect himself and his parts than he was moved by the chivalrous notion of saving his lady. Whether Lorenzo meant to murder his faithless wife and her paramour or to wound them – or merely to frighten them – would never be known. Probably Lorenzo did not even know himself. By now the fury had risen full in his face and he was crouched on the wooden platform with Novella and Aquilino at opposite corners.

Then there was an abrupt, twanging sound, like an axe striking the trunk. One of the cords securing the platform in the heart of the pear tree had snapped. The bower of love tilted on the side where the load was greatest. This put even more strain on the remaining cords and within the blink of an eye there was another thunk. This time the platform, never intended to bear the weight of more than a couple of boys, lurched as if it had been struck by a giant hand. All three of the occupants were toppled from their perches.

Aquilino found himself descending through a shower of leaves and blossom. He hit the earth with a thud. He was joined, seconds later, by the husband and wife. Perhaps the mercenary was more resilient than the Liparis, more accustomed to knocks and swipes. Or perhaps he had been more fortunate in the way that he fell. The bruises and aches would come later but some exploratory movements assured him that he was essentially undamaged. The other two lay on the grass, strange fruit of the pear. Lorenzo was curled up on his side while Novella sprawled on her front. They weren't moving but Aquilino could tell that they weren't dead. As if in proof, Lorenzo groaned and twitched. Panic screeched at Aquilino to get out of this place. He was sorry to leave Novella to Lorenzo's mercy, but they were husband and wife after all . . . no man should come between husband and wife . . .

The mercenary stood up. Luckily his discarded clothes had fallen with him off the platform and were scattered nearby. With fumbling hands he drew on his hose and snatched up his doublet from the ground. He started to run towards the entrance to the secret garden, blundering along alleyways and ducking under branches but came only to a stone wall, against which were espaliered fruit trees. There was no gate to be seen. In his panic, Aquilino had taken the wrong direction. He must escape from Paradise! What he was chiefly afraid of was that Lorenzo Lipari would clamber to his feet and set off in pursuit. Aquilino was not normally a coward but he was without a weapon and he was shaken by the events of the past couple of hours. Lorenzo, on the other hand, had a nasty-looking dagger and was possessed by jealous fury. And there was something deeply unnerving about the fact that the blind man could see, whether his sight had suddenly been restored to him or whether he'd been tricking them all the time.

Aquilino set off to his left, reckoning that if he did a circuit of the garden he must reach the gate eventually. All the time he kept one ear cocked for sounds of pursuit. Sure enough the gate lay beyond the next angle of the wall. It was slightly ajar, just as it must have been left by Lorenzo when he first crept up on the lovers. Aquilino slowed down to catch his breath and, to his alarm, saw the door begin to swing further open.

Through the gate there appeared the figure of his

commander, Tomaso Falcone, accompanied by that Englishman who'd questioned him in Donna Michela's, the Chaucer fellow. He was as surprised to see them as they were to see him. For an instant no one moved.

"Aquilino!" said Falcone in English. "I have been looking for you, man. Discipline must be maintained, by God!"

"So is the rest of the world looking for me," said Aquilino.

"What has happened to your face, Peter Hodge?" said the Chaucer fellow. "Been in a fight?"

Aquilino supposed that the marks of the fall from the tree must be on his face and hands. No time to stop and account for himself, though. There was a madman in the garden, a man who was blind but who now could see, a man determined to exact vengeance for his cuckolding, a man who'd killed his brother. Let the others deal with him.

"Watch out for Lorenzo," he said, gesturing vaguely over his shoulder.

Then he circled past Falcone and Chaucer, ignoring their shouts and raised arms, and sped through the door. Thank God he'd left Fuoco tethered nearby. Thank God no one had thought to remove his mount, which was contentedly cropping the grass. There was only one idea in Aquilino's head: to put some distance between himself and Paradise.

As he emerged near the main house he saw some of his fellows milling about at the entrance together with the notary who'd accompanied Chaucer to the *bordello*. What was going on? The company hadn't noticed him yet. Turning his head away, Aquilino urged his horse into a canter down the path which led to the main gates. They were unguarded, and he shot through them and into the open. Then, more by instinct than by conscious decision, he turned in the direction of the city.

"What is the matter with him?" said Falcone. "Aquilino is a young fool but he's no coward. Why should he run?"

Tomaso Falcone and Geoffrey Chaucer stood inside the entrance to the secret garden. They'd found themselves here almost by chance, one of the Lipari household having seen Aquilino ambling in this direction earlier in the morning. Falcone had identified his man's horse tethered outside. But, if finding Pietro Hodge had been their aim when they set out for Paradise, the two men now had different business in hand.

"I've heard rumours that he is in pursuit of Novella Lipari," said Chaucer, not revealing that he and Bartolomeo had seen Lipari's wife at Donna Michela's the day before.

"By God, I have heard the same but I did not believe it," said Falcone. "Lorenzo Lipari is a jealous man. Why go after a jealous man's wife, when there are so many other women, willing and able?"

"Lorenzo Lipari must be here," said Geoffrey. "He must be somewhere in this garden."

"Aquilino said we should watch out for him. Why? He can hardy watch out for himself."

"He is not blind, I tell you."

"I don't understand you, Geoffrey. Why would he pretend to be blind?"

"You remember Jack Abbot, he who was with us in France more than fifteen years ago and escaped without a wound? I said I had another tale to tell about him."

"What's a blind Florentine got to do with lucky Jack?"

"I saw him in London a few years afterwards, saw lucky Jack that is. He was on the street, begging in the guise of a veteran. He didn't recognize me at first, nor I him. It wasn't surprising that he did not know me for I've changed over the years – and besides he could not see. His eyes were pitifully sore and weeping sad stuff. It was only when I passed over a coin and spoke some words to him that he seized my hand and said, 'Geoffrey?' He was a fine-looking fellow once but now he had other wounds apart from his sightlessness."

"Not wounds from the wars surely?"

"Some he had given himself, real wounds but slight. The effects of others he had created with lime and rusty iron. They were very convincing. He was able to see as well as you or I, of course, although he claimed to have lost his sight at Rheims during the siege. He had three or four different stories to account for it."

"In God's name, why was he doing this?"

"Everyone pities the blind. And many are fearful of them too. It's as if to compensate for their lack of sight they can see in some other way. See with the mind perhaps."

"That's too deep for me, Geoffrey," said Falcone. "I mean why was Jack Abbot doing this? What possessed him?"

"He was the younger son. Everything had gone to the older one through some whim of the father. He'd simply found an ingenious way of earning his daily bread. He ate well, I should say."

"A gentleman as a beggar, a sightless beggar!"

In his surprise, almost his outrage, Falcone had forgotten that they were standing by the gate to a garden where some secret or danger was concealed.

"We had a drink together," said Geoffrey, "though well away from his begging haunts. With a bit of liquor inside him, he unbent and let me in on his tricks. He made more money out of begging than he would have made out of any gainful employment. He'd even bought a house off Bishopsgate and had a wife. She thought he was something in the city. His neighbours thought he was something in the city. Often they used to pass by him but they didn't know him, his disguise and wounds were that good. He still had the gentleman's manner though, and that was how he won his custom."

"God's bones," said Falcone, "I've been rated for my way of life, but I'd never stoop as low as begging."

"Jack Abbot sees it as an opportunity for people to show their charity – he's speeding them to heaven, he says. Or he was. He's dead now. I heard he'd died in a fire at his Bishopsgate house. They buried his remains like a gentleman's. His wife never knew."

Suddenly Tomaso Falcone, who'd been listening attentively to Geoffrey, seemed to become aware of their surroundings once more. He glanced at the trees in blossom, the warm stone of the garden walls.

"Geoffrey, this is an interesting story, a sad one too, but what has it got to do with Lorenzo Lipari?"

"Only this. That there is often advantage to be gained if the world believes that we are in a sorrier state than we really are. Think of Jack Abbot pretending to blindness and other wounds he never had, and resting on the pity and alms of others. And think of Lorenzo Lipari who has presented himself these many years as a blind man, a simple and scholarly fellow by contrast with his worldly brother."

"It is beyond belief. To act blind!"

"See for yourself," said Chaucer.

Out of the nearest alleyway of trees emerged Novella Lipari. Her dress was disordered and there was a look of confusion and fear on her bruised face. There were red smears on her shoulders and arms, though these were not blood. Close at her heels came the husband, his hands outstretched to lay hold of her. In one of them he was grasping a dagger. For a blind man, he moved in a very sure-footed fashion.

Novella, seeing Chaucer and Falcone, ran towards them. She took shelter behind the pair. Falcone already had his sword out. Geoffrey still had the dagger with which he had fended off Giuseppe Orioli and the bald-head, but his injured right hand was incapable of holding a weapon and he was unpractised with his left. Even so he unsheathed his dagger for the second time that morning.

Lorenzo Lipari halted and looked at the two Englishmen. There was no doubt now that he could see, and see well. His eyes flicked from one to the other with malevolent intent but he kept his distance, threatened by their weapons. Meantime Novella hovered to their rear.

"Be careful," said Chaucer quietly to Falcone. "He is dangerous."

Falcone whispered back, "From the way he is holding that knife, the scholar is no stranger to it."

"He is not just a scholar but a murderer also. He murdered his brother as surely as Cain did Abel."

"Murdered Antonio?"

Though Lorenzo Lipari's understanding of English was limited, his ears were sharp enough to pick up some of the conversation – or perhaps it was nothing more than the reference to Cain and Abel. He nodded and brandished his right hand.

"*Si, è vero. Ecco la mano assassina.*"

Then, still maintaining a distance between himself and the other two, he mimed pushing over some heavy object.

"The statue of Mars," said Chaucer. "He toppled it over on his brother."

"In God's name, why?"

"Something to do with hell and the seventh circle. *Specialmente il settimo.*"

They saw Lorenzo's gaze flicker past them. More, they all heard the creaking of the garden gate. Chaucer risked a quick glance over his shoulder. Novella was still behind them but coming through the entrance were Falcone's mercenaries together with Bartolomeo Gentile.

Although Lorenzo Lipari might have risked an attack on the two Englishmen, he was not prepared to take on a whole group. Instead he turned and hared off down an alley towards the orchard.

Falcone asked Novella whether there was another door out of the garden. She shook her head. He signalled to his men that they should split into two groups and cut off the fugitive's retreat. In their practised way they slunk through the long grass and the hanging blossom. Meanwhile Falcone and Geoffrey Chaucer waited by the gate, like huntsmen who'd sent off their best hounds and were now waiting for the barking and baying which would indicate the quarry was cornered. In fact, a peculiar kind of leisure descended over the scene, although the two men kept their weapons drawn. Bartolomeo, who still hadn't fully recovered from the effects of the drugged flask, remained by them without speaking.

"Explain what you meant, Geoffrey, by the seventh circle of hell, *il settimo*."

"It is the circle where the poet Dante Alighieri put blasphemers and suicides — and usurers. The money lenders. Lorenzo referred to the city as being such a place — a seventh circle — and no doubt he was thinking of his brother in particular. He believed that Antonio had agreed to do business with the English crown. In my hearing he picked up on the fact that Antonio had signed and sealed letters for me to deliver to court. I saw the brothers whispering together. I believe Lorenzo went to Antonio's office to settle accounts with him, to lay his hands on the letters."

"So there he killed him. But what happened to the letters?"

"No doubt they have been destroyed by now — thrown in the Arno, put in the fire, I don't know," said Geoffrey. "But that wasn't the only reason for the murder. Lorenzo had long hated his brother. Almost any occasion would have served for his death."

"Hated him? But . . . but Antonio Lipari arranged his marriage, for God's sake," said Tomaso Falcone. "Novella was offered to Lorenzo. It is said that he was atoning to his brother for having caused his blindness all those years ago."

"Except that Lorenzo isn't blind. Pretending that he was blind was his lifelong revenge on his brother," said Geoffrey. "And who knows whether Antonio wasn't having a very clever revenge on him in turn, by arranging a match with a beautiful woman who might lead him a merry dance. What a torment to be blind and yoked to a spouse who likes to stray! Maybe Antonio hoped that his brother would never have a restful night or day again but would be eaten up with jealousy and worry."

Chaucer looked behind him once again but Novella Lipari had disappeared through the gate. Somehow he'd expected it.

"If so," said Falcone, "Antonio's plan to torment his brother worked a little too well, and he procured his own death."

"I do not know whether Lorenzo intended to kill him. All that's certain is that he was in the long chamber when he was surprised by Antonio's appearance. Perhaps he was seen taking the letters. Perhaps his fury simply boiled over. They fought maybe. Or Lorenzo tried to conceal himself behind the statue of Mars. As his brother approached, Lorenzo pushed at the statue, so – "Chaucer imitated the pushing motion already demonstrated by Lorenzo – "and the banker was crushed under the weight of the stone."

"When we capture Lorenzo, we shall question him about these matters," said Falcone.

"Any questioning is better left to the *gonfalonier*, isn't it?" said Geoffrey. "And first he must be captured."

As if in answer to this remark, there were shouts from somewhere near the centre of the orchard. Falcone set off at a half-run followed by Geoffrey and, some way to the rear, by Bartolomeo Gentile. They came to the very pear tree where Lorenzo Lipari had surprised the lovers. Chaucer didn't know exactly what had happened here but he observed the leaves and branches strewn over the grass and a spilled bottle of wine (which explained the red staining on Novella). Nearby was a discarded ladder, the grass poking through its rungs. He thought of the device on the Lipari *scudo*, the golden ladder which led slowly but surely to fortune. Looking up, he could see the tilted platform which had once been a bower of love.

Also up the tree was Lorenzo Lipari. Like a cornered animal he'd taken refuge in the place he knew best, sitting astride a fork which had until recently supported one side of the wooden platform. Some of the mercenaries were jabbing with their lances at his lower legs. If they still believed him to be blind, it was evident from their taunts and actions that they didn't care.

To escape their attentions, Lorenzo moved as far up among the branches as he could. Geoffrey Chaucer was reminded, uncomfortably, of a gang of boys standing at the base of a tree and throwing sticks and stones at some half-starved cat. Except that Lorenzo Lipari was no wretched beast but a cunning murderer.

"Call your men off," he said to Tomaso Falcone.

"Let them have their sport. It is called treeing the rich man."

"Call them off now, I say. He will have to come down eventually."

"An axe is quicker. A few strokes and down will come rich man and tree and all."

"As you please," said Geoffrey, seeing that he had little authority here.

Among the group of soldiers clustered about the pear tree was Ruggiero the crossbowman. He was wearing the red cap belonging to the man he'd killed earlier this fine morning. Now he was inclined to kill another. He raised his crossbow to his shoulder and sighted along its length. Lorenzo Lipari was a sitting target. Ruggiero seemed to toy with him, dropping the bow and making small adjustments to the mechanism before putting it to his shoulder again. Yet a child of five, having the strength to wield the weapon, would scarcely have missed his mark.

Lorenzo Lipari, seeing his danger, tried to put branches and foliage between himself and Ruggiero's bolt. It was futile, of course. A bolt will penetrate such feeble defences. Futile and dangerous too, for in seeking to protect himself from the one

287

peril, Lipari lost his footing and exposed himself to another danger. For the third time in his life and for the second time on this fine morning he tumbled from the pear tree and landed with a thud on the ground. This time he fell further. This time he did not rise again, but lay with his neck awry and his eyes staring up at the unclouded heavens. Now he really would never see again.

26

" I know you," repeated Aquilino to Lisabetta.
They were standing at the edge of the quarry. Down below, the body of Giuseppe was already halfway to the city in the back of the quarry cart. Down below, the sounds of work, of cutting and sawing, proceeded as though they'd never been interrupted by the fall of a man. Down below, in the depths of the rock, lay the mouldering body of Guido Greco.

Lisabetta's scream tapered off as it sank in that this individual, with his bruised and scratched visage, intended her no harm.

"How . . . where . . . ? I don't know you," she said.

"I . . . I have seen you in the streets of our fair city. I have long admired your . . . "

Aquilino paused, uncertain whether to say exactly what it was about this woman that he'd admired, specifically her *cioccie*. Some women wouldn't mind, others would object for form's sake. Until he got to know her a little better he couldn't be sure which type of woman he was dealing with. Neither did he mention that he had glimpsed her in the long chamber of Antonio Lipari, nor that he had recently implied that she might be a murderess. He couldn't say any of this without revealing his own presence in the Lipari household – and at the moment he wanted nothing more to do with the Liparis.

"Who are you?"

"My name is Pietro Hodge, but everyone calls me Aquilino on account of this."

He indicated the nose and waited for her to name herself.

"I am Lisabetta."

"What are you doing here outside the city walls? Why aren't you at work? You are no *contadina* for sure but a city woman."

"The spring morning was so fair that I thought I would enjoy the fresh air."

"I also, Lisabetta," said Aquilino, not believing her. "The morning is too fair for work and I thought I would enjoy the fresh air beyond the city walls."

"Your face is scratched," she said, not believing him.

"So is yours," he said.

"The fresh air is dangerous," she said.

"We are safer inside the city," he said. "Do you know, Lisabetta, of anywhere a man might lay his head for a night or two in this city? I had lodgings here once but I'm not inclined to return to them."

"I may know of a place," she said.

"Forgive my forwardness, lady," said Aquilino, "but are you married? I observe that you are wearing a ring."

"I am a widow," she said.

(But one with a child in her belly, she thought. He doesn't need to know that yet, she thought.)

"I am sorry to hear it," he said, though he was delighted. "So young too."

"And you, Pietro?"

"I am single," said Aquilino. He took her by the arm, pausing for an instant to see whether she would object. She did not. In fact, she pressed herself to his side. "Yes, single," he repeated.

As they were riding back into the city and before they reached the Oltrarno, they again passed the straggly smallholdings which were not quite urban nor properly rural. The cock was still strutting in his dusty yard, attended by his faithful hens. The woman stood in the crooked doorway as if she hadn't moved since the morning. The germ of a story began to stir in Geoffrey's mind until he was interrupted by Bartolomeo who by this time had recovered from the drugged flask.

"You must explain how you knew that Lorenzo Lipari was not blind," he said.

"Yes, Geoffrey," added Tomaso Falcone. "Explain."

"It was to do first of all with a book of poetry. Antonio Lipari gave me a present. It was the *Inferno* by Dante Alighieri."

"I saw the gift," said Bartolomeo. "It pleased you, Geoffrey."

"Very much. But as I was receiving the book, Lorenzo Lipari said something. He said, '*Lasciate ogni speranza voi ch'entrata.*'"

"All hope abandon, you who enter here," said Falcone, putting it into English.

"It is inscribed over the entrance to hell, so says our Dante Alighieri," said Bartolomeo.

"But how did Lorenzo Lipari know that I had been given a copy of the *Inferno* by his brother? Because he saw the gift, that's why, and he quoted one of the most famous lines from it without thinking."

"Perhaps his brother told him what he was going to do," said Bartolomeo. "Perhaps he mentioned the title of the book which he intended to present to his English guest."

"Not very likely," said Geoffrey. "The brothers entered the room separately, and I had the impression that they had not met for some time. And, when they did talk, it wasn't to exchange pleasantries and unimportant news to do with gift-giving. Then Lorenzo looked angry when they were whispering together. He was being told about the English loan."

"That I didn't see," said Bartolomeo.

"You were busy watching out for Philomela," said Geoffrey. "It so happened that I was watching. I had less to say in the buzz of Italian which was all round us, and more time to watch. At some point later in the feast Lorenzo must have gone off to the long chamber, intending to confront his brother. We heard that

Novella had been out of her husband's company for a time. But it was the other way round. He had been absent from hers. He confronted Antonio in the long chamber – or he hid and waited for him – but one way or another he procured his death."

"And all the time he could see?" said Bartolomeo.

"I believe so," said Chaucer. "It would take incredible self-control to pretend to be blind for all that time. But it was his way of tricking the world and keeping a hold over his brother. Remember, Bartolomeo, it was you first told me about the emnity between the brothers, how they'd fought over some girl Antonio had stolen from Lorenzo. Lorenzo was still a jealous man – and a murderous one. Both Aquilino and Novella were lucky to escape with their lives."

"I'd like a word with Aquilino," said Tomaso Falcone. "And I wouldn't mind seeing that Lipari woman again. I wonder what's happened to them?"

At that moment, Aquilino was crossing the Ponte Rubaconte with Lisabetta Greco. They were both on horseback. In the midst of the foot-passengers and mule-drawn carts, Lisabetta couldn't help looking at the little house where her friend Donna Maria had lived and died. She couldn't help it that tears were forming in the corners of her eyes and beginning to run down her cheeks. It was small comfort to her that the individuals responsible for the deaths of Maria and Guido were themselves no more.

"What is it?" said Aquilino, feeling her distress as she clung to him, so as to keep her seat on Fuoco.

"I am thinking of a friend who used to live here."

"What happened to your friend?"

"She was foully murdered."

Indeed, Aquilino had heard something of this crime when he was at Donna Michela's, but without having any idea that Giuseppe and Bruno were responsible. He felt the firm jut of her jaw pressing into his shoulder, he felt the pleasant swell of those fine *cioccie* of hers in the small of his back. He recalled the fresh scratches on her face, as well as her presence in the *palazzo* on the Via dei Cerretani where he'd seen her holding a knife. Again he wondered what she'd been doing at the edge of the quarry.

"Has the villain who did it been caught?" he said.

Lisabetta hesitated an instant before shaking her head. He felt that too, the hesitation and the head-shake.

"But justice has been done," he said. It was barely a question and Lisabetta answered it with an almost inaudible, "Yes."

Aquilino saw more and more to admire in this woman. Unlike Novella, she would not seduce someone else into doing her dirty work for her. Unlike Novella, she did not give herself airs and graces but answered simply and plainly. There could be no deception in her.

For her part, Lisabetta was well aware that Aquilino was growing interested in her. He was pressing back so as to feel her against him. She thought he'd taken the horse at a faster downhill trot than necessary as they approached the city, all so that she'd clutch him tighter. Lisabetta knew that this man had been in trouble, just as she had been in trouble herself. She was still in trouble, as a woman who lived by her needle and who would quite soon have to provide for two mouths. A woman who had recently recalled the old saying about a mouse with only one hole to go to being poorly provided for. Lisabetta took one hand from around Aquilino's waist and wiped at her damp cheeks. For the first time in many days, she smiled to herself.

And what happened to Novella Lipari? If Lisabetta Greco – by now Lisabetta Hodge (which she pronounces 'Odge) and with a swelling belly – had crossed the Rubaconte in the autumn of this year and once again searched for the occupants of the *romite* cells on the bridge, she would have found that the one formerly occupied by Maria was now tenanted by another well-born woman. Novella Lipari, who knew Monna Apollonia of old, had concluded that it was safest to keep her head down for the time being. What better way than to throw oneself on the charity and goodwill of her fellow Florentines? If her reputation had suffered – if stories about her and some nameless mercenary were spreading about the place – what better way to restore it than by taking shelter as a religious? There was often a gaggle of men around Novella's cell on the Rubaconte. Indeed, it seemed to have become a popular place of resort. But the fellow she had her eye on was a slightly older one. He looked as though he had a florin or two . . .

27

A few days after the events in the garden Chaucer and Bartolomeo were summoned to a meeting at the *palazzo* on the Via dei Cerretani by Emilia Lipari. The widow had recently attended the funerals of her husband and her brother-in-law. The deaths of the Lipari brothers had both been taken as accidents, despite the initial doubts of the authorities about Antonio's demise. Both had been buried in the family mausoleum in Paradise, side by side in death in a way that they'd never been in life.

Chaucer's realization that it had been brother Lorenzo who had toppled the statue on top of brother Antonio was not one he chose to share with anyone except Bartolomeo and Falcone, who'd been witnesses to that strange, final scene in the secret garden. In public, it was thought that Lorenzo had run mad, perhaps overcome with grief for Antonio, and had taken shelter in their childhood tree-house from where he had suffered a fatal fall. This was not so surprising. Blind men ought not to climb trees perhaps. The part played by Falcone's men was minimized.

Novella Lipari's role in all this was similarly overlooked. In fact she had disappeared, and was not to be seen for several months until she took up her new (if temporary) life as a *romita* on the Ponte Rubaconte. The savage murder of Donna Maria was never solved, although there was a laundrywoman in a tenement in the poorer quarter of the city who might have been able to provide an answer or two. She was busy, however, with a new husband and the discovery that she was expecting a child, too busy to bother much with old crimes. If it was a boy, however, she was going to call him Guido in memory of her first husband – her only concession to the past. Aquilino, who preferred to be called Pietro these days, had no objection. After all, he was sure that the child was his. Lisabetta had told him so; more, she had complimented him on his potency in making her pregnant so soon – so very soon – after they'd wed.

Chaucer had already packed to return home when the summons came from Purgatory a few days after the death of Lorenzo Lipari. He had nothing to take back to England with him, except for the copy of the *Inferno* presented to him by Antonio Lipari and the little clasp which he'd picked up from the floor near the man's body. Chaucer had no idea whether this ornament belonged to Masetto Cennini, the pocky-faced individual who had entered the long chamber. If he wanted it so badly he could come in search of it.

He assumed that the request to visit the Via dei Cerretani originated with Matteo Peruzzi but this could not have been the case because as he and Bartolomeo Gentile were approaching the house they saw the red-bearded secretary exiting through the *sportello*. He was carrying a small bag. He looked with his customary hostility at Geoffrey and the notary, before brushing past them without a word. Bartolomeo raised his eyebrows at Geoffrey.

Once inside Purgatory, they were directed to the long chamber. They passed through the counting house. Clerks clicked on the abacuses while their pens ranged across columns of figures. The life of the bank continued as silent and undisturbed as an underground river. Inside the long chamber the statue of Mars had been restored to its upright position but with fresh cement securing it to the pedestal. The statue appeared to have sustained no damage from its fall. The marble floor had been scrubbed clean. There was little trace that a man had died here only days before.

Chaucer was surprised to see the wife of the late Antonio Lipari sitting in her husband's place behind the desk. They sat down in front of her. She glanced at them, the slight smile on her face giving no suggestion of recent grief. Chaucer had not so far heard her say more than a few words. In fact, not a word of hers has been reported in this story. But now she had a great deal to say, and Bartolomeo struggled to keep up with the flow of her tongue. Emilia Lipari spoke with authority. She reinforced her points by tapping on the desk with the tip of a paper-knife. The knife was of the type that her husband had also used, the one whose absence Geoffrey had noticed on the night of Lipari's death. Hadn't the woman called Lisabetta Greco taken it, according to what she'd told Bartolomeo? Chaucer wondered whether it was the same knife or whether Emilia had got herself another one. Or had possessed one all the time . . .

Meantime Bartolomeo was translating the opinions and instructions of the flame-haired Emilia Lipari.

"Monna Emilia," he said, "she says that now her husband is dead and gone, and now that his brother is dead and gone also, the control of the Lipari banking house has fallen into her hands. She says that it will be a good thing to have such an enterprise in the hands of a woman. Throughout the life of Antonio Lipari, she often desired to intervene in business but he always shut her out. Well, he cannot shut her out now! She has also dealt with Matteo Peruzzi or the *volpacchiotto* as her husband used to call him. She never had any time for the "little fox cub". She never trusted him. Now he is gone from the house for good.

"As far as existing business is concerned, Monna Emilia assures the *messere* from England that the loan to the English King will be honoured. In fact, she has signed documents to that effect – documents signed by her husband, she wishes to make clear – and Master Chaucer may return home with good news for his Edward."

Emilia sensed the point that Bartolomeo had reached in his translation and, reaching for a sealed pouch on the desk, handed it to Chaucer. He realized that inside were the very documents he'd been searching for on the desk. So Lorenzo Lipari hadn't got hold of them after all. They hadn't been thrown in the Arno or put on the fire. He raised an eyebrow at Emilia Lipari. She was quick – oh, how quick she was! – and, before he could speak, she said something which Bartolomeo rendered as follows: "Monna Emilia, she took these items for safe-keeping on the tragic night of her husband's death. She says furthermore that she believes you have a saying in England about gifts and the mouths of horses."

Chaucer smiled and kept quiet. Emilia, however, did not. When she finished eventually, Bartolomeo had difficulty in resuming his version.

"And . . . and . . . "

"What's the matter, Bartolomeo?" said Geoffrey, seeing his friend too moved or disturbed to continue with his translation. Meantime, Monna Emilia was tapping impatiently with the knife-tip on the desk. Chaucer feared the worst. But soon Bartolomeo recovered himself. He was smiling.

"Monna Emilia, she says that she knows the wishes and desires of her daughter Philomela. She knows too the wishes and desires of one Bartolomeo Gentile – that's me! – and she has no wish of her own to stand in their way. She is aware that her husband intended her daughter for that red-bearded secretary. But now that Antonio is dead in the tragic accident, there is no need to take account of what he wanted any longer. Accordingly, as soon as the official period of mourning for her husband is over, the couple may marry. That period of mourning will not be lengthy. Oh, Geoffrey! I am to marry Philomela. Philomela is to marry Bartolomeo!"

And that was it, more or less.

Geoffrey and Bartolomeo bowed to Emilia Lipari, who was

happily ensconced behind her desk. Geoffrey did not doubt that she would run her husband's business with the same efficiency as him, but with a touch less ruthlessness perhaps. He thought of how women had been hidden at the heart of this business. Novella Lipari, Lisabetta Greco, and others perhaps that he did not know of. Now there was Emilia Lipari. Perhaps all the time it was the women who pulled the strings – or wielded the knives.

They walked back down the long chamber, past the pictures of the works of Venus, past the scenes of slaughter presided over by Mars, past the statue with no head and the raised sword. Chaucer wondered how Emilia could tolerate the presence of this statue which had, indirectly, been the cause of her husband's death.

It was at this point that Geoffrey Chaucer stopped. He looked back over his shoulder. Emilia Lipari – the woman who has been silent until now, the woman who had submitted to her husband – was examining some papers on her desk. She looked up at Geoffrey and again smiled slightly.

Suppose, thought Chaucer, suppose that we were wrong about Lorenzo Lipari. Suppose that it wasn't the brother who toppled the statue over on Antonio but the -

"Come along, Geoffrey," said Bartolomeo Gentile. "We must go now. I have a marriage to arrange."